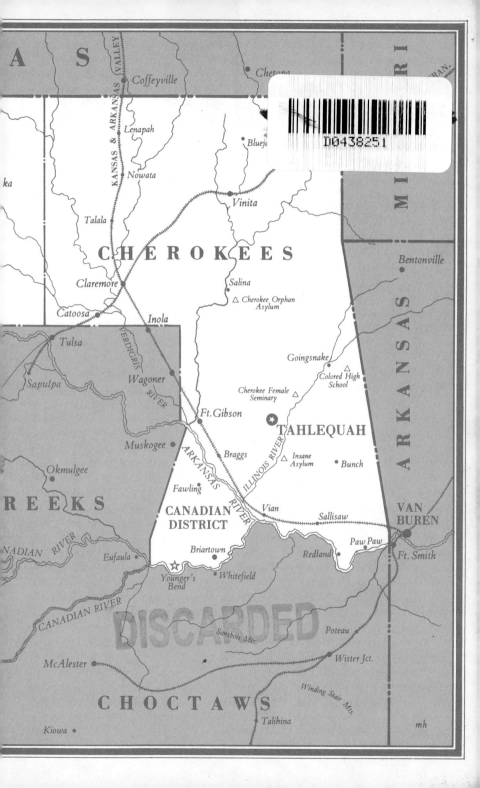

Also by Speer Morgan

Frog Gig and Other Stories

Belle Starr

Belle Starr

A Novel by

Speer Morgan

An Atlantic Monthly Press Book
LITTLE, BROWN AND COMPANY
Boston — Toronto

FIRST EDITION

T 01/79

LIBRARY OF CONGRESS CATALOGING IN PUBLICATION DATA

Morgan, Speer, 1949–
  Belle Starr.

"An Atlantic Monthly press book."
  1. Starr, Belle Shirley, 1848–1889—Fiction.
I. Title.
PZ4.M85137Be [PS3563.087149] 813'.5'4 78–10278
ISBN 0–316–58296–4

ATLANTIC—LITTLE, BROWN BOOKS
ARE PUBLISHED BY
LITTLE, BROWN AND COMPANY
IN ASSOCIATION WITH
THE ATLANTIC MONTHLY PRESS

*Published simultaneously in Canada
by Little, Brown & Company (Canada) Limited*

PRINTED IN THE UNITED STATES OF AMERICA

For Virginia Lee Morgan and Ralph Speer, Sr.,
who never told me any of this.

Belle Starr

1

A woman stood on the drought-cracked clay in a storm of grasshoppers. They rattled through the air, veering in all directions, bouncing off of her, holding to her. She filled a black kettle with water and prepared to wash her hair. A rusted cricket plow lay at the edge of the garden, a few stunted melons all that was left of a thin harvest. The plow had belonged to old Tom, although she doubted that he ever pushed it.

The grasshoppers were thinning out today. A couple of days before, they had been so thick in the old orchard, millions of them climbing over each other on the trees, that they broke off limbs with their weight. They stuck to her hair as she washed it in borax and egg. The sun crawled in the rattling sky. She saw the outline of her face in the water. It had never ceased to be strange to look into a mirror at that image, a mask with wet dark eyes moving behind it.

She rinsed her hair in gyppy-smelling water from the shallow well. Down the hill the river was low and sluggish, crows stalking the bank for dead fish. It was the driest sickly season in many years.

She squeezed the water out of her hair and called up Faith.

The horse had a felon on her lip, and she decided to use a hackamore instead of a bit. Faith was a chestnut mare, not young anymore. She and Jim Reed had stolen her off of . . . somebody . . . some dirt-faced breed, but that had been a while back.

Right now she had to decide whether to go to Catoosa after her boy Ed or Fort Smith after Jim July. No reason to go after Jim July except for the fun of it, and there was a damn good reason to go after Ed. He'd taken her palomino and three hundred dollars and disappeared into the Territory, and if she didn't catch him pretty soon he'd surely lose the horse and the money. But then it was more complicated than that. She was getting down the Texas saddle, so she guessed it would be Catoosa. To Fort Smith she generally rode sidesaddle and ladylike.

Fort Smith was the courthouse — and Parker. Parker was a fact, a force as solid and indisputable as the weather or the turning of the years. Fat man. Six days a week, twelve hours a day, he sat behind the gavel of the Thirteenth District, Western Arkansas and the Indian Territory. She held no grudge against Parker, even for the nine months he sent her up to Detroit to weave cane-bottom chairs. It wasn't all that bad. Her nervous headaches had actually gotten better during that time. Her husband Sam Starr had received the same sentence but didn't make out quite so good busting rocks. Sam never did have the right idea about Parker. You played his game, or acted like you were playing it, and you had him half-licked. At the trial, Belle hadn't spoken a word out loud. She had written careful notes to her lawyer. She had worn nothing that could be considered gaudy. *Act right,* she had told Sam, *act like a gentleman of your tribe.*

Why was she thinking about Sam? Perhaps because Faith had threaded the maze of trails under Hi-Early Mountain virtually on her own, and right now they weren't two hundred yards from old Tom's graveyard, where Sam lay. The saddle was stiff and squeaky. She noticed that she had forgotten her shotgun. She reined in Faith. It was only thirty minutes back to Younger's Bend, but it would be an annoyance to have to retrace herself in this heat. The air smelled of ironwood and something rotten.

4

The horse skittered backwards, and Belle checked to be sure the hackamore wasn't rubbing her sore.

Lately she'd been doing this a little too often, forgetting herself and daydreaming through whole spaces of time, finding herself down a trail or at a crossing and scarcely knowing how she got there. An old woman with bad teeth and stiff bones and now, it appeared, addled wits. W. F. Wailes in Briartown sold these Phoenix Pills, and it seemed like they did some good for the stiffness but not much for the wandering mind. There were more different kinds of patent medicines than there were Arkansas whiskey peddlers these days — medicines for your head, your heart, your bowels, liver regulators, Black Draught, Bile Beans, Swamp Root, Stomach Bitters, Ague Busters, Botanic Blood Balm, Dromgooles English Female Bitters, Syrup of Figs, Dr. Miles Heart Cure, Nerve Seeds, Electric Bitters — and from what she'd seen, a lot of folks out here spent more money on medicine than anything else. As if a bottle of pills could keep down what starts happening to you after forty.

The graveyard was on a little plateau above the trail. Tom and Sam were both there, and a whole passel of other Starrs. She didn't particularly like visiting the place. Some of the graves had little houses over them, Indian style. She got down and found Sam's stone. It had cost her forty-five dollars from a sculptor in Whitefield. Just his name and years and a simple legend: SON OF TOM STARR. Who was the meanest son-of-a-bitch Cherokee in the Nation, it ought to have said, but didn't. Grasshoppers clung to it.

She felt nothing but tired. It was too early in the day to feel tired. And irritated at the prospect of going all the way back to the house for the shotgun.

If she could talk to Sam what would she say to him? Funny she'd never thought of that. What would she say after three years? "Hello." Maybe that was all. She really couldn't think of what to say. They had talked a pretty good bit while he was alive, a lot of it business, horses and cattle and shipments, but then Sam hadn't always been interested in that. He wasn't what would be called a real hardworking thief. He did business in fits and starts somewhat like his daddy had done. During the in-between times, he could be just about as lazy as any old fleabag Cherokee — lazy and gregarious and improvident and hospitable and loving the kids (everybody's damn kids) — and sometimes in the summer when it got real hot, his clothes would fall away piece by piece until he even looked like an Indian, and he'd be happy puttering around in the squaw patch for two months, talking about nothing but squash, corn, beans, horses. But then he'd get started, steal a few horses or get up a whiskey deal, and one thing would lead to another until he had ten deals going and a half-dozen warrants out on him, and Parker and the Lighthorse and the Choctaws all looking for him at once, and then he'd have to make himself scarce, keep moving, keep working, which was not his true nature, she supposed. Not really. He'd get crazy in his nerves and start acting like a wild buck. She'd been with him when he did it for the last time — over at Aunt Lucy Suratt's at a green-corn dance. . . .

Forgetting the shotgun, she mounted Faith and headed on out of the hills. Tom and Sam always used to get onto her about the trails, telling her to be careful and not take the same one every time and beat out a regular road to the homesite. It was a habit with them, keeping the place as distant from the law as possible. Which wasn't hard considering where it was. About as far south from the capital of the Cherokee Nation and as hidden in the hills as Tom Starr could have put it, right north of the Choctaw boundary and not a day's ride from the Winding Stair Mountains; Younger's Bend was below, between and beyond, and there weren't too many people crazy enough just to go out looking for it.

On the plain north toward Okmulgee, she ran into a locoed steer, his hair bristling up like quills. He stood in the scorched grass, ears cocked up listening, eyes clouded white. He was blind. A lot of them, including the hundreds and thousands of cattle up north in the Cherokee Outlet, were sickly or dying this year because of the drought. The cattle business had been down for two or three years — seriously down — because of bad weather and overinvestment and now the land being taken over by settlers. The Indian Territory had the "last free land in the west," the railroad posters said. And last April over in what had been Seminole country there had been a "land rush," an interesting new invention of the railroads and banks and federal government which enticed armies of people to abandon the northern plains and move here just in time for the drought. She had seen cowboys plowing the creek bottoms for water. She'd seen steers like this on sale for a dollar a head.

He rared feebly, rolling his white-globe eyes, skin dangling off his bones like a dirty robe. He was — or had been — wild as a deer. He tweaked his ears around and nodded his head.

Over two slow rises she came across a shack that she didn't remember seeing before. Nothing special about that, since there were now whole tribes in the Nation that she didn't know anything about, as well as about five times as many white settlers because of the land madness. There was no immediate sign of anyone around the shack, no crop or garden visible from there, but something about it seemed occupied. The door wasn't barred, and one of the windows in the lean-to kitchen was open. Through that window she saw what looked like the outline of a person standing, holding something out — as if to show her. . . . A strong urge came out of her body — up her spine — to get the hell out of there. She spurred Faith around the cabin and out across the plain.

A woman, was it? Offering to share food? Maybe an Indian, her man out hunting or something, wanting to show that she was friendly. Not a bad idea, the way things were. Punk breeds following their pistols around like bulls following their balls, knocking over anything that got in their way.

Had she noticed that Belle was a woman? A white woman? Probably not. Her skin had gotten to the point that she looked like a field hand. Of course her daughter, Pearl, was a different story. She kept herself white as a railhead hussy. Which at her present rate was just about what she was going to be.

She hit the Okmulgee Trail at the North Fork but decided to head east of Okmulgee, cross the Arkansas at Tulsa and go from there to Catoosa. Okmulgee was the "capital" of the Creek Nation — a huddle of shacks on the prairie which she had no reason to visit.

The sun was going down when she reached an old campsite that they had used back in the cattle business days. There was a little spring nearby, which she was glad to see still flowing. The water was so chalky that it would probably give a kildee flying too close a case of diarrhea, but this was the last water until the Arkansas, and she didn't want to ride into Tulsa after dark.

After tethering Faith on twenty feet of rope within reach of the spring, she went about making herself a place on the ground. Mosquitoes and grasshoppers weren't too bad, probably because they couldn't stand the smell of the water. Tin cans littered the ground around the spring. Jim July wasn't far from wrong when he said that if it wasn't for canned tomatoes, most of these settlers wouldn't make it. She gathered some weeds, piled them up and arranged her blanket. She hadn't slept outside in a good while.

Faith's boil was swollen to the breaking point, and she decided to drain and cauterize it. That required a fire, which was okay, she supposed. She hadn't heard of any trouble out here lately. Gathering dry sticks and heating her knife, she thought of the woman in the kitchen back at that shack holding out whatever it was.

When she lanced the felon the horse flinched and snorted but then went right back to nibbling weeds. Belle pressed the heated blade against the draining sore, and the horse started backward, shaking her head vigorously. Belle felt a little better then.

She didn't have anything to eat but a little salt side that she'd carried along, and chewing on it with her front teeth, she smelled the evening air for signs of trouble. She felt . . . almost nothing.

It had been a while since she had been on a good ride. All summer she'd been no farther than Eufala. And now where was she going? She ought not to go chasing after her boy. She ought not interfere with his doings any more than she already had, no matter how stupid he acted. If he called her it would be different, but just chasing after him like this wasn't right. She was what he was trying to get away from in the first place. Well, he'd be sending word for her pretty soon anyway, into some kind of trouble, tangling himself up like a steer with its head through the fence. Catoosa was the place for it, all right, a poisoned town like only some of these little Creek and Seminole places a good way out in the Territory could be. Ed had gotten in trouble there before and sent after her. He was a pretty boy, all right, and no coward; he just wasn't mean enough. He was mean enough to get himself into trouble but not to get himself out of it. She had been trying to teach him ever since Sam died.

Sam, Sam, it was a day to think about Sam.

The night at Aunt Lucy Suratt's when Sam shot Frank West, and Frank West managed to shoot Sam, and they were both dead within three minutes, the dance didn't stop and she didn't leave it. She danced all night.

The kids. She remembered the afternoon — when was it, maybe a week after they put Sam into the ground — when she watched Ed out in the river, naked, wading in the shallows. She realized that he had a good stout man's body. For sixteen years she had lived in one- and two-room cabins with the boy. She had changed his rags and taught him how to sit up at the table and feed himself, helped teach him how to ride, read, shoot, cipher, and a dozen, dozen other human tasks, and in all those years she'd never had anything like the feeling she had at that moment. He was unaware of her, daydreaming in the water, thigh deep. He was getting away from her. She was aware of his body and of the fact that it was not a mere forgotten appendage of hers. She watched him and perhaps in that moment made a decision.

She thought now: was it a decision? It was her belief — her assumption — that whatever she did she meant to do. So had it been at that moment when she decided to deserve her name?

She lay down now, the sky opening up above her. She had good eyes. Wondered if Jim July was having any fun in Fort

9

Smith tonight. Doubtless was. He was probably down on Front Street in one of those prim little two-story whorehouses, playing cards, drinking and showing off how he could talk six languages. Trying to get a piece of ass without paying for it.

The stars were like gauze across the sky. Faith nickered. She didn't sound too bad off.

2

Earliest morning, when night had gone to sleep, the smell of the spring hovered in her face. Ah, here she was, back to the land of milk and magnesia. Something had awakened her. Faith was kicking and raring against her long tether, doubtless caught scent of a skunk or coyote. Belle sat up, stiff as an old table. Her jaw hurt. God damn teeth, what she ought to do was drink some whiskey and get every damn one of them pulled out of her head. "Heyyy-you! Heyyy-you!" she croaked at the horse. "Cut the shit, will you. Nothing wants to eat you — old stringy fool." Damn horse wasn't anything but a thousand-pound rabbit. Put her up against a determined field mouse and she'd run for cover.

Belle ignored her and went for a drink of chalk water. She'd like to ask a scientist sometime why the Nation had so many foul waters and noxious minerals. The whole place smelled like a mule fart. She splashed some against her face, cleaned out her mouth with a hackberry root and squatted down to relieve herself. Damn bowels hardly worked anymore. . . .

Something about Faith's fretting made her uneasy. By the time she rolled up her blanket, the horse was standing still — quite still — with one of her black hooves curled up like she did sleeping. Maybe it was just a bad dream. "Heyyy-you! Get over here!" The horse remained still. "Heyy-you!" So she was going to make Belle carry the saddle to her. Okay.

She slapped down the blanket on Faith's back. She was drooping her head down and blinking her eyes in a funny kind of rapid way. Belle hadn't known that she was this old and worn out. "Wake up you fool horse, we're going to Catoosa." Her voice sounded muffled in the dew-laden air. The horse sighed and laid her bulk down in a patch of rusty cans. She farted and drooped her head down. Belle saw then what was in her right flank — a small feathered stick.

She looked around. They were not showing themselves yet. Okay. She would think clearly. This was something new: in fourteen years in the Territory she'd never come up hard against any horse Indians. They seldom came this far east. They waited until she was forty years old, alone and with a toothache, to jump her, the sons of bitches. Her shirt was not buttoned, and for a moment she feared that they'd see she was a woman and move in. At least her hair was up. Buttoning her shirt slowly, she put on her hat and cartridge belt. They could have been on the hillside above the spring or out behind some brush, there was no way to tell yet. If they were shooting arrows there was probably more than one of them, and if they saw she was a woman they'd probably try to take her. She'd heard plenty of stories.

No motion yet. They were waiting for her to leave so they could cut up the horse. She should move, not show indecision, but she had no clue regarding which direction to take. She'd have to decide. The Arkansas River Road was only a few miles north of there — the direction she'd already been headed. With the little sack off her saddle horn and a couple of small items from the saddlebags, she took off walking. It irritated her to leave that saddle. They'd probably cut it up and eat it in favor of Faith after they got a taste of her. They had the drop on her and could have shot her. Apparently they just wanted the horsemeat.

Up over the shoulder of the hill she realized too late that she had made a mistake. A band of them were waiting on foot in brush just over the crest, seven or eight of them, some in buckskin, some chest naked, single feathers in their braids. A couple had rifles, old long-barrels. Down the rise about a mile to the north was a whole population of them — women, horses, mules, travaux. These were the scouts and must have seen her horse and strung a poisoned arrow.

For years and years she'd been hearing stories about the western Indians, especially the Comanches, since they were the biggest and closest tribe of them. How their raids up through eastern Oklahoma were the worst part of being a "Civilized" Indian. It was hard on a farmer when somebody came around every year and ate his plowhorse. So now she was finally getting her taste of it. Funny thing about it was that this wasn't a raiding party but a whole gaggle of them, probably another poor bunch being stuffed into the Nation, lost their way and wandered too far east.

Well now. If she kept on straight ahead she'd walk right into them. She couldn't figure out why they were on foot, unless to be quiet coming up over the hill. Crow, Comanche, Kiowa, Arapaho, most of them would fight or hunt from horseback if they had a choice. So they hadn't intended in the first place to do any fighting — she told herself that. She still walked toward them but grazed off just enough to avoid a direct encounter. She had absolutely no chance if they chose to cut down on her. Zero. There was not enough cover for a holdout. If she turned heel they'd chase her down. She'd heard enough stories of what horse Indians did with women captives. She knew a Creek woman in Briartown who had lived with the Comanche for a few years. Her fingers had been frozen and cut off, her legs were swollen and useless, eyes hollow in her skull. They'd driven her with the livestock all over the western Territory until her legs gave out, then just left her behind like they sometimes did with their own old people.

The God damn lice-jumping sons of bitches. There was only one way to handle something like this, and that was flat out. She wasn't scared. Her teeth hurt too much to be scared, she told herself. They were holding steady, but talking among themselves

— fifty yards away. If she kept on she'd come real close to them. They could see her pistols and probably wanted them. She had no advantage, there was no prudent course of action, her thoughts began to race and stagger beyond logic. Beyond reasonableness. One of the bucks had an old Sharps rifle and could pick her off in a second at three times this distance. If she tried to suck up to them, they'd take her like a squirrel. Nothing a wild Indian hates worse than pleading. Made them sick.

Good. Good, sons of bitches. She drew a pistol, careful to keep it aimed to the sky, and pulled off a round. It was a gesture of amicability to empty your guns at a great distance, but she didn't intend that. She intended something not quite understood to herself. Still headed in their direction, she pulled off another round. They were restless now, an arrow was strung, the Sharps was leveled at her. She should get down but didn't. With her free hand she took off her hat and flung it in an arc across the hill, and snapped loose her hair to fall down past her shoulders. She didn't know until she unbuttoned her shirt what she was doing. She pulled off another round and began to let loose a high-pitched death gobble. She holstered the pistol, threw down her shirt and slipped off her camisole.

She was showing them that she was a woman. That was not good sense, but there was no such thing as good sense at the moment. Somehow — maybe — she could slip through their superstitions. They would kill a woman in a raid, all right — but a single woman? They would have to mutilate her body if they killed her, and did they want to do that, the body of a single woman shot at sunrise? She didn't know. She gobbled like a dying Cherokee. She'd confuse them if nothing else. Shooting into the dawn sky again, she continued to walk in a straight line over the hill. She could see their faces now. A couple of them were wearing war hatchets. All of them had little purses tied to their belts, probably with "good medicine" in them. They ain't scared to die, but they are afraid of bad medicine, Sam used to say. So maybe that was what she was trying to do.

She walked in such a way as to bounce her tits, much as the poor old dugs would bounce.

At the closest point, perhaps twenty yards, she stopped and untied the little sack from her belt and laid it down on a rock. An offering of some kind? But she continued to hold the pistol high and gobble to beat hell. She could just about see the copper head down the fat barrel of the Sharps. One of the bucks was grinning. She moved on down the hill, back turned now, walking briskly as though knowing her destination. Would they shoot her in the back? Spread her over fifteen yards of hillside. *This very dust.* Her throat was hoarse and raw from gobbling.

She had an odd thought. If Cole Younger could see this, he'd get a chuckle out of it.

At the bottom of the hill she chanced to look back and see that they'd lowered their weapons. One of them was picking up the little sack she'd left. It had some money, her headache and soreness medicines, and a couple of other little doodads in it. She hoped it would interest them. She had to walk a little eastward to keep from bumping into the big tribe out on the flats. They seemed to be going about their normal business. Only a few of them were even watching her. There was a ravine off to the right — very inviting — but she sensed that trying to conceal herself might tip the balance and make the scouts curious about her. She would walk in the open at a normal pace and not look back again.

Even though they might just look at her trinkets and decide that she was not a demon woman but your regular old fleshly kind, good for certain tasks. Maybe it was a mistake to leave the sack. And right now they could be gliding down the hill like they do, quiet as cats, fixing to turn her into a herd cow.

She was hot and sagging by the time she made it to the Arkansas River Road. For four hours grasshoppers had been rattling out of the dust, bouncing off her face, gluing onto her tits. There was no one in sight. She felt ridiculous without a shirt, and there was no way to cover herself up. She had no choice but to head toward Tulsa. She'd stop at some shack and beg or steal a shirt of some kind. After getting a drink in the river, she climbed back up to the road in time to see a wagon coming up not far behind.

Walking on slowly ahead she let it catch up with her. Good brace of mules. One man in the seat, canvas-covered wagon with a sign on the side: PHOTOGRAPHS TAKEN. The man had a puzzled expression on his face, something between a smile and a gape. "May I offer . . ."

"You can offer but you best not ask, mister."

He was still gaping.

"Got anything I can wear?"

"Indeed, I . . . must . . . yes."

She swung up onto the seat and looked at him with ice in her eyes. "Then get it."

She took the reins while he got a shirt out of the wagon.

"I hope this will do." He looked chastely away while she put it on.

"It'll do. Now you can take back the reins and get us to Tulsa."

"Pardon my asking, but . . ."

"How did I lose my shirt? The same way I lost my horse and almost my ass. To a band of Crows."

He nodded slowly and finally thought to close his mouth. They rode on for a while, and he spoke again. "Are you Belle Starr?"

She glanced at him. "Who wants to know?"

"I'm a photographer. I've seen pictures of you. In fact I had once thought to visit your home."

"Where'd you see these pictures?"

"They were studio portraits taken at Mr. Griffin's in Fort Smith."

She didn't respond.

After a while he went on. "I am taking pictures around the Territory. The last of the great Indian Nation, you know. It's a very popular theme. I took pictures at the land rush last April."

She looked at him.

"Popular, you know, on stage and with stories in the magazines

16

and so forth. I've sold a number of photographs to published albums. The noble warrior, beautiful squaw . . ."

"Maybe you ought to go back there and take one of them sawing up my horse to eat."

"I do try to take some candid scenes, but the Indians prefer posed portraits with the backdrops. Many of them won't allow their picture taken at all except with the backdrop — boulders and waterfalls, you know, no relation to this part of the country. I think they deem it exotic."

"Where you from?"

"I make my home in Arkansas City, Kansas. My name is William S. Prettyman, proud to meet you, ma'am. This is not my first trip down into the Territory. I grew tired of the studio, the smell of mercury and the ruby lamp. Oh, there's always excitement. . . . A Mr. Bob Dalton came in last winter. He mentioned your name. It was the first I'd heard of you."

"What'd he say?"

"I don't recall exactly. He was very nervous. A peculiar man. He combed his hair with so much water that he would not photograph well. I objected in the strongest language. He was so nervous that he had to use the headstand."

"The only good thing I can say about Mr. Bob Dalton is that his folks are from Jackson County, Missouri. His momma was Adeline Younger."

"He served as a marshal for Judge Parker, I believe."

"Marshal and horsethief. His brother Frank was shot down in a scrap with some rustlers. Three or four of his brothers worked for Parker at one time or another. About like most of them that work for Parker. I believe they're robbing trains now. Ain't got any class. Pinkertons will get them before long."

"May I ask the destination of your interrupted journey?"

"Tulsa, right now."

"And may I ask the purpose?"

"No."

They rode on in silence a way, through a little cluster of Indian shacks built right on the road. Piles of rusted cans. Sullen, droop-shouldered children, naked, with fever and hunger-glazed eyes. Patches of oat, kafir, and sweet corn out back frying in the sun, sweet corn every bit of thumb size this season. One old gray-muzzled mule tied with a lariat in exactly the spot and with the same look of unconcern that Belle had seen every time she'd traveled this road. Wasn't for the flies, he'd be more a statue than a mule.

"You can tell me what pictures you saw of me at Griffin's."

"I don't know . . . they were various. . . . If I remember correctly, one was a dual portrait of you and a man named Jack Spaniard."

She nodded slightly. "What else?"

"That's all."

"You said 'various.' "

"That's all I recall." He was somewhat ruffled by her manner.

"Well re-call a little bit better, Mr. Prettyman."

"Madam, I don't believe it necessary . . ."

"You brought it up. I don't like pictures of me being shown around. Who's the jackleg that was showing them? Was it Griffin?"

He was genuinely upset. "I would remind you, madam . . ."

"I would remind you that I might pull out one of these pistols and shoot your dick off, Mr. Prettyman. I've done worse. Was it Griffin?"

He was truly distressed and didn't answer.

"Was it Griffin?"

"It is not necessary for you to threaten to shoot . . . me. I brought up the topic merely as a gesture of friendliness."

"You brought up the topic because you want to snuggle up and get a few pictures of me to sell for fifty dollars apiece."

"I never suggested that. And I beg your pardon for turning my casual conversation into threats and disputation. If you don't mind, this journey may be more felicitous in silence."

"You sound like a lawyer." She reached into the back of her mouth and pulled on a tooth, wincing. "You got any laudanum?"

He looked ahead with exaggerated coolness. "I do."

"I need it for these teeth."

After another dignified pause he reached into a box behind him and dug out a bottle of syrup. She took a chug and kept it. She didn't feel very friendly right now. There was always some turkey buzzard waiting to eat out your softest parts. She didn't appreciate Griffin showing around her portrait with Jack Spaniard. The worst part of it was that she couldn't remember having it taken. Nothing about it. But one thing was sure, every time her picture was taken it caused her grief. Just looking at her own face . . . And then some prosecutor would get a hold of it and use it in court to put her and this character together for one spurious reason or another. Jack Spaniard was out of jail right now, running horses last she'd heard.

Not far from the crossing, the shacks and crops became more numerous. There were some Cherokee along here, but the main part of them were lower Creek. They were the first bunch of the Creek Tribe to come to the Territory, mostly breeds to one degree or another who settled this good cropland along the Arkansas. They weren't as fierce against the white man as the full bloods. Belle had heard more than once about how Roby McIntosh, Chief of the lower Creek, tried to get the U.S. Army to herd the full bloods back east, claiming that their presence threatened property and government. The split in the Creek was like the split in the Cherokee between the Ridge and the Ross factions: their worst enemies were their own tribal kin.

The Creek had no constitution, no schools, and there were lots of stories of missionaries getting kicked out of the Nation. They had stayed old-fashioned longer than the Cherokee. And when they got down and out they could be worse off than other tribes, pride bruised more deeply and likely to go bad all at once, if at all. Where a Cherokee could shrug his shoulders and make a joke, a Creek would get worried, brood, find himself a bottle.

With Jim July she knew about that firsthand.

Things had changed now that Oklahoma was filling up with white settlers and wild tribes. The government had used the war as an excuse to take land away from the Civilized Tribes (the Chickasaw and Choctaw had joined the Southern cause outright, along with slave-owning Cherokee, Creek and Seminole), and ever since then they had been squashing every kind of Indian from all parts of the country into the Territory. Belle had never seen a tribe of horse Indians as far east as she had today. The woman back at that shack holding out her rabbit — maybe she'd heard they were coming and mistook Belle for a scout. Belle would like to tell that gal, it'll take more than a skinned rabbit to head off that bunch, honey, you better clear yourself out of there.

By the time they reached the Tulsa crossing the laudanum had given her some relief. She'd taken several more sips and was feeling almost friendly with Mr. Prettyman. He was still sitting there with a plug up his ass. A sign painted with green letters was nailed to a tree near the landing.

10¢ FOR A FOOTMAN, COW, SHEEP, HOG, HORSE
   OR ANY OTHER ANIMAL
25¢ MAN AND HORSE
35¢ TWO HORSE VEHICLE
50¢ FOUR HORSES

They rattled onto the wooden planks of the ferry.

"Hello Esco. You remember me?"

The old man glanced up from his ropes. He was beardless, and old enough to have been born in Alabama or Georgia. "Yep."

"You seen Ed Reed lately?"

"Nope."

"He'd a been riding a pretty little palomino horse. Wearing a silk neckerchief, probably green. Might have had him a female companion along."

The ferryman shook his head vaguely, long since hardened to such urgent questions.

"Think hard, Esco. I'll make it worth your while."

"Nope." He shuffled off the ferry.

She drew one of her pistols and shot into the mud not far from him.

"What are you doing?" Mr. Prettyman demanded.

The team of mules on the ratchet at the front of the ferry grew restless. She pulled off another round, and they began to pull and rattle against their harness. Esco climbed back onto the boat and stepped up beside her. "Wouldn't do that if I was you."

When she shot again the barrel was one foot from the old man's face. He staggered backward. The ratchet mules were about to break out of harness.

"Which side of the river is my boy on, Esco?"

The old man blinked and rubbed the powder sparks from his face, shuffling his feet around in a little dance of miff.

Belle laughed at him. "You old spook, get this thing across the river."

Prettyman swung down from his side and walked up front to calm the ferry mules. One of them bit him on the forearm. Belle howled with laughter and took another swig of laudanum. Esco was very wrought up, but he finally managed to push off and get his mules walking in a circle. On the other side of the river the photographer, having poured some carbolic acid from his medicine chest onto the mule bite, turned to Belle. "You may keep the shirt, madam. Good evening."

"Trying to get rid of me here?"

"We have crossed the river. I see no use in further accompaniment."

"You don't like me do you, Mr. Prettyman?"

He looked away from her and sniffed.

"I can't say as I blame you. A woman ought not introduce herself with no shirt on. It makes for a strain."

"I think you have had entirely too much of that laudanum."

"Well now, is that right? Too much? Far as I'm concerned, Mr. Prettyman, God couldn't make too much laudanum for me to take. Whip up those mules. You don't want to get rid of me until we get into Tulsy Town, anyway. Can you see me, a lone woman, walking this dangerous road at sunset? Ah," she sighed. "I am a woman much misused. My back teeth are falling out all at once. My only boy stole all my money and my best horse and ran away from home. Plus, if what I heard is right, he went and found a two-bit strumpet that couldn't make a living in Fort Smith to trail after him. I know the type. Only kind of meat they got on their bones is the kind that jiggles when they walk. They'd reject her at the rendering plant. And now he's running with her. Son of a bitch. Where are we?"

"Mrs. Starr, we are in Tulsa now. I am leaving the wagon at Jenkins' just down the street."

". . . Which ain't half my troubles. I haven't got a dime to buy a drink. I haven't got a change of clothes to shake off the dust. Tell you what I'll do, Mr. Prettyman. You want pictures, you can have them. I'll pose five pictures at a flat rate of five dollars apiece for you, no more, no less. Hell, you'll get fifty apiece on my name. Five pictures, twenty-five dollars, in advance. You pay now, I'll pose tomorrow morning right here at the stable."

"I am sorry Mrs. Starr, I do not have twenty-five dollars for such a project. Now if you will . . ."

"Well then what do you need, three pictures? I won't settle for less than three pictures at five apiece. That's fifteen dollars now."

"I might be able to offer two apiece for four pictures," he said.

"Twelve dollars for four and I won't go any lower. Twelve dollars right now."

"Ten dollars for four, and I take one pistol as mortgage that you'll show up."

Belle gave him a pistol and took the ten dollars. At least now she'd be able to get something to eat and a place to stay.

At Beckman's Inn she drank three fingers of whiskey and waited for some supper. Old Mrs. Beckman was as busy and grumpy as ever. She warmed up fried chicken and beans and cornbread and tiny little potatoes at the big open fireplace in the common room, muttering about the weather and fate and whatever else came to mind. Belle had some food and began to feel a little more human. She chewed with her front teeth. The old woman had no news about her boy, only about the boomer raids. From what she'd heard, big portions of the Cherokee Outlet across the top of Oklahoma had been set afire by raiders out of

Kansas, who were coming down and dragging burning logs through the grass in an attempt to run the cattlemen out.

The Starrs had always scoffed at tribal government, calling the chiefs incompetent (Ross faction) fools and disaffiliating themselves from tribal business. Belle hadn't always entirely shared that attitude, but she was skeptical of the big leasing operation. For several years the Cherokee Tribe had leased to the big cattle operations its "outlet" lands. Although the cattle business had been in trouble the last few years, she heard that the new contract between the Livestock Association and the Tribe called for $200,000 in lease money over the next year.

"Well I'll tell you what they're going to do, Mrs. Beckman. The feds are going to take that land away from the Tribe and give it to the boomers. They'll have another one of them damn runs on it, and Oklahoma will get so top-heavy with people it'll turn upside down and sink. The railroads and wholesalers are putting on an advertising campaign to make it look like a battle between the big cattlemen and the poor white settlers, as if there wasn't a tribe that owned the land at all. What it really comes down to is the Tribe on one side and the white boomers and the money men that'll get rich off their settlement on the other. And there ain't no way on God's earth that the Tribe has a chance. The government doesn't want them to stay together anyway. Wants them to break down into individual property owners. Free enterprise, whoopie. Thanks for the food. I enjoyed it. Where's Mr. Beckman?"

"Dead."

"Mr. Beckman dead? . . . Well I'm real sorry to hear that."

"Yeah, he died, the lazy old devil. Not that he helped me much. At least there was a man around. It was one day last April. He finished breakfast and went back to sleep. There wasn't anything unusual about that. It was dinner before I guessed that there was something wrong. Old Beckman, he'd sleep all morning, but he sure wouldn't miss dinner. Now I haven't got a man and I'm too old to get one. Don't know what I'm going to do."

Belle leaned forward in her chair and smiled at the old lady. "You may be seasoned out, Mrs. Beckman, but you've got some money you can waggle just about as good as you can waggle your bustle. You own this place outright, don't you?"

Mrs. Beckman reddened somewhat. "Well, of course the land is leased from Okmulgee."

"You got the bills and Mr. Beckman's stone paid for?"

"Yes."

"Well I'd say you're in good shape. Just don't be so modest. This town's growing. You let them know that you're on top of it. Long as there's breath in you you'll look pretty. You've got good bones and haven't spent too much time in the sun. Me, I lost three husbands and looked like an old prune before I was thirty-eight, and you don't hear me complaining. Now don't let me hear it from you, you sassy old thing. Where do I sleep?"

She awakened before sunrise with her mouth a volcano of pain. It reached through her jawbone into her skull. She didn't think of breakfast, coffee or anything except walking out in that street in the first nitch of light and finding a dentist.

In the middle of town a crew of men were inflating a big hot-air balloon. FREE LAND said a sign on the platform. A LADY FROM THE EAST, exotic in a glittery robe, was being instructed in how to HANG FROM HER TOES and scatter thousands of pieces of paper in which were going to be included FREE LAND DEEDS.

She bet they'd be free. Tulsy Town was just beginning to stir when she found the dentist sign at the Masonic Building (the only brick building in town). There she waited while the sun began to peek over the hills and the morning train from Sapulpa arrived with a crowd of passengers who'd apparently come for the balloon ascension and FREE LAND. The smell of coffee in the air failed to entice her. She had a broken mouth and had to get some relief for it now. A barkeep across the street was sweeping out, and she asked him if he knew where the dentist was.

"You'll find him at Jenkins' Blacksmith. Works there in the morning and here at the dentist office in the afternoons."

She didn't like the implications of that, but had no choice. At his wagon in the blacksmith shop, Mr. Prettyman had already gotten out his camera for pictures of the balloon. The town was all in a tizzy. The man working at the forge was not Jenkins but someone she seemed to vaguely remember.

"Got time for a tooth-pulling job? . . . Do I know you?"

He looked up from his work, thin moustache, brown face, very handsome. He put down his hammer and looked into her mouth. "You have two teeth that need to be pulled. I charge fifty cents per tooth for those kind."

"All right, but I can't wait."

"There's no need to wait. Lie down."

"Where at? . . . I don't want no funny business now."

His manner was gentle and quiet. There was a strangely soothing way about him — soothing and distant. Belle had seen this man somewhere before. "What's your name?"

"Blue Duck."

"Ahh . . . ever make it down to the Canadian River District?"

He still smiled, lightly. "Would you lie down in the stall, please?"

She lay down in a patch of hay, and the man's right knee descended to her chest. He kept the weight off until putting the pliers into her mouth, then pressed down hard on her chestbone and grabbed hold of a tooth — she heard all kind of squrshing around in there but hardly anything new in the way of pain — and he withdrew one bloody stump, gave her a breather and descended for the second. All the while Belle was watching his expression, which was utterly fixed and showed no thought nor mood nor irritation, even when the second tooth broke off in her mouth and he had to use a small knife, sterilized in the fire, to dig it out by the roots. By the time he finished and packed her mouth with salt, she was choking on blood.

She sat up coughing, and he went back to work on some horseshoes. She was nauseated but so glad to be rid of those rotten teeth that she almost felt good. "Boo Duk." He looked up. "My 'ame's Beah Stharr, by th' way. . . . You got 'ome whisk'?"

He turned up his hat a little. "No ma'am. You can get whiskey over at Jaycox."

His calmness was intriguing and irritating. She hadn't seen such a pleasant, lineless, worryless demeanor in a long time. "How owd awe you?"

"Pardon me?"

"Owd. How owd?"

For the first time a light perplexity crossed his face. He went back to work without answering. Prettyman rushed back in to pick up more plates for his camera. "She's taking off! Less than five minutes! There must be a thousand people out there. She's going to hang by her ankles and fly over town dropping deeds. It's the most ingenious thing I've ever seen. Her costume is quite . . . well, theatrical, to say the least. Some bank up in Coffeyville is sponsoring the event. You've got to see it to believe it."

Belle sat in the straw trying to get her stomach under control. After a while she wandered out into the street, which was a regular dust storm of excitement with children selling parched kafir and sugar candies and all kinds of people milling around — tellers and clerks from town in short coats and high collars, burning-eyed men who'd come in on the morning train and Indian farm families from the jacks, some of whom were trying to sell bushels of poor-looking corn and oats and even flowers for buttoneers. Over in a side street a choir of Indian kids dressed up in their best — suspenders and calico dresses — stood all at attention staring out with wide glittery dark eyes, singing temperance songs. A man with curly golden hair harangued a crowd on the virtues of Dr. Rinaldo's Magic Belt and Suspensory.

She went to Jaycox's for a drink of rye whiskey to calm her stomach, and went back out in time to witness final preparations for the ascent. The LADY FROM THE EAST had taken off her robe and was standing in the middle of the main street wearing a little leopard-skin outfit. They were trying to tie her ankle so she could hang upside down. Women gasped and men pushed to the front. Belle could tell by the confused way she acted that she was not an acrobat but some poor Kansas whore they'd hired for the job. She blinked her eyes and giggled at the men while they secured the rope. A dude in a vested suit made a big show of tying a bulging pocketed belt around her waist — apparently with the FREE LAND DEEDS in it. He was explaining to her how to scatter them.

The balloon was tied to posts on both sides of the street, and they eased it higher while the woman got ready to hang. Men were offering their opinions and advice on how to do it more safely, and she was agreeing with everybody. Mr. Prettyman pushed through the mob, camera over his shoulder, looking for a better angle on the balloon. She was secured by one ankle when an officious drunk who claimed to be a "knot expert" came up and retied her.

Belle had a premonition that Ed was going to show up here. She didn't want to get into it with him now, her mouth swole up and feeling puny like this. The dentist had come out for a look and was standing beside her, impassive at the excitement.

Men were riding and running down the street out across the fields in the direction they thought the balloon would fly. An old leathery-skinned woman stood outside her mud-chinked cabin down the street, crushing corn with mortar and pestle, fiercely uninvolved in all this nonsense. An orator was making some kind of pitch for the bank that was sponsoring the event, but his listeners were either too inebriated, excited or suspicious to pay him much mind. One anchor rope popped loose and the LADY was wrenched off her feet and levitated somewhat prematurely. She was still smiling, however, trying to make the best of it, although indeed her bosom was about to fall out of the leopard skin and her face was already turning red.

A number of drunks in the crowd, including the "knot expert," were taking the whole thing very seriously, shouting directions at her and the boys on the anchor ropes. Others, including a group of old Seminole men, were standing apart. Wearing turbans and the usual six or eight shirts, the old men talked among themselves as if unsure about the reality of this event. A couple of them were old enough to have fought in Florida. Belle had always admired the Seminole for being the only one of the Five Tribes to have held out in the South. But these men had been around here for years and years — you could see it in their faces — hanging around waiting for rations, not dead, most of them, only because they hadn't been able to scrounge up enough corn liquor to kill themselves on.

The LADY was hanging upside down with the blood running to her face, trying to unbutton her belt. "Not yet! Not yet!" yelled the man in the double-breasted suit, as they cut the remaining anchor cord with an ax. The crowd cheered while she flailed helplessly down the street, BY HER TOES, the balloon catching in a gust of wind that prevented it at the moment from rising. It ascended above the Masonic Building, and at a speed of several miles an hour the LADY ran square into the chimney. She ceased to flail as the balloon dragged her off into the sky. The banker rode after her yelling "Now! Now drop the deeds! Begin to drop them!" But she was apparently out cold.

Belle spat blood and laughed. Everybody had joined the banker now in yelling "Drop the deeds!" but she flew across the fields as unresponsive as a side of bacon. The wind carried the balloon toward the river, pulling it downward across the brown sludgy surface, and the LADY was just about to be dipped head-first, arms dangling, when she flew out of sight. Blue Duck shook his head and went back inside the shop.

Belle listened to the clanging of his hammer and tried to remember who he was. Everything about the man was familiar, but she couldn't quite place him.

Prettyman reappeared, huffing and puffing with his camera over his shoulder. "Are we ready for those pictures now? The light is good at this hour."

"I had some dental work Mr. Prettyman. My jaw's swole up. You'll have to take them later."

"We agreed on the hour and the place, Mrs. Starr, and I will remind you that I paid you in advance."

"That's too bad. My face hurts. Besides which, I haven't got any decent clothes. You'll have to do it later."

"Madam . . ."

"I ain't a madam, you fart-faced cob-eared son of a bitch. Now lay off. I got a quart of blood in my gut, and I don't feel like putting up with you."

Belle went to the wagon, opened up the medicine chest and reclaimed the pistol, leaving the photographer once again at a loss. She went looking for Bill Whittington, an old acquaintance from her horse-running days who used to loaf around the pool hall. He might be able to advance her a little loan so she could buy a nag and get out of this hellhole. But he was not there now, and she didn't see any other old friends. It was always a pain these days to walk into a smoke-swirling ball-cracking manplace like this and not know anybody, or not at least see by the look on somebody's face that they knew who she was. They were always ready to wisecrack at a woman. As many hours as Belle had spent in this joint dealing livestock, she didn't see a single friendly face. All these galoots were drunk and clamorous after the balloon ascension.

"What is it?" someone yelled.

"Is it the lady from the east?"

"If it is she sure as hell fell onto a rocky slope."

"I'm Belle Starr, you creampuff. Say something else and I'll make you sit on that pool stick."

Her threat was absorbed in the general hubbub of the place, no one apparently hearing her.

Toothache congealed into a headache, mood soured, she wandered back out onto the street rubbing her forehead, trying to decide what to do. She'd been out of action too long. The flow of scum through this town was faster than the river current; it was a whole new place now. She headed back toward the blacksmith shop.

The crowds in the street had broken up. Everybody with a horse was out chasing the LADY. There was speculation on whether she had drowned or flown off the river and perhaps descended into a tree somewhere with all her deeds intact, and if so, whether a man might take possession of all of them. Were the deeds clear titles, or was there some kind of catch in them that allowed a person to possess only one? "Why hellfire," she heard one old whiskeyface splutter, "I ain't greedy about land, I only want what jines mine."

Which reminded her of nothing so much as her own poor old daddy. It had been his favorite joke, maybe his only joke.

Standing in the middle of the street holding her headache, she heard a rig rattle up behind her — Prettyman with the dentist beside him on the seat. "Mrs. Starr, I am on my way out of town. Do you still intend to forfeit on our agreement?"

"Where you going?"

"Catoosa."

"Tell you what I'll do. You give me a ride to Catoosa, and I'll let you take my picture. I think that jaw's going down okay."

"And what guarantee do I have that once we get there you . . ."

"Halfway, we can stop and you can take my picture, nice little grove somewhere, then we can head on to Catoosa."

"All right. Mr. Blue Duck is our witness."

"You going to Catoosa, too?"

He looked at her, expressionless as before. "I pull teeth there on Saturday."

Belle swung up and sat beside him. Prettyman got into the back to prepare his wetplates. She couldn't help but glance at the dentist. "Did you ever ride with Jack Spaniard?"

"No."

"Cole Younger?"

"No."

"Sinker Wilson?"

"No."

"Who then? I've seen your face or heard of you, one."

"I rode with you once, if that's what you mean."

She stared at him. "You rode with me? I don't remember that." Her mind raced through possibilities.

"Many years ago. Watt Grayson."

"Oh Jesus Christ, Watt Grayson. My God in heaven, were you

that boy Dan Evans brought along? I'll be damned. What ever happened? Parker got Dan. Fact he was one of Parker's first six, if I remember right. Got him for something else, and he confessed to the Grayson job on the gallows. Maledon had the rope around his neck, and he told the whole damn story. Big thing in the newspapers. So what happened to you? How'd you get loose?"

"Never got caught."

"Blue Duck isn't what you went by then."

"I had many names."

"And you were about eighteen years old, if I estimate right. You been a dentist all these years?"

"A good while. Traveled some. Tried out a few different things."

"I'm trying to remember . . . you didn't say a word that whole time. I thought you were just some wild Indian Evans hired on for a horseboy."

"I was."

Remembering the Watt Grayson robbery put her in a funny state. It was not only her first robbery but really the only big one she ever participated in herself. Fourteen years ago she and Dan Evans and Jim Reed and this boy had ridden to Grayson's house, not far from Eufala, and tortured him into revealing where he had stashed the tribal annuities. Grayson was an upper Creek chief, and like most of them he didn't do anything with the government handouts, year after year, but hide them; he certainly wouldn't have considered giving any more of it than he had to to the common people in the Tribe. An old dried-up walnut of a man, he hid behind two wives out in a smokeshack, and Jim Reed beat him on the fingers with a hammer and kicked him on the legs and finally hanged him from a crossbeam in his cabin, half choking him to death before he would reveal the location of his treasure. It was hidden in a cave up the hill from his house, all the governmental gifts and allowances from years past that he'd managed to hoard, including bars of iron and steel, anvils, black-smith tools, saws, knives, wedges, four-pound axes, blankets, a frock coat laced with gold, pairs of lavender pantaloons, beaver hats with scarlet plumes, several pairs of calfskin puttees, a stack of medals with inscriptions on them (CHIEF, TREASURER, SHERIFF, etc.), also a drum, fife and flag, several hundred long-barrel Derringer rifles, together with lead, powder and bullet molds, and even spinning wheels and plows of outdated design, and most significantly, one chest of gold coins amounting to $30,000.

Watt Grayson told them where the treasure was, all right, after Jim Reed nearly tore his head off — but then what happened?

Belle had almost forgotten about the Grayson robbery. After so long it had grown to seem unreal to her. As with any big job, she couldn't go around talking about it with outsiders, and as her accomplices disappeared over the years, the event receded into silence and obscurity. Not unlike a lot of the rest of her life these dry days. Yet this one was special in two ways. Not only was it her first big job, it was also one of the biggest hauls she'd ever heard of. Even bigshot Cole Younger couldn't brag of anything much bigger — bank or train. He could sit up in the pen writing letters to the newspapers calling Belle Starr a "horsethief" in the Cherokee Nation who "used my name for the notoriety it carried," she doubted that he'd ever looked square in the face of $30,000 gold.

"What happened to it?" she asked Blue Duck.

He watched the road, reins asleep in his hands. "I don't know."

Prettyman clanked around behind them in the wagon, and she spoke more quietly. "Evans and Jim were going to get it changed to silver and paper. Next thing I knew, Jim was bushwhacked and Evans was on Parker's gallows. What happened to it?"

"I heard that you and Jim Reed spent it in Dallas."

"Who told you that?"

"Evans."

"He's a sweatbacked liar, too — no offense to the dead. Jim and I took one thousand dollars to squander and not a cent more. Lived high for a while at the Planters' where I used to deal faro — bought a horse and buggy, kept me a riding horse, hired a hostler, stayed around town drinking and shooting dice there for a few months."

"All that on a thousand?"

"I ain't saying we didn't do a little work on the side. But as far as that gold went, we took one thousand dollars' worth. You don't have to flash a lot of gold to get up suspicion. Jim knew this old scalawag down in San Antonio who'd change it at a pretty fair rate. But Evans never did make it down to Dallas with the chest. Just about the time they called me out on the prairie to identify Jim, I heard that Evans was going to be hanged. Were you with him before he got arrested?"

"For a while. I hadn't seen him for over a month when he was taken to Fort Smith."

"Was he guilty?"

"Probably."

"Who'd he kill?"

"A white man named Seabolt, I think, nineteen, twenty years old. Put a bullet in his head, stole his horse, saddle and boots. They convicted him on the boots."

"I heard that Dan was riding with Cole Younger just before he got hanged. Is that true?"

"I don't know."

"Why would he kill somebody for a horse and boots when he had twenty-nine thousand dollars in a chest?"

"Perhaps it was too dangerous to spend the gold."

"Why'd you leave him? You knew he had the money."

"I didn't care about it one way or the other."

"What do you mean?"

He shrugged. "Like I said, I didn't know he had it. He told me that you and Jim Reed had taken it to Dallas. I didn't care."

"Didn't care? Now why are you trying to tell me a lie like that? Us meeting up after all these years, you ought to be straight with me."

He didn't reply.

"Come on, mister, I'm trying to talk serious to you."

"Also I was very young."

"So now you're old enough to think different, fished in enough old rotten mouths for fifty cents a throw to get better sense, I hope. Where do you think he hid it?"

Blue Duck glanced at her. He had a very closely trimmed moustache that made his expression look somehow lightly ironic, which irritated her. And there was something about the way that he talked which made a joke of what he said.

His dark eyes twinkled. "May I look into your mouth?"

"What? . . . Oh . . ." She opened up.

He took her by the jaw and scrutinized, frowning.

3

Somewhere down the road they passed the line between the Creek and Cherokee Nations, invisible except for hints of somewhat less destitution. They passed a saline with a couple of wagons out front packing in bags of salt. The few farms along the road included not just single-room shacks, twelve by sixteen, but more spacious two-room dogtrot cabins, like the ones in the Ozarks where Belle had grown up. They passed a little clapboard building, recently whitewashed, with a sign out front: DRIPPING SPRINGS SCHOOL.

Belle agreed with the Starrs that the Cherokee Tribe wasn't well governed, but they made the Creek look like something out of the Dark Ages, some lost tribe who had wandered into this dust-eaten world out of a storybook.

Three horsemen reined up beside them, blowing and going and stone drunk. "You seen a balloon out here?"

"Balloon?" Belle said innocently. "Why yes. Right up over that ridge, looked like somebody was fixing to fall out of it."

"Come on boys, we got her now!" They went blasting off across the field.

"What if they come back?" Blue Duck joked her.

"Oh well, the fools, they ought to know better than to chase around after a hot-air whore financed by a Kansas bank. Serve them right if they ride to Missouri."

Mr. Prettyman informed them that the plates were ready, and they stopped at a grove for the pictures. Belle's headache and mood had not improved, despite her scheming with Blue Duck. The idea of posing and being captured in Prettyman's box made her uneasy. He stood her up next to a deeply lined old walnut tree, and then against one of his painted backdrops, a big picture of Niagara Falls, which he lowered on pulleys down from the wagon; he asked for a third pose with her pistols drawn, and another with her sitting in the wagon seat holding the reins. She had to hold each pose unmoving for several seconds, and it made her conscious of her skin, its dryness, thickness — like a damned buffalo hide, she thought, stitched up tight around her. Holding self-consciously quiet and still like that, for whatever purpose, always made her feel unnatural, trapped almost as though in iron. He fluttered and fooled around, toting his camera here and there, and took all four plates immediately for development, the smell of acid and alcohol emanating from the wagon.

She sat against the walnut tree and rubbed her temples. The day had gotten unusually hot again. Blue Duck had gone off somewhere in the grove, probably doing his morning job. She got out the laudanum bottle, swallowed a good horse dose and wondered vaguely what she was going to do with her boy when she found him. Lord have mercy, that was one mess. She couldn't deny that she was half the cause. He'd never amount to anything. There were rumors about it, too. Ed Reed was a gone cat and his own momma was the reason for it. She was what made him that way. . . .

Staring at the wagon, she suddenly had an irrepressible urge to see the developed plates. She yelled at Prettyman that she was coming in, and he fretted and fumed and told her to stay out. She pushed in anyway. The plates were lined up one by one in dim candlelight, three still damp, one in a bath of acid. Her eyes took a moment to adjust to the dimness, and then the detail of the four plates emerged.

The person on them was ugly. The absoluteness of that fact never ceased to startle her. Her chin looked like a bag of beans. Her eyes squinted up like she was sun-blind. And with that dirty shirt on, it was hard to tell that she was even a woman.

"I don't like them."

"They aren't studio settings," he said somewhat petulantly. "But the subject is better outdoors."

"I think the subject looks like a hunk of shit, Prettyman. We'll have to do it again when my mouth isn't swole up. I don't want people looking at those pictures."

"They are quite fine, Mrs. Starr. I am satisfied."

"I'm not." She picked up the plates and stacked them on top of each other.

"Please! Don't touch the collodion, they haven't fixed yet."

She pushed her way outside and dropped them into the dust. The images began to dim in the sunlight. Blue Duck was back, and picked up one of the pictures as it dissolved. She didn't want anybody seeing any of them and so jumped down, taking the plate from him, throwing it onto the ground with the other three and with her heel smashing all of them. The photographer emerged in a blue-faced fury, shouting about agreements and words of honor and lawsuits. He got down from the wagon and stood up in her face, shrilly reprimanding and threatening her in the highfalutin way he had done before.

She watched him like a rat.

He told her that she would have to find her own ride to Catoosa, since in his opinion she was a common brute criminal without any of the qualities of honor or civility that he had seen all over this Indian Nation in even the poorest folk, and further-more as far as he was concerned her reputation as a "bandit queen" was the most ludicrous chicanery ever perpetrated by newspapers and ignorant rumor, she was a foul-tempered, selfish, intemperate, cruel and heedless person, all on the most basic and despicable level, and having been in her presence for the last two days he could say frankly that he hoped he never had the ill fortune to ever come upon her again in a state of need, with her nakedness uncovered, because he quite honestly did not know whether given a second opportunity he would raise a finger to help her, much less give her clothing and money and make agreements with her. . . .

She backed off, he kept walking up in her face, so she pulled out her pistol and shot him in the foot.

His yelling monologue thus interrupted, he looked down at his foot and up at her, down and up. "You can't do that. You shot my foot." He looked morose in a sudden weird sort of way. "You shot my foot."

"I made a mess of your foot."

Blue Duck made no move.

"Now get up against that tree, fatmouth."

"You shot my foot."

"And I'm going to give you something to chew on unless you get up against that tree."

Face transformed by fear and wonderment, the photographer hobbled a few steps and fell down, moaning. She stood over him and cocked the pistol. He looked up in complete astonishment and began to crawl on hands and knees toward the tree. She laughed. One minute ago he was spurring her like a rooster.

"Tie him up to that tree."

Blue Duck looked at her.

"We'll take his wagon."

"Somebody will be along this road pretty soon," he said.

"So you want me to kill him?"

"Of course not. But he'll be found and come to Catoosa. If we take his wagon that'll be evidence of assault and theft."

"Smart figuring there, Mr. Blue Duck. What do you suggest we do — walk? Time we get there he'll have caught up. Besides which, what difference does it make? Lighthorse aren't going to get up a posse because we borrowed this twirp's wagon. Go on. Tie him up."

Blue Duck looked thoughtful. ". . . It's possible too that he might be here for some time. He's bleeding."

She sighed.

"Why don't we take him to Catoosa. Let him get his foot fixed. If he's in the wagon with us, he can't claim theft. If he tries to press charges, you can say that it was a mutual squabble and you acted in self-defense."

"He can't press charges anyway, unless he uses the telegraph. There's no place to press them." She was irritated and gloomy. "Okay, okay, throw him in the back. But you better watch him."

Prettyman was sitting at the base of the walnut tree, looking at his foot with tenderness and remorse. Blue Duck helped him up. "Come on man, you'll be all right."

Belle scowled down at the broken plates and kicked dust over them.

Blue Duck rigged a bandage for Prettyman and tried to keep him calm in the back of the wagon. He would doubtless have liked to make a speech, to delineate in clear language why he did not like his foot having a hole in it. But he knew better. By the time they rolled into Catoosa he had worked himself into a sullen tempest.

Belle pulled up before a saloon and invited them both in for a drink. Prettyman hobbled along behind groaning and making what were, for him, rather indelicate comments. Belle propped up on the brass footrail and ordered bonded whiskey.

"You go to the wine room," the bartender said. "The womans go to the wine room."

"The womans stand right here, buddy."

"The womans go to the wine room," the bartender repeated.

Belle wiped at the side of her mouth with a bar towel. "I don't like the wine room in this place, little buddy. It's about as big as an outhouse. Get us something to drink."

39

He eventually poured, annoyed.

Belle toasted Prettyman. "Here's to the end of our dispute."

He glared at her. "You apologize as though this were an insignificant event? As though you had splashed mud on me?"

"I'm not apologizing. Shut your trap before you swallow a bee."

"This is egregious," he muttered.

"Drink your whiskey, it'll numb you down."

"That isn't a bad idea," Blue Duck said.

She turned to the bartender. "Ed Reed ain't upstairs, is he?"

The bartender didn't answer.

"Go find out for me, Blue Duck. Black hair and a piece of a moustache. About six foot. Has a sneaky, glancy-eyed look to him. Find out if he's up there."

Blue Duck went upstairs and returned shaking his head.

"Nobody there except the dealer setting up."

"Did you ask him?"

"He saw him last night."

She nodded and took a deep breath. "Where are you sleeping?"

"I board with a friend here."

"You want a woman tonight?"

"I beg your pardon."

"You heard me."

"A married woman?"

"Widow woman, if you're talking about the record."

"But in common law . . ."

"What would you know about that?"

"Word gets around."

"What word? You been hearing rumors about me?"

"For many years."

She looked at Prettyman. "See there — rumors. I'm famous."

Prettyman held his drink and stared at her, deflated. He stood favoring his wounded foot, sipping resentfully.

"I can rent a room at the inn," Blue Duck said.

"No you can't. To hell with it. . . . I've got my boy to find." She drained the whiskey and walked out of the bar.

She found an inn with an upstairs room and went immediately to rest. She felt broken up, nervous, scattered. There were about six bars in Catoosa, half of them with gambling rooms. It was too early in the evening for much action, but Ed would be down there after a while, playing at being a grown man and getting fleeced, as usual. He was a fool about gambling, a perpetual tinhorn. Belle had pulled him out of more than one mess he didn't know how to pull himself out of. Recently she'd helped finagle him a parole after less than a year of a seven-year sentence for larceny at the penitentiary in Columbus, Ohio. And what did he do but steal away from home after a few weeks, find a whore off the row and start running with her all over the Territory.

She'd have liked to forget about Ed, but for some reason every little thing he did hit her hard. She got those strange feelings. She had them now — in bed, fully dressed, pistols still around her waist, in a room that she hardly noticed. They were like deep winter dreams, seeing his eyes, the way they took a while to blink, lazy-like. . . . And Jim July (not five years older than Ed) living there at the Bend pestering her to death served only to make things worse. Some nights she would wake up scared, unable to move, eyes open, mind flowing with darker and darker thoughts. Her body would feel heavy as a stone. On the morning that Ed ran off a few weeks ago, Jim July took to pawing at her when she was in a spell like that, and she knocked the hell out of him. It was before sunrise. She remembered it now, how she got out of bed, weak in the knees, and went to look at her babies.

Only they weren't her babies now, and it seemed like she could hardly get them to come home anymore except through some kind of careful strategy.

Pearl — sweet-tempered fat Pearl, a little stupid, with her pretty pale skin and big eyes. Belle had once hoped to make a dramatic star of her, but she collapsed onstage in her first performance with what the doctor called a brain hemorrhage. She was now the mother of her own bastard child, whose name Belle hated and would not repeat and whose unknown father had best keep himself unknown. Pearl slept like a baby with her little rosebud mouth partly open, her white unlined face showing no signs of distress or pain even in passing dreams. Belle had managed to get her home from Kansas, where she had gone to live with the child, only by trickery. She sent word that Ed was dying of a bullet wound. He had been shot in a bar all right (less than two weeks after his parole), but was only slightly wounded. Once she got Pearl back home, she figured she could keep her there and leave the child with relatives. She didn't want it to come between them. She wanted Pearl to marry a man of prominence. She wanted her to find a place in the world. She had no doubt that she could engineer a fine future for the girl if she would just do right. There were rich men to be had in Fort Smith — owners of livery stables, hardware stores, even professional men — who would be proud to marry the daughter of Belle Starr.

Belle knew how their eyes followed her when she rode into Fort Smith, how they waited for her to appear — straight-backed, plumed, dressed like a goddess, regal on her sidesaddle. How they really liked it when she clattered onto the wooden sidewalks up Garrison Avenue scattering onlookers, and circled around her when she played the piano in bars, waiting for what she would say next, unwomanly words that opened strange possibilities in their minds. How their expressions toward her tried to be humorous but then would grow intrigued and oddly worried. How they loved what they could not figure out she was.

(It was hardly that way here in the Territory, where there was no prosperity, no standards, no fixed order. Here she was only one more odd creature in the circus.)

Belle knew that she could set Pearl up handsomely. She had been away from home these many months eating the bitter fruits of her foolishness, but now back home sleeping so quietly, she was untouched as a virgin in appearance and still ripe for the market.

But on that morning, over in the feather-tick mattress that she and Sam had used for seven years, was a different story. Ed slept in a curl as he always had. She didn't know what it was about Ed that made her feel this way. Maybe he looked a little like Cole

Younger. Maybe it was the desperation she felt about his life or the strange mood that had been building up this last couple of years. She wanted to hold him down and scream in his face. She wanted to do things that were not fit for a mother to think. It wasn't thoughts so much as the flow of blood, her legs tingling like getting off a horse after a long ride. She went to the foot of the bed and looked down at him. Earliest morning light through the glass and chinks between the walls made the room transparent, uncertain, and his naked curled-up body looked as though it might disappear in the blue shadows. He hadn't said much about the penitentiary, nor had he been much concerned about how she got him out. He was spoiled that way — all her men were — they took for granted her ability to perform legal miracles.

His head rolled to the side and his body straightened. He had a hard-on. Unexpectedly, his eyes blinked open and after a moment he noticed her.

He lay that way on his back, head unmoving, looking at her. Through the leaden paleness she saw a kind of smile on his face. She wanted to move, go about making breakfast or something, but was unable to. She was dizzy. His eyes looked down across his body at her. They blinked that slow way. Was there a challenge in his face? His dick was hard and flat across his belly.

"*What's the matter with you?*" a voice said.

"What?" She spoke as if across a clouded distance.

"*What's the matter with you, old woman?*" Was it his voice? She was stiff with confusion.

Her frozen body cracked, melted and was finally able to move. A rawhide horsewhip, off the wall, was in her hand. She lashed his body. Cut down hard across his thighs, across his penis, chest. His face exploded in fear and pain, he writhed back and forth trying to find a place to hide in the mattress. He was a little boy again, helpless, croaking.

"Stop! Oh Momma, stop!" Pearl shouted from the other side of the room.

She lashed him out of bed and followed him across the puncheon floor, striping his back as he fell and struggled to get up off his knees. Out the door he ran zigzagging in every direction, wild hoarse exhalations pushing out of his throat. He stumbled over the iron kettle, fell flat, got up and went into the barn.

Belle stood in the doorway looking at the quirt in her hand. A great fear bloomed inside her skull.

"Oh Lord Jesus!" Pearl breathed. "Oh Lord Jesus!"

Belle ground her hurting teeth. Jim July appeared with his usual silly smile. "What's the matter?"

She stared into his face and tried to collect her thoughts. "Take some britches to him," she said. "In the barn."

Ed was gone within a half-hour, stealing her palomino and three hundred dollars, and that was the last she'd seen of him.

Now he had to be found. Lying in the strange hotel room, the fact became clearer and clearer. He had to be brought back home. He was a dead man if she didn't get him back. He would kill himself. He went on binges that were bound to end bad. Showed off, talked loud, stepped on toes, and all the while kept about as alert as a snake in winter. She hadn't *seen* him act this way so much, because she wouldn't put up with it, but she knew from what people said about him and just from things that she picked up. She had a special connection with him, could read his mind almost and know what he was doing halfway across the Territory. He was an open book to her. It was one of the things that made her perpetually angry with him — the availability of his thoughts and weaknesses. He had to learn to be meaner, closer, to hoard things better. You couldn't be half blue jay and half chicken and expect to live very long out here.

She couldn't sleep. Downstairs she got a boy to bring her a bottle of whiskey. It was going on suppertime, but she had no desire to eat. Back in the room she drank from the bottle.

It was a large room in the old style, built for as many people as the innkeeper could pack in. Her daddy had run an inn just about this size in Carthage, Missouri, when she was a little girl, before he got burned out in the war. He was prosperous in Carthage, owned a blacksmith shop, livery stable, and also — she thought, but was never quite clear on this fact — a tavern. That was about half of Carthage. She sipped on the Indian whiskey and tried to remember those days.

It was sad how little she could recall. There was a slave girl — Leanner, was that her name? Leanner? It didn't sound quite right. They'd been best friends and she couldn't remember her damned name. She stood at the dining table fanning away flies and mosquitoes and going to sleep on her feet day after summer day, meal after taciturn meal. Her old daddy would reach out with his big hand and thump Leanner when she nodded off. He thought that was a great joke. Dried beans boiled in salt pork. Fried chicken. Chicory coffee. Her momma jaundiced, gaunt, dry-skinned, working like a mule seven days of the week . . .

School, she remembered that better than the hotel. Mr. Cravens, headmaster, a worried and distracted man in all subjects but one, he labored through French, Latin and Hebrew, dutifully plowed through *Ray's Arithmetic*, drudged through McGuffey, expounding dully upon Keats and Byron — but then, wonder of wonders, Mr. Cravens would sit down at the piano and a great change would come across him. He would grow quiet and self-possessed, a gravity would descend upon his otherwise ravaged and nervous countenance, and he would quickly lose himself in the keys. He was a damned good pianist. That was how Belle picked it up, she supposed, and why the little cabin at Younger's Bend had a good-sized upright taking up half of one room. Pearl could play, but she didn't have the knack for much more than simple accompaniments. Pearl, Pearl, her sweet Pearl . . .

And Ed. She ought to get out of bed right now and find him. Catoosa was waking up for the night: shouts in the street, doors slamming. But the whiskey was beginning to taste good and she was so tired. . . . A mother on top of it all. It was putting her in a mood. She drank from the glass and felt sorry for herself.

She slept the night away but the next morning was up before sunrise trudging down the potholed main street toward the hotel she knew he would be in. An expression settled across her face like an iron mask. She pounded the bell until a bedraggled man in one suspender appeared.

"What room is Ed Reed in?"

"Who?"

"Reed. Ed Reed."

"Who's inquiring?"

"Belle Starr."

He coughed and hocked up a big wad, expertly disposed of it in a can across the floor, and looked back at her. "Who's that?"

"Me. His blood mother. Now which room is he in?"

He squinted in mild perplexity. "Three."

Tramping up the stairs, she knocked twice on the door and pushed in. The walls of the hotel were plastered and wallpapered, probably the only such in Catoosa. Ed was in bed with his whore, as expected. She stood at the door until they awakened, the girl, then Ed. He groaned. The girl started digging at her eyes to get the sleep — or this illusion — out.

She walked to the foot of the bed and looked down at them, a light quilt covering them. She could feel the smile on her face — hard, mean. "That's real pretty hair you've got, honey."

The girl grinned confusedly, her face stiff with sleep.

"Real pretty. I always like a good black head of hair. Especially when it's kind of oily like yours. Makes it easy to see what you are."

"Oh," Ed groaned into the mattress.

"I have a couple of things to talk to you about. Like to do it in private. You don't mind that, do you honey? Put some clothes on your little fanny and go to the crapper or something. My boy and I have to talk."

The girl squirmed out of bed, trying to take the quilt with her, but Ed held it down, and for a moment there was a struggle to see who would stay covered. Flailing turbulently around under the covers, she managed to get her bloomer panties to cover herself, then quickly slipped out of bed, dressed and disappeared.

Ed lay face down.

"You're too smart to ride with a whore, Ed."

"She's not a whore," he said into the bed.

"You stole money from me when you ran off. That's the first thing that we have to talk about. If you've lost it I'll take it out of your hide. I got waylaid by a tribe of Crows coming to find you. They killed Faith and stole my clothes. I had to walk seventeen miles naked across the Creek Nation. Nearly died. Had to stand up before a two-bit photographer and have my picture taken in swap for a ride to Tulsa."

He turned and looked at her, face clouded. "What?"

"That's right. You shamed your mother once again, Ed Reed. Where's that three hundred dollars?"

"Coat."

She found his wallet, counted out $210 in paper and took all of it. "Ain't as bad as it could be. I assume you've already paid for this little frolic in the hotel. What horse do you have besides Zero?"

He put both feet on the floor and sighed, looking down. "An old cayuse. Cost me twenty-five."

"That what you put your whore astraddle?"

"She ain't a whore," he said resignedly.

"She's a whore and a breed. Looks like part of a nigger. You're too smart for that, boy."

He glanced up as though to speak but didn't. He looked like he'd had the breath knocked out of him. Cheap perfume and the smell of sex mingled in the air. Thighs covered by the quilt, moustache bristling in all directions, he was a big gangly boy caught once again with his hand in the sugar bowl, and looking down on his helplessness she experienced a feeling she'd had before, a flood of pity and love and bewilderment. Bewilderment because she didn't know why this had to happen again and again — why she had to break his back. It was against her philosophy. She knew better. A boy had to sow his wild oats. But there was an instinct behind it. An absolute certainty that gripped her stomach. He was going to be dead if she didn't make him do right. *He was going to be dead.*

Standing up naked and trying to put on his britches, he had trouble with his balance. By the way he hopped around the floor, he must have gotten drunk as a wheelbarrow last night. He looked like he was dancing a hoedown. She scolded him for it. She helped with his shirt and picked up a few things around the room and scolded him good.

They had breakfast together downstairs. Belle ordered up three eggs and a pot of sheepherder's coffee. "And don't put no water in it, either." The girl entered the common room and sat down beside Ed. After a cup or two of good solid coffee and some eats, Belle felt slightly more generous toward her. "And what's your name?"

"Laura Ziegler Reed."

"You from Fort Smith?"

"Yes," she said prissily.

"Well you're a pretty girl, Laura, a pretty girl. You know how to take care of yourself, don't you?"

Laura looked at Ed for an interpretation of that question.

"How old are you?"

"Eighteen."

"Well good. You're old enough to ride the train alone."

Ed spoke after a moment. "We're married, Momma."

"Who married you?"

"Pete Ishtonubbe in Sallisaw."

"Pete Ishtonubbe doesn't even speak English. What'd he marry you with, a stick and a piece of cornbread?"

"He married us with the Book, Momma."

"You ain't old enough to take care of a horse, much less a wife."

"I'm nineteen."

She took another few knifeloads of egg, swallowed a fist of coffee, and asked quietly, "Which house did you get her out of?"

"You can't talk to me like that."

"I can talk to you through my butt hole if I want to, Ed Reed, and don't forget it." She made a noise like a fart. The fierceness in her face was barely controlled. She turned over a cup, splashing hot coffee across the table onto the girl. "Oh now, excuse me. Did I spot your little dress? That's too bad."

Ed gave her his green neckerchief and she dabbed at the coffee and sniffled. She was not flinching, and that made Belle madder by the moment. She wanted to be rid of the girl immediately, abolish her dirty brown eyes. Mad energy rattled through her body. It was hard to hold back from using a pistol. Level metal in the little trollop's face and she'd flap her wings all the way back to the row.

Blue Duck walked into the common room. He looked amiable and composed — but saw that something was strange and held back. He didn't speak.

Belle went silent. Laura's eyes darted. Ed sat with his head down.

"How old were you when you married Cole Younger?" he finally muttered.

"Didn't marry him. Run off with him. And God knows it's been my sorrow ever since."

"How old were you when you married Jim Reed?"

"Old enough to raise two babies back and forth across this continent from California to Missouri is how old."

He muttered even more indistinctly, "How old is Jim July?"

She looked into his eyes. "I don't know and it's none of your business if I did. Quit asking questions. Any asking, I'll do it."

"Not anymore," he said doggedly.

She turned to Blue Duck. "How do you like this? My son I raised — gave him everything I had — he goes off and gets married without even telling me. What kind of thing is that?"

A hint of a smile came to Blue Duck's face. "Looks like he's man enough to handle it."

Her back grew stiff. Standing up slowly, she went around to the girl and leaned down beside her with one hand on the table.

"There's some mothers that cry when their sons go to the dogs. There's some that pray to the Lord. I don't do neither one of those, honey." She took a handful of scrambled eggs and allowed them to slip down the girl's blouse. The girl was astonished. Belle stuffed a ten-dollar bill after the eggs. "Now there's a train out here. It's called the Arkansas Valley. It'll take you through Fort Gibson, Vian, Sallisaw, and Fort Smith. I advise you to get on it."

The girl tried to weep but for the moment could only choke and turn red in the face. She left the room very quickly. Ed fell into a helpless rage. He pounded his cup on the table, geysering coffee all over the place. "That's my wife, God damn it!"

"She's no more your wife than every drunken drummer that pays five dollars to see her."

"She wasn't in Fort Smith a year."

"Fresh whore's like a fresh corpse. She'll stink pretty soon."

Ed broke a plate with his cup, then proceeded to break the other two. He was white-faced, huffing, smothering in fury. He pounded his fists among the broken shards of plate.

Blue Duck stood back watching, impassive as when he pulled teeth. Belle walked out to the front desk, where the hotel owner, still in one suspender, was squatting down fiddling with an old squirrel rifle, apparently loading it. "What do I owe you for breakfast, plates included?"

He answered quickly, as though he had been goosed. "Three dollars!"

She put down a bill and waited for change. He fumbled around, ridiculously trying to hide his money box even as he got it out to make change. Seven silver dollars. She left one of them on the counter. "That's for the mess."

Down the street, Blue Duck caught up with her. "Where are you going?"

"Buy me a bath. Haven't had one in a while."

"Prettyman has gone to the district sheriff, by the way."

"Ain't no district sheriff in Catoosa."

"He's on his way through."

"Who is it?"

"John Eno."

"Eno's okay. We used to have some transactions together in the cattle business."

The little town was awake now — fresh manure in the street, a cotton wagon rattling by, a stream of dirty water poured from an upstairs window, Indians squatting at the corner of a building sharing a pipe of sumac.

As they approached a hotel/bathhouse, a shout echoed down the street, *"What about you?"*

People turned to look. Belle paused for a moment but did not turn. She looked at the sign: BATHS GIVEN/PURE WATER/ PRIMROSE SOAP PROVIDED/CLEANSE YOURSELF TODAY/30¢.

Her son's voice reverberated down the main street. *"What about you?"*

She went inside the bathhouse. Blue Duck followed.

4

Blue Duck normally took his bath here on Saturday afternoon after a strenuous day of gazing into the mouths of Catoosa and the surrounding area — an activity which had after so many hundreds of hours become somewhat routine, the many mouths becoming one collective and generalized Mouth of Catoosa, and the many rotten molars, canines, incisors — whether in the delicate and difficult to Open Wide mouths of chaste young maidens or the whiskey-scalded canker-scarred hell-breathing mouths of old Cherokee drunks — becoming one of two kinds, either one that had to go or one that didn't. In the course of a few years he had lost his original shyness and concern, and what began early in his apprenticeship as painful encounters with different personalities became something more like mining in a small bloody sometimes loud and dangerous enamel mine. Dangerous because it could snap shut at any minute, causing damage to his tools or even his person. The Mouth of Catoosa was not much different from the Mouth of Tulsa, except perhaps that it tended to be somewhat more truculent, abusive, and slightly more decayed. This may have been the result of the fact that while Tulsa was one of the more hopeful spots in the Creek Nation, Catoosa was a distant outpost in the Cherokee, and most of its inhabitants were either whiskey-criminals, cowpunchers, or poor farmers, none of whom tended to go to the dentist until their teeth were clattering in their heads like piano keys.

He normally waited until after Saturday's work to take his bath, washing away the collective blood and gore of the day and week and leaving Sunday as his one day outside the Mouth. But now she was going into the bathhouse, and he would have to follow her.

The old squaw who prepared the baths was surprised to see him at this hour. She hung a blanket between the "men" and "women" sides of the little room.

"You want it hot?"

"I sure do," Belle said. "See if you can't boil some of the sulfur out of this Oklahoma water."

"One already hot. Man's."

"Well Grandma, I smell like a man — and worse. Why don't you just let me go first. You mind, mister?"

Blue Duck was taking his shirt off. "No, please, go ahead."

"Man's!" the old lady said, somewhat alarmed.

"It ain't gonna hurt me." She proceeded to disrobe and step into the steaming water. "And I know it ain't gonna hurt this rusty old tub. . . . Ohhh . . ."

Blue Duck hung his shirt up and waited on the other side of the blanket. After some splashing around there was a moment of silence, a groan and a sigh.

"What tribe are you from — Sioux?"

He sat on the edge of the tub and pulled off his boots. The old lady came in lugging two buckets of hot water, poured them and tugged Blue Duck's pants off at the cuffs. She folded them and went out for more water. He stepped gingerly into the water. "Don't know for sure."

"Don't tell me you don't know where you got them scars on your chest."

53

Settling into the tub, he looked down at the swirls and bumps of scar tissue on his chest. "They put in wooden screws. We were supposed to hang off the pole until we had a dream."

"Must be Sioux."

"Perhaps."

"Why don't you know?"

"Because I left the tribe when I was young."

"Kidnapped?"

"No. I was cast out."

"How come?"

"I don't know. It's unclear in my mind. We traveled from place to place. There wasn't much to eat. I didn't fit in. Didn't understand what was going on most of the time. I was an orphan with impure blood — white father, probably. I didn't have the dream. Got the scars for nothing, I guess."

"What's it like to lean back on that rope with screws in you?" She sounded very curious.

He looked at the blanket and shook his head to himself, as if he didn't know or care to remember.

"That little trick always has sounded crazy to me," she said. "I think about a woman doing it and that's bad enough, but a man — hell, most of them have more delicate tits than a woman."

He shook his head again, as if in mutual wonderment.

"You don't hardly act like a wild Indian."

"I didn't ever make it to wild. Too hungry."

"It didn't dry you out."

He picked up a bar of perfumed soap and went to work on his feet. The old lady came in with two more buckets of hot water and without hesitation or warning poured them over his thighs.

"I mean most of them, living that way, it kind of cures them out. They get tough like an old hide," Belle said.

"I was young when I left. I didn't have the dream so I didn't become a man. They gave up on me. I followed along after them, sitting outside the tents like an old mother-in-law." He leaned back in the tub and simmered. "Ate scraps. One day they left and

I didn't have the energy to follow. I just stayed. On a green hillside — I sat and watched them disappear. I took out east, snaring rabbits and so forth. Ended up at Fort Gibson."

"Starvation capital of the world," she muttered.

"Yeah. I stayed there eating out of the garbage. There was a storekeeper named Daley who used to be a trapper; he found a few words in common with me, and after a while he let me run errands for him. Gave me food and a bed. After four or five months of that I was outright fat." He smiled. "I learned English. There was a teacher from back east. Her grandmother had taught Cherokee kids at a school in Maine back in the twenties. They used to send a few kids up there every year. Anyway, she took a special interest in helping me learn the language. She was very correct."

"That must have been quite a job."

"Three and a half years, she taught me during after-school hours at her cabin. She was rigorous and made me want to study hard. I would stay up all night reading and learning the grammar."

"What did she look like?"

"Very white."

"You in love with her?"

"Of course."

"What happened to her?"

"I killed her."

"Oh? How's that?"

"She married a man named Birdsell from Ohio. He ran a store there. I was jealous and I killed her. I meant to kill him, but I got her instead."

"How's that?" she repeated.

"I put arsenic in his water barrel. He didn't die, she did. She was supposed to be out of town at the summer normal."

"Then you got hooked up with Dan Evans?"

"After a while."

"Pretty rough character."

"Yes."

"I don't remember Dan that well, to tell you the truth. I don't remember anything very well. . . . How old are you?"

"Thirty-four, thirty-five. How about you?"

"A hundred and fifty." There was a noisy splashing on her side and then silence in the hot little sulfurous room. The old lady came in and poured more water over Blue Duck and, clucking at him, took the forgotten bar of soap from his hand and went to work on his back. She did this every Saturday, each time pretending disapproval at his laziness in the tub. Blue Duck would not have said — would not have admitted to himself — that the main reason he came to Catoosa on Saturday was not to pull teeth but to relax and lie back in the tub while this old squaw washed his body with vigorous and very un-Cherokee minuteness, muttering and disapproving of him as she did now in a tone somewhat the mother, somewhat the harried functionary. Her name was irrelevant to the transaction, and she would have considered him calling her by it an intrusion, an immodesty, a downright violation, whereas the act of washing him with her hands head to foot anonymously was entirely within the bounds.

Belle spoke up again. "You say you don't remember enough about your raising to know what tribe you were from. What language did they use on you?"

"Daley had been a trapper, like I said. He knew a little of this and that, without knowing exactly which was which. He thought I was Sioux, though — my name and all."

"What name?"

"Blue Duck. That's what it means."

"You use the name the tribe gave you?"

"Yes. I do now. I tried others. Put them on and off like hats there for a while. Then I just went back to it. When I was a kid I found this blue feather and kept it. It was my friend. I talked to it — you know how kids are. So they named me by it. I kept that feather for the longest time."

"Well. I'd say you've been around. How in the hell did you ever get to be a dentist?"

"Apprenticed myself."

"You didn't go to school?"

"No. And the man who taught me was a drunk. Bad drunk. I got only what he hadn't burned out of his head on clear whiskey. A good man, though. In Tulsa."

"You didn't murder him, did you?"

He put his chin to his chest as the old lady washed the back of his neck, up his scalp. "He took care of that himself."

"I got a taste for whiskey myself. Not that I go swimming in the jug or anything. . . . You know Sam Starr, my dead husband, he was a full-blood Cherokee, and he hated Sioux and Comanche and all them worse than anything. He just hated a wild Indian. Called them flatheads, and that long hair, the tattoos — he hated all of it. He'd go on about it at the dinner table, how he'd like to see them exterminated."

"I ran up against that. But I was used to worse."

"When you were an errand boy, you mean?"

"Yes."

"They treat you like a nigger?"

"A nigger would get a penny. They didn't give this boy anything but a knuckle on the head. But I had plenty to eat. It was paradise in Mr. Daley's store. All those cans and packages and bins, and I could just eat come mealtime. I tell you . . ." He smiled. The old lady was washing his face now. For all of her gruffness, she washed his temples, his nose, around his eyes, very gently.

"I haven't ever been real hungry," Belle said. "My old daddy went from rich to poor, but he always managed to keep scratching."

"Yeah . . ."

"Why you reckon you went back to 'Blue Duck'?"

"No good reason. Maybe I thought it would be easy for folks to remember — 'Blue Duck the Dentist.' "

"You're a damn good dentist, if I can go by the job you did on me. It don't hardly hurt at all today."

He rinsed the soap from his face. The old lady scrubbed his

chest and legs quickly today, splashed more water over him and went out with her buckets.

"That the way you do all your women customers — lay them down in the straw and put it to them?"

"Only when I don't have my chair. I've got a nice chair, made in St. Louis."

"How about the blacksmith job?"

"Temporary. Jenkins was low on help."

"You make a pretty good living?"

"Tolerable."

"Why are you all the time smiling like that? You're always looking like you know something."

"Oh? How's that? You can't even see my face."

"Satisfied like."

"Oh I'm not like that" — he stood up and reached for a towel — "except on Saturday. I like my bath."

He did have other thoughts. He put on his clothes while the old lady hauled more buckets to rinse Belle. He didn't tell her that she'd been his companion more than once, that she had come to his mind many times in the last thirteen or fourteen years, dreams and memories of the woman he saw the night they took apart old Watt Grayson. A fierce mean plain woman who rode a horse like she had been born to it, strapped into two big .44s that climbed up off of her hips under her arms. He had heard her name many times and wondered about her, what had happened to her, whether she was still the person he met that night with Dan Evans and Jim Reed, father of the boy whom Belle had now shamed before his bride. Not a likable man by any reckoning, Jim Reed: he operated like a snake, close to the ground and quiet and not particularly smart. Blue Duck had wondered, that night and later, how it was that Belle married a man like that. It looked a little like she had married the runt so she could run with the pack.

Blue Duck was himself only a boy then, a confused reticent boy running from what he had done. Women were for him an idea and a curiosity from which he had to turn away, to the work of forgetting. He was a penitent without the forms of penitence. He could speak of it lightly now, without elaboration or appearance of guilt, because it had come to a certain perfection within him. Like all penitence, it left him free in some ways, put him outside the usual course of things. He would have no women.

The woman he had killed was not just the first in a young man's life, she was also the first person to care for him, his wife and mother and friend, loved in too many chambers of his heart, the person who with Puritan diligence taught him how to speak and act, how to stand up straight and eat his food with manners other than the coyote outcast. She stood behind him, surrounding him, arms down his arms and hands over his hands, the knife and fork irrelevant in his grasp, the lesson too amazing to be learned. He was a strenuous challenge to her strenuous will. And no matter how she submitted finally as a woman, her Yankee backbone did not bend. She was not his own until he made her so irrevocably.

Belle Reed, fourteen years ago, was the first to penetrate a mental door he had locked against all women, and in the years since then there had been no others. She had remained memorable because she seemed so unlike a woman. Because she was as desperate as he was, and seemed to care — then — as little as he did for the gold. He remembered precisely how she picked up a twenty-dollar piece, held it close and squinted at it as though nearsighted, threw it back into the chest and said, "We better get out of here. That breed's wives are gonna start beating the pots and pans."

And of course he remembered her because people in that part of the country talked about her. There were stories about her, articles in newspapers and the *Police Gazette*. People hated her venomously, admired her; he had even seen a book about her, a pamphlet printed in Denver for sale at twenty-five cents in the general store in Tulsa.

Now she had appeared out of the past, her face different — dark, hard, eroded by sorrow — and it did not seem quite real to him. She sat in the bathtub on the other side of the blanket cursing the rinse water for being too hot. He put down fifty cents and was about to leave when she called him. "Come here a second."

He stopped.

"Come here."

He hesitated and finally came around. The old squaw clucked and muttered and bustled out with her two buckets. Belle looked up at him from the tub. "Would you let your one boy marry a whore?"

"If I had a boy, I guess I wouldn't want him to."

"Of course not, but would you *let* him?"

"After a certain age, it wouldn't be my decision."

She looked away, frowning. "Well he hasn't got good sense, that's the trouble. Older he gets, the less sense he has. I get crazy thinking about it." She glanced back at him. "Now get out of here so I can get dressed."

He pulled a few teeth and stuffed a few cavities that morning, but it was a mercifully slack day. He disliked the dental profession for the most part. Not the least of the usual problems was payment. A good number of his patients had to pay him in some kind of trade — bundles of dried corn, jugs of molasses, clear whiskey, sacks of chitlins, prairie potatoes, cornmeal, kafir, popcorn, pieces of cloth or hardwood or pottery — so that after a busy Saturday he rode back to Tulsa with a little of everything strapped onto his mule, like a general-merchandise drummer riding out into the Territory to gyp the Indians. It was not a good idea to let people go without making any kind of payment, because the word spread remarkably fast and every swollen mouth and goggling face in the Indian Nation would begin to line up outside his door moaning and rocking and talking out loud to Jesus, expecting, demanding to be relieved of their agony without thought of recompense. He had to be firm about payment in order to get any at all.

There was a baseball game at noon, and partly in order to get away from the station when the southbound arrived — when, presumably, Belle would herd her son's bride onto the train like a stockyard heifer — he closed down the office and wandered out to the field. The feel of things today was strange. At first he had thought it was just Belle — with whom proximity automatically seemed to spell trouble — but that was not the case. In the last several months, the mood all over the Territory had darkened. Boomer raids, quiet for three or four years, were on the increase in the Cherokee Nation, compounding the burdens of drought and a bad previous winter for cattlemen. From the dentist's chair he had been hearing more predictions of ruin, theories of calamity, and dire ruminations than usual, from the Mouth of Tulsa and the other little towns that he visited in the Creek Nation as well as that of Catoosa and the Cherokee. It was not just lawlessness, it was not just crops, nor the tribes which had been stacked like dominoes west of the Arkansas in the Cherokee Outlet — Kaws, Nez Percés, Poncas, Otoes, Pawnees — but all of that plus something less tangible. People smelled trouble as clearly as a prairie rainstorm, but they seemed to have no more idea of precisely what trouble than a man in the moon. "It's politics," one old man today spluttered through a mouthful of blood. "You can bet your ass it's politics."

Blue Duck walked out to the baseball field, at least to avoid any more of the Starr family troubles today. Seeing Belle had been salubrious for him. Perhaps now he would stop wondering about her. Over the last several years she had been not exactly an obsession, but certainly a persistent visitor to his thoughts, reminding him of the path he could have taken — did take for a few years and then abandoned in favor of an honest living. The sight of her in the bathtub was hard to put out of his mind. He had grown accustomed to her as an idea, and it was unnerving to see her in the flesh. After fourteen years this female-who-was-not-female had walked out of his memory and reconstituted herself before him in a bathtub, very female. Very female, and aging, nervous, mean, homelier and more vital even than he remembered her being. "Belle Starr" with a stretch-marked belly, sagging breasts and close-boned hips. He preferred, almost, the memory.

The baseball game was in progress. The out-of-town team wore outfits, CHEROKEE BANK, and had a good country pitcher on the mound striking out one after the other of the locals. The local players and watchers were unhappy and restless. Sheriff John Eno was there and he glanced at Blue Duck but did not come over. Blue Duck had seen Prettyman talking to the sheriff earlier and was a little worried about the shooting incident. He himself would not be charged with anything serious, or if he was, the chances for conviction were slight, but he did not relish the idea of getting hauled in for a trial, having to pay lawyer's fees, and missing a week or two of work.

The pitcher for the Cherokee Bank had a long pumping windup, pushing forward and pulling back, pushing and pulling as though the ball was very heavy, then on the fourth swing letting it fly like a hot bullet. The local batters were helpless against him. By the time the southbound train had come and gone, the score was thirteen to nothing. The locals stood in little clumps, kicking dust, spitting and talking quietly among themselves, trying to pretend that the game wasn't there. They passed around a pint bottle, horsed around nervously, slunk to bat.

"Come on! Put one down his throat!" Astride a palomino, in new denims and blouse, it was Belle with Ed following along at some distance behind on a ragged cayuse, an underfed, runty, swaybacked pony with parts of its coat missing and blue skin showing through, which the boy did not ride so much as sit astride with his long legs hanging limp outside the short stirrups just about dragging the ground. She dismounted at the watering trough and came over to Blue Duck. "Hey, what's going on here?" He told her the score, she groaned aloud and started yelling at the pitcher. "Look at that Indian! He ain't got but one eyebrow!"

A few people laughed. It was true. He had what looked like one thick eyebrow running all the way across his forehead. He glanced in her direction and took a stick of green from his pocket for a chew.

"Well, well," she said. "Look at him bite off that good cowpatty chaw. Bet you he pays a dollar a foot for that stuff in Tah-le-quah."

The pitcher looked at her again, not deigning to show irritation. John Eno came wandering over with a crooked smile on his face. He was a middle-aged full blood with an easy way about him, like most of the Cherokee district sheriffs, better at gossip and the masculine social graces than law enforcement. Although he wore a sidearm now, it seemed less a weapon on him than a ritual sign of authority to discourage the baseball game from erupting into a riot. He smiled and tipped his hat at Belle.

She smiled back. "How you doing, you old horsethief?"

"Pretty good, pretty good."

"What's wrong with these boys — a-scared of the big city team?"

"Ain't hitting very good today."

The pitcher threw a ball, and she exclaimed in a fake high voice, "Why my goodness! Did you see that? That boy is wearing tight pants!"

The crowd laughed again, some of them. Others grew stiff at the suggested lewdness. He pitched another ball, and someone on the Catoosa team yelled, "That's it, keep him honest!"

Belle put her hands to her mouth. "If the Cherokee Bank can't afford underwear, who can?"

She yelled a few more things at him and the crowd started joining in.

"Is them socks or stockings?"

"He's lost it now!"

"Arm's wore out!"

"It's them windups, throwed it out of joint."

Chewing that green a little faster now!"

"Keep him honest, Homer!"

Homer, who was fat, got hold of a ball just like Belle had told him to, line drive right through the pitcher that gave him time to waddle to first. The hometown folk were feeling better all of a sudden.

Ed did not join in. He remained back at the trough, hat down over his forehead, as apparently uninterested in the game as the gelding that he sat on. Mules and plowhorses stood this way and that, none tied, most of them grazing in their sleep, heads low. Ed stayed with them for now.

John Eno was still smiling. "Got a complaint against you, Belle."

"What's wrong, pitcher? That an ant mound or a pitcher's mound you're standing on? Got 'em in your pants?" She looked at Eno. "So what's new, John? Won't be much more than a jawbone left, time the complaints against me run out."

"This photographer said you shot him and busted up some of his equipment."

"You remember me enough to know I wouldn't do something like that unless I had to."

"He swore out a complaint. Said Mr. Blue Duck saw it all." Eno glanced at Blue Duck.

"What are you going to do, John, arrest your old fence?"

The sheriff seemed very uneasy. "I ain't got any choice, not when this man's got a big bullet hole in his foot."

A little mad now but still level — "You can't arrest me, not for that snake-oil twirp. If I was to put him on his tripod and rotate him for pistol practice, it would be no loss to the world, and you know it. He's still walking and talking; he ain't dead."

"He swore it out. I ain't got any choice."

"Besides which, it ain't your jurisdiction. If he's going to bring in the law, he's going to have to do it through old Ike Parker, and I figure he'll get cooled off before he can ride all the way to Fort Smith."

"There's a Lighthorseman in town right now, and I think you'll do a lot better getting this taken care of in Tahlequah."

"I'm as white as a picket fence, John."

"You're a Cherokee widow living in the Cherokee Nation," Eno said, looking away.

"John, John" — she sounded like she felt sorry for him — "Are you serving a warrant on me?"

"I ain't got papers on it yet. I was hoping you'd just ride over to Tahlequah and settle it with Wailer or somebody."

"You want me to turn myself in to John Wailer?"

"Why not? I don't want to arrest you, and I sure don't want to send out no telegram on you."

"That's good. Real good, Eno. I wouldn't want to talk too loud here at a public event, but if you were to send a telegram on me I might just have to start my mouth flapping like a pair of bloomers on the clothesline with certain memories about the good old days, back when there weren't no telegrams to send and certain respectable people weren't so respectable."

The sheriff's smile melted. "Them skeletons are dried up, Belle. You ain't pushing me around with that." He walked back over to the game, where Catoosa was taking the field.

Cursing under her breath, she turned to Blue Duck. "You're the witness. You going to testify against me?"

"No."

"Son-of-a-bitch Prettyman, he ought to be tarred and feathered. You know what that vulture does for a living? Takes pictures of drunk Indians and sells them as the last 'noble warriors' for tea-table books. . . . I have to get back to the place, get this boy back there before he goes off mooning over that slut. And Pearl's coming home. . . . I haven't got time to fool with this twirp. Lucky I didn't shoot his liver out. . . . Maybe I just better talk to him. You staying here?"

Blue Duck looked at her.

"If you'd come with me, maybe we could tell this horse's ass he ain't got no case. I could walk out of here and John Eno wouldn't turn a thumb. I've got enough things on him rattling around in my skull to put him on about five front pages and he knows it, but if Prettyman was to go to Tahlequah or Fort Smith it might get rough. The Starrs don't exactly get the red carpet in either one of them places."

"Why?"

"What do you mean why? Frying pan and the fire."

"What's the feud with Tahlequah?"

"You've heard about that. How the Starrs got on the outs. It goes way back to the homeland, eighteen thirties. There were some Cherokees that figured the only way to deal with the white man was to get the hell out. Leave the east and find a new place where they could live independent. It was just getting worse trying to protect their lands against the Andy Jackson types. This part of the Tribe signed a treaty giving up all their lands in the east in swap for a new, sovereign Indian Nation out here. . . . You know about all that. Anyway, James Starr, Tom's daddy, was one of the signers, along with lots of other big shots in the Tribe. The treaty party left the east and came out here right away, settled into some of the best farmland. Back there, the Ross faction kept trying to hold out, until they got drove here on their bare feet, half of them strewn out dead across Arkansas. They scrapped over land and such, and the Ross faction took hold of the government and ain't let go since. James Starr and a bunch of the other treaty signers were assassinated in forty-five. Tom was still smoldering over his dead daddy twenty years later, getting meaner by the year. Lit Ross shacks like candles over the territory. And I lived in the same house with him, too. Not long, thank the Lord. I was always worrying when he'd lose his fancy for me as a daughter-in-law. The Tribe had come up with some kind of 'treaty' with Tom way back before I knew him, but he wasn't much interested in it anymore. Tahlequah learned a long time ago not to like a Starr. You knew something about that, didn't you?"

"As a matter of fact I did, barbershop kind of. What about Fort Smith?"

"What about it?"

"Why aren't you welcome over there?"

"People like me all right. Streets and saloons, you know. But Ike Parker ain't above a feud himself. We holed up some big names out there sixty-five miles from his gavel. That's *his* district, buddy. . . . Looky here, I got to ask you now, will you talk to Prettyman?"

"Yes."

"You're the only gentleman in sight. You can ride with me."

Prettyman was not to be found. They looked in every bar and inn. Ed clopped along behind on his swaybacked pony. He followed his mother, or rather allowed the pony to follow her, and in town allowed his own legs to walk along at some distance behind, hat pulled down over his forehead, without words, expression or any other sign of attentiveness, a sullen ghost not quite successful at disappearing from the dusty streets. Blue Duck assumed that Belle had gotten his bride onto the noon train to Fort Smith, and he had gone now into hibernation from the shame of it. The town was too small to hide the photographer, but they nevertheless piddled the afternoon away looking for him. They did find his wagon put up in a livery stable — but no information on his whereabouts.

Belle grew preoccupied and nervous; she muttered, complained, drank whiskey. Folks wandered back into town from the baseball game, and without asking the score she cursed them. "One-horse chumps — they ought not to waste their squatting and flea-picking time getting whooped by Tahlequah. They're scared of the bank is what it is. They could send a boxcar of monkeys over here wearing BANK on their uniforms, and these okabillies would strike out. Hell what am I doing in this place?"

By dark she was in a lowering drunken mood, with her boy still hanging around like a somnambulist at what seemed like a peculiarly exact distance from her, wordless and blank, and Blue Duck was glad when they separated for the night. Glad to go off alone and get a good night's sleep.

At seven o'clock they met for breakfast at the hotel that Belle had chased Ed and his bride out of the previous morning. The owner was nervous and ingratiating. Ed sat hunched over his plate chewing with regular solid horse-jaw motions, elbows stuck out, hat still down over his face as though he had slept in it. Belle chided him for bad manners, but in small matters like this she seemed not so insistent. She played the fretful mother this morning.

Blue Duck was getting tired of her and her boy. Being around them was like being in a haunted house. It was time to leave and head back to Tulsa. Monday was always a big tooth day. Seeing Belle had been instructive. Maybe it had cleared out an old preoccupation. The woman was not the memory or dream of the woman, nor the name, Belle Starr. She was ornery, stingy, selfish, theatrical, and just a little bit crazy in regard to this boy. Blue Duck was satisfied to let this breakfast be a farewell.

But before they had finished, a young man appeared at the hotel. He hung around the common room for a while with a drink, watching their table, then came over as if casually and proceeded to serve a warrant on Belle. He was a handsome young man sporting a fresh cowboy haircut — shampooed, tonicked, shaved, bay-rummed and powdered. He looked like a picture.

"What's your name, boy?"

"Henry Carp," he said. "Deputy marshal to the Thirteenth District . . ."

"I've heard all that." She glanced at the paper he'd handed her and put it aside on the table. "These John Doe warrants aren't worth the paper they're written on. Might as well flash a piece of buttwipe at me. What are you trying to charge me with?" She sounded bored, as if with a bad salesman.

"Introducing spiritous liquors to the Indian peoples of the Thirteenth District."

"Shit boy, I haven't introduced any spiritous liquors in the last geological age. Are you nuts?"

The young man flushed. He stood away from the table, very stiff-backed. Everybody had stopped eating. "I received a telegram this morning. That's why I'm using the John Doe warrant. The charge will be changed when you get to Fort Smith."

Belle laughed as though at a preposterous joke. "Look Mr. Crap . . ."

"Carp." His eyes glanced around.

She watched him closely without watching. It appeared to Blue Duck that he was high-strung, maybe volatile. He wore a short-barrel .45 with a white handle. There weren't any general truths

about Parker's marshals except that there were a lot of them —
from 185 to 200 at any one time riding the Territory — and they
didn't get much: six cents a mile and a couple of bucks for
arrests, plus occasional rewards. Parker's jurisdiction was supposed to cover all federal crimes and all crimes committed by or
against whites. Most of it was liquor-related, and the marshals
rode into the Territory with bundles of John Doe warrants, making as many arrests as possible.

"I don't believe you, Mr. Carp." She pushed back her chair and
stood up to him.

He glanced around. "What? . . ." He seemed very uncertain.
"What don't you believe?"

"I don't believe anything you're saying. What telegram?
Where'd this telegram come from? How'd this telegram know I'd
be in Catoosa this morning? I didn't know it myself until yesterday."

He handed her a piece of paper from his back pocket. She
unfolded it, carefully maintaining her unconcern.

To: ALL STATS CHEROKEE CHOCTAW CHICKASAW SEMINOLE CREEK
NATIONS
    WANTED LIVE BELLE STARR WIDOW OF SAM STARR LOCAL REWARD
FIVE HUNDRED DOLLARS STOP AUTH HECK THOMAS US MARSHAL FT
SMITH

"Well, well, Heck Thomas — I'm coming up in the world. And
five hundred, they're careful to say that it's a local reward." Her
voice was neutral, somewhat softer, as she handed Mr. Carp back
the telegram with an expression almost of solicitation. "You can't
collect a federal reward, so it's good for you that it's local. Means
you could make a lot of money. You could. Only one problem.
There ain't a charge on this telegram, and I ain't going with you
on one that you just made up out of your head. My son here and
my friend, they agree, don't you boys?"

Blue Duck and Ed sat still over their plates.

"I am a duly empowered deputy marshal of the Thirteenth . . ."

"I heard you. You heard me, too. You'll have to get something better than a John Doe to haul me to Fort Smith on."

The young man pulled his white-handled revolver slowly from its holster. His eyes were very bright and nervous. Holding the pistol to the floor uncocked, he was about to speak when the table exploded and his head snapped up. He dropped the pistol and staggered backward, but remained standing long after it had become evident that the bridge of his nose had been obliterated and the cap of his skull taken apart. He remained on two feet, one hand brushing oddly at the air as though to knock a bug off. Opening his mouth to a slow round shape, he said nothing, went limp, collapsed on top of his knees.

Belle was onto Ed before he could put the pistol away. She slapped his face and head with both hands. He raised his hands to protect himself, pistol still held, and she took him by both shoulders and pushed his chair over, feet flying, crashing backwards. She kicked him hard in the ribs. "You stupid punk."

She left him and went over to the marshal, who was solid dead. "Oh . . ." She shook her head. "Oh boy . . ."

Ed stood up, still holding the pistol. The room went quiet. She looked at him standing there with his pistol. "Now you've done it. Aren't you something. You're going to spend the rest of your natural life jumping through your asshole no matter what, aren't you boy? Well congratulations. You've got a real good start. Now wrap him up, get something and wrap him up. And get his brains off the wall."

Blue Duck went out into the street and stood there, just breathing. Belle went after horses, but John Eno and two other men were there by the time she returned with them. Others gathered at a distance.

Belle tried to sound sure of herself. "John, my boy shot that man. He tried to serve a trumped-up warrant on me. Pulled a gun. Ed shot him. I didn't have no choice in the matter."

Eno just stood there, nodding, the same embarrassed smile on his face that he'd had yesterday at the ball game.

"I didn't want him to do it, but he did. He is my boy. You and I have known each other for a while; you know I can't go against my blood. I hope you stay out of it. I'll trust you to. That man was doing wrong. Now he's dead. You throw us in jail over that and it might get rough."

Eno was shaking his head now, still smiling but with a tinge of sorrow.

"*Okay, John?*"

"Belle, you know I can't let this go."

"I don't need to tell you that there are other Starrs in the Nation," she hurried on. "Something happens to me and my boy and it'll be worse than if old Tom was to rise from the grave."

He shook his head. "I want you to go in there and get that boy's gun. Bring it and him out here. We'll have to ride to Tahlequah."

"John . . ." Blue Duck watched her face. It was the first time he'd seen her at a loss. She was suddenly and utterly depleted. The two pistols strapped around her waist were irrelevant — silly theatrical props. The sheriff was unarmed today.

"You were in there, weren't you, Mr. Blue Duck?"

He nodded.

"Well you have to come for a deposition."

Belle looked blank now. "You're taking us to Tahlequah?"

"Yeah and I'd sooner take you to Fort Smith the way things are up there right now." He took a pair of light manacles from one of the deputies and pitched them to her; she caught them, surprised. "Better put them on the boy so he don't cause any more trouble. Be back with a wagon." The sheriff turned and walked away.

She held the manacles, awkward, staring, eyes cataracted by the grieving certainty that was not new or sudden but only closer to fulfillment.

Sheriff *Eno and two deputies* got them on the noon train to Fort Gibson. They would stay the night there and head on over to Tahlequah by road the next day. South of Inola, a dust storm raked the train, sifting through imperfectly sealed windows and making it hard to keep their eyes open.

Belle had managed to buy some Phoenix Pills before leaving Catoosa and was feeling a little better, but she was worried. The three of them sat on a bench together. The two deputies, across from them, had shotguns. John Eno drowsed.

"There are only two possibilities I can think of. Either Prettyman took the train to Fort Smith, claimed a charge against me and put up a private reward, or your whore got to Fort Smith and made up some kind of bull that Heck Thomas was willing to go along with just to give me some trouble."

"She's not a whore," Ed said dully.

"I don't know what she'd claim against me unless it'd be assault with scrambled eggs — or where she'd get the reward money. Does she have money in Fort Smith?"

"No."

"Tell me the truth, boy."

"No, I said."

"Probably took out some short-term loans using her ass as collateral."

Ed shook his head. He was tired and sour and didn't seem to care too much what she said. "I saved you," he muttered.

"What?"

"I saved you from getting took off." He looked down.

She sighed. "Ed — boy — are you really that dumb? Do you think the way to keep out of jail is to shoot a deputy between the eyes?"

"He had a warrant on you."

"You can't do that kind of thing anymore, boy. They got this country strung with wires, don't you realize that?" She rubbed her face with both hands, blinking, sighing again.

"What about Jim July? He's in Fort Smith up for trial."

"What about it?" she snapped.

"Maybe he made a deal with the prosecutor, testified against you on some old charge."

"Oh shut up. Jim wouldn't do that. Just close it down. The thing that worries me is the five-hundred-dollar reward. That's unnatural. I ain't had a five-hundred-dollar bag on my head since before my teeth started falling out. I can't think of anything I did worth five hundred dollars. That'll cock a lot of guns out here."

Dusty wind enshrouded the train as it labored southeastward toward foothill country. Everything on the train was covered in fine silt. It was very dark for a cloudless day. Belle took a couple more Phoenix Pills and worried. Tahlequah was not a good place for her to be at anybody's mercy without a roll of money to buy a decent lawyer. It was the capital of the Cherokee Nation, and Starrs had never gotten along very well there — from before the time old Tom waged his one-man war against the Tribe. There had been a tribal election recently, and she didn't know much about the new Chief, except for the rumor that his winning had almost resulted in warfare in the streets of Tahlequah. She'd heard too that he was an educated man, a talker, educated back east somewhere. Whoever he was, he would doubtless not take kindly — nor be happy if any of his judges took kindly — to the widow of Tom Starr's son.

In this country, Belle was more identifiable as Tom's daughter-in-law than as the friend of Jesse James and Cole Younger. Bandits were born every day, but only one man carried the Cherokee civil war on his back and kept it alive when it flagged, all his born life.

With this in mind Belle had to think about jurisdiction. It was very unlikely that she could keep Ed out of the U.S. Federal Court in Fort Smith. She did not know why Sheriff Eno was taking them to Tahlequah if only to be hauled immediately from there to Fort Smith, but she was certainly not going to protest it at this stage. Judge Parker would hang Ed Reed without a second thought, whereas judicial matters in Tahlequah, complicated by the ancient Ross/Ridge passions, the new elections, and numerous other splits, were usually more confused. It was at least feasible that she could get together some kind of defense in Tahlequah if there was time.

The jail at Fort Gibson was full of squatters whom the army was holding before escorting them back to Kansas. The Illinois District sheriff recommended that they leave Ed there in chains and the rest of them stay overnight at a schoolhouse on the east side of town. By the time they had built a fire in the schoolhouse stove, it was almost dusk. They roasted a mess of rabbits that the sheriff had bought in town. Belle was despondent. The mosquitoes all seemed to have come inside the schoolhouse to avoid the high wind. She was very tired — too old to be riding around the Territory camping out. Too old to be taking her own boy to be hanged. There was a way to get out of this — there always was — but she hadn't figured it out yet. Maybe through Eno. Her mind just wasn't working.

When dusk fell — indigo and purple in the receding dust storm — Blue Duck went out into a field and picked some popcorn, and all five of them sat around the stove eating a few panfuls cooked in rabbit grease. Belle nibbled at it with her front teeth. Crickets rattled outside. Blue Duck talked to one of the deputies in Cherokee. They talked about the drought, crops, baseball, whatever came to mind. It was fully dark before she remembered that this was the place where Blue Duck had grown up — indeed, this might have been the very schoolhouse where his tutor and first love had taught. But there was nothing different in his manner, nothing outside his usual easy familiarity. She liked that. She liked a man who didn't read too easily.

He was good at talking about nothing in particular. He was good at staying cool. He was reserved but he wasn't stiff. He was light. It was an odd manner for a man of his blood. He was so light he seemed empty, and pleasant, which was the oddest thing. A pleasant man who was quiet. So quiet and light and pleasant that she really couldn't tell what he was after. She could usually tell what a man was after in five seconds.

One of the deputies had gone outside to sleep. Another had put his head down on a school desk for a nap. John Eno had been asleep or drowsing most of the day. He amazed and irritated Belle. He seemed fearless. Rather than guarding her or even watching her carefully, he slept. Rather than staying on top of a tense situation or surrounding a place or calling out the deputies, he had given the manacles to her and walked away. The son of a bitch, he would probably be the longest-lived sheriff in Indian Territory. Used to be a pretty good livestock thief, too. He never let anything get him off-center. Hardly ever let anything wake him up.

"I need some damn whiskey is what I need," she said.

"Would you like some tea? I saw a patch of clover. Good for sleep." Blue Duck offered her the pan.

She nibbled on the last of the popcorn. "A regular yarb doctor, ain't you. What do you prescribe for my boy? . . ." She sighed and looked out a window. A new moon was coming off the horizon. "I knew a family back in Carthage, name of Morgan, had a crazy boy, they fed him walnuts. Walnuts are supposed to be good for that. Must have fed him a thousand trees of walnuts over the years, they was feeding him walnuts when he had gray hair. It was the joke around there; we used to wonder when that old loony boy was going to grow roots and sprigs out his head. I mean those people believed in walnuts. That's how they are, you know, the old hill folk, get an idea and, buddy, that's it. And of course he didn't do nothing but get crazier. . . . Used to do that kind of stuff when I was a girl. Put cow pies on my face to stop the freckles. Didn't comb my hair at night for fear I'd lower my nature. Do just about anything to take a cuss off — drink a fly in a cup of water. . . . You ever do that kind of thing?"

Blue Duck smiled into the stove.

"Put an ax under the bed to cut off the birth pains. That was out in California, two thousand miles from where I learned it."

"That was when Ed was coming?"

"That was when Ed came, buster. Came like rolling thunder, too. That ax under there was about the only hope from home there was. His daddy was out drinking, having a high old time, celebrating the boy before he was done born."

"What were you doing in California?" Blue Duck asked.

"Oh . . ." She looked around at the sleeping law. "Ain't much story to that, really. Jim Reed and I went to live at Rich Hill with his family right after we got married, and he got into a scrap there with the Shannon Clan. They bushwhacked his brother Scott, probably on a mistake, and Jim took after them. Shot down two of them. It got hot in Missouri and we went to California. James boys were already out there visiting their uncle. We took Pearl and moved to L.A. They did a job or two out there, but it wasn't much." She got up from the desk that she'd been sitting in and walked to the window. The horned moon was orange and fat with dust.

"Why did you marry Jim Reed?"

"Ha!" she laughed once at the outrageousness of the question. Didn't ask for much, did he? How would she answer that one even if she was inclined to? . . . Well maybe it wasn't as complicated as all that. Cole Younger got her pregnant is what happened. That's what got it all started. And you might say that Jim Reed, formerly a member of Cole's gang, saved her from the dual curse of her daddy and the Dallas night life, between which she vacillated after Cole left Texas and Pearl was born.

But all that was a long story which made her tired to think about. Tired because it seemed like when she thought about one part of it she couldn't help but remember the whole damn story, how when they found out she was pregnant and Cole left the country, her daddy locked her in a closet for three weeks. Mr. Shirley didn't lock her up when Cole was sparking her because the truth was he was scared of Cole — scared of him and Frank and all of them. On St. Valentine's Day of that year they had committed the second bank robbery in U.S. history, at the Clay County Savings Association (the county in Missouri where they had grown up), getting away with $15,000 in gold currency and $45,000 in useless bonds, and a few months later they had robbed a bank in Richmond County, Missouri, and killed several men in the process; and even though Mr. Shirley didn't know the details he could see that there was something peculiar about these boys, something wild and free and queer. Cole read *The Corsair* aloud one night at the fireplace with real emotion, and to Mr. Shirley it was just a tad bit strange seeing a true Ozark boy, raised to be grim, taciturn, suspicious, open up his heart like this reading a book of poetry. Mr. Shirley didn't know quite what to think about that, or about Jesse, whose dim blue eyes appeared to be fixed on some distant goal, some Absolute Place that he saw looming off across the heat-shimmering prairie. Jesse was strange, unreachable, cold, dreamy, to the point that he made you fret in his presence; he tried your patience. He lived inside his own thoughts. Now, Frank James was as solid and regular as a banker. His feet were on the ground. He hadn't spent one day of his life in jail, to Belle's knowledge, and probably never would. Frank had an air of honesty about him, and even though you knew he was the biggest crook ever to straddle a horse, he still felt like your good wise uncle.

Cole was dark, fervent, romantic. He was self-conscious. He read books constantly. He read the Bible and talked about becoming a wandering preacher back in the burned-out wastes of

Missouri. He was serious about it. One minute he'd be talking about Jesus and the next minute about Faust. Belle had read books herself; she'd done pretty well at the Carthage Female Academy back in Missouri, and not just in ornamental needle-work or piano, either — but here was a man who read and studied and worried about books. She'd never seen anybody go that far. Cole worried about sin, depravity, purity, true love, loneliness, the wandering spirit, courage, the end of the world — matters of great portent. Sometimes he'd sit Jesse down and talk to him about these things. Jesse seemed to be the ideal listener with his faraway look and quiet manner, but if he replied it would be to mutter, "You're just a-talkin and a-poopin, aren't you buddy?" and Cole would grow genuinely indignant.

When Cole left her pregnant, Mr. Shirley got hateful and locked her up in a closet. Her momma wept and screamed and carried on to get her out, but it didn't do any good. He told her to give the girl food and lock the damn door. They made her use a slop pot right there in the closet. Every once in a while her daddy came to the door and said something about how she had sinned. His tone wasn't righteous; it was more confused than righteous, but he laid it all to her, of course. Said he could tell at a glance the night that she and Cole had done it because her face lost its shine. Said he always knew she had a high nature and would go to the devil. Now she was just proving him out. He made her smoke pennyroyal and tobacco to cause her to lose the child. It didn't work. He had Momma give her cedarberry tea, which didn't work either, except to make her sick to her stomach. Then he put all the knives he could find into the closet with her and stood outside the door reading chapters from the Old Testament. Nothing worked, but he persisted.

At first she wanted out. She screamed and hollered and made up stories to get out. She said that the baby had been birthed, that she was dying, that an animal had got in there. Then there was a long time when she was tired. This was after a few days in the closet. She slept sitting up in a corner. When she began to come awake again she had no sense of time. Mice walked over her in the dark. She got headaches — the first time she'd ever had them. The food began to seem strange and unnecessary. She saw her baby born with two snakes for a head, writhing up to her breasts for milk. She could feel it biting her in the darkness, slipping across her skin with its fixed diamond eyes and sinking its white thin fangs into her brown nipples. It had arms and legs and perfect tiny little baby hands and feet, and out of the mouths of the snakes, as if from very far away, came a dim crying. She struggled with this vision for what seemed like many days.

When her father came to the door and declaimed at her, she listened but could not understand the words. She was not entirely mad; she knew basically what he was saying, but there was a veil of perplexity that she could not quite get through. She put herself to the task of understanding him, but the words just wouldn't stay glued together in her mind. And then there was a while when any sounds, even his voice, began to sound beautiful. The booming of a prairie chicken, the wind, the mutter and dim clanking of meals, her mother weeping and wailing at the door after she'd just delivered another tin plate of food — all the sounds became oddly soothing and interesting. Her emotions grew as thin as a glass of water. She thought, *I should hate him,* but her supply of hatred just wasn't big enough. She couldn't find enough to direct at him; by the time she managed to get some of it up, she forgot what she was supposed to do with it.

When they let her out, she was different. Face twisted in fear and hatred, her father asked her what she was going to do now, where she was going to have her bastard. She watched him and felt only a glimmering of interest. It was as though in that three weeks he had taken on a new identity — no longer her father to be feared and obeyed but a person . . . just some person.

She wasn't clear on anything. She didn't feel particularly strong or weak, just disinterested in a lot of things that she had previously assumed were the very substance of her life.

He decided that she was a Fallen Woman. This was apparently a hard-won theory that took him over a month to reach. Locking her in the closet and cursing her and acting disgusted by her very presence were all preambles to this definitive decision. Once he had made it and pronounced it a few times, he seemed to grow less worried. He had arrived at a way of understanding it all, and it was apparently no longer necessary to torture her. She was a Fallen Woman.

Being a Fallen Woman offered certain benefits, she learned fairly quickly. For one thing she could learn how to ride a man's saddle without the usual jokes and trouble a woman got. Since she was already fallen, it didn't much matter what she did, so they didn't watch over her nearly as much. In fact, they didn't watch over her at all. After Pearl was born and she began going off to Dallas for several days at a time, staying there with her brother Preston, who was a faro dealer in the Planters' Hotel, and trying out certain little jobs in the bars around town, her folks assumed that this was exactly as it should be; she was fulfilling her new role. And when she did come home she was not expected to help feed the men, as had always been the case before, nor to do any of the usual chores like fetching water.

She'd never liked fetching water. Scyene had a communal well, and her family had gotten a bad reputation about it right after they moved there. Her daddy would take three rain barrels out on a drag sled and fill them all, draining the well dry and making the neighbors mad. The Shirleys had always been outsiders in Scyene, really. They didn't have any friends. They still lived like Ozarkans — independent, suspicious, hoarding — in country where something else was called for.

But even Dallas wasn't all too great, to tell the truth. She just couldn't run away to it once and for all. She danced in the hotel bars, showing off ruffled knee panties, and sang a few places, but without much luck. She had trouble smiling and blinking her eyes just right. Her brother got her a job dealing faro at the Planters'. She did this well. He taught her how to swipe change. She learned how to dress herself up real nice. She learned that her face wouldn't rot off if she put whitening on it. She wore black velvet, chiffon waists, long flowing skirts, high-topped boots and a Stetson hat with an ostrich plume in it. She had been raised to think that costume — any costume — was an unnecessary and suspect thing. To wear a costume was to break the law. And so she would look at herself for long periods in the mirror, posing, trying on different things. She knew she was not pretty; there were no illusions about that. But it was possible to look wild and dashing and interesting, and she enjoyed it more than anything.

But then Dallas would get to her, she would grow lonely for her child and head on back out to Scyene. And it wasn't long before she began to leave her city dresses on when she went home. Although he understood that she was fallen and therefore such dresses were to be expected, the actual sight of them drove her father into dithers. He argued and denounced and covered her with scorn, but Belle would neither quit coming home nor wearing the fancy dresses. It was almost as if she wanted to drive her daddy crazy.

When Jim Reed appeared in Scyene with a bunch of Missouri boys, it reminded her of Cole and them a couple of years before. She was getting tired of going back and forth to Dallas, and her daddy was worse all the time. She had grown up with Jim in Carthage — he was as familiar as a weed. So he "rescued" her. She rode off with him and his boys one night, heading north for the Territory. A man named Fischer — big man who chewed tobacco all the time — married them on horseback. He claimed to be some kind of preacher. Jim knew the Indian Territory pretty well. For some time he'd been friends with old Tom Starr, who was always happy to accommodate outlaws of the southern persuasion. Together, old Tom's tribe and the Missouri boys were what might be termed the last Confederates. And since a good half of the Nation had not committed itself to the South, they had a good field of "enemies" to harvest from.

Jim Reed got killed back down in Texas and she married Sam Starr. She called the old home place Younger's Bend after Cole, and the name stuck. She fetched water and cooked meals, got a piano out there and sang to a dozen men in a night, ducking around and acting as sweet as she had to while she got her feet on the ground. Mainly she was *out* from under her daddy, the old stingy mean hypocrite, wearing a plume in her hat and loud-jingling spurs. Wasn't nobody going to put her in a closet again.

She stood looking at the red horns of the moon, remembering those early days in the Territory. "One thing you can say about Jim Reed," she spoke quietly to the window. "One thing about him you can't take away. He knew the Territory, every creek and spring and jackrabbit well to the other side of Cross Timbers. Sam, too — both of my legal husbands were dogs in Oklahoma Country. You'd be surprised at how many of the roughnecks that camped out with us at Younger's Bend over the years didn't know their butts from a hole in the ground when it came to this country. It comes from flashing your gun around too much. Gives you some kind of vertigo. Set some of these boys aloose for Dallas and they'd end up in St. Louis. I ain't naming full names but there was one started with Cole and another Jesse. Bob Younger had a nose. Jesse couldn't smell shit on his own boot, and Cole was so busy reading Byron and the Bible and drinking whiskey to make them fit that he couldn't pick out the east at sunrise. He was, I mean to tell you, one dumb turkey when it came to getting some-where. Some of them could, some couldn't, and mostly the ones that could didn't strut around getting public attention so that their mommas back in Missouri would get blowed up with dyna-mite. The ones that could, they didn't have to put on no stage plays."

"And you could?"

"What do you mean 'could'? Honey, I have a nose for Okla-homa like a redbone hound. Which is why all those bumpkins hung around me so close. Sure ain't because I was pretty. Jesse couldn't find the crapper in the morning without an Indian guide and a government map. That's why they come out here in the first place — seventy thousand square miles of Territory with no local law to speak of, outside the United States, only one judge, and him operating through these underpaid deputies, most of them as stupid as a post. There is no better place to hide if you know how to get around yourself. Now Sam Starr, he was a lazy man but he could sure get his hot tail into the Winding Stair and leave behind Lighthorse and the Choctaws and everybody else for as God-blessed long as he wanted to. Half the time we were married, he was on the scout for one reason or another. The other half he was at home sleeping. His temperament was about like Sheriff Eno here. Him and me and Bob Younger and Dan Evans and a few others, we could cipher north from south."

She gazed at the moon, her voice dreaming and proud and somehow hateful. She turned toward the stove and Blue Duck. John Eno was snoring lightly in a corner. Despite the Phoenix Pills, she was alert. Coals in the stove cast a dim glow across her face. "Tell you something else. I've had a few men out here, some of them legal, some not, but all of them have been the same. All of them have been a son-of-a-bitch man trying to hire me for cooking and washing. All of them have been him and his buddies waiting till after dinner to stand around outside spitting and swigging whiskey and talking about the real business. You could say Younger's Bend was a regular hideout for outlaws in the Territory. And you could say that nine out of ten of the boys that come through there wanted to see Belle Starr do her regular woman work real quiet and get the hell out of the way. They wanted her to feed the men and then eat the scraps with the children after dinner, like all the other women in this God-forsaken place. That ain't right, you know." She looked up at him. "They kept it from me. They kept it from me as regular as if I was going off to knitting to tell the ladies all about it the next day. Cole Younger started it. He gave me a child and he took me on the trail, but when I wouldn't get down real regular in the stream and wash the cobwebs out of him and his brothers' underwear, he started a-quoting the Bible at me. Jim Reed wasn't no better, he was just sneakier. And Sam, shit, he was a full-blood Cherokee Indian with a maniac for a father — what could you expect out of him? Only good thing about him was that he was gone half the time. You get what I'm saying?"

Blue Duck sat in the pupil's chair, watching her.

She came over closer to him. "And now they're all dead and hanged and in jail and left me with the last thing — make something out of these kids. I haven't got a chance. That boy is bound and determined to kill himself. He's spinning like a top, I'll tell you."

"Maybe you ought to leave him alone."

"It's too late for that, mister." Her glance snicked around the darkness and stopped on Blue Duck. "Been too late."

"What do you mean?"

"What do I mean? . . ." She sighed. "If you can't see with your own eyes . . . What are we talking about me all the time for? What about you?" Her voice got quieter, changing the subject. "Didn't you tell me something about this schoolmarm from Fort Gibson. Was this her school?"

Blue Duck didn't answer.

She searched his face in the dimness. "This right here the place? You spend many an hour in here?"

After a moment he answered her — very precisely, "This is not the schoolhouse where she taught. This is a new building. I did not spend time in the public school, anyway. I was alien."

"This isn't where she taught?"

"No," he said quietly. "It is not."

"Well here we are in Fort Gibson anyway, and I don't see you mooning."

"Sometimes you go on, don't you Belle? Get pretty rough."

"It must have been pretty rough when she walked away from that rain barrel."

Blue Duck went quiet.

"I like to test a man out — see what I got," she almost whispered.

"Why don't you just end it at that?"

"It won't be ended until you tell the judge how that deputy pulled his gun and was fixing to shoot my boy."

"Is that what you want out of me?"

"You owe it."

"Owe it for what?"

"You know what you owe better than I can tell it to you."

"Excuse me, Mrs. Starr, but I don't owe you anything."

"Excuse me, Mr. Blue Duck, but you might just change your mind."

6

Having *seen her,* he remained nearly as fascinated as he had sometimes indulged in being while *not* seeing her over the past fourteen years. Yet whether because he had grown too tame reading books and pulling teeth or because there really was something, as he imagined, strange about her, a way she put her shoulder against every moment of time and tried to push forward just a little faster than it could possibly go, in what seemed almost like an effort to *get it all over with* — whether because of this or simply because he was growing middle-aged and set in his ways, there really was something hard to take about her. Something that made her almost not worth it. She was hard, she was imperious, she was theatrical, she was selfish, she was stubborn, she was a liar, and yet all of her faults did not define her nor give her her peculiar essence. There was something worse and more amazing about her than the sum of it all.

She was a weird blue fury of a woman, and he was satisfied that he had seen enough of her for now.

But events conspired against him. He had hoped to make a deposition as soon as they arrived and then get on back to Tulsa. But the sheriff required that he stay at least the afternoon. Ed was put in jail immediately and no bond was set. After they had been at the sheriff's office a while, a deputy came in and asked if they would like to wait at the National Hotel.

"Wait for what?" Belle asked.

"The Chief wants to talk to you."

"We've already talked to him. What else does he want?"

"Not the sheriff, ma'am. The Chief."

"Chief of the Tribe?" Belle was surprised.

"That's right."

"What the hell for?"

"I can't tell you."

He escorted them to the National, a two-story brick hotel, where he asked them to wait in the salon. Belle ordered a straight-up whiskey, and Blue Duck followed suit.

"Real sippin whiskey . . . You know there's something funny about this place."

"The hotel?" Blue Duck took a drink; it was indeed good whiskey. He loved the taste of good whiskey. If he wasn't a dentist, he'd be a drunk.

"I mean Tahlequah. There's something strange-turned about the town. Must be this boomer deal."

"May be the drought."

"It's the drought and it's something else, too. The new Chief, he must have half of them scared to death, hiding up in their houses or something, scared these boomers are going to sweep down on Tahlequah. He's standing up against them, I've heard. What in the world does he want to see us for? I know he's got better things to do than handle extradition cases."

"You think that's what he'll do?"

"I don't see why Eno brought us here in the first place. You don't shoot one of Parker's boys and get took to a tribal court. That don't balance out."

"Maybe the Chief already wanted to see you."

"That don't make sense either." Belle took a good slug and settled into thought. "There's just something real funny about this place."

A while later, three Cherokee Lighthorsemen entered the hotel bar and escorted them to a room on the second floor. A man sitting in an armchair with a file of papers in his lap stood up and introduced himself. "Joel B. Mayes," he said. "I am Principal Chief of the Cherokees. You're Belle Starr and . . ."

"Blue Duck, from Tulsa."

"Are you Creek?"

"No."

"Oh? Excuse my probing, but are you and Mrs. Starr in each other's confidence?"

"Yes, he's in my confidence," Belle said.

"Well . . . I brought you here for a purpose — obviously — and you're curious about that. No mystery is intended. Your boy is in trouble with the law, if I'm not mistaken, Mrs. Starr."

"That's right."

Chief Mayes smiled. He had a pleasant smile, his lower lip protruding somewhat underneath quite a thick moustache. He was a half-breed. His white shirt, although buttoned at the top, was wrinkled and spotted, and his double-breasted suit was marked with the stains and sediments of office — whiskey, tobacco, food. Right away he gave the impression of an intelligent, slovenly and effective man. "You must know first of all, Mrs. Starr, that I was already in the process of sending you a message when this business with your boy came up."

"Is that right?" She sat down.

"That's right. I don't know what effect this will have on our discussion, but I wanted you to know it before I began. I am going to ask you a couple of questions. My purpose is to save time — yours and mine. First of all, do you know what this is?" He gave her a handbill from his file.

OKLAHOMA
Capt. Couch's
Oklahoma Colony

Will move to and settle the Public Lands in the Indian Territory. Arrangements have been made with the Railroads for

LOW RATES

14,000,000 acres of the finest Agricultural and Grazing Lands in the world open for

FREE HOMES

For the people — these are the last desirable public lands remaining for settlement. Situated between the 34th & 38th degrees of latitude, at the foot of the Ouachita Mountains, we have the finest climate in the world, an abundance of water, timber and stone. Springs gush from every hill. The grass is green the Year round. No flies or mosquitoes.

THE BEST STOCK COUNTRY ON EARTH

A committee was appointed by the citizens of St. Louis, and their legal opinion asked regarding the right of settlement, and they, after a thorough research, report the lands subject under the existing laws to Homestead and Pre-emption settlement.
Some three thousand have already joined the Colony and will soon move in a body to Oklahoma, taking with them Saw Mills, Printing Presses, and all things required to build up a prosperous community. Schools and Churches will be at once established. The Colony has laid off a city, which will be the Capital. In less than twelve months the Railroads that are now built to the Territory line will reach the Capital. Other towns and cities will spring up, and there never was such an opportunity offered to enterprising men.

MINERALS!

Copper and lead are known to exist in large quantities — the same vein that is worked at Joplin Mines runs through the Territory to the Ouachita Mountains, and it will be found to be the richest lead and copper district in the Union. The Ouachita Mountains are known to contain GOLD & SILVER. The Indians have brought in fine specimens to the Forts, they have never allowed the white men to prospect

them. Parties that have attempted it have not returned.

The winters are short and never severe and will not
interfere with the operations of the Colony. Farm
work commences here early in February, and it is
best that we should get on the grounds as early as
possible, as the winter can be spent in building, opening lands and preparing for spring.

For full information and circulars and the time of
starting, rates, &c., address,

T. C. Craddock	Geo. M. Jackson
General Manager	General Agent
Wichita, Kan.	508 Chestnut St.
	St. Louis

"Of course I know what it is," Belle said.

"Do you approve of the boomer settlement of Indian lands?"

"No I don't."

"You don't?"

"I didn't approve of it in eighteen-eighty, I didn't approve of it
when what's-his-name Payne was leading those raids, and I don't
approve of it now."

"Why not?" Chief Mayes was still smiling quite amiably.

"Why not? Because they're taking back land from the Tribe
that they gave to it in perpetuity seventy-five years ago. That's
no good. The way the weather's been — the way everythin's
been — this ain't no time to rue back on the Tribe. That's the way
I see it."

"Do you know what's happening in the Cherokee Outlet right
now?"

"What is this, a test? I ain't no schoolgirl anymore, Chief
Mayes. Just tell me what you're getting at."

Mayes leaned back in his chair, still smiling. He instructed two
of his Lighthorsemen to wait on the balcony, leaving one of them
in the room. "All right, you are acquainted with the fact that the
U.S. Federal Congress is presently contemplating forced purchase
of the entire Cherokee Outlet at a dollar twenty-five cents per

acre. That's seven million acres which have been ours since we were forced to move to the Territory, a strip of land sixty miles wide across the top of Oklahoma. And you're aware that for the last ten years we have managed the cattle leasing rights of the Outlet to great profit for the Tribe. Six years ago the Cherokee Strip Live Stock Association formed to deal with us and the federal government. Whatever their own purposes were, eighteen eighty-three was the first year we were able to handle the leasing rights in an organized fashion. In that year our arrangement with the Association was for a year's lease at one hundred thousand dollars.

"You must also know that I was just elected as Principal Chief of the Cherokee Tribe a few months ago, and that my election caused some controversy."

"I've heard something about it."

"There is a disagreement within the Tribe over how we are going to continue to handle the grazing rights in the Outlet, how we are going to deal with the renewed threat from boomers and the threat from the federal government of forced purchase. After my election, I insisted on open bidding on the lease rights. As a result, we have just signed an agreement with the Live Stock Association for two hundred thousand dollars for next year. That is a substantial increase, considering the weather and the state of grass. However, the government at this point is pursuing the policy — not entirely openly, but certainly in what is becoming a consistent pattern — of breaking up the various tribal governments. They are systematically weakening the tribes through purchase and settlement." Chief Mayes, still smiling, went silent.

Belle sat back in her chair and looked at him. "How does that touch on me and my boy?"

"Mrs. Starr, have you heard about the methods that have been used by certain railroads and banks which stand to profit by opening Oklahoma to white settlement?"

"If you mean tying strumpets up in balloons and all such as that, yeah, I've seen some of it."

"You mentioned David L. Payne. Mr. Payne, as you recall, began leading boomer raids on the Outlet ten years ago. He made highfalutin speeches saying that his poor settlers could not afford to bribe and lobby in the Congress and that the big cattle-leasing operations cut off poor white settlers from the lands in favor of the soulless beef monopoly. He said that the tribal government had been corrupted by the beef monopoly. Of course, it was certain equally soulless bank and railroad interests that were lubricating Mr. Payne's golden tongue. He was escorted a number of times back to Kansas, but because we had no way to prosecute, he simply came back again as soon as another band of squatters could be organized. Our means of dealing with these encroachments must be initiated in Tribal Council and move from there in a complex process through the U.S. Department of the Interior, the War Department, and back out to union post commanders. We have no right to act ourselves. The land is ours and yet it is not ours.

"David L. Payne died of natural causes in eighteen eighty-four, but immediately upon his death, his protégé William Lawes Couch — the man on this poster — led a raid of four hundred settlers on Stillwater. The cavalry eventually cut their supply lines and they were forced to surrender, but not before public opinion had swung in favor of the white settlers."

"That was the nigger cavalry, wasn't it?"

"The War Department sent a Negro regiment; that is correct."

"Whoever decided to protect Indian land using nigger soldiers against whites was either dimwitted or on the other side. They couldn't have cooked up a stupider move if they had plotted all year."

"Soon after that, President Cleveland signed legislation for money to buy some lands from the Cherokee Outlet. Negotiations were not begun, and for reasons that we do not entirely understand, boomer raids and political activity were relatively quiet for a few years. We have maintained on a regular and orderly basis the leasing arrangement with the Live Stock Association, and there are now some one hundred pastures, two hundred fifty thousand dollars' worth of barb wire, and perhaps three hundred thousand licensed cattle in the Outlet. Needless to say, this is the greatest source of income for the Tribe — virtually the only major source. The forced purchase of the Outlet, if it indeed happens, will mark the death of Cherokee sovereignty over its own lands."

Belle sat back in her chair very still, eyes fixed on Mayes. She was waiting for his proposition, remaining diplomatically blank, almost bored.

"By which I mean the Cherokee National Council will become a piece of paper and a few colorful rituals if the boomer raids are successful in exciting further public opinion against us and the lands are taken. It will mean the end of the Cherokee Government. They will make a fine offer of ten million or so dollars, suggesting that it should be a very generous incitement to the leaders of the Tribe, should in fact promise to set most of us up *as individuals* for life. It will be a very difficult offer to resist, because common sense will tell us that we have no choice."

"No choice but to take your bundle and set back. That doesn't sound bad."

Mayes looked at her with what appeared good humor. "The Starrs have enjoyed that approach for several generations now, haven't they?"

Blue Duck watched her. She was suddenly awake, ready to scrap. "I'll tell you what, Chief, it ain't exactly settin back living under Hi-Early Mountain. That old clay's made for bricks, not vegetables."

"You've done all right in cattle, I believe." He continued to look friendly.

Belle looked back at him with a kind of smile on her face, too, but didn't reply.

Mayes picked up a newspaper from his lap. "Boomer activities have started up again in the last few weeks. There have been night burnings in the Outlet, cattle slaughter and cattle theft, and right now there's a small army of settlers organizing for a raid out of Caldwell, Kansas. This means further publicity and further losses with the government. We can't afford it, but neither can we afford to operate through the U.S. Army. That's like trying to train a bull to kill a plague of grasshoppers."

"So what do you want from Sam Starr's widow?"

"Mrs. Starr, I know about the grudge held by the Starr family against the tribal government. I am aware of the history of Tom Starr — at least, as it's told to little boys growing up in these parts. But I'm also aware of the fact that you have an independent mind."

She looked at Blue Duck. "Really talking like a chief now, ain't he?"

"And I'm aware that your boy Ed Reed shot a U.S. deputy marshal yesterday, and that he should be extradited immediately to Judge Parker, and that there is right now a warrant for your arrest out of the Fort Smith court."

"What do you want out of me, Mayes? Say it to me flat and straight before you start waving my boy like a flag in front of my face. You want me to scatter some of these boomers? That's called warfare — you got an army?"

"Are you concerned about your boy, Mrs. Starr?"

She flushed but spoke evenly. "I take care of my blood, mister. Now are you talking about burning people out or what?"

"We aren't as interested in the settlers as we are in finding out more about the financing of these activities and taking action at the source. Action against the settlers invariably swings more public opinion in favor of forced purchase. Anytime some poor white settler's shack burns down, they start beating the drums back east. I think you understand that."

"What 'action at the source' are you talking about?"

"I can't give you a detailed answer to that now. If you're interested, we can discuss it more later. . . . I want to say that the reason I sought you out is that you are known for being fearless and extraordinarily resourceful."

"I'm not fearless, Chief Mayes. I wouldn't be going on an old lady and alive out here if I was. Why are you tapping a woman for this?"

"An inspiration, Mrs. Starr. You have a reputation for knowing the Territory. You also have a reputation for knowing the cattle industry — and much of what we're concerned with is our inability to protect the lands that we have leased to the Live Stock Association. At two hundred thousand dollars, they expect us to provide some protection for their fences and stock. We are forbidden to outfit a border-guard army. Our only alternative is to employ agents."

"I'm not sure I understand the purpose of these agents. You want somebody to go out there and strip down these boomers? That's a little bit farfetched, isn't it?"

Chief Mayes's smile had melted away now. He got up and spoke with the one remaining Lighthorse guard, who went out on the balcony with the others. He poured three short drinks from a flask kept in an inside coat pocket, and handed drinks to Blue Duck and Belle. "It is difficult to define and even more difficult to face, Mrs. Starr. You can see, you have doubtless heard rumors to the effect, that the Tribe is in a state of turmoil over this subject. I was elected chief over Dennis Wolfe Bushyhead because he was not dealing with the Outlet question at all. He was in effect waiting for the boomers and the federals to take it over. Now that I am in his place it has become apparent to me why Dennis was helpless. There doesn't seem to be much that we can do. The law appears to be on the side of the Tribe, but in point of fact it renders us helpless against the white settlers. If we notify the Department of the Interior of incursions and they eventually send out troops, the newspapers claim that a band of poor deserving whites has once again been denied their due acreage by the heartless federal government, which is protecting rich Indians and cattlemen. It is the present policy of the United States government, as I said a moment ago, to break up and weaken the tribal governments. The tool that is being used for that purpose is severality — the institution of private property. As long as the tribes are unified and as long as their governments have sources of income, they represent a force and a threat repugnant to the government. Speeches to this effect are being given every week in Congress, and the powers-that-be in the Department of the Interior are moving further in this direction with every bulletin, every issuance.

"The most peculiar thing about it is that we recognized it as the federal policy before the government did. It is believed by certain very high-ranking persons in government that the Indians are not capable of understanding the complexities of federal policy. In fact, we understand — and have understood — quite well. We are not part of the United States. We are by law a separate nation, the whole Territory a patchwork of separate nations uprooted from our homelands and put here to be out of the way. But now we are in the way again. By virtue of our existence we are in the way. And by virtue of the fact that our land is owned communally. There is something very undesirable about that to the federal government. So the land is being taken away. It is happening now before our eyes, and we are quite fully conscious of it. And of course the white settlers, while appearing to be breaking the law, are serving exactly the function of the government. They are pawns in a larger partnership. . . ." The Chief ran out of words for a moment. He seemed to drop away into private thought.

"What do you want out of me, Mayes? Be straight."

He took another slug of whiskey and frowned. For a moment he appeared to have lost his powers of articulation. When he finally spoke there was a new tension in his voice. "Mrs. Starr, I do not relish the idea of warfare. The idea is in fact ludicrous. But the land is being taken. Banks, railroads, and settlers are readying themselves for final expansion into our territories. There's no recourse for the Cherokee Tribe but to operate through agents. It can be an extremely dangerous strategy. I am asking that you serve in that capacity."

"How many agents are you hiring?"

"I don't know. If the idea is successful, a number of others. A cooperative network."

"And what are you hoping to get out of it?"

"What anyone who's desperate hopes for, Mrs. Starr — time. If we can keep the lands clear for another few months, perhaps we can reach Congress. There are problems within the Tribe that have to be cleared up. We have to get better organized, and quickly, but lobbying tactics shouldn't take too long, now that we have the new lease money arrangement." Mayes glanced down at the newspaper in his lap and looked back up at Belle. "Are you interested?"

"What about my boy?"

"Your boy is in the Tahlequah jail. If we can come to an agreement, I will see to it that he is tried for manslaughter in the tribal court."

"That ain't good enough."

"I cannot have him released. The best I can do is try to have the case handled in such a way that he doesn't have to go to Fort Smith for trial."

"You're asking me to risk my tail on guaranteed manslaughter?"

"At present, that's the best I can offer. As an agent, of course, you will be paid."

"Yeah . . . Well Mr. Mayes." Belle finished off her glass and stood up. "I don't know where you got your college degree, but it must have been up north somewhere. You talk a real Yankee bargain."

"Can we come to an agreement?"

She looked at him for a moment. "No offense, but I don't think so."

"Would you explain?"

"It ain't no kind of deal for me. The Tahlequah court just might skin my boy alive. Is that supposed to be a deal? I think we *could* make a deal, but I haven't heard any offers yet."

"What kind of offer?"

"Well, for example, you might just offer your personal word that the judge, I guess it would be John Wailer, no matter what the jury decides, won't give the boy more than a certain sentence with a regular parole — something like that. At least, that would be an offer."

"I do not have John Wailer, nor any judge, in my pocket, Mrs. Starr. I wish I did. But I can assure you that every influence within the limits of propriety will be exerted."

"Boy, you're really talking pretty now. Make a stupid old woman dizzy in the head, make me think I'm getting something for nothing."

"It's not for nothing, ma'am. On the contrary."

"I like you, Mayes." She looked at him.

He appeared somewhat ill at ease. ". . . Well, that's good."

"I believe you. I believe the sound of your voice. If I can get your word that my boy won't get his neck broke over this thing, I'll talk to you. Your word is good. That's all I need."

"I want you to appreciate that I cannot do that, Mrs. Starr."

"I don't appreciate it for shit. Until you guarantee me my boy's life, we ain't on good family terms, Chief."

"We do not know yet what we can get away with in regard to Judge Parker. I cannot even guarantee you that we can keep the trial here, in fact. I can guarantee you that I will do my *best* to keep it here and that I will do my best to lighten the sentence. I will assure you only of what I *can* assure you, and I will certainly hope for the best."

"If you can hire special agents, you can decide a trial. What you're doing real politely is just waggling my boy in my face, and that's getting old real fast."

Mr. Mayes was growing somewhat irritated, but digging in and remaining patient. "Unfortunately, my powers are limited and what powers I presumably do have are in dispute with the National Council. We have been limping along with the bicameral democracy for many years now. The Principal Chief has been a figurehead. This is ideal for the federal government, since lack of a strong executive has made it impossible for us to deal with them effectively. Without an executive, resistance is impossible."

"The Starrs used to talk about that."

"Everybody talks about it."

". . . About how no account the Chief was."

"That has certainly been the case. Now we must either have a chief who can act or we will have no tribe at all."

"So act and get my boy loose."

"Mrs. Starr" — he leaned forward — "I am admitting something to you. At this point everything I do is tenuous. Every decision I make is a balancing act. When I began to take executive actions after my election, we very nearly had a civil war in this town. The Lighthorse were dividing up allegiances. Citizens were burying family treasures and all such nonsense. Had it been another season, we would have seen trouble. Hostilities dissipated because of the heat and drought as much as anything, I think. There isn't enough water to drink, much less to throw on burning houses, and I think the people understood that. Things are quiet for now. But I have enemies. Very strong enemies who would be delighted by nothing so much as an open act of malfeasance. That is all I can tell you." He stood up and faced her. "I've said more than necessary already."

Blue Duck saw that Mayes really did look disturbed. He was a good talker but not entirely sure of himself in this situation.

Belle looked scarcely interested. "What were you going to offer as payment to these agents?"

"About that I can be fairly certain. I will put in your hands ten percent of the lease payment for this year if you can disrupt the present illegal activities of the boomers in the area of Enid."

"Disrupt them how?"

"Again, I cannot be entirely specific about that. I can give you a list of some of the principal financiers — or who we think are the financiers — and I can offer you free choice in tactics. I do not in fact want to be personally involved in tactics. I believe you can understand that."

"Ten percent is twenty thousand dollars. You want me to pay my boys out of that, I suppose?"

"Yes."

She looked at Blue Duck, who had been sitting back quiet during all of this. "Well Mr. Dentist, what's your opinion?"

99

7

hey lay naked in the hot night, the list of financiers between them on the bed illumined by a coal-oil lamp. The streets outside were quiet. She was a little drunk. She seemed to have a very unambiguous relationship with good whiskey. Cradling her jaw in her hand and staring at the list, she spoke quietly.

"That's one modern Indian chief. Which is okay with me — I'd sooner talk to him than one of these feather dusters. He's lying about my boy, though. He's holding Ed for insurance. And I don't see nothing to do but go along with him. If he can keep him out of Fort Smith, it's a good swap. You know what Fatman Parker would do with that boy? Whew! Parker was mad, I mean to say hopping, when word got around that Ed was paroled. Some newspaper reporter asked him if he had any comment on it, and he nearly cleaned that young man's plow right there in the courtroom. He had sentenced Ed Reed to seven years and he wanted Ed Reed by God to sit in that pen seven years. Now if he gets a second, better chance at him, he'll have old shovelface tarring the rope before he calls the court to order. Nosir. Any way I can keep him out of Fort Smith is worth it."

"What about the reward on you?"

"I've been thinking about that. I could go on the scout or I could turn myself in. I think what I better do is get over there and find out what it's for. Once I'm feeling solid about Joel Mayes keeping this shooting from Parker, and if it's just Prettyman over there bitching about assault, I'll probably do better to put up a bond and face him down in court. With you the only witness, he can't put me in jail. The ticklish thing will be making sure Mayes is quiet about this shooting. I don't know what kind of tricks he'll pull on that. I'll just have to trust him."

"How's he going to account for a missing deputy in the Cherokee Nation?"

"He doesn't have to. Nobody knows where them guys are usually. They're just out there — running whiskey half the time. What I'm worried about is somebody poking around Catoosa and just stumbling onto it."

"What about making some deals in Catoosa?"

"You can't make deals when it's gossip-sized. What I'm counting on — fact, what I should have made sure about with Joel Mayes — is him making up a story about the deputy that throws them clear off. That's about the only hope."

"Do you understand what Mayes wants?"

She looked at the list. "He wants us to break the law bad. He doesn't want any traceable connections between him and us, that's for sure. Wants to come down on some of these big boys. He isn't saying it outright, but I suppose he's aiming for us to burn some of them out. But look here" — she pointed at the list — "Arkansas Bank of Commerce, Kansas and Western Railroad, *Oklahoma War Chief Newspaper*, Waldrop and Myers — that's classy stuff. I mean, for a broke-down little Indian tribe, that's some big business. And one way you look at it, it sounds kind of off-center. If you had a grudge against Mayes and heard about this, you might decide that he was stupid. Hiring an old locoed woman to do this. He's paying tolerable wages, all right. . . . But him and me have to do some talking before I'll make any arrangements. It'll be a messy deal because it all has to be kept secret. The last thing he can afford is anything public with me."

"It doesn't sound like a very safe arrangement."

"Safe!" She glanced up at him. "If we get snagged, we're on our own. I think that's where my boy comes in. Mayes will keep him here with the unspoken threat that if I spill the beans about a deal with him, he'll extradite him to Parker."

"It still doesn't sound like a very safe deal for him."

"Well it ain't, but what can he do, send out the Lighthorse and wage war against the white man? He tapped me because I was the only one crazy enough and yet with the sense to pull it off."

Blue Duck lay back and looked at the ceiling. "He's asking you to go out there on your own and close these boomers down?"

"Not on my own. I'll have to get together some kind of troops."

"Who would that be?"

"Don't know. I could probably find four or five old thugs. Strong Man J. B. Stampp is living right here in Tahlequah, I believe. He's worth about three natural men. Crick Watson, I believe he's living over to Fort Smith. . . . I can tie into a few old crooks. They ain't all whiskey-soaked and lamebrained yet. . . . Hey. Let me ask you something."

"What's that?"

"Am I going to have to wear false teeth?"

"False teeth. . . . Well, I can't be sure about that. You've still got your incisors. Your molars are pretty bad, of course."

"I don't want to wear false teeth."

"You're still able to chew, aren't you?"

"Yeah, I can kind of chew *at* it, I guess you'd say. But I'd rather eat gruel than put one of them ridiculous machines in my mouth."

"I'll make you one for eight dollars, upper and lower. As long as you can chew, though, you can do without."

"How do you like going to bed with me?"

"I like it."

"You ain't feisty in bed."

He looked at her. "Oh?"

"It ain't because you're dreading it, is it?"

"Dreading it? No. What makes you say that?"

"There's just something kind of held back."

"I haven't . . . I mean, I've been living pretty much without a woman."

"Pretty much or sure enough without?"

He didn't answer.

"Ain't no shame to that. Many's the time I'd just as soon be without an old mangy man. Been living with this Jim July. . . . Have I told you about him?"

"No."

"He's about Ed's age. Good head, you can give him that. Speaks five or six languages. Could probably talk Cherokee in circles around Joel Mayes. Got a knack for it. He's also a pretty good crook. But he's awful young. Like if he was to walk in here right now, he'd get on you."

"Oh?"

"Oh yeah. He gets hot under the collar. I expect to bury him one of these days. . . . Hey, any more of that whiskey over there?"

"No."

"So you don't chase the skirts? Is it because you killed your teacher?"

"I wouldn't know."

"Don't get mad. I ain't asking it to dig at you."

"That's all right. Do you want me to get more whiskey?"

"Oh, I reckon I've had enough. Going to see Mayes again tomorrow. Want to go to war with me?"

Blue Duck lay on his back looking at the ceiling without, for now, an answer to that.

The talks with Chief Mayes turned into regular negotiations held three nights in a row at midnight in a room of the National. Each night Mayes was accompanied by the same wordless firm-jawed Lighthorseman, apparently chosen over the others because of his inability to speak English. There were very few Cherokee who spoke no English, whereas quite a percentage spoke English and only smatterings of the native tongue. This young man stood back and at least pretended to not understand a word. Blue Duck grew more amazed each night at the tenor of the discussions. Chief Mayes was a politic man, intelligent and quite capable of dealing with Belle. But the meaning that emerged from those three nights of confusion, arrangement, amendment, veiled threat, accusation, breakdown, patch-up and general turmoil was that this was indeed, as Belle had said, an act of unparalleled desperation. At stake was the ability and right of the Cherokee Nation to transact its own business and to exercise sovereignty over its own lands. Chief Mayes was not deluded about the probable outcome. Lands had been taken from the Tribe before, north of the Arkansas River in the Territory of Arkansas, and south and west of the River in the Cherokee Outlet. The "ceding" of lands had been going on virtually ever since the federal government first removed the Cherokee to northern Oklahoma on the theory that this land was part of a vast and undesirable "Great American Desert." It had happened again and again. As soon as the whites came into competition for the land or the government needed it for a place to squeeze more western Indians into the Territory, a reason was devised and more of it was taken.

As the three of them perused maps and discussed details, it became evident that in his own modestly reckless way Chief Mayes regarded the threatened forced purchase of the Outlet as the final and irrevocable depredation of Cherokee power. Looking at the map, it was easy to see why: the whole top of Oklahoma would be taken from them. The extent of tribal lands would be reduced by more than half. That Mayes was desperate was most apparent in the fact that he did not seem to know how to deal directly with the federal government on the question of the purchase. An articulate and educated man, sovereign Chief of the Cherokee Nation, he'd so far had no more success dealing with this problem than a naked Comanche. What diplomatic moves he had made had been ruthlessly blocked. There seemed no choice but to deal with it on a local level, and here the law was entirely against him. He was forbidden to use his own police against the boomers. And it was the boomers who were — most successfully — keeping the wound open and the question of purchase constantly in the foreground. They, in turn, were largely supported by white entrepreneurs and interests.

It was the latter against whom Mayes wanted to act, but a measure of his desperation could be seen in the fact that he didn't seem to know — or at least Blue Duck could not determine after three nights of talk — what kind of action to take against them, nor precisely what effect *any* action would have. At times, he seemed bent merely on revenge. At others, he seemed to be hoping that his "agents" could warn the boomer entrepreneurs in the only language they understood and that this warning would cause them to desist. His greatest hope, apparently, was to buy enough time to organize a lobbying effort in Congress.

Blue Duck understood that one reason for his ambiguity was that he wanted to maintain a certain distance from the illegal activities that he was licensing. In making arrangements for payment and so forth, he expended a great deal of diplomacy in trying to insulate himself from future direct contact with Belle. It became more and more evident that Ed Reed was indeed his ace in the hole. The murder of Parker's marshal had been a propitious event for Chief Mayes.

Belle demanded partial payment in advance, total volition in deciding the size and constitution of her force, clearance on any spoils that might arise from her activities, freedom to visit her boy in the Tahlequah jail and numerous other details and footnotes that she spelled out as carefully as if this were a lifetime contract. The details all made sense, and all seemed to testify to her meticulous awareness of what she was entering into — and yet the whole project, the whole idea of the thing, was half-cocked and weird. It seemed to Blue Duck that in her concern with the details she was missing the obvious larger point that it was a suicide mission.

But then perhaps he had gotten too chickenhearted in his life as a decent citizen. Too addicted to his easy chair and books and rather orderly bachelor's life. He missed his books already. Here he was riding with a woman who had haunted his brain for fourteen years, and what did he think about but the stack of cheap novels waiting to be read back on the table in Tulsa. Being with her was an act not yet understood. It was not as it should be, as his dreams or memories or even his books would have it be. His first love had been a state of being, a madness, a crime. This was no more than an enigmatic little tap at the door of his spirit. Yet perhaps there was promise of something. No very grand hopes, but something. He decided to go with her at least to Fort Smith. He sent a telegram to Jenkins back in Tulsa: ON VACATION WILL RETURN SOON PLEASE PUT NOTE ON MY OFFICE DOOR.

Belle saw Ed one last time and rounded up "Strong Man" J. B. Stampp, who agreed to be her first recruit. He was not a remarkably big man in any of his proportions, neither particularly tall nor hugely muscled, but his posture and long angular Cherokee jaw suggested strength. In past years he had been an outlaw, but lately he had been a farmer. At first, Blue Duck thought he acted like a farmer — lanky, sullen, self-contained — which stirred up a hidden prejudice in the dentist: he would rather work on the teeth of just about anyone than a farmer (unfortunate since the great majority of his patients were farmers). Not that they complained in the chair; in total measure of stoicism they were perhaps higher than any other type. Nor that their persons were especially unkempt or unpleasant. Nothing could compare in that regard to the greasy, stinking hunters who occasionally wandered into his office with their buckskins growing like permanent funguses on their bodies. But there was something about a farmer as he sat strapped into the bib, something more than just his breath — God knows the dentist had grown inured to the manifold possibilities in human breath — but beneath or beyond that, some effluence out of the farmer's deepest nature: the habit of grudging acceptance, the touch of lunacy that came from battling grasshoppers and weather and slow fever and malaria and living in flea-ridden houses eating the same corn, roots, and bacon in the same silence amidst a family that grew and atrophied, flourished and died like so many limbs on a tree, and working always in the shadow of the chattel mortgage, everything payable at harvest — implements, crop, livestock. Never owning anything.

Farmers. All of it a little melancholy emanation that sputtered out of their mouths along with the blood and saliva and hung above the chair like a cloud.

On the Arkansas River ferry at Paw Paw, just south of Fort Smith, he talked some with J. B. He had started out an honest family man, of all things. Then his family got burned up one night in their farmhouse outside Tahlequah in a fire set by an incendiary. It was during one of the waves of incendiaries in the Nation. J. B. found the man, extracted a confession from him and beat him to death. That was how he had first gotten outside the law, and he soon found himself operating as a highway robber, mostly in the eastern part of the Nation, and then riding with the Youngers and later with John Middleton on a few bigger jobs. Middleton had been one of Belle's beaux, and J. B. first met her at Younger's Bend on a visit there after Sam Starr's death.

He had never been convicted, although he had stood before Parker on two occasions, the latter being one reason why he'd gone back and tried to make another go at farming. Parker told him in his acquittal speech that he did not believe J. B. was innocent and would be very happy to have another chance at him, and if he did he could promise a conviction that would warm his own heart deeply. J. B. believed him. He ended up back in Tahlequah and eventually got himself fitted out to make another go at the dirt. But the problems with weather and money had grown insuperable over the last two growing seasons. He had lost part of his acreage last year, and this year his entire corn crop was burned out.

"I know two farmers that drunk Paris green this season."

"Lost their crops?" Blue Duck said.

"Crops, sickness, loan coming due and nothing to pay it. There'll be a lot of them out there next spring with nothing to start on."

"So what's new?" Belle said, playing with her quirt. "An honest living is a desperate living. I stay away from it as much as possible. Which reminds me: we're going to have to keep pretty low in Fort Smith. I figure we take the Poteau River ferry at dark and we'll be better off than if we went busting right across onto Garrison Avenue. We can check around the hotels and find Jim July. He ought to know something about this warrant on me. After I get that straightened out, we can decide what we're going to do for Mr. Mayes over here."

"What are you thinking about with the bank?" J. B. got out a little bag of tobacco, shook some onto a paper and rolled a fat cigarette with one hand.

"Ain't much choice." Belle glanced over at the ferryman.

"You thinking about robbing a bank in Fort Smith?" He licked the cigarette and looked up at her.

"What do you think we're going to do with them, start a savings account?"

"It just don't make much sense is all. You rob a bank in Fort Smith and you'll have two hundred deputy marshals on your tail. Heck Thomas would consider it a direct insult."

"There's a branch of the Arkansas Bank at Guthrie. That may be our target. We can worry about it when we get there."

They rode the short distance to the Poteau crossing and waited on the Choctaw side for full darkness. An old Negro man there, bank fishing, had caught a pile of gar, two- and three-foot-long armored monsters with toothy mouths. Belle talked him into letting her hold the pole and bring one in.

"Let him swallow that hook, Missie. They got a bony old mouth, hook don't catch till it's down in their guts."

The cork did not bob and sink as with other kinds of fish, but scooted across the surface of the water. Belle was getting excited waiting to hook him. "Now? He's had it long enough? . . ."

"No'm, not yet. You let that fish alone. Let him play. When the bass fish bite, you got a fight. When the gar fish play, give him all day."

"Line's running tight."

"That's okay. Just let him be for a while."

"This is ridiculous." She stood perched, cocked over the pole like a spring. Blue Duck and J. B. sat on the bank watching her.

She finally pulled in a three-footer that put up remarkably little fight. The fisherman got out a knife and hunkered down over it.

"You have to take the hook out that way every time?" Belle asked.

"Yes'm. It get way down there."

"I don't think I like gar fishing," she said. "Ain't good for anything, are they?"

"No'm, not much of anything. I have knowed a man, claim he can cook up a gar as good as catfish. He smoke em, loosen up their bones. But I ain't had much luck with it myself. I just mostly does it for the sport, you know. When they's biting, I'll pull em in. Good to get em out of here, cause they eat up the good fishes. Now they's some gar fish in here, get pretty big." He finally managed to get the hook loose, threw the fish onto the pile and stood up. "I wouldn't even say pretty, I'd just say big."

"How big?"

"What I ain't seen, I don't talk about," he said somewhat mysteriously.

"What have you seen?"

"Well now." He squatted back down over his hook to bait it with gut. "Wasn't this year. Wasn't last year, wasn't the year before, it was on back. This nigger seen a grandaddy."

"Five foot, six foot?"

"Friend of mine hooked him out of a johnboat, and that old fish just drug him up and down the slough like a steam engine. He about to give up. When he finally reel him up close and got a look at his snort, he decided he must be Jonah, cept'n the whale done got *ugly* since the Bible days. Yessah. He couldn't pull him into the boat, but after while that fish caught hisself in the shallows."

"How big was he?"

"Ohhh . . . I hate to speculate."

"Big as the boat?"

He assumed a still more serious expression. "No'm, wasn't quite that big. But I'll tell you this much. He took that fish's head home with him. Had to haul him in a wagon, get it sawed off at the sawmill — they say it dulled the blade. Then he went into business trading the tooths out of that jaw — you know, for a little trick, some folks wear it on a necklace — trade a tooth for a jar of whiskey. But before that jaw done run out of tooths, he was a solid drunk. And that's the truth. Done broke his head drinking all that whiskey. I done traded him for one."

"Oh yeah? You still have it?"

"Yes'm, I always carries it for good fishing luck." He reached into his pocket and brought something out. Blue Duck stood up to get a look at it. It was growing dark now. Belle took the thing and brought it up close to her face, squinting at it the way she had squinted at the twenty-dollar gold piece at Watt Grayson's fourteen years ago. A funny chill went up Blue Duck's spine. He looked at the tooth: it was as long as a cigarette.

"What'll you take for this tooth, Grandpa?"

He chuckled. "No'm, don't want to sell it. That's my good luck piece."

"I'll give you two dollars for it."

He looked somewhat surprised at the offer but really didn't want to sell it. She put on the bullying, cajoling manner that Blue Duck had seen her use the last few days and eventually talked him into taking four dollars for it, a ridiculously high price, yet he did seem a little unhappy parting with the thing. She was oblivious to that. She had taken a fancy and was not to be deterred.

Darkness had fallen when she counted out four coins into the old black man's paw. She held out the tooth to Blue Duck. "There. Something to remember me by in case we get over there and have to part ways."

"Oh . . . thanks, but I don't want it."

"A souvenir . . ." She looked surprised at his refusal.

"As many teeth as I see, that's like offering a clod of dirt to a farmer." He was kidding her, trying to keep it on the level of a joke, but he really did not want the thing. He did not want a "souvenir" in case they had to part ways because of Jim July. She had referred to July several times now, to what a mean, jealous lover he was and how he couldn't tolerate anybody messing around with her. Blue Duck had made no decisions about Belle, no commitments, but he was certain that he wanted no damned "souvenirs" of her.

"What's wrong, that in bad taste or something?" She was irritated. "You're the damndest horse Indian I ever saw. You ought to get into schoolteaching. I think you'd be a real fine schoolteacher."

She pocketed the tooth and headed off to the ferry.

He looked after her, a little bit mad actually, although not showing it. (He hardly ever showed it.) That side of Mrs. Starr kind of irritated him, to tell the truth, kind of lit another candle in the dark room of his fourteen-year dream.

8

he Poteau crossing was a back way into town. From the
dock they ascended the road up Coke Hill, conversationless in an
early night chorus of owls, crickets, frogs and one shrill hopeless
loon flapping out of the trees behind them and over the federal
cemetery. Belle was nervous about seeing Jim July — in particular, she was unsure about introducing Blue Duck to him. It wasn't
her nature to be demure about these things, but Jim was unlikely
to be too accepting about any newcomers. He was young and
Creek-proud and tight as a trigger.

The Negro and Choctaw saloons on Coke Hill were relatively
quiet tonight. The tinkling of a ragtime piano could be heard
from one, and they headed there for a drink. Inside, Belle recognized the owner tending bar, a portly, dignified black man with
graying muttonchop sideburns and a vest under his apron. The
pianist, in a derby hat, sat laboring hunch-shouldered at a cheap
upright in the corner. Belle had played that piano. There were
only two customers at this early hour — a cowboy and a prostitute sitting across a table in a cloud of lavender tonic.

"How you doing, Parko?"

"All right, all right," the owner said.

They ordered up drinks at the rail. "Parko, what's going on?"

"You coming out of the Territory?"

"Yes."

"You hear about they caught some horse Indians over there?"

"That right?"

"Yeah. Whole troop of them. Army went out and put an escort on them. Look like they was going to cause some trouble, but the Army took them on past Cross Timbers."

"Well I'll be." Belle glanced at Blue Duck.

"And . . . let's see. Biggest thing happen around here, I got me a telephone."

"You're lying to me."

"No ma'am, I ain't lying. Go back there and look at it."

"I've seen the damn things. I don't like them." She popped down a shot of bourbon and chased it with water. "Ahh, the water. Only good thing about this town. I'd almost ride here to drink it."

"It ought to be good," Parko said. "You know they spent five hundred thousand dollars putting in the new system."

"Ain't that much money in the world," J. B. muttered.

"Parko, let me ask you something serious. Have you heard anything about a warrant on me?"

"Not lately."

He didn't appear to be telling the exact truth, but then Parko generally avoided ticklish subjects. "Okay, let me ask you this: you seen Jim July in the past few days?"

"Don't believe I have."

He was flat lying this time. But a lie was as good as the truth when you could read it. Jim July had probably sashayed through here a couple of times with some strumpet.

"Can you call up a place or two for me on your new tele-phone?"

"If they got one, I sure can. Exchange stay open till ten o'clock. It cost a nickel a call." He seemed proud of his new instrument.

"Call up some of the houses over on the row and ask for Jim July — whichever ones have a phone. When you get him, I'll talk."

"James. Hey James! Sit the bar, will you?"

The pianist broke off mid-tune and wandered behind the bar. He was fairly sodden with Parko's barrel beer.

Belle looked at Blue Duck. "God damn headaches."

He sipped at his drink. "You have one now?"

"A touch."

Parko cranked the phone. "Hello! Good evening! I want the Riverfront Hotel!" He stood just behind the backroom door shouting into the thing. "Yes! Give me the Riverfront!"

"Do better to stand outside and yell across town," Belle grumbled.

J. B. Stampp bought a cigar and leaned against the bar trimming it. "Think we ought to split up? Maybe meet here later?"

"Maybe so. You have things you need to do. I got things. That's a good idea. We can meet here at nine tomorrow night."

"I believe I'll stay," Blue Duck said. "Like to meet Jim."

She inhaled another shot of bourbon and made a face. "Maybe you wouldn't like to. I mean tonight . . ." She held out the chaser glass for a refill.

The dentist had put on his blank look. There was something ornery — not on the surface but deep-down ornery — about him. She didn't know what mood Jim July would be in, but she was pretty sure that the three of them would make an awkward party. Yet something — some curiosity — prevented her from insisting that Blue Duck leave.

Parko was on his second call. "Miss Miller! That you? This is Parko over to Coke Hill! Is Jim July there at the Athenian? . . . Yes'm, *Jim July!*"

The cowboy and prostitute were still sitting with their heads tipped over toward each other as if swooning in the haze of his tonic. J. B. smoked his cigar peacefully. "Look J. B., can you scare up Crick Watson? Test him out on this deal, see if he might be interested. Same terms you're on. And if you can find John Hotsie and Ralph Bunch — don't mess with them if they're in the bottle too deep. And don't tell them too much. Keep it general. I'll talk out the details tomorrow night. Don't mention nothing about my boy. Nothing. That information goes no further than it is right now."

J. B. puffed his cigar and nodded slightly.

"Jim July? This heah Jim July? . . ." Parko emerged triumphant. "I got him! Got him on the line!"

"Can anybody hear what you say?" Belle asked. "Others listen in?"

"No ma'am. Complete privacy."

Privacy except for the city block square in which people could hear you declaiming into the thing. But at least she would avoid having to traipse around the row looking for him. An appearance over there was the quickest way to advertise one's presence in town since the sheriff's boys were all over the place making arrests and handing out summonses, and the madams remained in the good graces of the authorities by paying their "fines" regularly and reporting anything unusual. The row houses were as regulated and public as streetcars.

"Talk into this thing?"

"That's it. Easiest thing in the world."

She yelled into the horn. "Hello, Jim! You there?"

After a moment a little voice crackled out. "Who is this?"

"Your mother, who do you think? You sound like you're in a hole. Talk Cherokee so I can understand you."

He did. "*Where are you?*"

"Parko's. *Get over here right now. And don't say anything to anybody. Just get over here right now. I'll be waiting.*"

She replaced the receiver, thus completing the first call of her life. It wasn't bad — but she'd never get one for herself. There was something eerie about throwing your voice through these electric wires that hung all over town. It made her throat feel tight. She was cranky about wires — wires draped out across the country so thick a person couldn't go any direction without hitting them sooner or later. Couldn't move without setting wires to tapping and clattering and talking all over the place. That was something she didn't like. It made her itchy. Telegraph. They were using it to round up the horse Indians, following every move they made until they were worn out and fit to be corralled. Not that she felt sentimental about them, but it did seem just a little bit of a dirty trick. It wasn't going to be people or cities that tamed and killed off everything wild, it was going to be wires. They'd take care of it. They made her feel old, like her day was done and some new bleak thing was rising up to take over. Why it was bleak to her she couldn't say. Maybe just a silliness. There was a lot of silliness to her lately.

J. B. had left and a few other customers had arrived by the time Jim July got there. The gaslights were up and the pianist played a mesmerizing little rag. Blue Duck stood up to meet him, Jim touched his hat desultorily and slipped into a chair. "What's going on? I didn't expect you here."

"I'll bet you didn't. Honey, I've lived two lives since I last saw you. I'm trying to find out about this warrant on me. What's it for?"

"What warrant?"

"The warrant for my arrest, what do you think? And reward. What's the charge?"

"Don't know nothing about it."

". . . Guess I need to make a little visit to William S. Prettyman myself. What about you, Jim — you okay?"

He looked a little shifty-eyed at this point. "This horse-thieving rap, been trying to shake that. Been pretty much taking it easy, though."

"I bet you have." She looked at him coolly. His fine Creek face was pallid from poker games and whorehouse whiskey. Blue Duck was sitting back with his impassive look. Jim was uneasy — which meant that he would probably take on a mood pretty soon. Facing him coolly implied something about her and Blue Duck, and she almost wondered why she was doing it. Briefly, she told him about what had been happening and the deal with the Cherokees. He seemed unamazed.

"Where'd you and Mr. Duck meet?" His smile was a little green.

"Blue Duck. I usually go by the whole thing."

"Blue Duck . . . Well why don't I just call him Blue, huh Belle? You know like that old black-and-tan we got out at the house." He continued to smile.

"That's amusing, Mr. July, but I had not known grown men to make fun of names," Blue Duck said.

"Oh you had not? Well pardon me. I had not known you to be a gentleman so well spoken. What is your profession, sir?"

"Dentistry."

"Oh? And have you worked on any interesting mouths lately?" Blue Duck looked at him as though at a wall.

"Belle, you were complaining of a toothache. Did he work on you?"

"Yes he did, matter of fact. Laid me down and took care of it before I knew what to think."

Jim glanced at her. He was getting that look in his eye, and the strange thing about it was that she didn't care to hush him. Didn't care to but ought to.

"That right? . . . ," he breathed.

They sat there a while, at an impasse. Jim finally spoke up again. "Well. You know I've been having some dental trouble lately myself. Would you mind, sir, taking a look into my mouth? It's in the back. I fear I'm experiencing wisdom tooth decay. Quite painful."

The mocking in his voice excited her in a funny way. When Jim took on that tone there was no telling what he'd do. He was a mad dog when he was riled. But she couldn't afford that right now, that was the main fact of the matter. She leaned across the table and spoke quietly to him. "Looky here Jim. Listen to me. There's a five-hundred-dollar bag on my head right now. Everything is going to have to stay real cool until I get that straight."

He put on an innocent look. "What are you talking about?"

"Just keep that in mind. And keep it in mind when you go back to the Athenian tonight."

"Ain't you coming with me?"

"No."

"Oh? Where will you stay?"

"On Coke Hill. I want to stay low until I get this warrant straightened out."

"I see. Uh . . . Mr. Duck here, is he going to stay low with you?"

"You're a funny one to be asking that question."

"Why is that?"

"Because you've been wallowing in the clap palace of Arkansas for the last week is why. Which is another reason I ain't going near it or you."

July turned to Blue Duck. "I'm serious, sir. I am experiencing severe dental pains. Would you mind taking a look?"

"It's a bit dark in here."

Belle saw what Jim was trying to pull. He'd done it before. It was his favorite story about himself. When he was sixteen he bit a man's finger off. She'd heard him tell it a half-dozen times. She started to say something to prevent it, but again a strange curiosity kept her quiet. She knew pretty much what Jim was capable of doing, but she had no clear idea about Blue Duck. The curiosity was more than just in her head. It rode her neck like a chill.

Jim's eyes had assumed a look of mock earnestness. He opened his mouth and pointed into the back of it. ". . . ack here. Hurts somethin terr . . ."

Blue Duck looked into his empty shot glass. He picked it up and looked toward a lamp through the bottom of it. Then he brought his thumb back and forth as though examining it through the glass, testing its powers of magnification. "All right. Open wide," he said to Jim in a professional voice.

Jim leaned back a little and opened up. Blue Duck approached slowly with the glass, peering through it. He hesitated for a moment and then put the glass into Jim's mouth. "Now close down."

Jim did so, apparently still waiting for his chance. He closed down over the shot glass, his expression dampening slowly to confusion.

Blue Duck settled back into his chair and said to Belle, "Do you have a place to sleep lined up?"

Jim remained with the shot glass stuffed in his mouth.

Belle looked back and forth at them.

"Because if you don't, I know an old fellow who rents out a few rooms down on the Choctaw strip. I've stayed with him before."

She was surprised at how long it look Jim to realize that he'd been played with, and to reach up and take the shot glass from between his rounded lips. Blue Duck showed no special interest in him.

Jim took out his pocket Smith and Wesson and checked the chambers. He gazed upon Belle with exaggerated dignity and spoke in Cherokee. "*Where did you pick up this shit?*"

Blue Duck answered in Cherokee. "*In Tulsa. I operate my business there.*"

Belle got serious pretty fast. "Don't start flashing your rod, Jim. You'll get these niggers to screaming and have us all in jail."

Jim aimed the gun off the table, casually, at Blue Duck's chest. His face was cold. "I might blow this punk down and get it over with."

"You do and it'll be over all right. Put it away."

"*Are you bedding with this punk?*"

"*You take care of your bedding and I'll take care of mine, young man.*"

"*I do take care of mine. That's why I may aerate this punk.*"

Belle threw a glass of water into his face. It splintered the concentration he was building up in the pistol — made him madder but broke him. Noise in the room sputtered down to near-silence. She put on her sternest countenance. "Listen to me good, Jim. You been living with me at Younger's Bend. Even calling yourself 'Starr' sometime. Okay. But I'm Belle Starr, sole owner of that name and what goes with it. You ain't gonna be herding me nor picking my friends. You're too damn young, for one thing."

"You like my young dick, you bitch."

"Your young dick was a tadpole pissing on itself when I was riding with the names, so just relax. If you're going to sit here, relax. Where's that hotel, Blue Duck? I think we better go."

"Are you trying to shuck me?"

"Of course not, damnit. You think I rode all this way over here and called you out to Coke Hill to shuck you. Do you think I'm stupid? I came to ask you to help on this Cherokee deal, for one thing."

"What do I have to do with Cherokee?"

"You won't be doing it for them, you'll be doing it for hard cash money — better than you'll get in a long life of stealing heifers. I'm talking about some wages, Jim."

"For doing what? Riding barb wire?"

"Come tomorrow night at nine o'clock here, and I'll tell you the whole scheme. Until then, just go on about your business. Don't say nothing about me to nobody."

"Don't worry." Jim was mad — or some combination of mad and sour and still volatile. It had occurred to Belle before, and for some reason did now, that his face was a little like Ed's, except with spark and intelligence. She didn't want him to go away mad.

"Hey Jim." She stood up. "I ain't trying to make you mad. You and me will take and iron this out tomorrow or the next day. . . . By the way — you know anything about Laura Ziegler Reed?"

He arose glowering. "No."

"Down on the row somewhere . . ."

"That the one Ed married? No, I don't know her. I'll see you maybe." He glanced at Blue Duck.

"Your teeth are fine, by the way," Blue Duck said in Cherokee.
"Eat some shit, chickenface."

"I heard that you were a smart fellow. Glad to have samples of your wit."

"You don't know how dead you might get talking like that, buddy."

"Thank you very much for the demonstration."

"Now boys, now . . . we're being good boys. Let's say good night and get a fresh look at it tomorrow."

Jim put away his revolver and departed stiffly. Noise in the bar slowly leveled back up to normal. Belle looked darkly at Blue Duck.

"Take it easy, friend. Just take it easy. I seen men perish on less than that."

"Where'd you get that kid?"

"None of your damn business." She tried to maintain a disapproving frown, but the sight of Jim sitting there with the shot glass in his mouth struck her and she laughed. "You're getting scrappier by the minute, ain't you? How'd you know to play him?"

"Oh come on."

She managed to get serious. "Anyway, you just keep it down tomorrow. He's a good boy if you treat him decent. He don't necessarily hold a grudge. I want you two to get along."

"I'm afraid that's impossible," Blue Duck said, putting on his hat. "I can't stand civilized Indians."

She woke up with her butt against his in a narrow bed. She had no headache, no toothache and no special pains. She felt downright young. It was almost simpler this way, with Ed in jail and her not having to deal with him in person. Every time she got close to him she started to feel crazy — crazy like real crazy, all in a tangle. Her own boy was her nemesis, and it was because of what *she had done*. . . . But why start thinking about that the minute she woke up? That was the reason she got these headaches, letting her mind get to worrying and whirling around like it did.

Rising to dress, she watched the dentist sleep. He was a strange man. He was sure a handsome man. The Lord didn't make too many like that to put in the Territory. Most of the white men out there looked like one kind of old jacklegged frizzy-jawed, Adam's-apple-bobbing trash or another, and most of the Indians looked like they had clear whiskey for blood and had been eating old rusty-canned love apples all their lives for nourishment. It was a hard place to find a good-looking man. But who was she to talk? Her face looked about like the bottom of the potato bin.

The thing that struck her most about Blue Duck was that he was a gentleman — a natural gentleman, she supposed, since it wasn't so much his manners as his attitude that made him that way: the way he held back, staying quiet and within himself. Yet there was something in his face that bespoke an entirely different possibility. Whether because of the plains blood or the years he'd spent living as an outcast or the woman-killing, she didn't know. The gentleman, anyway, didn't seem fully to be trusted.

Maybe he was just too damned good-looking to be trusted. Or maybe she'd gotten beyond trusting any man. Most of them had been so outright bad that there wasn't any puzzle to them. You took one look and saw a lying, thieving, short-fused, woman-bleeding rascal. She'd always thought of Cole in a little different light — her first man, a name, a cut-free outlaw — but he wasn't really. He was just a little more insane than some of them. He had wanted to "make a woman out of her" like all the rest, the only difference being that he walked around bung-eyed reading the Bible and spouting poetry.

She almost wanted to kiss the dentist, lying there looking so pretty, but would feel a little silly. . . . She hadn't intended to leave with him last night, but that was the way it happened. Jim July did seem awful damn young up next to him.

His eyes opened.

She looked away, a little embarrassed at being caught staring at him. "I'm getting some clothes and a bath. You find the photographer if you can."

He spoke after a moment. "What are you going to do with him?"

"Not sure yet."

"You don't want to get in deeper with him, do you?"

"I'll figure that out. You just locate him."

Blue Duck swung his legs out to the floor and rested his elbows on his knees. Head in hands, he appeared to meditate. Then spoke quietly. "I haven't decided for sure I want to get involved in this."

"In what?"

"That's just the problem."

"If you're talking about the work for Joel Mayes, it's not that big a deal — a little scouting and bushwhacking."

His voice remained oddly quiet, as though not quite awake. "If I ask you something, will you tell me the truth?"

"I doubt it." Her admiring mood was rapidly disappearing. Him waking up so serious and inquisitive unsettled her.

"How many big jobs have you been on besides the Watt Grayson robbery?"

"That don't sound like you."

"Pardon me?"

"It don't sound like you to ask me that."

"Why not?"

". . . I don't know. . . ." It had been a musing thought, and she really didn't know why. Perhaps because she had seen him as a man who essentially had no questions to ask.

"Then tell me."

"What?"

"Just what I asked," he said. "How many big jobs have you been on besides the Grayson thing?"

"What's a 'big job'? Are you talking about bowel movements or what?"

He sat up straight on the side of the bed. "Banks, trains . . ."

She wrapped a shawl around her head and checked her face in a tiny mirror on the wall. "What difference does it make?"

"I mean jobs that you rode on."

She pinched her cheeks and flicked at her eyebrows. "None. What are you going to make of it?"

He looked up at her with no answer.

"Because I didn't doesn't mean I can't. I ain't a cripple. And I've been the brains and fence and legal expert on more deals than you could shake a stick at. If you took me out of the Territory a lot of them big boys would just walk around in a circle till their tongues swole up."

"Why now?"

"Because my boy's neck's going to get broke if I don't."

"You don't sound like you want to talk about this."

"About what? What are you getting at?"

"Nothing in particular. I just wondered if you'd really thought about it."

"Well I guess I have. You were there with me and Mayes. Don't you think I thought about it the ten or twelve hours I spent jawing with him? You think I was in a daze or something?"

"No . . . it's just the whole idea. I mean you aren't going to meet up with these guys tonight and suggest out of the blue that they rob a bank. You do that and they might not think you're right in the brain."

"Honey, this ain't no straight-head contest. Now if you're not with me, that's okay. If you are, why don't you try to find Prettyman. I'll be back here around noon."

9

It was already hot. She went to a joint on Coke Hill and had a hoecake with butter and molasses and a quart of coffee. She was feeling good today and wasn't about to let the dentist put her in a mood. What was he being so damned careful about? He hadn't been an ounce of careful the night before, neither at Parko's bar nor at the room later. For a man who'd lived without a woman so long, he was a quick learner. Not that there was all that much to learn, little more than a cat or dog could do, and not that it gave her any more pleasure than usual. There had been only a few times in her life when that kind of thing happened, and it was not exactly the stuff of sweet nostalgia. The thought of it was in fact enough to send her into a pharmacy looking for some Phoenix Pills. They didn't have them, so she bought two papers of morphine in case the day kept worrying on like this. It could conceivably get worse, what with Prettyman and Jim and Blue Duck and these other thugs to deal with. She could only hope that there'd be any thugs *to* deal with. If J. B. couldn't get anybody interested, the whole plan might fizzle out before it got started.

She bought a bath and headed over to the Boston Store on Garrison Avenue for clothes. On the street she kept her head down, face partially hidden by the shawl. There were any number of people on the sidewalks and chewers-and-spitters at the corners and clerks in stores who might recognize her, and on a better day she'd be saying hello to them and passing the time. They looked upon her with respect. She thought of herself as a kind of public entertainer when she came to Fort Smith, someone who livened things up and maybe laughed and amazed a little of the pain out of their guts. She was glad to do it, to play in a bar or ride down Garrison in silk and ostrich plumes with them looking after her and pointing, shaking their heads and pretending to disapprove.

A few times over the years she had hired on regular at Fort Smith saloons just to keep her hand in. Folks came more to look at her than to hear her play. Once a few years before they'd hired her to be an "outlaw" in the Fort Smith rodeo. They had her "rob" a stagecoach, chasing it around the circus shooting in the air and whoopin it up, stopping it and making everyone get out and deliver the goods. Old Ike Parker himself was one of the "prominent citizens" that she got to rob that night, which tickled her pink. He lined up outside the stagecoach with the rest of the prominent citizens and handed her over a big fake watch — soberly.

Blue Duck had hinted that she was getting out of her element by taking on this job for the Indians. Maybe he was right. Maybe not only Joel Mayes but she herself was being taken in by the image of Belle Starr. Maybe a middle-aged rodeo queen ought not leave the show to go out chasing wild horses. And then again, maybe she should. Maybe it was *exactly* what she should do.

She fiddled around in the Boston Store for a while buying a petticoat linen dress with a front-ruffled blouse and a sculptured jacket with peplum trim and a feathered hat that could be pulled down over her forehead and eyes. She looked at herself in the mirror and wished there was some way to hide that chin. Permanently. She was being waited on by a clerk who didn't know her, but as always when someone was buying, other clerks were beginning to buzz around, and she had to get out of there before this became an appearance.

On Garrison, she hesitated a moment. Up the street a ways was the Arkansas Bank of Commerce. She hopped a mule streetcar and rode up in that direction. It was a six-story brick building — nothing like the clapboard joints Cole and them had gotten famous for holding up. It was a fortress in a civilized town. Fort Smith made the Dallas of her youth look like a boomer camp. She got off the streetcar and took another one going back down toward the river. A bridge was being built at the end of Garrison. Within a year or two a person could just ride his horse or wagon right on across from Arkansas into the Indian Territory. She felt a little quirky about that. It seemed like the Territory was being opened up wide as a barn dance. All the barriers were coming down, and it damn sure wasn't the tribes paying for those bridges and laying that track.

A big sign was stuck in the dust:

THE JAY GOULD ARKANSAS RIVER BRIDGE
TO BE COMPLETED 1890.

Who was Jay Gould? Probably some banker. That's who was behind most of these big projects. Big eastern bankers, they were stitching the country up tight with their progress. They'd make a state out of the Indian Nation before long — call it "Oklahoma, the White Trash State" and fly strumpets all over the sky dropping leaflet invitations.

At Speer Hardware Company and the Carriage Repository, she got off the streetcar and walked over one block to the federal courthouse. It was a brick building which had been the officers' quarters in the old fort. In the basement was the "new" jail — new for ten or fifteen years now — where they shoveled in crooks and whiskey peddlers up to 160-175 at a time. Over by the gallows enclosure were parked a couple of tumbleweed wagons with cages on the back designed to hold six or seven men. They scoured the Territory with those things, hauling them in at two bucks a head. She walked up the pitted wooden sidewalk a ways, trying to decide what to do. It would be nice to just walk in there and look on Heck Thomas's bulletin board for her warrant. That way she could be one-hundred-percent certain that it was Prettyman who had put them on to her. She had a lingering uncertainty about Miss Laura Ziegler Reed, but that may have been just because she felt a little bad about running her off so harsh.

She sat on a bench in the yard for a moment thinking about it. Court would be in session, as usual. The old man would be there on the job as he was twelve to fourteen hours a day, every day of the year except Sundays, Christmas and Easter. She kind of admired old Fatman Parker, for sitting on his butt that much of his life looking like a judge if nothing else. Spent that much of his life looking like one then she supposed he must *be* something of one by now. She'd read in a newspaper article that he'd tried over ten thousand cases on the bench in Fort Smith. And of course they always mentioned that he'd hanged more men than any judge in history. Newspaper reporters came from St. Louis and New York and New Orleans to cover the hangings, writing about how they were inhumane and so forth.

She didn't know for sure what she thought about executions, but most of the crooks she'd ever been around didn't worry about whether they were "inhumane" or not, and most of them had a certain respect for a man like Parker. The way some of them talked, it almost seemed like they believed in Parker and the law more than honest men. The law and breaking the law was the game they chose to play, and maybe a person just naturally tended to respect what he did. Most of the guys who ended up on the gallows were poor sorts, wrung-out breeds and niggers who grew up hungry and just cut loose on a spree one day until they got caught. Very few professionals ended up dangling off that crossbeam. They ended up dead all right, but not with a broken neck. There was a certain ignominy to it that the professionals shunned. She worried about that for her boy as much as anything. To be hanged alongside two or three other drained-out sad whiskey-broke punks who got caught shooting somebody in the back for twenty dollars and couldn't afford a good lawyer to confuse a jury — the thought of it made her stomach turn over. What was she supposed to do, stand out on this lawn in front of four or five thousand people while they slipped the rope over her boy's head? That was ridiculous.

She got up and went toward the courthouse. She really shouldn't, but what the hell. She pulled the hat down low over her forehead and tried to walk up the steps unobtrusive and humbled over. Maybe she would pass as a witness. She sure couldn't pass as an observer, because Parker didn't allow females to sit in on his trials. The weaker sex were positively forbidden from anything but the formal proceedings, and he always gave little speeches to any of them taking the stand. He thought that they would all be — or should be — horrified at what went on in court.

The marshal's office was at the end of the main hallway and the courtroom off to the right. There were a half-dozen men standing around outside. A voice, not Parker's, droned on and paused, a chair dragged the floor. It was a common day in the courtroom, justice piddling along under the heat. She stopped in front of the bulletin board and looked for her own warrant. What was it Parker had said when she stood before him to be sentenced? That by her actions she had *clearly and flagrantly abandoned the virtues which nature to render the sex amiable had implanted in the female heart, that the verdict was an entirely just one and must be approved by all honest men, the offense of which she had been convicted shocked all persons who were not brutal and brought forth shame from the hearts of honest women, the ex-ample set by her being a pernicious and . . .* Somewhere near the end of a pretty long speech he remembered to mention that she'd been caught stealing some horses, too. She'd been in his court a few times before and he'd never gotten a chance to sentence her, and he was sure enjoying the opportunity.

Standing in front of the bulletin board remembering that day, she heard him say something now — the tone of his voice if not the words. He sounded bored. She'd never thought of how bored he must get sitting up there looking at one bum after another. The funny thing about his face — which she could see in her mind — was his eyes. They were dark and bright and flashing like a young man's. They were passionate and somewhat bulging eyes, strange in his otherwise judicially dulled countenance.

She found her warrant. It was for assault on Mr. Prettyman. That was fine. She could deal with that. Now she just had to get her bustle out of this place. Which she was about to do when something caught her eye. The door to the marshal's office had just opened at the end of the corridor and a deputy ushered in someone who'd been sitting out of view among the old kegs and broken-down chairs that served as a waiting room. It was Jim July.

Jim July was talking to Heck Thomas. What about?

Surely she'd remember if he'd said something last night about going to see the marshal today.

She hurried out of the courthouse and over to Coke Hill. Blue Duck was back already, napping on the bed with his hat over his face. He told her that he'd found the photographer.

"So you're going with me?" she asked.

"You look pretty in your new dress," he said.

"Well . . ." The remark confused her for some reason. ". . . Helps me to pass. I've been getting around without anybody noticing me so far. I'm going right directly over to see Prettyman now. You want to come?"

"What do you have in mind?"

"Don't know yet."

"Are you taking a gun?"

"Oh I've got a gun when I go to the outhouse. But don't worry, I don't aim to do him any harm. That don't ever do any good."

"What's that?"

"Shooting people and such. You usually have to eat it, worse than what you did in the first place."

Blue Duck laughed. One surprised burst. It was the first time she'd heard him laugh.

"What's funny?"

He shook his head.

"What?"

He stood up, shaking his head.

10

Complaining *about the onset* of a headache, she drank some morphine before they left.

He told himself that it was curiosity which kept him following her, curiosity about what her next trick was going to be. He did not want to get involved in any further trouble between her and the photographer, yet something, as before, drew him on.

She paused as they were leaving. "There's something funny going on."

"How's that?"

"I saw Jim over at the courthouse. He was talking to Heck Thomas."

"The marshal?"

"That's right."

"Jim's up for trial, isn't he? On bail?"

"That's right. . . . I don't know, maybe it's nothing."

"What are you thinking?"

She put a finger to her lips. "I guess I don't need to say. It's silliness."

They went to the photographer's studio where Blue Duck had seen Prettyman earlier, and Belle barged right into the backroom looking for him. He was there buffing a stack of copper plates, which he continued to do after she began talking.

Blue Duck hardly heard what she said he was so surprised by her reasonable and apologetic manner. She approached him with the deference of a salesman. The photographer continued vigorously rubbing plates one after another with a piece of lamb's wool. He held up each one inspecting its sheen and pretended to be scarcely aware of her. His foot was bundled up in a ragged dressing. He went to the high windows and pulled shut a thick curtain, plunging the room into darkness. Belle went quiet until he lit a candle, and Blue Duck saw an instant of confusion in her eyes as if she thought the photographer was trying to pull something. But he was simply going on about his business. He poured iodine crystals into a cylinder and began sensitizing the copper plates.

Blue Duck almost admired Prettyman. He wasn't a bad man, certainly. A little bit huffy but certainly no coward or fool.

When he finally spoke it was not in direct response to her. "Will you please stand back. These fumes are poisonous."

She moved back a few steps into the shadows. "All I'm saying to you, Mr. Prettyman, is that I will give you ample recompense for whatever damage I caused. I was in a state. You saw me on the road. A woman with her bosom exposed to God and all the world is not a steady woman. I'm sure you can understand that. . . ."

"Madam" — eyes on a plate — "I do not care to hear of your stability or lack of it."

"I said I'll pay you for the plates and the doctoring."

"Pardon me, but I will not be advised further by you in this matter."

"You put up a five-hundred-dollar reward on me. Well I'm bringing myself in and I'm offering to pay you one thousand dollars: the five hundred you'd have paid for the reward plus five hundred cash for the trouble I caused you."

He glanced at her over the candle.

"That's a thousand cash. I guess I owe it to you. I owe it and

I'm gonna pay it, and that'll be that as far as I'm concerned. It's worth it to me not to have to hire a lawyer and waste my time in court. All you have to do is go over to Heck Thomas and tell him you're dropping the charges."

He went on about his plates, taking them from the tube one at a time and holding them over a limy-smelling brew in a shallow bucket. He was not going to be intimidated by her.

"Of course the other way — I mean if you was to keep up this reward and all — it'd be a mess and I imagine a pretty good one. A person can't sit on their butt with somebody trying to sic the law onto them. I'm just saying that now, I ain't threatening you."

She went on, and after a while Blue Duck could see the photographer's stubbornness falter a little. If not impressed, he was at least surprised by her reasonable attitude. It was of course his pride more than his foot that she was offering to pay back, and she was suggesting that if he did not accept her bargain his pride might find itself more imperiled than it had already been.

". . . And one more thing. I realize that I agreed back there that you could take a few pictures of me. I made that deal with you and broke it because of the mood I'd fell into. Well I can see how that would get your goat. What I'm offering in addition to a thousand cash is for you to go on and take that picture of me. I'll sit for you. I hate it worse than hell, but if you can get it over with, I'll put up with it."

Prettyman did not respond. In the candlelight he continued to move plates back and forth from the iodine to the lime solutions. Blue Duck could see that she'd found his weak point. He stood in the darkened room behind her while she pleaded reasonably. Despite her mollifying tone, tension was building up. She was a little like a mother who is sweet and motherly up to a point, then might just do anything. Her reasonableness teetered on the edge. Without saying anything, Prettyman eventually put away the plates and loaded the tripod camera with one that was prepared, opened the curtain and set an armchair before a flat backdrop.

"All right," he said, "I have a great deal to do today, but I will take a portrait. Mr. Blue Duck, will you sit?"

"It's not up to him," Belle snapped.

"I'm asking him to sit," Prettyman said. "His physiognomy is interesting. Please take this chair. Mrs. Starr, you can stand beside him here."

"He wants both of us," she said.

He bustled around imperiously, ordering them to alter their postures, move their hands, Blue Duck to leave his hat on, Belle to remain expressionless — as though by each direction further restoring the pride that had been wounded on the road to Catoosa. The exposure took five seconds, and he required them to sit for two more in case plates had been ill prepared or they moved during the exposure. Belle went along with him without further comment, but it was apparent by her drained looked that either she was just barely able to stand this or the morphine had taken hold.

After they had finished she produced five hundred dollars, counted it out hand to hand and laid it in one tottering heap on the table. It was most of Joel Mayes's initial payment. "We're just about even now, mister. I've done right by you. Drop the charges and you get five hundred more." She smiled wanly. "What are you going to do with the pictures?"

"It depends on how attractive they are. If they are good I may sell them to an album about the west. If they are imperfect I will throw them away. They are of no use to me personally."

Her smile melted. She was again teetering on the edge, but she restrained herself. "I'll see you around."

Outside the studio, she hurried down the street at such a pace that Blue Duck had trouble keeping up with her. At a saloon on First Street she went in and drank down a couple of belts of whiskey. Elbow on the table, she put the back of her hand to her mouth and looked at him. "All right, I've kissed his ass. Now maybe we can get something done."

Back at the hotel, she sat propped up in bed worrying and staring and talking to herself. She seemed to fall into an almost delirious condition, dulled, mind wandering. Blue Duck understood from some of her disconnected remarks that she was fretting about tonight when J. B., presumably, would show up at Parko's with some guys to talk about the Cherokee scheme. She had taken enough morphine and whiskey to knock herself out but instead just sat there propped up looking awful. When he spoke to her she either stared at him in silence or said something irrelevant.

He sat beside her on the bed with a newspaper. She made him uneasy. Pale even through her dark skin, mumbling to herself, she seemed to be in a daze. In the time he'd known her, she hadn't acted this way before. Her usual control — the wariness and cunning — had receded into a fragile vagueness. Her eyes were dim, strange, stupid.

For just a moment he remembered — or almost remembered — something from his childhood, eyes like that. When everyone was hungry . . . Those days were like old dreams that he could never fully recall, and it always slightly turned his stomach to try. . . . The eyes were those of an old woman. She was no good and being left to starve. She walked sometimes on her knees. Her teeth were gone, hair cut short, legs gashed and scarred from some past time of mourning. Her eyes blinked a lot. What else? It was just a face. He had no memory of her name or where she died. . . .

He could not read the newspaper. When he left the room she glanced up at him through what appeared to be a great cloud of worry and distractedness. She said nothing.

He walked the town brooding. His life was ordered. He treasured his rituals. He worked, he read books, he kept his house as clean as any white person. She threatened those certainties. The Cherokee scheme was ludicrous. Worse than that was something about her, the way she was. It was to be expected that she both reminded him of the schoolteacher and seemed her opposite; that was understandable. But she did more than that.

It was that she was hopeless. Even before seeing her drugged and stupid just now he had sensed it. He should know about that, after all — something in the heart that one has given up.

So why was he following her? Was it because she was that way — cut-free, poison, moving faster than life? He didn't know.

He wandered the streets without attending to his direction. The streets were of brick or macadam, Garrison was of wooden blocks, busy this hour with commerce. He ended up heading toward the old officers' quarters that stood squarely at the end of the avenue (where Zachary Taylor had lived), and on from there toward the old Butterfield Road.

It was a pretty nice town, really. He had even thought of setting up practice here, but that was not realistic. Fort Smith was a white town, after all. Dark skin was not an asset in the outpost from which the whites "kept order" in the Indian Nation. An Indian dentist in Fort Smith would not do well unless he stayed down on Coke Hill and catered only to Choctaws and blacks, and he wouldn't move here to live on Coke Hill.

The population of the town was around eight or nine thousand, he guessed. Somewhere he'd read that the population of Oklahoma was 61,000 in 1888, but that already this year it had doubled and was heading toward tripling. The Indian Nation was staggering under the influx of whites. Soon the separate domains of the tribes would be shattered by the pressure of growth. The idea of trying to hold back the flow of those settlers was hopeless. The Cherokee were the strongest of the Five Tribes, and if the best strategy they could come up with to protect their borders was hiring a small band of outlaw ruffians to harass the boomers and their financiers, then there was little hope indeed.

Oklahoma would be a state soon. This town was building its bridge across the Arkansas River just in time to lose its dominion over the Territory. There was already talk of a federal court in Muskogee. Judge Parker would become obsolete — a prospect hard to imagine.

Blue Duck was not as pained by the white takeover as were some in eastern Oklahoma. His own dark skin had been no asset in the Cherokee or Creek Nations as long as he was known to be of a western tribe, for as Belle had said, an eastern Indian hated nothing so much as a western, unless perhaps another eastern, the Creek and Cherokee having lived in enmity for decades; or unless it was another faction of one's own tribe — full bloods against breeds, noble class against common people, treaty party against resisters — or unless Negro, who were numerous in the Territory and at the bottom of every heap, having been slaves to the eastern Indians and, except for the mysterious gentle Seminole, treated worse by them than by southern whites, although not quite so badly as by the horse Indians, who had regularly kidnapped slaves from the easterners and sold them back for ransom — one of the causes of a lingering hatred between the civilized tribes and the Comanche, Sioux, Crow. . . . There was no end to it. Whether the whites or the Indians ruled seemed irrelevant. Pile a bunch of people together — white, brown, red, black — and they'd find plenty of reasons to hate each other.

He'd been walking on dirt for a while, out Rogers Street, which branched toward central and southern Arkansas. There were several plantation homes out this way which he'd never seen before. Come to think of it, he'd never been past the barrier that this town provided between the Indian Nation and the eastern states. He sometimes wondered what the east was like. He read books and so probably had a better idea than most, yet still it was a mystery. To be in a city like New York or Boston — that would be nice. Or even to visit the southern lands, the home country that fewer and fewer old people talked about nowadays — the green and lush forest land, easy town life, crops that grew by themselves — a loss to him not because he had any blood claim on those lands but because of his nostalgic temperament. An orphan of the west, he lived on this border dreaming of the east.

He stood at the front gate of a white, columned home. Children played in the yard. A mammy sewing in the shade of an oak tree glanced up suspiciously at him.

They had been right, after all, to cast him out. He had been a cat amidst dogs. There had been a silly mistake in his birth. And in private moments when he let his mind wander freely, it seemed that the schoolteacher had prepared him for another place, a second birth that would never be possible. To live among civilized people. What would that be like? Morning until night, people who were not falsely civil — who did not act civilized but were civilized. She had been that way despite a somewhat stiff nature. She put him at ease and allowed him to talk. She brought him warm things. She talked of high and distant matters. He would not say that the Indian people he had been mistakenly born into and wandered with across the grasslands were barbarous, but as the coyote he had been on the periphery of their ways. He did not learn them. She was the first to really teach him, and what she taught had become the pleasures, weaknesses, the secret core of his life.

The mammy had glanced up several more times and was now walking toward him. She stopped ten feet the other side of the gate.

"What you want? You got something to deliver?"

He shook his head.

"Well then get on."

He smiled at her, pushed up the brim of his hat. "I was just noticing how pretty this house is."

" 'Pend on which way you looks at it," she grumbled. "Now get on. Mrs. Kelly says don't allow no characters round the yard."

"Characters."

"That's what she said."

"You think I'm a character, grandma?"

"I ain't no grandma."

"Well I ain't no character then." He smiled.

"Get on anyway. I'm *busy*." She turned and walked back to the children, gathered and took them into the house.

He remained at the gate looking through. It didn't bother him. Very little bothered him. There were advantages to orphanship. One's investments must eventually be put in distant accounts. The foolishness, the pettiness roll like water off a duck's back.

But now he had to turn back to town, and there were things there that did bother him. What had Belle to do with his secret world? She was its opposite. If he was going to take a "vacation" from work, what in the hell was he doing it in this way for? Pedaling the drill, wielding the hypodermic, molding vulcanite teeth, packing arsenic in dead nerves, mixing up gold fillings — his daily work was better than following her from mess to mess.

He walked on vigorously back into town, shunning the slow streetcars.

The meeting that night was held in a room above Parko's saloon. J. B. showed up with four men. John Hotsie was a full-blood Choctaw, squat, taciturn at the start, of undiscernible age, with a round face and an awkward manner. Belle slapped him on the back and reminisced about some horsethieving they'd been involved in together. Hotsie smiled, embarrassed, making vague comments until certain particular horses were mentioned, then he began talking with loving and detailed appreciation about the animals whom he remembered individually by marks on their bodies, musculature — talking to her as long as she'd listen and when she wouldn't any longer, talking on to whoever else would hear him about bays and ponies and sorrels and Morgans and forty-dollar horses and seventy-five-dollar horses and horses that could not be bought at any price, only stolen, and on and on talking like a drunkard about horses, horses, horses. He was Choctaw all right.

Ralph Bunch was apparently the youngest man there. He had very pale skin and black hair, and the habit of spitting through his top front teeth. He did it frequently both when silent and when talking, in the latter case punctuating his sentences or adding emphasis at the end, bowing his head slightly and spitting with great ease and accuracy. He was a cold-blooded sort of man, who for some reason appeared to Blue Duck to belong in another time and place — not this town, this year, but some other, whether in the past or future he could not guess. He held his body and shoulders hunched over, and with his pale pure skin and blackest hair, somehow gave an impression that he was capable of sudden extreme actions.

They milled around drinking whiskey for a warmup. No one asked any questions yet. Belle was waiting for Jim July to show up. The piano rinky-tinked up through the floor. The room smelled of kerosene, tobacco, whiskey, nervousness. J. B. sat leaning back against the wall chewing a cigar, talking to Crick Watson. Watson was a cowboy. He walked like a cowboy, so awkwardly that his legs seemed deformed. He was pleasant and quiet, maybe fifty years old, plenty old enough to have ridden the Goodnight and Loving and the other northern drive trails (which had been closed now for three or four years because of the railroads), to have eaten a lot of dust in his trail life and worried about a thousand thunderstorms and crossings and prairie fires, to have ridden night herd on many a cold wet night — performed all the tasks and surmounted all the crises that tempered a real cowboy. He had long shaggy hair down over his ears. He listened with apparent seriousness to J. B.'s conversation.

Blue Duck talked with Maynard Evans, who was the only one here Belle didn't already know. He couldn't get much of a fix on the man except that he had a venomous mouth and acted mean as a sow.

When Jim July came in the door, Belle went to him immediately and began talking in a hushed, private, worried way — which was kind of irritating. Blue Duck had no reason to be here, after all. He had only come because he was afraid that she might not make it through the evening. Having been in nearly the state he'd left her in when he went on his walk, she'd only barely managed to get herself together to come. He advised her not to, which ticked her off enough to get her here. So far, she was kind of giddily on top of things. She was friendly and talkative with a shadow of craziness in her face — the dulled flamboyant glaze.

She talked passionately to Jim. He was drunk. Eventually she gave up on him. "Hey! I guess we can get started now." She paused while conversation petered out. "First thing I got to know, are there any big mouths in this room?"

"Only one, Belle," Ralph Bunch said, spitting.

"Well good. Because if there are any other big mouths here, that'll be bad for our little enterprise. I guess you boys know we're going to talk about breaking the law."

"No!"

"That's right Ralphie, and it'll be one mean son of a bitch on whoever carries a word of it outside this room. I mean not just to the law but to your hot sweetie or your wrinkled old momma or anybody else. That's what I have to start out with. Are yall with me so far?

"Next I got to repeat, we're going to talk about breaking the law. If any of you don't want to talk about that subject, you got a case hanging over you or something, I'll advise you to just melt away and forget this tea party. I mean now. It won't hurt you none. I'll wait for you to think on that one a minute."

"What's the idea, Belle?" Watson asked.

"I'm offering you seven bucks a day each, plus an equal split of profits."

"Seven, did you say?"

"That's right. Seven the minute you sign on."

"Where's the pencil?" Watson said.

"Take it easy Crick," she laughed.

"Easy hell, you're talking seven times anything I ever earned."

"What's the plan?" Hotsie asked.

"None of you leaving? . . . Okay. We're going to the north Territory, maybe across into Kansas, and try and run out some of the trespassers in the Cherokee Outlet."

"Boomers?"

"That's right, boomers and maybe some boomer moneybags."

"Who's that?"

"You'll have to settle for the main idea right now, John. I guess you can understand that."

Hotsie frowned.

"We're being paid by the Tribe. I'm making a little more because I'm putting my name to it. But anything big we knock over, you'll get a fair bite. Ain't nothing tricky or sneaky about it. Whatever I can't explain right yet, there's a solid reason for it. I'm just feeling you boys out. . . ."

"What in the hell is this?"

The room fell quiet. The voice sounded angry.

"What's the question, Mr. Evans?"

Evans snorted. "Question? The question is what in the God damn hell are you talking about? J. B. comes and brangs me to this God damn nigger saloon, puts me up in front of a woman talking what don't make no sense. Who in the hell are you?"

"If you don't know who I am, it's not likely I can tell you."

Evans looked at her for a minute. "I know your shittin name. Who are you talking for?"

"Herself," Jim July slurred. "She don't talk for nobody but herself."

Evans looked outraged. "Who's heading up this operation is what I'm asking."

"I am."

"Well God damn!" he exploded in incredulous laughter. The other men shuffled around some. "I don't have anything against a woman, I figure ever man ought to own at least one of them. But what in the hell kind *are* you?"

Belle stood there with a lantern on the table before her. She glanced at July but said nothing. Eyes tired, silent, she seemed to give up for the moment, receding into herself at exactly the time when her wit was most needed.

"No!" Maynard blustered on. "I like a good one. You know I heard about a schoolteacher out in the Territory, there was a tornader comin and she fell onto the schoolhouse floor and that there wind whooped around so as to strip off her clothes, stripped off ever thread she was wearing. Didn't flatten the walls or kill nobody, just sucked that woman aloose of ever thread on her body. Storm passed and she stood up nekkid." He looked around wide-eyed to see if everybody was as amazed by his story as he was.

Belle continued to stand there looking at nothing, lantern light cast up her rough face, hands dead at her sides. The mood of the place was getting very confused.

Blue Duck acted without thought. He arose and opened the door leading downstairs, picked the man Evans up by his shoulders and rammed him out of the room. He banged and rattled down the stairs, the piano downstairs stopped, and a long sad moan came up from the landing; when it started up again

Belle looked at Blue Duck with a smile creeping onto her face.

"Where'd you get that cull?" she asked J. B.

He shook his head.

"Son of a bitch is right, you know," July said. "This idea is as full of gas as a plowhorse's asshole."

"Why don't you wait until you're straight, Jim. Right now you're a little bit cockeyed, I'd say."

"Oh you would?"

"We have some things to talk about, all of us. You hold off for a while. . . ."

"I'm straight enough to know that you're going out there to get some people killed for that no-good boy."

"What's that?" Hotsie asked.

"What boy?"

Belle put a hard look on Jim. "That's right, and you were straight enough to talk to Heck Thomas today. What'd you and him have to discuss, Jim?"

"That's my business," he hissed, getting about half as drunk in a second.

"Uhh . . ." Crick Watson scratched his jaw and held a finger up as though to speak.

"Jim went to see the marshal today," Belle said. "I saw him walk into the office. I'm just curious about what the subject of conversation was."

"I'm trying to straighten up a rap. You know that."

"I'm just wondering how you're doing it. You wouldn't be making any funny deals, would you?"

"God damn you. Don't you talk to me like that. You're just trying to change the subject. I've seen the way you work. You're gonna ride out there and get your ass full of turkey shot because of that boy you carry on with like a God damn . . ."

"That's enough," Belle said.

"What is all this?" Ralph Bunch spat onto the floor. Hotsie was still frowning darkly. Even J. B. looked vexed. The meeting was threatening to break into complete confusion.

"Spend a week at Younger's Bend and you'll know what it is,"

July lowered. "A week and you'll know good. Stay there a few months and you'll be screaming with it. Talk about the old days gone. Talk about how it used to be out there. If that's the way it used to be . . ."

"What's he talking about?" Crick Watson asked.

"Drunk," Hotsie said. "Drunk as an Indian."

Jim spoke in Cherokee, face swoozy with anger, whiskey — *"Go through one after another. Always talking about the real ones. The originals. I get to put it where Cole Younger put it. So God damn what? Who else puts it there? What other kind of God damn dirty use do you put it to? Got this Comanche dentist now. What's next? You tell him the truth? You tell him the facts? Any of it? Just carry him along for a while, he'll catch on."*

"Did you make a bargain with Heck Thomas, Jim?"

"Whatever I do is my business."

"Not when it's me that's part of the bargain."

"You've been through more bargains than a forty-year-old mule."

"Get out, Jim."

"I'll tell you one more thing. You asked me if I knew Laura Ziegler. I know her. Sure I do. Everybody knows her. I even know how your boy got to know her, who first introduced her to the stupid son of a bitch. Your daughter Pearl Starr introduced her. That's at the Riverfront Hotel where she's selling it for five bucks a job. Which I don't blame her for, not a bit. If I was her, I'd rather do that than live in that insane asylum you call Younger's Bend."

"Get out Jim. I've said it twice now."

"Say it three times and put it up your ass."

"You're getting real ugly, Jim."

"Eat my cock, you dirty bitch. And don't start giving me that I'll-mess-you-up shit. Only messing up you ever do is out of both ends — your mouth and your cunt."

Belle shook her head. "God, boy, what have you been drinking?"

Blue Duck was surprised by her. She was not fierce and quick like before. She was stunned, uncertain. Was it reference to her children — Ed Reed, Pearl — that always made her strange like this? Jim was berserk, drunk on more than whiskey. She descended into a chair and looked out over the lantern.

Blue Duck acted again without premeditation. "We can get on with the basics if you boys want to hear about them. . . ."

Embarrassed, frowning, looking confused, they were all glad to hear someone else talk. They coughed and nodded, yeah, sure. . . .

Blue Duck started talking. He talked about the boomers and the law and the Cherokee problem with the cattle lease. In the dignified, quiet way that he employed to tell people they needed false teeth he rambled on and tried to smooth over what Jim July had breathed into the room. They all acted like they were listening hard but in fact were obviously not. They seemed to appreciate that someone was talking.

Belle interrupted, looking at Jim, "I'm just wondering how bad you must have gone to get up that much poison."

"You talk about me going bad, you dirty mother? I've had it. I'm leaving your shit." He looked at Blue Duck. "You better think about it real good, Mr. Dentist. Put your mind to it. Because something stinks out there. Something real funny. You understand that?"

"I understand. I'm asking you to leave now. Do you mind?"

"*You hear me?*"

"*I hear you.*"

Jim stood up swaying blowsy-faced over the table. "*You'll be dead in a week.*"

"What'd he say?" Hotsie asked. "I don't speak *Chalakki.*"

"I said you'll be dead in a week," Jim said in English. He leaned forward at Hotsie. "*Fiopa tapa.*"

"Thanks for the free advice. We'll be seeing you," Blue Duck said.

Belle spoke very dimly, almost below hearing, "You're lying about Pearl."

"Oh? Why shouldn't she? Couldn't take care of herself any

other way with you squeezing her to drop the kid. *That's what kind you are.*"

Belle sat there, diminished, quiet, with the lamp in her eyes.

Blue Duck tipped his hat at July. "Thanks again. We'll be seeing you."

"I'm going." A certain complacency settled into his face, as though for now he had satisfied his pride. "Keep your fork clean — which'll be hard in present company. And just remember that after the shitass way you acted, Jim July did you a favor." He headed for the door.

"Jim . . . Ji-im . . ." It sounded almost like a lamentation. He stopped but didn't turn. "Pearl's in Kansas," she said.

"Pearl's riding some drummer over there about eight blocks across Garrison." He pointed with an arching finger. "I've heard she's a pretty popular piece of ass. They all get a kick out of the fact that she's Belle Starr's daughter. Be seeing you around."

Jim clunked down the stairs. Belle remained seated, staring at the lantern. There was another embarrassed silence. Blue Duck finally started talking again. "I apologize for the confusion, gentlemen. That young man was, uh, drunk, as you could see. He apparently wanted to start a fight. I'm glad that we managed not to have one. Now we've discussed the basics. If, uh, there aren't any more questions . . ."

Ralph Bunch shook his head and spat. "Je-sus."

11

It *had happened before.* Feeling all ragtag like this. It was because she was aging. Her body was getting tired, her mind soft. What people thought got to her in a way that it hadn't when she was younger. She hated the fact that she cared what other people thought, but the hell with it; one way or the other Pearl Starr ought to marry somebody decent.

She ought to. The way things were going she would end up in the same kind of mess Ed was in. God help them, hadn't they seen enough of that kind of trash? Live that way, and you can't let up. Let up and it carries you off like a flood. Let up and you get the way she was getting right now — weak in the head.

That was the trouble with her kids. They were a little bit simple, both of them. Pearl acted helpless all the time, like she didn't know how to get through things. She wasn't tight-enough strung. She tended to hang around soft-eyed letting everybody else do the thinking. She didn't act outright simple like Ed sometimes did, but she was on the verge of it. Now look where she was.

They'd always wanted to call Belle a whore. A lady didn't do the things she did — deal faro, ride proud on a silver-trimmed saddle, all that — so they called her a street whore. Then they called her Cole Younger's whore. Later they called her the outlaw whore. She didn't know what kind they were calling her now. Probably the old beat-up whore that rode around the countryside chasing after her kids.

Which was the problem. She was worn out, too tired to do what she had to do. She knew the dentist was worrying about her, but he was the kind who wouldn't turn on her. He might disappear, but he wouldn't do her harm. Maybe he had done all the womanharm he needed in one life.

If she felt like talking to herself, well then she'd just have to go on and do it. If she felt like taking a little medicine now and then, she'd do that too. She might look like she was coming apart at the seams, but it wasn't quite that bad yet. She was down inside there hanging on, and it'd take more than a bum boyfriend and an errant daughter to knock her loose.

That's what she told herself.

What she had to do now was get Pearl out of that house, which was not a happy prospect. She wasn't in the mood to put up with all that. It made her weary to death in her *bones* to think about it. She had as much energy as a sick turtle to start with, and something about the Riverfront made her feel dead.

To walk in there and find Pearl sitting around...

God help them, how had they come out like this? All she ever did anymore was try to keep her children from going to hell. For years she hadn't thought twice about them, just went along making out the best she could, assuming that all this kind of thing would come out okay. Now she was past the age of assuming. Her house was falling apart and she had to work twenty-four hours a day just to keep the son of a bitch standing. Any time she turned her back or let go for a minute, the worst things happened.

She walked around Coke Hill, down by the old Commissary below Garrison and up the railroad tracks toward Front Street. Thank God for the dentist. He had saved her back there at the meeting. She hadn't expressed her full appreciation, but then she wasn't able to talk very good just yet. One thing at a time.

The row houses were on both sides of Front Street, a couple of hundred feet back from the river. The Athenian, where Jim had been staying, was at the west end of the street facing toward the river. The Riverfront was across the street and down a ways, its back toward the river. They looked all alike except for different paint jobs, square two-storied frame buildings with modest Greek decorations — wooden "vases," partial facades around the entrances with little triangle pediments above.

"Hey Betty, you got somethin for me?"

The voice shocked her. She turned and a big man was coming sideways drunk toward her. She put on her face. He sidled up close and peered squinty eyed at her. "I guess you don't." He stumbled off down the street.

The madam at the Riverfront, last time Belle heard, was Rosetta Hegel — a fat woman of some local renown for her choice of whores. She was known for making big appearances at the opera house with her girls trailing along after her. The whores always sat in the balcony at the opera house. That was one of the tacit rules, along with curfews and medical examinations and regular fines, whereby civilized society managed to tolerate the "lawless element." Belle had seen Madam Hegel there sitting in the balcony with her neck and ears and wrists dripping with cut glass, her hair piled in an unimaginable heap on top of her fat head, vast body swathed in an ocean of silk, tiny face expressionless in fat, overflowing with chins. The thought of her daughter being one of the ladies-in-waiting to that giant dungheap of a female made her heart rattle in her chest.

But for some reason she still couldn't clear her head out to march across the street. She retreated to the shadows beside the Athenian and tried to get straight. She couldn't just drag Pearl out. She'd need her wits about her. It didn't matter that her stomach was churning with disgust for that fat pig of a woman, her four chins and little round eyes, nor that she was feeling now almost like she could pick Pearl up bodily and carry her out of the place like a baby — it didn't matter how wild and blustery she was feeling, if she didn't have her sense about her she'd just go in there and stumble on her own tongue.

Words. She'd always been able to sling them like lightning. She could wrap a man up in them and send him home to his momma. It was her art. It was how she got where she was, and to do it she had to be ten times smarter and twenty times quicker than any of the sons of bitches. They wrote books about Jesse James; he was getting to be a regular celebrity now that he was dead, and she used to be able to talk the pants off of the big old rolling-eyed clodhopper and put them back on again before he ever knew the difference.

But right now she was about as smart as a goose in a thunderstorm. She kept swooning into crazy thoughts. Her eyes glowed with pain — a headache, ten God damn headaches — all concentrated in her eyes. Her heart was gulping and whanging and her legs were so numb they didn't feel real. If she decided to go across the street she wouldn't walk, she'd let herself loose and glide over there. But then maybe she'd glide right on back to the river and fall in like a rock.

This was crazy. She should go — carefully — back to the hotel. Maybe she was dying of old age and dissipation. Maybe the Lord was taking her early so she wouldn't have to put up with any more of this shit.

Lord Jesus Christ, she was crying. Tears were running down her cheeks. She didn't feel like it but she was, squatting in the shadow up against the building crying like a girl. For what?

Maybe it was inevitable. The daughter had to be what the mother had not been all her life.

Because she had not been a stinking whore. She had cut loose, she had told them to put their lady's ways up their butts, but by God she had *not* been the only thing they said she could be. "Not a whore," she whispered. "Not a whore," she whispered it again.

She waited until the tears had stopped.

But she couldn't go into the Riverfront. She couldn't walk in there and ask that big sleazy Christmas tree of a woman for her daughter. To even walk through the door would be humiliating. It would get in all the newspapers. It would appear on the third or fourth page of the *Fort Smith Elevator*, a neat little entertainment rumor all written up in smart-aleck language so everybody would get a double kick out of it. "DISAPPROVES OF DAUGHTER?" "A SINGULAR APPEARANCE."

Rosetta Hegel was not that dangerous really. When you're that ugly who needs to be dangerous? All she had to do was shake her chins and rattle her jewels and, like a tarantula doing push-ups, she'd put a chill on your neck. Waddling around her perfume-stinking "salon" with men slavering after her asking for this and that girl. Blinking her little pig eyes and saying, "All right, so-and-so, go with him."

Maybe what she was afraid of was not Rosetta Hegel herself or whatever house thugs she had over there to keep order, but the fact that if she walked in there in this state something really bad was likely to happen. She was likely to ventilate that womanheap and thereby change the whole relatively prudent course of her own life in a minute. Oh boy, wouldn't Ike Parker just love it. He'd set a hundred deputy marshals on her trail, get her in court and bore her into decrepitude with a lecture on female morality.

She walked back down Front Street and over behind the railroad station. Whether by previous notice or simple instinct, she walked straight to the shed out back where the kerosene and oil and such were stored. She could smell it. She shot the padlock off the door before the full idea of what she was doing went through her mind. It was not a decision exactly. She rattled around inside and found what seemed to be a three-gallon tin of kerosene, put it into an empty box and hurried out of the shed. Nobody was onto her yet. Circling around to the riverbank, she came back up toward the house from the rear.

There were voices, a couple on the bank just ahead. It was Pearl with some man, walking with him pretending to flirt, some peddler or horsecart driver out on the town trying to get his cigar lit. She sank down in a clump of cockleburrs. They strolled by making insipid noises. It might as well be Pearl. Her heart ached, her mouth tasted like seven days of whiskey.

Pearl Starr, it sounded like a whore's name. And she'd chosen it.

She hurried to the house and got under the back steps. It smelled of piss. After waiting a minute to catch her breath, she crawled underneath the house dragging the kerosene tin with her. There were about two and a half feet between the dirt and the floor joists. She bumped the daylights out of her head and then caught her dress in a tangle and had to rip it loose. She could hear people walking the floor and little gobbets of conversation. Splits of soft light shed down here and there through the floorboards. Mosquitoes tickled along her skin. There was no telling what kind of bugs, snakes, possums, and wild dogs lived under this whorehouse, what kind of eyes looked out of the darkness. She'd be lucky to get out in one piece, without a good case of slow fever or the clap or whatever was carried in the spillings and leakages seeping down through the floorboards of a place like this. God knows, it was a sad place for a forty-year-old woman to be crawling around on all fours in total dark. She felt with her palms each move forward. There were broken bottles, pipes. . . .

She tried to smear kerosene on the floor joists, but that wouldn't do. She'd just waste it and get it all over herself. Light a match and she'd go up in flames herself. Wouldn't that be something: catch herself afire and walk upstairs saying her daughter's name. She'd say Pearl, Pearl, until her eyes melted. Her hair would crackle like weeds, her teeth would go black. . . .

She crawled through the reeking dampness, looking for some way to do this. With her face close, it smelled of perfume and butts and liquor and rich bottom dirt and other less identifiable substances. A chair dragged overhead and she heard the businesslike tones of a card game. A woman said something and giggled. That was how they made their money — off the gambling more than the girls. The girls were there to hang around and make them feel like studs losing their money. A man would empty his wallet twice as fast when there were some tits showing.

She found a heap of something — lumber and old empty boxes, it felt like. Which was perfect. She spilled the kerosene on it.

Something hissed. Not three feet from her face. It had to be a coon. Nothing else could make that sound.

She didn't have a match. Well that was typical. She'd have to get one *now* if she was going to finish what she'd started. Crawling to the opening and waiting under the back porch a moment, she came out, stood up and tried to brush herself off. She was a mess, shaking, scared like a little girl doing something naughty.

Something told her she shouldn't go out in the street looking for a match. She walked up the back steps terrified. Inside the back door she would see Laura. Or Pearl. Or Rosetta Hegel. She walked down the corridor trying not to pause at the partially opened door where the card game was going on. She stood at the foot of the stairs. There was intermittent conversation coming from what appeared to be a reception room off to one side. The girls' rooms were probably all upstairs. A door opened and shut. Someone was coming down. She imagined them all three descending at once, catching her here looking like this, stinking of kerosene with a torn dress and petticoats hanging out and dirt on her face. But it was one person, not three, for an instant still obscure on the landing, and she saw them as one — Laura Ziegler, the Madam, Pearl — gliding down out of the darkness into the circumambiance of the wall lamp, the coarse black hair and weak mouth and pig eyes — her son's wife, her daughter, what-she-was-not-and-never-had-been in one face which now descended the stairs to discover her dirty and helpless and ashamed, and to watch her with the little quick wet eyes judging her by her weakness until her legs gave way underneath her. Because they were. Very weak now. One hand on the balustrade.

It was a man. He appeared shocked at the first sight of her, but then quickly hurried on by.

"A match," she said.

"What? Pardon me?"

"Do you have a match?"

"Yes. Yes of course." He fumbled in his pockets, drew out a box and struck one: the face of a clerk, a married one. She took the box from his hand and left him with the lighted match and a puzzled look on his face. Out the rear door without further encounter, she crawled back under the house and made her way to the wood and trash pile. She rubbed her hands and forearms in the dirt to take off the spilled kerosene. She would have to be very careful now. Clear her mind. She thought of taking off her dress so it wouldn't ignite, but decided to take her chances on that one. She'd rather burn alive than be caught running down Front Street naked. She got as far away from the pile as she could and still reach it, and lit a match.

It took three tries and crawling a little closer, but she got it started. The darkness around her flickered as fire walked quickly over the trash. She saw the coon sloping away from the light toward the same opening that she hurried for. There were kits hanging off her back, scrambling to stay on. She split her palm on a piece of broken glass but didn't pause.

She made her way straight for the river and cut back around toward Coke Hill. Passing under the new bridge, she heard the bells ringing. They clanged and clanged. She waited there under the bridge until a glow could be seen in the sky. Her hand was bleeding pretty bad. She remained there for a time wheezing like a wind-broke horse, hearing the bells, seeing that momma coon like a picture against the burning sky.

She'd take them out to Younger's Bend to get things set up. She wanted to get started on home ground.

Riding out, all of them were pretty quiet. Nothing much happened. They met at Red Land across the River, and rode at a leisurely pace to Tamaeha, which was bordering on home ground; the next day they crossed the Canadian and took the road to Briartown, where she bought some supplies and Phoenix

Pills at Bill Wailes' General Store, then headed on south the few miles to Younger's Bend.

There was feeding and watering and currying and combing while Belle wrung a half-dozen chickens' necks and got together a meal. The whiskey was intact, amazing considering the fact that the unconscionable old drunk Indian of a neighbor who took care of her animals while she was away usually found the jug faster than a fox could find an egg.

Everyone perked up under the good influences of rest and a drink. She still didn't feel like talking much. Shaky in the insides, she had the odd feeling that if she started talking she'd run out of words midway. Just run out and maybe start laughing or crying or something strange.

Blue Duck was quiet and half-formal, as usual. He ate his dinner with washed hands and face, hat off, hair plastered to his head with water. He sat up very straight and used a knife to take apart his chicken. Cowboy Crick Watson ate with long slow rolling chews, and big neck-muscling swallows. John Hotsie consumed his food with abandon, smacking his lips and burping and roving his eyes jealously over the table for more. J. B. didn't sit at the table. He stole a bit of this and that and went out on the front porch by himself. He'd said something to Belle once about not liking to take his meals at a big table because it reminded him of his family. Ralph Bunch sat hunched over his plate eating like it was illegal.

After supper she boiled up a half-gallon of coffee and played a little on the dusty-keyed piano. She wandered out into the garden at sunset to take a look at the vegetables. They weren't much good. The pond had been too low to channel any water from. Water could be hauled up from the river but she hadn't been able to keep up with it by herself.

When he wasn't on the scout, Sam used to make a pretty garden. He had a way with vegetables, generally preferring their company to people. He'd hang around out in the patch pulling a weed here and thinning something there, but mostly just loafing for a half-day at a time. She didn't know how he could tolerate that. It was inbred patience, so deep that it wasn't patience at all so much as just the natural way to spend his time — standing among the plants while they grew. But then he'd slip into a deal, selling a horse, riding out with John Middleton or somebody on a job, and within a few weeks he'd be in his outlaw mood, all high-strung and tight and head-on mean. He reminded her of his daddy at those times, the kind of man who sat on the front porch after dinner reminiscing about the men he'd shamed or killed or almost killed.

The vegetables were bug-ragged and shriveled. The corn never had gotten anywhere from the start. The cobs were tiny. The carrots and radishes had long gone to seed.

The gourds looked like dead okra — which was okay; it took a fool to raise gourds anyway, as her daddy used to say. Pumpkins were wrinkling in on themselves like an old lady's face, and the peas had given up crawling months ago. The red pepper was doing all right, but then it'd grow in the dry sand. She dug up some potatoes. They were about the size of rabbit pellets.

Blue Duck wandered out with a cup of coffee. "Crick is asking where to put down his bedroll."

"In the house if he wants, or the barn, or out under the honey locust. It don't make any difference."

"They're talking about the money, how they'll be paid."

"They'll get paid."

"You gave most of Joel Mayes' money to Prettyman, didn't you?"

"I got money. I'll work all that out."

He sipped his coffee looking off toward the sunset. "I have to head back to Tulsa pretty soon."

"What for?"

"Work."

"You can pull teeth anytime. Ride with me. I need you."

"I have a practice to keep up."

"There'll be plenty of rotten teeth when you get back; don't worry about it."

"What kind of deal do you think Jim made with the marshal?"

"I don't know. Probably said he'd witness against me on some old case. Or maybe told him about what we're doing now."

"You worried?"

"He's got to prove it, whatever it is, and I ain't easy to prove against."

"Did you burn down the Riverfront?"

She looked at him, brow wrinkled.

"It was in the newspaper yesterday."

"I didn't notice."

"They made mention of your daughter."

Belle's face flashed hot. "What mention?"

"They said that she was among the persons who escaped the fire."

"Which paper?"

"*The Independent.*"

"That figures. They're a flock of buzzards, circle anything that stinks. I'll burn them down next."

He looked out over the meander of river in the valley below. "I'm not the man for this."

"What do you mean?"

"I'm not the same as you."

"Well I hope not."

"I don't care about all of it."

"I don't expect you to."

He looked at the ground. "It just doesn't hook up very well. It's all out of the air."

"Yeah. It's always out of the air. Even when you claim it's solid as dirt. I don't mind that. I don't mind riding it out to see what happens. It's better than the chickenshit I've been shoveling most of my life. And I don't mind doing something for the God damn poor old scrawny Tribe either. All those years I listened to the Starrs talking against Tahlequah — it was a bunch of manure. I can tell you Joel Mayes ain't a bad man."

"No. I agree."

"Better'n stealing plowmules."

"What are you going to do?"

"We'll figure it out."

"Like I said before, that's the thing I don't like. You've got four men who don't know anything about this, or care, and they're supposed to set up a border guard on twelve thousand square miles of Territory...."

"That's not how it works. You know better than that. You don't set up a guard, you find out where they are and hit them. You sound funny talking this way, you know it?"

"Oh?"

"Get that look off your face, smarty boy. I didn't think you were so careful by nature. Always plotting everything out."

"Pardon me for not being what you thought."

"You're just smarter than a coachwhip, aren't you?"

"And you're feeling better, I see."

"Why, cause I'm sparking you? What else did the paper say?"

"Nothing really. Just that Pearl was among the survivors."

"Anybody hurt?"

"One person killed."

She flicked a grasshopper off a pepper leaf. "Who was it?"

"They speculated that it was a resident of the hotel."

"... Always wanted to burn a whore. Maybe it was Rosetta Hegel, she'd be the only one who couldn't waddle down one flight of stairs and out the door. Did it say anything about Laura Ziegler?"

He was silent, looking at the ground.

"Did it?"

"No."

"What's wrong, do you disapprove of me?"

"I guess so," he said speculatively. Then he nodded his head slowly. "I guess I do."

"Well then go on back to Tulsa and pull teeth. I can get along without you."

12

But *she was smiling*. Her face looked odd when she smiled, the gesture of the mouth inconsistent with the fixity of her eyes. It was a smile on an unsmiling face. For the second or third time in a few days, he saw briefly another face out of the forgotten center of his memory. It was even less clear than the others: time-ravaged, a smile overladen by sadness. The memory unsettled him. He could not quite grasp it.

Belle was seducing him. She always started it with this smile. And then she went quiet for a while. Without further conversation they ended up back in the house in a bedroom taking off their clothes. They stripped naked and got into the bed and looked at the ceiling in silence for a while. She always seemed to think very hard during these moments. Her body felt hot and jittery next to him. And when they started to touch each other, their hands were wooden, her mouth limp. Memories of the schoolteacher made it seem futile. Before he could do this he had to give up and start from nothing. Blank out the last fifteen or twenty years of his life.

After a few moments she quit the rigid pressing forward of her body and lay back, daubing the back of her hand to her cheek and forehead. "How'd they do it in the Tribe?"

"What?"

"Courting — you know."

"For courting, they gave meat."

"Didn't mess around, huh?"

"No, I mean they gave presents of meat. They would send the present to the young woman and wait outside for her response."

"Did you ever do that?"

"I don't think so. I did not have my manhood yet."

"Why'd they put those screws into your chest if you didn't have your manhood?"

"The manhood of the body — I had that. I didn't have the manhood of the dream."

"Well to hell with the dream, you should have scratched around under that buffalo robe and got you a little bit of it preliminary."

"I guess . . ."

"I thought wild Indians did it every whichaway."

"I don't think so."

"That way you could teach me a thing or two."

"I didn't think you liked being taught."

She daubed at her face again. "Oh yes. I do. I like to be taught if you catch me in the mood. Like right now I'm in the mood."

"You have more experience than I."

"That's the silliest thing I ever heard."

He lay back and looked at the ceiling.

"Do you realize how silly it sounds for a big fine man like you to lie next to a woman and tell her you don't have no experience?"

"I didn't say that. I said you have more experience."

"So the hell what?"

"I did not mean anything by it. I was only making conversation."

"Why don't you quit making conversation and do something else."

"I was waiting for you to quit making conversation."

161

"God damn," she groaned.

"What?"

"I feel like I've been married to you for twenty-five years. Do you reckon we're too old?"

"For fucking?"

"Praise the Lord."

"What?"

"You said the word. I didn't think you used coarse terms."

"I'm learning."

She took his penis in her hand. "All right then. Let's do something else."

He moved up to her and kissed her lips. They were dry and hot. Her eyes shut, deep-socketed. She masturbated him with a stiff wrist. He kissed her sun-scarred neck, her shoulders, breasts. Her breasts were flaccid and damp, and he took the nipple into his mouth and rolled it around against his tongue. She groaned without pleasure, and he found between her thighs with his left hand and after a moment she began to relax a little, going quieter, but still frowning as though at some persistent small pain. His penis was hard in her hand. There was an outburst of laughter outside, and she groaned again and he pushed into her with his fingers, she was dry and he kept on until she was not.

She continued to frown, face sweating, head moving very slowly from side to side. Her whole body was slick and wet with sweating, as though she were performing a great labor. She pulled him to her, but her brow remained troubled. He found his way inside her and she gasped as she had done before when he made the full depth of her — and raised her legs slightly so that her knees were bent and he was between them, cradled, and beginning to move in an exploratory way that appeared to give her neither pleasure nor pain. She seemed to be waiting, or fighting thoughts within herself, perhaps just wanting to say something out loud but not doing it, just letting it continue until he began to move more freely in her and to prop himself on his elbows so that she was below him, breasts moving slightly as he fucked her, moving up tighter so that he came down more vertically into her and after while her discomfited brow gave a hint of fevered pleasure. She groaned. He kept doing it in the same way exactly. He did not hurry or slow down.

After a while it felt like they were coming into agreement, resistance weakening, and she put her feet on the bed with knees bent all the way and hips tilted up so that she opened wider and deeper to him. She began to move, but with the slight gasp of pain.

He asked her what was wrong.

"What's wrong? What's wrong is you're hung like a horse. . . . I ain't complaining . . . exactly."

"You mean I am . . ."

"You're fine, dentist. . . . ah . . . just . . . ah . . . now come down straight like you was . . . now . . . there's some good to it."

"Yes."

"I had . . . I . . ."

"Had? . . ."

"A man . . . I had this one man . . ."

"Only one?"

" . . . was . . ."

"Can you hold still?"

"I don't want to."

"Just for now," he said.

"Do it yourself. You're the one moving."

"Well stop me then."

"I ain't your momma. Stop yourself."

"Just for a second."

"He was bowlegged . . . ," she said.

"Bowlegged? . . ."

"Breed . . . a bowlegged breed. Oh! God damn you."

"I'm not doing anything."

"That's the trouble. You rile me up and then leave me to waste."

"I'm resting."

"You ain't hardly got the harness wet before you have to rest."

"What about the bowlegged breed?"

"I ain't telling you till you start up again."

"Can't they hear us in the other room?"

"They're big boys."

"Like . . ."

"Ah . . . now yes . . . now . . . that's right . . . come down like . . ."

"Down."

"Come down like you was before."

He wanted to stop or move more slowly because he was just about to go, and she would not be pleased. She would not be pleased because she was just getting hot. Her thoughts or whatever had finally receded and she was clear — no worry or preoccupation or sorrow — her face clear with lust.

He could try to stop, but if he did now it might be too late anyway so why even try, because he would only stop and it would be the same only he would be stopped and so why even try. He felt himself separating from the mire of his body, as though there were a being constituted of light which began to come free from the body and rise as he got closer to what there was no use trying to prevent because he was over the rise now and there was no delaying it, and the fact that she was getting like she was made it even more inevitable because she was moving in some different and more fluid way now, no longer forcing herself but being pulled along, if awkward then awkward out of the wet center of her body not her mind, and for the first time they had done this he imagined some special consonance between them, and the being of light was higher, as high and separated as it would get, ready to swoop back down on him. The moment of greatest pleasure was the moment of greatest separation from himself when the being of light was crouched ready to leap like a bobcat back through his flesh — and so it did with claws of fire hitting him in the small of the back and pulling bone and muscle apart so that the upper part of the body, head and chest, reared like a horse and there were noises like a creature in agony, yet before they had stopped he was inside himself again — aware, conscious — and the noises seemed a little loud, like the guys in the other room might hear.

"Son of a bitch."

"What?"

"Just like all of them."

"Pardon?"

"All of them — they'll do anything to get you here, talk sugar candy, make pitiful faces, waddle around like they got melons between their legs, look to be hurting with love and all that stuff, drag their ass like a cur dog around on the ground, then they get you here, slam bam thank you ma'am, what's for dinner."

"I did not bring you here."

"I could line a hundred and twenty-six men outside that door and they'd all be that way."

He didn't reply. He felt even less than usually perturbable now. A hand moved to her leg. "What about Jim July?"

"Jim?" She slapped his hand. "Get out of there. Jim July is treacherous is what he is. I don't want to think about him."

"I mean how was he with a woman?"

"I don't know how he was with 'a woman.' I know how he was with me, but that's none of your business."

"I'm sure he was superior horseflesh."

"What do I hear? What do I hear in your voice? You ain't jealous of him, are you?"

He looked blank.

"Let it be. . . . It doesn't matter. Jim's on my permanent pissant list, anyway. There's not much to worry about from him."

"Who else is on this list?"

"Oh. Ed Reed. He's shooting for number one."

"What are you going to do about him?"

"What can I do? Try to keep him from getting what he deserves. Hope they don't send him to the Hanging Judge. Hope they put on some kind of trial in Tahlequah where I can hire Walter Minko or somebody to get him off."

"Will you visit him?"

"Don't know. I'd like to have something to show Joel Mayes before I go back to Tahlequah."

"Think he can get Ed off?"

"Boy you ask a lot of questions, don't you? I don't know. I just don't know that. I reckon he can do something or he wouldn't have made me this deal. I'm just hoping he can get the charges right — manslaughter or something like that so we can get it finagled around to self-defense. You know these deputy marshals, they ain't all that certain a thing, their jurisdiction gets cloudy and exactly when they're riding for the U.S. and when they go private is sometimes up in the air. The feeling in Tahlequah isn't all that lovey-dovey with Parker's boys. If we can get our lies all reasonable and coordinated we might be able to save his simple ass."

Blue Duck sat up on the side of the bed and began putting his clothes on. "No chance of my getting on your list, is there?"

She looked up at him, back of her hand to her forehead. "Depends on how you do me, smarty pants."

There was heat lightning in the evening, little shudders like something imagined. The stars shimmered with heat waves breathing up out of the dry earth. Sirius rose at dawn. Belle rose with it and washed her hair in the cast-iron cauldron in the yard. John Hotsie was up early fooling with the horses. There were clouds on the horizon, mountains of impotent gauze.

Blue Duck had been up since before light. He'd made coffee and sat on the porch watching the dawn and slapping mosquitoes.

She walked past him as if unnoticing and pumped some rusty water and hauled it and washed her thick flag of hair in the cauldron. In the first sunlight a butterfly chopped the air around her. She squeezed her hair out like a cloth and went into the kitchen to make breakfast. Ralph Bunch sat up on his elbows from his bedroll under the honey locust and made no other gestures or signs of life for some time, not even a spit. He looked like a reclining statue. The boys had been up pretty late last night with the jug and the cards. Belle asked J. B. to gather eggs.

The others arose and went through their various ablutions, coughing and hacking and washing tobacco juice out of the corners of their mouths, plastering their hair down. They were taciturn, especially toward Blue Duck. He remained on the porch while they shuffled back and forth getting themselves awake.

There wasn't much conversation at breakfast. Belle disappeared for a while. She returned with a handful of money and slapped down twenty dollars beside everybody's plate except Blue Duck's. "That's for three days, boys. After we get to moving and you all decide you're staying on, I'll pay you by the week, fifty bucks per. That okay?"

They muttered assent and seemed to perk up pretty quickly.

"How come you don't get none?" Hotsie asked Blue Duck.

"He's gettin it, don't worry," Ralph Bunch said.

Belle laid a look on Ralph that would have poisoned a scorpion. He hunched down over his eggs.

Getting ready for the trail would take better than a day. There were guns and supplies and horses to get together. J. B. took his Winchester apart on the front porch and was cussing and fuming trying to put it back together, not having much luck but remaining deaf to advice from Crick or anybody else. Ralph saw a saddle in the barn that he liked and was trying to do a little trading with Belle. Blue Duck noticed that he was a lousy trader. He didn't have the pauses down right.

They needed a couple of extra horses and Belle rode off with Hotsie in the scorching afternoon to look for a deal down around Whitefield.

Blue Duck sat on the edge of the front porch talking with Crick. J. B. mumbled over his disemboweled rifle. Crick was finishing off a jug that had a little left over from last night, and was about ten times more talkative than usual. A man who'd spent the biggest part of his life away from the stuff, he drank easily, with guiltless abandon, like a young Indian. He talked about his work. He'd been making a living in Fort Smith at the stockyards' slaughterhouse. ". . . Hittin them between the eyes with a sledgehammer. Course, I don't do that every day twelve hours, but they've been putting me on it pretty much here lately. Don't particularly like it." He smiled a little at Blue Duck. "Not that I mind an honest day's work but to spend it slamming them between the eyes one after another, I don't like that so much. Gets you in the back. They used to shoot them, but somebody figured out it'd be cheaper and more certain just to knock their brains out. I drove a lot of cattle in my time — used to — and I'll tell you driving them's different from knockin them dead all day. I almost like it better on the gut row. Once they're cut open, you know . . . Except it's pretty hard work for an old man."

"What old man?" Blue Duck said.

"Yeah, well . . . I met Belle seventeen years ago and I wasn't no kid them. That'll give you an idea. . . . You know how it is, I've been making a decent living there — damn sight better'n I could get out of town anywhere. Now you drive them halfway across Texas and across the Territory up to Abilene and, time you make it, you've done got kind of used to them. You're drivin them up there to get slaughtered, but it's a damn sight different from wielding the hammer. You know, there's some people that don't eat beef. In the world, I mean, like way over in India and such places — they don't eat it. Nosir. Won't touch it. They don't drive them or herd them or do nothin. They think these cows are God."

"Is that right?" Blue Duck said.

"Won't touch them. Imagine that. I'd kind of like to see that before I die. You know? Just to see it. They got these old skinny-rump white cows, hump on their back like a brahmer. I seen some pictures once — they're just standing around on the hills and in the streets, right in the *town*, I mean these cows have got it made. They just about invite them in for dinner. These are heathens, of course. I guess they ain't got much sense . . ." Brow wrinkled, Crick trailed off. He sat for a while in silence, then burst out, "Imagine that, thinking these old silly-faced cows are

God. Hell. They ought to try to get them across a thousand miles sometime, maybe that'd change their minds. I have sung some nights until my throat was raw trying to keep down a stampede. I've seen them balk at a crick two foot deep and I've seen them jump into the Red River when there was a house floating by. I've seen them eat loco weed and chew holes in their own legs like they thought they was made out of grass. I seen them refuse to go north like there was a compass in their silly heads — go anywhere but north. . . . And Lord help me, I've eaten them for breakfast, lunch and dinner until the sight of another steak would just about get me sick to the stomach, until all I could see when somebody said Abilene was a big plate of green beans a-rising up into the sky. . . ." He looked at Blue Duck. "I have paid one dollar and fifty cent in my time for a slice of pie — anything besides another plate of beef. There was an old scoundrel that set up a store of some kind out on the trail in the middle of nowhere. He'd sell these cowboys apple pie for ridiculous prices. We held him up one time, ate a half-dozen pies with him tied up in a lariat. Boy, he *cussed*. They wasn't that good, but I'll tell you what: they wasn't sourdough and they wasn't beef. . . ."

He looked over at J. B., who was fiddling with his rifle and swearing to himself in a steady low patient voice. "J. B., that rifle ain't that bad off, is it?"

"This rifle is going in the river in about two minutes."

"What you got to do there is file off that flange at the end of the magazine. These bullets, I think they're just a little part bigger'n they used to be on the cap end."

"I'll figure the son of a bitch out one way or the other," J. B. grumbled.

"If it won't feed, that's what you have to do. I had an old fifteen-shot do that on me once."

"Yeah, well the son of a bitch cost enough money. They can't make bullets to fit it, that's pretty bad."

"You want a swig? There's a mouthful left."

"No."

J. B. was dead serious about this rifle, and Blue Duck eventually got up to stretch his legs. He ended up taking a nap, sweating and turbulent with dreams. When he awoke, the day was gone and his mind was fuzzy with sleep. In the living room, thick-headed, he noticed something he hadn't before, a big Bible lying flat on a shelf with a few other dusty books. He wondered how long it had been in the family. Since the homeland perhaps. It doubtless hadn't been too overworked in the Starr family. They may have put their names in the front pages, but they didn't put their trust in anybody outside these dirt hills.

He went out on the front porch. Belle and Hotsie hadn't shown up and it was past suppertime. Ralph, J. B. and Crick were leaning against the corral fence talking, their backs to him. J. B. was in the middle with his foot on the fence, and they were standing close to him on either side. He couldn't hear what they were saying. Heat lightning flickered through the dusk and one lone cricket lit up singing in the garden.

13

ometime deep in the night Belle collapsed beside him in the feather tick. She was up early in the morning pumping water and cooking breakfast and yelling at Hotsie to get the horses good and watered. There were new horses in the corral which she and Hotsie had ended up stealing rather than buying near Whitefield.

"They're rich down there," she said over the stove. "They can afford to loan me a couple of horses. Bastards are making a mint off of the walnut. They ship it to Fort Smith to mill, and they tell me it's all going to Europe for gunstocks. Guns for Africa — they're drawing the lines over there. . . . Any of you need more eggs?"

"Yeah," J. B. said.

"Well go find four or five more for me, would you? Those poor old hens can't hardly keep up with you studs. . . . Reminds me of old times."

After breakfast they hassled equipment and packing for a good three hours before they were ready to leave. Hotsie was unsatisfied at using one of the new horses for a pack animal, he was too spirited for it, and he argued with J. B. over letting them use his old farm horse for packing. J. B. stubbornly refused, and Crick finally offered his. They were on their way about the time the heat of the day settled in, threading the boulder-strewn jackpine labyrinth under Hi-Early Mountain out onto the Briartown-Eufala Trail.

The area between Briartown and Eufala was populated mostly by Belle's relatives through marriage, the Starr clan, who'd been in this remote part of the Cherokee kingdom for three and four generations, maintaining a feud whose nexus had been the murder by Ross-faction Cherokees of James Starr, father of Tom. Tom had dedicated his life to revenging that act and to keeping up the feud whose original source had been the signing by Starrs and other Ridge-faction Cherokees of the Removal Bill agreeing to leave the homelands in Tennessee and Alabama.

Blue Duck had heard about Tom Starr, as anyone from this part of the country had heard about him. He knew that Tom was the patriarch who had in effect owned this small part of Oklahoma, and that his brothers and children and nephews lived in fealty to him, that he was a cold-blooded murderer, an opportunist, an unreconstructed Confederate who had not owned slaves but believed in slavery, and believed in the South because it was the losing faction in a national feud. And Blue Duck knew that Sam Starr, his son, husband to Belle, had been a peaceful man compared to his father, a small-time and mainly local thief but friend to men who were not small-time and not local — the "great" Missouri outlaws about whom he had seen books and newspaper articles and monographs and heard drunken arguments as though they were athletes of some new kind, baseball players cherished for their infamy instead of their batting abilities. Belle and Sam had provided the final hideout for these men — some of them — in a place inaccessible to persons not approved by the Starr clan, an incredible network of spies and lookouts that old Tom had organized and maintained back when he feared, rightly, that the government in Tahlequah was considering sending an army of Lighthorsemen to extirpate him and his clan from these hills.

Blue Duck knew these things as all of the others probably did, and he saw irony in the fact that Belle was now riding out in service to the same government which she had supposedly held in abomination for all these years. It could not be entirely or simply because her boy was in jail. Nor — certainly — was it intentional recompense to the Cherokee government by the widow of the Starr clan for fifty years of civil war against that government, yet in some way Blue Duck enjoyed imagining it as such, an act of redress performed in time to be hopeless.

And he was riding with her, for no good reason except that she was hard to leave.

They bought supplies in Briartown and headed north over back trails through the Canadian District, over the South Fork and Georges Fork, both of which were dry, east of Rattlesnake Mountain and past Spaniard Creek, which was muddy but not running, and then westward out of the mountains into the rolling hills of Creek Territory. Camping on the high prairie that night, Blue Duck was saddle-sore. He brooded on the fact that he could ride straight north the next morning and make it to Tulsa before dark.

He awoke to the boom and cackle of prairie chickens and a mighty rhythm of wind and grass, a day that held promise of respite from the sickly weather despite a clear sky. Belle was crouched with her back to him over a fire. "All right you galoots, get up if you want this journey-cake hot." She went around kicking butts and cussing the boys awake, all except Hotsie, who was already unhobbling and saddling horses. Crick noted that Belle's fire ought to be better protected against the wind. She handed him a tin plate of dried fruit and journey-cake topped with ribbon cane. "You think it ought to be better laid, cowboy, why don't you take care of the fires from now on."

"Sure, sure," Crick muttered. "Never argue with a woman, a mule or a cook."

"She's at least two of those," Ralph Bunch said, sitting up in his bedroll.

"Watch out paleface." She put a plate on top of his sleep-mussed hair.

Mid-morning they hit the railroad line out of Muskogee and rode north on it a ways, crossties fuming with creosote in the sun. Then they took out straight west toward Okmulgee. It was the capital of the Creek Nation and a lousy little town, lousier than Tulsa by Blue Duck's reckoning, log cabins and storefronts lining a wide main street that was pocked and rutted with long-dried mudholes. The summer air of the place was normally somnolent with flies, tobacco, street corner bullshitting, but today farmers were in town with wagons of produce and cotton that had been harvested early against the drought, and buyers armed with hook knives swarmed over them slashing out samples. Puffs of white blew up the street in the stout breeze. There was a hint of autumn in the air, and Blue Duck was damn glad for it.

The saloon where they took a drink was busy. A man with a sad face turned to Blue Duck and said to him in Creek, "*My wheat is good for seed. How about yours?*"

"*I'm from Tulsa.*"

"*Oh yeah? . . . The oats and corn aren't worth harvesting.*" He smiled and held up his glass. "*Here's to the winter. I hope it does not take our babies.*"

Blue Duck drank to that.

They were on the trail again in a half-hour, following Deep Fork so that they would not be waterless, into the narrow band of hills west of Okmulgee. The next morning they rode out of the hills into prairie country which put him in mind of his youth — bluestem and switchgrass that was dry but not burned out, rolling in a breeze that continued to bless them as they pushed westward. At some point that day they crossed the Creek border into "Oklahoma Territory," an entity which had been in existence for about four months now — land in the middle of Oklahoma that prior to April 22 had belonged to the Indians and now belonged to the fifty thousand or so whites who had materialized in the land rush.

The horses went waterless that night. Deep Fork had dried up and they couldn't find a farm. They looked dejected the next morning, and Hotsie kept checking their tongues as they rode on northwest in weather that had suddenly become much less pleasant than on the previous two days. Dead thick heat breathed out of the motionless grass.

Something of an argument was brewing between Hotsie and Crick because of Hotsie's officiousness about the horses. Crick was particular about who messed with his horse, and on this dry and blazing day he was not at all pleased by the little round-faced Choctaw's intrusions in how tight his cinch was, how thirsty his horse or how fast he rode. Whether the horse was the one Hotsie and Belle had stolen or his own, it was *the one he was riding* and therefore not anybody else's business. A man's horse and gear were the privatest of property, not to touch or disturb or even discuss except according to a certain decorum. If a person saw some improvement that was needed with someone else's horse, he'd better be damn careful how he broached the subject. And here Hotsie was riding around telling everybody to do this and that because the horses were getting thirsty.

Crick finally spoke up, to Blue Duck's slight amazement. "Looky here Hotsie, I've ridden a few dry miles in my life. You think I'm stupid? You just let me worry about this mare, if that's all right."

"That mare is going to lie down pretty soon if you don't walk her slower."

"You think I'm going at a different rate from the rest of you? We're all going at the same rate; we wouldn't stay together if we wasn't."

"Then we all got to slow down. Yours is the worst off."

"Well now I'm not so sure about that. That slack-jawed heifer you're ridin doesn't look all too healthy. Maybe you ought to get off and let her ride you."

175

"What are you guys talking about?" Belle yelled back, without turning in her saddle. "Keep your peters in your pockets, we've got a ways to go here."

"Where the hell are we getting water?" J. B. asked. "I don't see no prospects."

"That's because there's a hill in the way, J. B. Just simmer down, all of you. We ain't gonna die."

They were packing enough water for themselves, but the horses were getting pretty low down. Blue Duck began to wonder if Belle had made some bad mistake in calculations and they'd ridden north of Guthrie and were now headed for nowhere.

"You tell me," she said. "You've been here before."

"Not when there was a Guthrie."

"Well quit worrying about it — and tell those saps to shut up. Guthrie ain't just a town. There's a hundred thousand sodbusters crawling in every direction out from it. I'm sure we can't miss it."

One of the packhorses, Crick's old *canelo*, strapped down with gunnysacks and pots and Dutch ovens, stumbled, got up wobbly and refused to go any farther. Hotsie checked the horse's tongue and eyes and rearranged his load, muttering at him in Choctaw that he was carrying the least weight of all and to get on now before they all started stalling. Crick got down and twisted the horse's ear and cussed him. Hotsie pleaded in Choctaw on one side and Crick cussed in English on the other, but the horse was not moved by either of them. He lowered his head and heaved gently as though sighing.

Hotsie stopped pleading and Crick stopped cussing at about the same time. They were both red-faced and sweating and angry. The rest of them sat around on their horses conserving energy. There was a moment of silence. Then Crick yelled at Hotsie, "Get the hell away. You don't know nothing about this horse."

"You make me, son of a bitch."

"I could thrash your little ass with a fishing worm."

"Try it, *imafe*."

They went for each other punching and grunting and tumbling to the ground, first one on top, then the other, administering body blows and cussing like it was Saturday night at the saloon and they were both nineteen years old. They pounded on each other for a good three minutes, Crick drawing blood but Hotsie not giving up. Belle pulled out her .44 and shot into the dirt. That didn't stop them either, but she was laughing kind of. They were wrestling right near the packhorse's lowered head, and he took a blow on the snout, rared up his head and walked away.

"You done it, boys!" Belle said. "You unstalled him. You can stop now."

They did stop eventually, when both of them were out of breath.

Belle was still amiable about it. "Pretty good. Give these fellows some water, J. B. And check Hotsie's tongue. He looks thirsty."

Late in the day they finally came onto a homesteader. The sun was low in the sky. Their horses were sluggish and dazed, trudging through switchgrass with their heads down. None of them had lain down yet, but they were getting close to it. A big wagon was blocked up near a creek branch. There were clothes of all sizes hanging on a line. Buzzards circled the sky. Belle hallooed and they rode on by to the creek. It was dry as a bone. The homesteader came out, a short man with big suspenders and a beard. Belle asked him where he got his water.

"Haul it," he said.

"From Guthrie?"

The man didn't answer.

"Suppose you could let us water our horses?"

He remained silent, standing there with his hands hanging down at his sides. He had a big pistol strapped around toward the front of his waist.

"These horses are about to fall out. We'll pay you for it," J. B. said.

"Ain't got water for anybody's horses."

"Where do you water them mules?" J. B. asked.

"I don't haul it for anybody else. Enough trouble to keep up with it myself. Now get out of here. This is my property."

"How far are we from Guthrie?" Belle asked.

The man nodded his head westward. "Over there."

"How far?"

The man stood there staring. Blue Duck had the feeling that something bad was going to happen. They were tired and thirsty and mad, their horses had just gone sixty or seventy miles dry, and here this little man in suspenders was denying them water. He had a big bushy beard that hid his mouth and hardly moved when he spoke. "Get out," he said again.

Blue Duck glanced toward Ralph and Belle, and spoke up quickly, "Hey mister. I'm a dentist. I'll swap you a full go-round on your family for letting us water these horses."

He looked at Blue Duck. Ralph snickered.

"I'll examine them for tooth decay and pull any that need it in exchange for the water."

"That's the best deal you're gonna get, mister," J. B. said.

He stood there, whatever expression he might have had hidden in the thicket of beard. Evening sounds were starting up. "Luke! Woman! Come out," he finally shouted.

They came out of the brush — a teenage boy with a rifle and a woman with a shotgun. They had been down there ready to bushwhack them.

"I'll swap you one barrel of water," he said. "Only got two. It's eleven mile."

The woman climbed up into the wagon. The man rolled out a barrel on its rim, and they watered the horses one at a time. Blue Duck heard whimpering inside the wagon. Hotsie, with a swollen eye and dried blood on his face, took over rationing water to the horses. Blue Duck unstrapped his little trail kit of instruments, got a stump to sit on, and went to work on the family's mouths. The mother brought them out of the wagon one at a time. There were three very young ones who required nothing, and then the older ones started coming out one after another. There were a lot of them. After the seventh or eighth one Blue Duck was tempted to ask how many damn kids were in there.

It was a big wagon, a Studebaker, but she must have had them stacked inside it on shelves. He noticed that the mother was apparently crying each time she got back into the thing. Whether for a minute or five minutes, she puled like a hen over her brood. Outside, bringing the next child, she made as little expression as her husband's beard.

He stood by Blue Duck while the children were being examined.

"Big family," Blue Duck said, after about the fourteenth one.

No response.

Big indeed. He began to suspect that she was running them in a circle. He poked around scraping wads of biscuit off, determining where there was decay beneath the gummy rot of food. They had decent teeth but otherwise didn't look too well off. Like their father they didn't talk much, and some had eyes that looked dull and sickly. They had rickets. One of them was seriously ill — a girl about ten who kept falling asleep while he looked into her mouth. She had big blisters in her throat — probably from diphtheria. She would choke to death if they didn't see about her.

The five extractions that were necessary he handled with the children on their backs and his knee on their chestbones. There were three who definitely needed fillings, but it would have taken up into the night to hand drill the teeth and mix the compound. He pointed them out to the farmer. "You better take them to town soon. And that girl, she needs a doctor. She's got diphtheria."

The beard stared at him and blinked once.

Belle managed to get a couple of words of direction out of him before they took off for Guthrie. Eleven miles or not, nightfall or not, they all wanted out of this place.

They rode by the stars.

A distance away, Ralph said, "That sombitch was strange."

"That's a homesteader," Belle yelled back down the line. "Ain't

179

you ever seen one? They come out of Illinois and Iowa and up in there. They don't talk much, just fasten down to that quarter section like poison ivy and multiply."

"Sombitch had a cob up his ass," Ralph said.

"He wasn't scared. I'll give him that," J. B. said.

"Doesn't have enough sense," Belle said. "I can tolerate an Indian that don't talk, but God damn those Germans or whatever they are. . . . They always have a look about them like they just farted in church."

They made it to Guthrie sometime late in the night. Blue Duck couldn't tell much about the place except that there were new storefronts up and tents, and a few card games here and there and, thank God, a good drink of whiskey, which he enjoyed as much as the horses enjoyed their water. They spread out to sleep wherever they could, agreeing to meet early the next morning. Belle and J. B. and Blue Duck wandered off looking for a hotel of some kind but had no luck. They ended up sleeping on the ground near a slow-burning trash pile.

Blue Duck was up early watching the town awaken. He walked the streets. There was a breeze again today, a downright wind, carrying the smell of excrement and garbage across the newly plotted streets. Dust whipped up around the buildings and tents. Children were playing in a quiet early-morning way. Cows roamed on drag ropes looking for something to eat. The buildings were mostly twelve-by-twelve clapboard boxes with barbed wire strung up around them. Fly-buzzing garbage lay in heaps near property boundaries. A couple of tents had red quarantine signs up in front of them.

The town woke up quickly. Horsecarts with lumber and firewood and food rattled by. Hammers pounded the air at all distances. Down near the BANK, ARMED GUARDS, men in bowler hats and high collars and short coats with revolvers sticking out stood around spitting and talking, deciding the future of Oklahoma Territory. Concessions took the place of finished buildings — GOOD FOOD, LAWYEAR CERTIFIED, OUT-

DOOR CAFE. There were dozens of lawyers. One of them sat on a nail keg whittling, with a little sign stuck in the brim of his hat: OFFICE.

There weren't many women, but they seemed to be dressed up fancier, in puff sleeves and silk, than what was typical to eastern Oklahoma.

There were notices everywhere. Notices of openings and meetings and set-tos and churches and temperance gatherings and advertisements for candidates and builders and job offerings of all sorts. The sides of buildings and poles and watering troughs and barrels flapped with paper annoucements.

The wind was getting fairly strong as Blue Duck wandered back to the OUTDOOR CAFE, where they were to meet. He got a cup of coffee and sat down to wait. Fine red dust swirled in the wind; he cupped his hands over the coffee and pulled his hat down low over his eyes. The others showed up eventually and sat glumly around the table. They were hung over from yesterday's ride and a bad night's sleep. Hotsie and Crick had been run off of two places where they'd tried to put down their bedrolls, and they hadn't gotten much rest. They seemed to be on friendlier terms all of a sudden. Blue Duck guessed it was because they had beat the hell out of each other on the prairie yesterday.

None of them was in much of a mood. Blue Duck shut his eyes against the dust and drank the rest of his gritty coffee. They found an indoor restaurant, but dust sifted even into the closed room. The place was full of busy, talking, coughing men. The food had a fine silt on it.

After they'd gotten something in their stomachs, Belle talked a little business. She wanted to check out the boomer promotion operations that were going on here. W. L. Couch was in town conducting meetings on the Cherokee Outlet. His posters were tacked up everywhere advertising THE INFAMOUS BEEF MONOPOLY/BRIBERY OF TOP OFFICIALS!!/YOUR PRIVATE PROPERTY THREATENED!!

The meeting wasn't until seven that evening, and Blue Duck was beginning to wonder if he'd live to see it. Dust was smothering out the sun. People in the restaurant put handkerchiefs to their faces but kept right on talking business. Outside the hammers slowed down some but continued to fall. Mules toiled their loads through the dust-choked streets.

Business was irrepressible. It was as different from the Indian towns in eastern Oklahoma as day and night. The biggest business in Tulsa was a three-day drunk every government payday. The railroads were changing that a little year by year, but they had fifty years of worklessness to get beyond in Indian Territory. Here, the whites were getting railroads before they even had the town set up. They were starting out busy.

There was motion, purpose, the vitality of greed. Fists pounded the tables, eyes glittered above bandit handkerchiefs held up so they could breathe while they bargained. Fingers pointed at chests with the true facts of the deal. The laughter of calculation rang through the room. Blue Duck felt intimidated by it, and he had the idea that the others were too. Even Belle. This room — the whole town — was rowdy with growth. He imagined the sun going out — extinguished by dust, and out of the darkness hammers would still be heard, bargains would still be struck. It would flourish in the blackness — the roving mania of possession, as swift and free-wheeling as daydreams, whatever could be imagined could be bought, sold. . . .

The townsfolk in a place like this were a different breed from the homesteaders. They were anything but farmers. They were looking for fast bucks. They would loan money to the farmers and buy and sell them land and outfit them for chattel mortgages. They would perform the services of commerce, turning bad luck into profit.

He was abashed by the loudness of it. Hat down over his eyes, hands cradling an empty cup, he remembered how the warriors bragged. They would sit on the ground straight-backed like they were riding, and smoke a pipe and talk very resourcefully about what mean sons of bitches they were. They spoke about how they could outride, outhunt, outcoup anybody around. When they came up with something good, the others would put their hands to their mouths in a gesture of amazement. That was what a warrior did. He got a few things to brag about and he bragged.

These men bragged, but not for gestures of amazement.

Belle found a hotel, rented a room for an outrageous price, and they all went up there to wait out the dust storm. A card game started up in the floor. Blue Duck lay belly flat on the bed and breathed into the straw mattress. He kept his eyes shut. He daydreamed and slept, somewhat sick to his stomach.

14

"*adies and gentlemen,* ladies and gentlemen, please! We are ready to start. Please let us have your attention! We are gathered here tonight to learn about an important moment in the history of our new land. Through the dramatic and forensic arts the true facts of the Indian issue shall be explained. It is an issue with which some of you, perforce, are already acquainted. Over the past several years the Indian tribes, especially that of the Cherokee, have attempted to retain possession of certain treaty lands, the very lands which we have broken with our own plows and sown with our seed, lands upon which our futures and the futures of our families depend. . . ."

The announcer turned and coughed into his sleeve. There was a haze of dust in the room. Outside, the wind continued to moan.

". . . And to make the dramatic presentation of those facts and details, we are honored tonight to hear the recitation of Mr. W. L. Couch. Mr. Couch is renowned in the states of Kansas, Missouri, Arkansas and the Territories of Oklahoma for his courage, eloquence and conviction. A man who has been called brilliant by the *St. Louis Democrat* and other newspapers of its ilk . . ."

"We've heard this three nights! Start the play!"

". . . This man has stood up to the hired brutes of the beef monopoly, to savage Indians and even to the United States cavalry for his beliefs. He has courageously held up the torch of white settlers who by right and virtue and Christian duty are the true heritors of this land. And here he is, the golden tongue of the Midwest, the Daniel Boone of the prairie, Mr. William Lawes Couch!"

Enthusiastic applause met the tall stern-faced man. He allowed the ghost of a smile. He waited until they were quiet and then waited some time longer. Just before they grew restive he began to speak — quietly, in a somewhat offhand way.

"It was mentioned in the introduction that in my time I have stood up to the United States cavalry. It is true. I must admit however that it was not the most challenging of my encounters. . . ." He shuffled his notes, as though to let the subject drop.

"Why's that?" someone in the audience yelled.

He looked up. "Because it was the Fourth Cavalry. They were all niggers."

Hearty laughter.

Mr. Couch maintained his serious demeanor. "Their captain was quite official. He presented me with a written eviction, which he tried to read aloud but could not. I finally told him that it was all right, he could just tell me the gist of it. [Snickers.] He said, 'Dis heah say you gots to get offen dis heah Indian country, get yo butt back to de Kainsas line.' Of course I did not want to distress the good captain. He was already having enough trouble with his troops. They had traded their rifles for beer and their cannonballs for watermelons [delighted laughter], and he was worried as to how they would do battle with the four hundred Christian men, women and children of our party. When I told him that we would comply with the wishes of the United States War Department, he appeared quite relieved. He said, 'Das good, dem white mens been on my ass evah since I loss my sword in a dice game.'" [Laughter.]

Belle watched the man closely. He was tall, with a high waist, narrow but strong shoulders and the eyes of a maniac. He was more commanding in appearance than Joel Mayes or the newspaper accounts had led her to believe. She had expected a stolid, zealous farmer with preacher leanings. This man was a regular stage show.

"Just north of here is an area of land that most of you know is claimed to be held by the Cherokee Indian Tribe. It comprises a strip sixty miles wide and two hundred miles in length running across the top of Oklahoma. It was called the Cherokee Outlet because, when the federal government granted it to these Indians, it was to serve as an 'outlet' into the buffalo-hunting lands of the west."

A small curtain opened and an Indian with an extravagant war bonnet stood there with his hand to his brow peering out from under it as though into the distance.

There were hoots and catcalls.

Hotsie whispered down the line, "That's a Cherokee?"

"But the Cherokee did not use the outlet lands," said Mr. Couch in a deepening voice, "for they were not buffalo hunters. Instead they were farmers."

The Indian took off the war bonnet and put on a floppy hat, another appeared with a similar hat and two cigars, they lit up and began to pantomime a conversation.

"And as you know, ladies and gentlemen, that is not all. . . . There is a worm in the fruit, an element to the disposition of these Indians which has yet to be curtailed by missionaries bringing the word of the Lord into that country or by the government with all of its soldiers and agents. . . ."

The second Indian drew out a bottle and glanced over his shoulder, took a drink and offered it to the other. They guzzled the contents and began to weave around onstage arguing over the bottle.

The audience guffawed, coughed, snorted and yelled. This was the part they'd come for — many of them for the second or third night in a row. "Watch out! He's got a knife!" someone yelled — but the two Indians had a long slovenly dance of a fight to get through before the second Indian pulled it, a huge stage dagger which he towered over the first Indian's head. Stabbed, red liquid burst out of his jerkin and he staggered around in rubbery agony dripping onto the floor.

Belle was for some reason surprised by that. The audience applauded and catcalled while the second Indian dragged the first, prostrate, covered with tomato juice, offstage.

"The habits of these Indians, long innocent of toil, temperance and the other Christian virtues, are not the best. [Knowing guffaws.] Paid by the United States government to maintain themselves and the tremendous tracts of land granted to them many years ago, their habits declined from innocent savagery to base corruption. While the honest white citizens of this nation labor for a meager living, these redskins loaf and enjoy the companionship of their several 'wives,' drinking liquor distilled by the tax dollar and aged in Uncle Sam's barrels — continuing to hold tribal 'ownership' over the lands which our government legally, by congressionally approved treaty, was supposed to have taken back in the year eighteen eighty-six. . . ."

The second Indian, now wearing a sign around his neck that said "Big Chief," lounged on one side of the stage with the bottle. Three squaws appeared in low-cut buckskins and pranced around while he grinned salaciously and drained the rest of it. The squaws were male actors with great padded breasts, huge bustles and lips painted with brilliant red grease.

On the other side of the stage a white farmer had appeared with hoe and straw hat. He hoed a while, took off the hat and wiped his brow. A fat man with "U.S. GOVERNMENT" on two bulging sacks appeared and demanded money from the honest farmer. He gave coins but the fat man was not satisfied.

"Don't do it, you stump jumper! He's a-goin to give it to the Indian!" shouted someone from the audience.

He handed over greenbacks, which the fat man stuffed into the sacks and carried over to the Big Chief just as he had run out of whiskey and was holding the bottle upside down. The fat man put down the sacks of money and rubbed his hands together. The

Big Chief smiled goofily and grabbed both of the sacks. The squaws came by and did a little teasing dance, and the agent's eyes got big as saucers. [Laughter.] He seemed for a moment to lose his balance but then got back to business. Looking over his shoulder furtively, he pleaded with and alternately threatened the Big Chief.

Finally the Chief offered back one of the bags. The agent stuffed greenbacks into his coat and pants pockets, wads of them sticking out this way and that. Running out of space in his pockets, he stuffed a handful down his pants. [Laughter.] Then he began, with absurd slyness, to make advances upon one of the squaws. She blinked her eyes and acted demure. He stuck a couple of greenbacks down her low-cut top. She still acted demure. He stuck some more money down her top. He reached out for her and she pulled back. He began to chase her around the stage, huffing and puffing and tripping over himself, dropping money all over the place while she danced on ahead, one moment horrified and the next moment coy.

The audience loved it. Belle looked over at Blue Duck. He'd put on his blank face. The others sat down the row, faces dimly visible in the dusty light. Hotsie was frowning and irritated, Ralph sneered pretty much as usual, Crick had an unlit cigarette hanging out of the side of his mouth. J. B. was at the end of the row. The meeting hall was jammed full of people. New lumber could be smelled somewhere through the dust and smoke and stench of people.

"As you may know," Mr. Couch proclaimed, "dealings between U.S. government officials and the Indians are not entirely lofty in their purpose. . . ."

Belle watched Couch as he narrated the events. He was a fierce man — tense, controlled, vital. She tried to imagine how much of his skit he believed and how much of it was just a put-on to rile up the Okies. He had the look of a dedicated man — a believer. He was sick-tired of this little entertainment, she guessed, but he didn't show it much.

The Indian now sat astride the tax collector like a mule, looking off woozily into the distance with his hand to his brow, taking drinks; Couch spoke with moderate theatrical passion, "This, ladies and gentlemen, is the Indian who holds, at your expense, twelve thousand square miles of good soil in *addition* to the entire northeastern quarter of Oklahoma. Not satisfied by the riches conferred upon him by our 'benevolent' government, he has in the past ten years managed to lease out those lands to massive beef enterprises owned by foreign concerns, thereby collecting even greater sums of money *at your expense*. Satisfied by the present arrangement with the so-called 'Cherokee Strip Live Stock Association' — an aggregation of foreign and domestic beef interests who are leasing the entire Outlet region for a half-million dollars per annum — that same Cherokee government naturally protests the orderly U.S. takeover of Outlet land. They do not want to give back these lands because for years they have lived in barbarous luxury upon their proceeds. . . ."

The audience was restive in the dust. They laughed and gagged and spat onto the new boards. The air was intolerable. It seemed to close in and close in, lightly, around Belle's skin and eyes. Dust storms were something fairly unfamiliar to her. She had not heard much about them until this summer. It made her fretful, almost to the point of wanting to bolt, run quickly and find some inner room where there was no dust.

". . . But there is a solution — a solution which responsible persons in both the federal and Indian governments have been calling for since the termination of the Civil War. It is so simple and so sure that there is no question of its adoption. It is the solution called for by the very history of this land, the solution of time and destiny. It is the hope which we build our own lives upon, the foundation of freedom and the proven basis of our great civilization. It is the gift which will banish the cowardly dependency of the past and inspire strength and dignity in these peoples. To the Indians of the Civilized Tribes we say: You must break up the corrupt tyranny of tribalism and assume the form of civilization. You must allow your peoples to become full citizens of the United States, and to possess their own properties man by man. You must take the only true gift which we have to offer, and that is the institution of private property."

Mr. Couch went on about the virtues of private property, while a Lady of Liberty bedecked in Grecian robe came out with a torch in one hand and little U.S. flags in the other. The crowd yelled and applauded. The Chief begged for money. He approached the Lady of Liberty, who was standing center stage like a statue. He hovered around her, pulling on her robes and pointing at his empty bottle. She remained perfectly composed. Moving only her arm and head, she popped him on the head with the torch of liberty. He wobbled around, holding his head, making hideous gestures. He came front stage and brandished his empty bottle at the audience, raising his eyebrows and twisting his face down in clownlike despair. They hissed and hollered.

"Go chew some pemmican, you dumb redskin!"

"That'll teach you!"

"Where's all them wives now, Big Chief?"

He wandered off stage holding his head.

When the curtain closed Mr. Couch went on with the presentation, but the part of the audience who'd come just for the sketch began to leave.

During the disturbance, Belle noticed that Couch did not lose his composure. He looked out upon them sternly but refrained from saying anything. This was the "practical application" of the lecture.

He talked about the courageous boomers who, under his leadership and that of David L. Payne before him, had tried to open up the Cherokee Outlet. He talked about how the tribes had attempted to block the opening up of Oklahoma Territory, the very land which they now occupied.

"This town, this settlement of Oklahoma pioneers, is the fruit of many years of labor in my life. I can almost weep looking out across this audience of strong white American faces, people from many states and backgrounds but common in certain ways: You are stubborn people. You have found the new land. Like the pioneers of the eastern mountains, you are undeterred by hardship. You are making these plains your home. You have waited on the border of a new life for many years.

"And by this act we align our fate with destiny. We loose the chains of the past. Common people — yes. Common in that we have backbone, common in that we are not afraid to claim the land and the life that are rightfully ours. From here, common people, we move northward. From here we take the lush prairies of the Cherokee Outlet from the corrupt hands of tribal chiefs and foreign speculators and make of it our garden. We move eastward and westward, possessing Oklahoma from its heart in every direction. . . ."

He paused and looked out across the half-empty audience, frowning with eloquence. Those who remained were coughing and blowing their noses, and Belle could see Mr. Couch make the decision to cut it short. For just a moment there was silence — no sounds from audience or stage, wind sifting through the walls, moaning gently over the newly plotted streets outside. Two or three stage lanterns blew out at once and Couch's eyes seemed to deepen in his face.

"Those of you who wish to discuss how we intend to proceed from here may come tomorrow morning. Weather permitting, we will have a public information session in front of this building at nine o'clock. I hope you have enjoyed it."

Leaving the stage in a smattering of applause, Couch looked drained and pale. Belle wondered how many hundreds of these lectures he'd given.

Back in the hotel room they got out a bottle and some glasses. They were quiet. When everyone had poured, Belle offered up a toast.

"Here's to the golden tongue of the Midwest."

"He's full of wind," Hotsie said.

J. B. started to speak and then paused. Staring into his whiskey, he seemed for a moment to go daydreaming. He rolled the amber liquid around and took a long tasting drink. "I don't like that guy."

"What he said was half true," Blue Duck said.

They all looked at him.

"More'n half," J. B. said. "But I still wouldn't mind plowing him a new asshole."

"He don't know shit from shingles about the *Chalakki okla*," Hotsie said, blotting his eyes and nose with a handkerchief. "I don't love them. They're always playing hot shit over the Choctaw. But I wouldn't go around telling those lies."

"What do you mean half true?" Belle asked Blue Duck.

"I mean he isn't a fool."

"Who said he was? He's tired of that little act, but he believes it. And he's getting paid good wages. I want somebody to go down there in the morning and see what he's up to. If he heads north, we'll follow him."

"You couldn't follow a locomotive in this weather," Crick said.

They listened. It gusted and howled outside, whispering dust that was like smoke in the small room. Belle looked around at their dirty faces.

15

R_alph talked and whimpered_ and whispered and sighed. J. B. sounded like a freight train on a steep rise. Belle didn't have much luck trying to sleep in the chorus. She was up before sunrise and out on the street.

A strange silence had settled over Guthrie. The wind was utterly gone. Dunes lay three and four feet deep against walls. The town was powdered, dry and as silent at this hour as some ancient city lost in the desert. New buildings looked old. Tents were motionless as stone. A milk cow looked dead on her feet. A black bitch fat with pups lying in the middle of the street moved only her eyes as Belle walked by. The moon shone very brightly in the lightening sky, like she could reach up and put it in her pocket.

She walked on down Main Street. It was her favorite hour, the time when ghosts were departing and people hadn't yet stirred.

Someone was coming toward her. At first she thought he was walking. But he wasn't. He seemed to glide down the deserted moon-bright street. She stopped at his approach. He came straight toward her, sitting on the seat of a metal contraption pedaling his feet up and down. When he was right upon her, she put her hand to her gun. He wore a big police badge. He tipped his hat and went pedaling on by.

Her heart pounded. It occurred to her that she was still back in the hotel dreaming. What the hell was that? She stood with her hand on her pistol staring after the thing as it went silently on down the street.

She turned and walked toward the bank. She was going to be nervous today, and she couldn't afford to be. She would have to take a good dose of Phoenix Pills. She walked by the bank. A big red sign outside said:

BANK,
ARMED GUARDS.

On the window:

ARKANSAS BANK OF COMMERCE
GUTHRIE, OKLAHOMA TERRITORY

It would be very hard to get away with. There were too many men around here wearing guns. She really had no plans about how to pull it off. J. B. would probably have some ideas; he'd done a little sure-enough gunslinging in his day. The rest of her boys were probably pretty green to it, although between them they'd handled a good share of thieving and rustling and small-time highway work. Ralph had a reputation with a gun, but most of what she'd heard about was after-supper entertainment.

She thought back on the Northfield robbery — the one that had ended it for the Younger Brothers thirteen years ago. They had been overconfident about pulling a job in Minnesota. They were used to sleepy little towns in Missouri where they could ride in shooting and whooping it up and everybody'd jump into a rain barrel. Northfield was a good-sized town full of tough pioneers who'd fought the Indians with their own minuteman defense. Belle knew exactly why the Jameses and Youngers had decided to ride all the way up to Minnesota on a job. She'd heard Cole talking about it years before they did it. Northfield was where old General Butler was from, the Yankee who'd used a Gatling gun at Petersburg. Always fighting the war. They fought it for ten years before it was declared and for as long as they were alive and free after it was over. It was what drove them. Furnished their ideals. They weren't robbing banks just for Jesse James or Cole Younger, nosir, they were doing it for the Cause.

It was strange thinking of Cole and Bob and Jim in jail all this time. The Stillwater jail was like a place in her stomach, something that stirred deep down. . . . Bob had finally died; he'd been sick with TB for seven years, dying and studying medicine, of all things, while in jail. The newspapers said he was an ideal prisoner. He'd taken a bullet through the lung in the robbery.

It must have been an incredible mess. Jim had been shot all to hell. He was the reason Jesse and Frank James split from the Youngers and didn't get caught following the robbery. They were wandering around in the sticks trying to get south, Cole with eleven bulletholes in him, Jim with five and in worse shape, Bob with a smashed elbow as well as one through his lung — and Jesse wanted to abandon Jim. Cole and Bob wouldn't leave their brother. So Frank and Jesse got away. The Youngers were caught and got life terms.

Now and then over the years she ran onto an odd little thing in the newspapers that set off a strange feeling inside her. Like eight or nine years ago there was an account in a Fort Smith paper about how Jim Younger had undergone an operation to extract a bullet that had been in his neck ever since the robbery. A surgeon attempted the operation but due to endangered blood vessels gave it up. Jim then begged an intern to try again, saying that the bullet gave him such pain that he would commit suicide if they didn't get it out. The intern operated on his neck for two days and finally got it out. Belle didn't know how you could dig in a person's neck for two days, but that's what the newspaper account said.

She also had never understood how Cole made it through alive so shot up. Every report she'd read said that he had eleven bullet wounds and was in fair condition upon arrest. Only Cole could ride around the countryside for the better part of a week with eleven bulletholes in him. She'd never known him to be wounded before, but it had always been obvious he wasn't made to break too easily. A lot of these big boys had a bullet in the back of their minds all the time. You could see it in their eyes. Cole didn't.

He was a small-minded hypocrite, too — a man who believed in his own lies. He continuously reshaped his doings with stories like a little boy living an imaginary life, going around talking to himself all the time. He'd brag about a robbery until the pressure came on, then he'd talk like he was innocent, like he couldn't possibly have pulled that job because of evidence to the contrary. Pretty soon he'd really seem to believe it himself. He'd be spending the loot and still believing his alibi. Truth was at the service of his will.

He wrote a letter from Northfield denying any close acquaintance with her. ". . . the fertile imagination of Belle Starr" — she remembered that phrase — "boasting of an intimate relationship with me, declaring that Pearl was our child. She used my name for the notoriety that it held in the Cherokee Nation. . . ." Just like Cole, that statement.

He'd shoot an innocent man in the face for having been a Yankee fifteen years before, but he didn't want people thinking he was a fornicator. The Bible was strict about such things. So he wrote his letters. For years before he went to jail, when he was still on the scout all over the country, he wrote them, in elegant and convincing rhetoric denying this and that, setting this and that straight. Trying to get on advanced parole with the Lord, she supposed.

She wished he was here now, the bastard. With his bull neck, his good medicine. They didn't make them like that anymore. Except that there was no telling what thirteen years of jail had done to him. A newspaper picture she'd seen made him look like a rotund businessman. . . . And if Pearl wasn't his daughter, then not only was she immaculately conceived, but the Lord took pretty poor care of His own.

She walked back toward the hotel. The policeman on the metal contraption went riding by again. He apparently rode up and down the street on the thing, tipping his hat like a penny bank.

Back in the room she swallowed a handful of Phoenix Pills and started waking the boys up. Dust covered everything. Their faces were smudged with it, noses clogged.

"Up fellers! Up! The sun's a-risin! The storm's gone. Going to be a fine day. Up and at it!"

They sat cursing and groaning and picking their noses. She stood with her hands on her hips. "God, I've never seen such an ugly crew of men! You all look like you died and rusted overnight. Get up!"

Ralph's eyes were glazed. His first morning spit was weak and imperfect, separating into two wads and rolling down the wall. He sat there staring at it. "God damn," he said.

"How come he gets the bed?" Hotsie gestured at Blue Duck.

"Shut up John. Ain't nothing but straw and corn shucks anyway. You're better off on the floor. Up and at em boys, we got some serious work today."

"You scheming on that bank?" J. B. asked.

"That's right. What do you think?"

J. B. wiped the clogs of dirt out of the corners of his eyes. "I think we'd do better to ride up to Philadelphia and rob the mint. There's too much going on around here."

She squatted down beside him and talked more quietly. "So what do we do?"

"I don't know. Depends on what you're after."

"We're after putting them out of business."

"You won't be doing that. No way I can think of. . . . I guess you could burn them out, but they'd just build it again."

"What good would that do us?" Ralph asked.

"We're working for the Tribe," Belle said. "That bank is against the Tribe. Been against it for ten years. They're the ones paying for the shit we heard rolling off the golden tongue last night. If we can't rob them, maybe we can put a little squeeze on them, make it a little less profitable around here."

"Don't sound to me like you know exactly what you're talking about," Ralph muttered.

Belle stood up. "We'll talk about it after breakfast. Go different ways and meet back here in an hour." She went with J. B. and Blue Duck to the Commercial Cafe, where they'd eaten yesterday, and ordered up breakfast. Everything was fried — bacon, eggs, corn, ham, chicken, potatoes. The coffee was better today, without the dust.

"So what do you think?" she asked.

"Already said what I think." J. B. spoke around a big mouthful of egg. He ate things one at a time in big bites: an egg in two mouthfuls, three or four hunks of bacon stuffed in at once, on around his plate. He seemed very uneasy at the table.

"What you said don't get us anywhere."

He went on eating.

She talked flatly, a little mad. "You're my top boy, J. B. I got you into this because you know what you're doing. You've had experience. You've done some big-time stuff in your life. Don't give me this junk. Put your head to it."

"Ask him." J. B. gestured at Blue Duck.

The dentist had on his blank face. He had said nothing so far.

"All right. What do you say?"

"I don't know."

She really did get mad now. It washed hot under her skin. "Are you riding with me or not? If you are, quit putting on the chicken-brain act. I can't keep explaining to you what we're doing. I've got these other boys to keep on the crew, which I ain't doing with you two acting like two piles of shit wax."

J. B. picked out a fried chicken leg and ate it in one tearing bite. He chewed as regularly as a steam engine, little beads of sweat on his forehead. After he'd finished, he got up from the table.

Belle glanced up at him. "Don't forget to wipe now, J. B."

He scowled and walked out.

"Have we talked money?" she asked Blue Duck after a while. He said nothing. "All right, let's talk it now. You're on salary, not wages. These other bums are getting fifty a week. You settle for four thousand? That's for however long it takes to make this run. We'll hit the bank, then go north and do whatever we have to up there. Any extra money is an even split between all of us."

"That's four thousand out of Joel Mayes' twenty thousand?" he finally asked.

"That's off the top of what Joel Mayes offered *if* he was satisfied. I'll be lucky to get a third of that. Plus I'm paying these apes two hundred a week to grumble around. I'm the one gambling."

"What about J. B.? You just told him that he was your number-one boy?"

"These galoots need somebody with class. J. B. just don't cut it. Besides which, he's getting kind of surly. You can't tell what they're going to do when you get them out there under the sky. I want you solid by me."

"And four thousand will take care of it?"

"God *damn*, you're acting just like the rest of them."

"It's your scheme, Belle."

"So what? So it's my scheme? Can't you pick up on it? Are you dumb?"

"I don't know what anybody else's reasons are. My reason is that I'm not a bushwhacker. I rode with Dan Evans for a couple of years when I was a kid. That was all." He shrugged. "I'm a dentist."

She leaned against the table and spoke very deliberately. "You're a fine black-haired man and you've got a wild streak in you two miles across. You've been rotting in Tulsa for years and now you're sick of it. You loved a woman that turned you from a scared little greasehead into a full-blood man. You killed her and buried yourself and haven't had the guts to get out of the hole since."

They sat for a moment looking at each other.

"Is that all?"

"No." She still looked him in the eye. "I've got something you want."

"Oh?"

"Maybe just a lesson. You want it or you wouldn't have tagged along this far."

"What lesson is that?"

"I don't know. The best ones don't put into words so easy." She sat back and glanced away. "All I know for sure is you'll get four thousand bucks out of it. That's eight thousand rotten teeth. Now will you go for that? J. B.'s coming back."

"I'll tell you. Before noon."

"You'll tell me within an hour."

He smiled. "You are very conceited."

"No choice in that. . . . Hello J. B. You didn't forget now, did you?"

He scowled, descended into his chair and stuffed a biscuit in his mouth.

Back at the hotel she told them what to do. They didn't want to decide things themselves. She had figured that much out already. They wanted her to tell them every move so they could bitch about it. She sent Crick out to buy some dynamite.

"Tell them you got twenty acres of stumps you're working on."

She sent J. B. and Ralph to the boomer meeting in front of the town hall. She wanted to send Blue Duck but he might stick out in the crowd with his dark skin.

They would hit the bank that evening. She wasn't clear on whether they should go after the safe. For now she tried to make it a mystery to them rather than an uncertainty. She would tell them later. Hotsie would get the horses in top trail condition. Blue Duck would hang around town and see what he could see.

She put on the dress that she'd bought in Fort Smith and went to the bank on the pretext of getting some change. She'd been carrying big bills from Joel Mayes in a little pocket in her underwear. There was only about two hundred bucks left. She'd have to ride back to Tahlequah soon.

Inside the bank, two guards with long drooping moustaches stood near the front door with Winchesters. The tellers' counter cut the room in half. The safe was right there at the back of the room, big and brand new. One look told her that there was nothing they could do with it locked. Not with dynamite or anything else. She stood in line up to the teller. Two executives sat behind the counter at their desks. Both of them looked up now and then in a vague, staring way. One of them slightly frowned at her. Probably at her dirty dress. She put a bill on the counter and asked for change. The teller was an older man with a city manner. He counted the bills twice, very quickly. Belle thanked him and went out slowly.

She tried to get a fix on the guards. You could sometimes tell whether a guy was likely to risk his ass or not. These guys were both youngish, not thirty — a bad sign.

She went to the Outdoor Cafe, across and down the street from the bank, and sat alone with a cup of coffee.

Men were gathering out front of the bank. It seemed to be the regular business and bullshitting rendezvous. Everything about this place — the flatness, the busyness, the number of men wearing guns, the hearty, almost inebriate mood of progress — everything said no deal, you'd do better to dance on a bear trap than try this heist.

Her time of the month was coming on. Perfect. She'd be stuffing rags down her pants just in time to try getting these galoots to pull a job that Cole probably wouldn't have tried if Jesus came to him in a Confederate uniform and ordered him to.

She looked at the sky. She looked in the bottom of her cup. Ed back in the Tahlequah jail. Another handful of pills. She was running low again.

16

She sat down on the edge of the bed and rared up her head to tie her hair back. A strange light was in her eyes. She looked at Blue Duck. "What's your answer?"

He still didn't want to make a solid agreement with her. He was wary of declaring himself inside her circle. The coyote was wary about anybody's circles. He shook his head slightly.

"Five minutes," she said. "Yes or no."

The others had arrived back in the room. They were in a better mood now.

"Did you get it, Crick?"

"Yep."

"How much?"

"Enough to blow up a lot of stumps."

"What'd you see at Mr. Couch's little meeting, J. B.?"

Ralph answered for him. "Couch wasn't there. Some other man — the one that announced him last night — talked about the settlement up at Enid, wherever the hell that is."

She looked away. "Smack dab in the middle of the Outlet. . . .

And he was trying to get people to go up there? What did he say exactly?"

"What did he call it, you mean?" Ralph leaned his head back. "Let's see . . . 'God's work in the Oklahoma Territory,' 'the vanguard of liberty,' ahh . . . 'the settlement of Eden,' 'Palestine on the prairie' — that enough?"

". . . Building them a boomer camp in the middle of the Outlet. . . . That's some old-fashioned straight poker. When are they leaving?"

"Two days. He says they'll be back here after a month to get another crew. He's been here before. This is his second roundup. He was talking a lot about the commercial possibilities in the new town. There's a morning train north in two days. They get free passage."

She appeared to be musing. "They've got the trains running before they've even got the towns settled."

"What about the bank?" Crick asked.

They all went silent at that one. Belle sat with her hands up behind her head still arranging her hair. Blue Duck watched her. She seemed relaxed sitting there in the bed with all of them watching her. She finally looked up — directly at him. He became uneasy. Her eyes were very heavy.

They were heavy and still and cracked with light. She looked at him.

The men shuffled around some. Someone muttered about the weather being decent, at least.

She just kept looking at him.

It was a minute before he understood what she was doing. He became irritated. He did not like being pressured.

"Well, are we going to burn them down tonight or what?" Crick said. "I wouldn't use that dynamite here. There must have been ten people saw me buying the stuff."

"The safe won't dynamite," Belle said, still looking at Blue Duck.

"Yeah?"

They were all getting uncomfortable. It was unlike her to just sit there. Her hands were in her lap now, her back straight as a board. Her face was the only thing in the room. Blue Duck looked away and tried to put on his Indian composure. It wouldn't stick. She was pushing him. He looked back at her, intending to call her on it.

Instead he looked at her and nodded. Eyes blinking slowly, he nodded once.

"All right," she said, "You boys get ready to start earning your wages. We're going public today. Whoever ain't ready for it, pack your saddlebags."

None of them liked the idea. Crick got quiet and withdrawn and slightly pale. Hotsie grew quiet, too — and shy-acting, as though he were suddenly much younger. Ralph spat between his upper front teeth at twice the usual rate and his sarcasm grew light and ineffectual. J. B. moved and spoke even more slowly than usual. He seemed almost drugged. Blue Duck was aware of them all, but he was most aware of his own intestines, which were a stew of snakes.

Strangely, none of them made serious protest. None of them decided to quit the job. Belle did almost all of the talking. He watched and listened to her sluggishly. At moments, watching her face, he did not hear her words precisely. The others seemed to do likewise, like little boys in a dreamy mood watching their mother.

They moved out one at a time after 2:30. The sunlight made him a little nauseated. He was conscious of the gun on his hip. Voices in his mind protested. They protested in every possible way, arguing, imploring and whispering at him. They talked one at a time like speakers at an assembly. They talked all at once like a swelling mob in his skull. They told him that this was everything that he did not want. He sat alone at the Outdoor Cafe slouched down in his chair over coffee, agreeing with them, capitulating to their arguments. Yet the voices were not as real as she was. She had become very different to him in the last few hours. He did not know why. No single thing had caused it. His accumulated friendship with her had perhaps totaled up somehow. Maybe he was getting scared of her. Maybe he was even more scared of her than of robbing a bank.

When the firebell clanged and people began rushing down the street, he hardly looked to see the smoke. Hotsie had done his job. He stood up and tucked his shirt in. Across the way he saw J. B. and Crick stalking toward the bank. Out in the street a little boy ran square into him.

"There's a fire! Down at the town hall!" The boy was so excited that he ran off and left his hat in the street.

Blue Duck stood looking at the hat with people rushing by him toward the fire. For a moment he forgot where he was or what he was supposed to do. When he saw Hotsie coming with three horses in tow, he remembered. Belle was at the rail in front of the stable on Main Street untying the other horses. She gave him the eye and nodded over toward the bank. J. B. and the others had not gone inside yet. They stood in a little group off the corner of the facade. One of the guards was leaning out the door looking up the street. A half-dozen of the regulars in front of the bank had not been drawn off by the fire. The diversion hadn't worked. A lot of people had gone off to see the show, but these old guys just chewed a little faster and looked a little more disgusted at all the hubbub. That could be very bad.

Blue Duck looked over at J. B. and the others. They huddled together without talking. They seemed scared. If they went in now it would be disastrous. All of the men in front of the bank were armed.

He hurried down the street toward them. He trotted right up to them with no idea in hell of what he was doing. His face was hot. He glanced over at J. B. and the others. On the verge of making a move, they held back now, puzzled.

"A woman!" he cried.

They scrutinized him lazily.

"How's that?" one of them eventually said.

"A woman in the fire!" Blue Duck said excitedly. "They said to come to the bank, out front, and get her man. Didn't give the name. . . ."

"Don't have a hemorrhage, buddy. What about this woman?"

"Burned," Blue Duck said, making it up as he went along. "All of her clothes were burned off. They got her laid out. It's horrible."

Two or three of the men seemed to get worried at that point. "What'd she look like?"

"I don't know. All of her clothes were burned off! They said to come down here and get some man. She's naked!"

"Get who? What was the name?"

"Was she fat?"

"The whole place is in flames!" Blue Duck looked over at J. B. and the others, hoping to God they'd stay back until he'd baited these guys. It half-worked. Four of them made off down the street. The two who remained stood there chewing like old steers, imperturbable. J. B. and the others closed in. The firebell was still clanging. A wagon rattled by. Belle started across the street with the horses. Blue Duck waited until J. B. and the others had entered the bank. The two remaining men were immediately suspicious.

There was a shot and yelling and another shot inside the bank. Blue Duck drew his pistol and aimed it toward the two. "Get in the bank." They hesitated. "I'll kill you." They finally moved.

Inside, there was a man on all fours on the floor and others standing against the wall with their hands up. He added his two to the group and helped Crick cover them. Belle came inside with her hair back, neckerchief up, hat down low over her forehead and spurs jingling.

J. B. was on the other side of the tellers' counter getting an older man to stuff the bags with money out of the safe. The man on all fours made a gurgling sound, looked around the room with a strange lost gleam in his eye and began to crawl toward a rifle off against the wall.

"Stop," Belle said. She stepped over and booted the rifle across the floor. He looked at her with puzzled bright eyes. Red foam dripped out of his mouth. Something hung out of his stomach. He started crawling toward the rifle again. "Stop." Belle lowered her pistol, following him.

"Up! Keep them high!" Crick warned. He had a shotgun.

One of the bank executives was making strange noises, something between a whimper and a catching in his throat. His eyes rolled up in his head and blinked rapidly, arms wavering.

"Up!" Crick shouted.

The executive toppled to the floor in a dead faint. The whole group seemed to panic at this point. One began to openly weep. Someone began to moan long deep lugubrious moans — Blue Duck couldn't tell who. Belle got between the crawling man and the rifle, and he pushed right into her boots, bumping her like a cow against a fence. She held her pistol cocked. He reached up, grabbed the boot and held it. He did not try to move her leg but just held on, face to the floor. She looked down on the top of his head. Halfway across the room, Blue Duck saw a combustion of terror in her face. She jerked her leg back as if from a snake. The hardness struggled back to her expression. The crawling man toppled over and went into seizure. His arms and legs stood straight out, his head lifted, he sat up and then stiffened flat, sat up and stiffened flat, blue-faced ugly mechanical laughter pushing out of his guts.

The room was exploding with craziness, all too fast to be real. Through the window Blue Duck saw a man approach the bank. At the entrance he turned tail and ran right by Hotsie, yelling, "Bank robbery! Bank robbery!" He had a good voice for it.

Blue Duck advised J. B. that they had about thirty seconds to get out. The old teller who was stuffing the bags stopped immediately and assumed an expression of composed distaste.

"Who's the boss here?" Belle asked.

No one answered.

"Who is he? I'll start shooting if you don't answer me."

A man pointed at the fainted executive. "Him. That's the boss."

"Tell him when he wakes up that this robbery was pulled by Cherokee Strip boomers. We weren't booming fast enough. The funds were slow coming through. Take it as a warning. You got that?"

The man nodded, confused.

"What'd I say?"

Lips moving, he couldn't speak.

"It's a woman," one of them muttered.

"What did I say?" Belle waved her .44 at the man, but he still could not talk.

The man in seizure was choking. Face white now, eyes turned-up bald globes, he was choking and burbling down his jaw and bleeding extravagant pumping slops of blood out of his belly. He was very unreservedly dying. Blue Duck went over and turned him onto his side to relieve the choking. "Tend this man. You in the ribbon tie, get over here."

A man in a black ribbon tie ventured over, hands still up. "Keep him on his side," Blue Duck said helplessly. "Get a . . . get a doctor."

"Sure," the man said venomously.

"*What did I say?*" Belle repeated.

The old teller, hands now on the counter, head erect, replied, "You requested that we inform the manager that the robbery was performed by Cherokee Strip boomers, that certain funds were slow in coming through."

"All right, grandpa, you got it. The rest of you get behind the counter. Now! We'll have you covered for three minutes after we go out the door, so don't try to leave. Time it or you'll get your face shot off. That's three minutes. Now all of you get behind the counter and put your hands flat on it. Get their guns, one of you."

Blue Duck gathered them up off the floor and threw them out. A gangly man who looked like a farmer stood outside near Hotsie. They burst out of the place with neckerchiefs up, waving guns and toting bags of money. The farmer stood in the swirl of dust and horses with a big smile pasted on his face. "What yall doin?"

"Robbing the bank, what the hell do you think?" Ralph yelled.

A man with a badge rode down the middle of the street on what looked like a bi-cycle. He dragged his feet, dropped it in the street and went for his gun. They blasted out in a clump right at him, J. B.'s horse trampling and for a moment entangling a leg in the machine. The policeman got off two wild shots and dove for a barrel. Belle fired off her pistol and yodeled out a high-pitched Cherokee gobble that raised the hair on Blue Duck's neck.

They were out of town in seconds and crossing the almost-dry Cimarron, two hundred yards of cracked clay and mud, a piss-trickle of water and a wagon toppled half over, stripped of canvas and baked solid in the clay. The two packhorses were on the other side of the river, tied up in some brush and loaded light. Hotsie loosed them without dismounting and gave one of the ropes to J. B. Belle took out ahead and they followed her straight and furious.

Crick was shot. Blue Duck didn't notice it until they finally stopped for water. Blood was soaking down his shirt into the top of his pants. He had been wounded low in the ribs. Blue Duck found out that the shooting before he had entered the bank was between Crick and the guard. The guard shot Crick and Crick blasted him in the stomach with the shotgun. Crick seemed disoriented. Belle got him to lie down.

One of the horses was heaving badly. Belle had made so many changes of trail, cutting down dry creeks and game trails and no trails at all, that it was hard to tell exactly where they were or how far they'd gone. His estimate was twenty miles northwest of Guthrie.

The water was a clear running spring in a patch of oaks with watercress growing in two pools. It was the best water Blue Duck had ever drunk in Oklahoma. Ever. He sucked it down his throat like a horse.

"Is this where we were heading all afternoon?" he asked Belle.

"Best hotel in the Glass Mountains," she said. "Sam and I used to bring livestock through here north for market. The ten plagues of Egypt wouldn't dry up that spring. It'll water a herd of cattle if you feed them to it slow enough. . . . Crick, let me see that hole in you." He unbuttoned his coat and she poked around on him. "Get your shirt off. We need to put some acid on that. Blue Duck, you're used to such things. I can't stand the sight. It gives me the vapors."

Hotsie chuckled. He and Ralph were counting the money. They had two feed sacks stuffed with bills and coins. The others groaned and hobbled around. They didn't talk much.

Blue Duck got out the carbolic acid and wound dressing and went to work. Crick sat back on his elbows and began to talk distractedly. He was worried about having shot the guard. "He pulled down on me. Course, I was the one that walked in the door with a shotgun. . . . I shouldn't never have toted that son-of-a-bitch bird gun in there. You ought to give a man a chance."

"He shot you in the gut with a Winchester, Crick. It's a fair trade," Belle said.

"Yeah, but you level a shotgun on somebody at ten feet . . ."

"Shut up. You gave that bum one chance too many as it is. Just keep quiet and think about cherry pies and vegetables. You got a respectable hole in you there."

Blue Duck worried with the wound. The bullet had entered on his left side around the lowest rib and made a fairly clean exit out the back. It hadn't apparently damaged any organs, but that was a guess based on how unpainful he kept declaring it. "Just a graze, nothing to it. Knocked off a roll of fat, that's all." Blue Duck wrapped him snugly around the belly and got him to lie back.

"Nine thousand six hundred, thereabouts," said Ralph, after a while. "What does that divide out to?"

"Sixteen hundred apiece," Belle said. "But I want to tell you something right now. We've got other business to attend to. We are going to be as strict as Pentecosts about any loot that we're carrying. We don't divide it and we don't worry about it. Just keep your mind on the work. If you start ogling the money, we're ruined. I've seen more gangs bust up on account of sloppy money than anything else. It's yours. You've earned it. But we're sticking absolutely to the plan — fifty a week plus an even share of loot. So get your mind off of it right now. We're on the trail and we're working together. You start slavering after the score and it'll sink us faster than anything."

"I think we ought to divide it up," Ralph said. "What if we was to lose you somehow?"

"It ain't good politics. Put sixteen hundred dollars in everybody's pockets and we'll be like a table of pool balls all heading for different holes. I'll keep the money, all except for the two or three hundred dollars of small money. Divide that up right now for pocket cash. I want the big bills in my saddlebags. J. B., pack them in, would you? And keep a close count on exactly how much goes where."

Blue Duck went for another drink. He was more saddle-sore than he'd ever been in his life, and he'd just gotten off the horse. Tomorrow it would be a sight. He hobbled over to the lower pool and submerged his face in the water. He withdrew and sat on his knees with it dripping down his skin. He took off his shirt and allowed the whole top of his body to fall into the pool, arms outspread. His neck and face and arms melted in the icy water. He sat back on his heels and felt his heart beat hard in his chest. He looked at the others all spread out resting, and beyond them across the rocky scrub oak hills toward the southeast. It was evening, the side of the hill just going into shadow.

Among the larger trees near the spring was one that grew at the very edge of the upper pool. There was a hole between roots that a small animal might use for a den, and the trunk looked like two separate trees grown together. He looked up at the limbs and down at the pool of water. The water had gone smooth again and he could see his face. He had a strange thought: I have been here before. It was a thought and a loosening feeling in his stomach, and it was not without a slight menace. He had been here before.

The night sky filled with clouds of light. Belle and Blue Duck had laid down their rolls off alone. At supper Belle had been talking at some length about what they were going to do next.

She seemed in good spirits. Blue Duck still felt numb from the ride.

"We're safe." She was leaning back on her saddle. "They won't get to us. We could spend the winter here and they wouldn't get to us. There aren't ten white people in the world that know about this spring. We're a few miles south of the Outlet. I guess it's 'Oklahoma Territory' now. It used to be nowhere."

"When did you first come here?"

"I don't remember. Back when I was learning the Territory. We had some stolen cow ponies, I do remember that. Sold them up in Caldwell."

"I have been here before."

"Oh yeah?" She looked over at him.

"Yes."

"I wouldn't doubt it. There were always signs of horse Indians around that spring. Fact of the matter, I found a flint bird point nor far from here one time. Pretty little thin thing, looked like it was fashioned for hummingbirds. Gave it to Pearl. . . ."

"*Iktomi.*"

"What?"

"*Iktomi.*"

"Who's that?"

Blue Duck sat for a moment gazing off, tasting a name long unremembered. "He was a giant. He made flint arrowheads in the ancient times. We made them out of steel, but we found flint heads and used them when we could. It was a big deal to find an *Iktomi* point."

She looked at him, for a moment silent. He could feel her eyes in the dark. "Are you scared of me?"

"Scared of you?"

"Yes."

He thought about that. "No. Why do you ask?"

She looked away sighing. "Anyway, what do you think? I mean the feel of it — the crew?"

"I think you better keep them very busy. We also better get Crick to a doctor."

"That old crowbait, he'll heal; don't worry about him. What do you mean 'keep them busy'?"

"Their minds will wander."

"We'll hit that morning train day after tomorrow. Put a squeeze on Enid. Maybe bust up the boomer newspaper in Kansas. Get that one out of the way and I won't be ashamed to go to Tahlequah. I don't want to go back there without something to show Joel Mayes."

"You think he will then release your boy and give you twenty thousand?"

"Don't be smart. I think he'll get Ed scheduled in John Wailer's court and pay me maybe half the money. If these galoots are still alive and ain't sulled up on me at that point, maybe we'll do some more work."

"You are very optimistic."

She grew quiet at this. They sat for a while without talking. He looked at her darkened face and saw the shadow of an expression. Without really seeing it, he knew it was the funny dead-eyed smile which was both unpleasant and remarkable to him, whether an awkward invitation or a satanically complacent demand.

Her hand touched his leg and it jolted him. He suddenly felt angry at her. It came out of nowhere and was strong, almost a ragefulness. It had no definition except that she was the cause. Her presence, her request. He had not felt anything like this toward her before. He hated her. It made him confused.

He got up and walked away, stumbling down the rock-strewn hill toward the spring. He heard the water and knelt down on all fours and drank long and deep. Sitting back on his heels, he closed his eyes and waited for it to go away. His mind was running very fast. He opened his eyes and the pool was full of stars. He must have drunk from it at night before.

17

*C*rick was not well the next morning. He looked pale and worried. Belle tried to feed him and he just held the plate. Blue Duck followed her over to the spring and said that they'd better get him to a doctor.

"He'll be all right. He's just a little rattled." She took a drink of water.

"He might be bleeding inside."

"Aren't we all." She shook off her hands and went back to the fire.

She asked Hotsie where her Phoenix Pills were. He didn't know and she complained at him for not having packed them. They sat around drinking coffee, not talking much.

Blue Duck spoke up. "Where's the nearest town?"

She threw the utensils inside the Dutch oven and tied the lid down. "Nearest real town is Caldwell, Kansas, eighty miles north."

"What's the fastest route?"

"Straight north through Enid, I guess," She slapped the other things together, carried them over to Hotsie and came back to speak more quietly to Blue Duck. "I think you better wait until we do something with this train. I wouldn't want you out there by yourself. We ought to stay together."

"Crick should be looked at by a physician."

"Crick will be looked at. Haven't you ever seen a man shot? What do you expect him to do, jump up on his horse and sing 'The Old Chisolm Trail'? He's shot. He's got a hole through his body. Now let him alone, let him sit back and look green a while. We'll get him to a damn doctor. Probably sooner than's good for him." She tightened Zero's cinch and mounted up.

On the trail they were all aware of Belle's low mood. She had neglected to bring her pills and also seemed to be having woman troubles. She was using the bit pretty hard on Zero.

Crick had no problem riding, but it was not because he was well. He could ride more comfortably than he could sit still — but he looked pale and beat. Hotsie kept doubling around asking him how he was. Hotsie was also worried about the packhorse that had been heaving last night. He was close to windbroke from the ride and kept threatening to stall.

They ran onto what looked like a temporary line camp around noon. Belle hallooed and rode toward a couple of wagons parked in a grove of dusty sweetgum near a creek. The canvas had been taken off a chuck wagon and was stretched out on the ground to protect food from flies. A cook was handling dinner for nine or ten cowboys with sowbelly and biscuits and sop and fruit and sorghum and three or four airtights of tomatoes that he was opening to pass around. He moved among them in sullen omniscience over their meal; they took things from his hand without looking. They all seemed to be very curious about the strangers; their eyes were clear as little boys' and steady as snakes'. Blue Duck had always admired a cowboy. They put up with dental work — to a man — like champions, and when they were sober they paid cash.

These were mostly younger fellows. There was one Negro among them. They appeared to be suspicious but didn't slow down on their food. The boss was quite suspicious when Belle told him, after some conversation, that her crew was out checking on the cattle situation for the Cherokee government.

"Mind if I ask your handle?"

"Don't mind, no." She smiled without giving it.

"We've been having a little trouble down in this quarter is all the reason I ask," the boss drawled, waving the flies off his plate. "In fact I've had so damn much trouble I've just about lost my sense of humor." He smiled back.

Belle looked at him for a moment. "That's why we're here. Have you been having night burnings?"

He still smiled. "Yeah, we get a few now and again."

"Lost any cattle to them?"

"I guess we've lost about two hundred head of beef to lit fires. That's this season. Outright. That's two hundred outright."

"Know anything about who's setting them?"

He stood up and put his plate down, stiff-backed. He straightened up with a menacing apology in his smile. He wore old-fashioned high-legged boots. "I'm still not sure who I'm talking to."

She told him again that they were agents of the Cherokee Tribe, serving at the orders of Joel Mayes.

"Mayes, huh?" he said. "Don't believe I remember what he looks like. Can you remind me?" He did up his brow in a fake look of curiosity.

Belle smiled at this little test and for a moment didn't answer. "You wouldn't be a Texan, would you?"

"Yes ma'am. I'm from west Texas."

"I had just about forgotten the way a sure-enough Texas man talked. . . . Joel Mayes looks like one thing in the world. He looks like a catfish and he talks like a professor and he could charm a wolf to play the fiddle."

The Texan appeared to seriously consider that. "Yes. I believe I remember meeting him now. What was it you were asking?"

"Who's been nightburning you?"

"There's some say one thing, some say another. It ain't all agreed on."

"Who do you think it is?"

"Personally? I think it's some of these hay shakers down from Enid. Can't prove it though. It ain't much work to start a fire right now. You can smoke your cigarette sloppy out here and barbecue a hundred head — either that or spread them out so far it takes a week to round them back up. Whoever it is, they don't have to be too smart to get away with it."

"Have you seen any strangers riding in your quarter?"

"Oh you always see them coming through — on their way down to the Territory and so on. I ain't got no time to mess with them. Try to keep them from cutting the fences is all. I have enough to occupy me with five thousand thirsty cows."

"Are you keeping them alive?"

"Well I wouldn't go so far as to say that. We're doing the best we can, I guess. Biggest problem is water. I've rode this range for eight years and I sure ain't seen anything like it. Water and crowding. The Association is paying big money for the lease, and they're packing them in to make up for it. Circle Bar brand — that's Wilson and Brothers, my outfit — used to border on the North Cimarron. Last year we was cut off from it to make room for the Drumm outfit. That's Cross and Crescent. All we got for water now is a few dry creeks and mud wallows. I ain't saying Drumm is tight. We've drove over there for watering a number of times now. But you can't go on a drive every time your cows get thirsty. I've had my boys digging in the creek beds as much as riding. I'd say if it doesn't break pretty soon, we might have to just take out north with the whole herd come season."

"Be a mighty big drive," Crick said. He had a feverish grin on his face.

The Texan looked over at him. "Yeah. Well. Last year was bad, this year it's a die-up. The Lord and the sodbusters are putting a squeeze on us."

"Have you had any theft from your herd?" Belle asked.

He waved the flies out of his face and off his neck with a languid gesture. "That's the one thing we haven't been worried with too much to my knowledge. The brands up farther north now — I've heard some tales from Texas Land and Cattle and a few others. The outfits on the Kansas border have always been bothered with it, and nowadays you hear the ones around Enid — Coffee Pot brand and them boys — talking some about it."

"Did you ever catch a thief on your range?"

"Nothing that walked on two legs." He stirred the flies with the same slow gesture.

"Why night burnings and no theft?"

He looked down and considered for a moment. "Maybe because they ain't after beef much as something else."

"What's that?"

He looked up and shook his head once. "Don't know. Excuse me, but what did you say your name was?"

"Becky Sharp. This is my *segundo*, Mr. Bird." She gestured at Blue Duck.

Blue Duck had some trouble with his expression at that point. The Texan didn't quite know how to respond. Belle obviously had a number of reasons not to give her real name, one being that it was a dirty name to honest cowboys. To tell this man that her name was Belle Starr and she was here to help him would have been about like saying her name was Santa Ana and she was organizing Sunday picnics.

"Well glad to meet you. . . ." The Texan tipped his hat and started to walk over to the wagon.

"Let me ask you one more question. If you could request the Tribe to help you in any way, what would you have them do?"

He considered that. "Dance a rain dance, I guess." He didn't want to talk anymore. He looked burdened and tired and a little impatient.

"I don't believe they're much good at that." Belle persisted. "Could they help you with these boomers?"

"They'll have to answer that themselves. For the money they're being paid, they ought to keep their borders, I guess. I've got work to do, Miz . . ."

"Sharp," Belle said, "Becky Sharp."

"Oh, yes. Miz Sharp. I knew it started with a 'B' and an 'S.' "

Belle laughed out loud and her face flushed. "Good luck, Circle Bar. By the way, you don't know where we might find a doctor, do you?"

"Nearest is Enid. They've got a couple of old crackers up there that call themselves doctors."

"Have you ever been to Enid?"

"We get up there now and then. It's mostly canvas. They ain't too friendly to us."

"Do you mind if we water our horses here?" Hotsie asked.

"There ain't really a place to do it here. We've dragged a hole out in the creekbed, but it ain't what you'd call big swimming. It'll hardly keep our ponies watered when we're over here. You might do better over on the North Cimarron. There's a drift fence out there. Take around east of it if that's where you're going."

They rode across the dry creek and out onto the prairie. The wind came at them head-on, so steady and hot that it seemed like no wind at all. The country was flat and treeless and rimmed by low hills at great distances. They rode across a vast flat-bottomed bowl of grass that seemed almost to have been shaped for big herds of livestock. The scars of what looked like two separate fires fingered across the plain. Some of the loners — even at a distance — looked sick. There was a smell of death in the air. Buzzards coasted low on the wind as thick and busy as flies. In a bald spot, an old mud wash, was a heap of burned corpses still smoking, and out on the prairie were more of these pyres scattered around, being visited by the buzzards.

Belle led them at a good pace across a corner of the plain to a rim of hills. From the top they could see railroad tracks off to the northeast, a shimmering line across the flatness. They descended and rode toward it. The sick packhorse had been getting worse and worse, and finally she lay down. J. B. and Hotsie tried to get him up. The others waited, hot, depressed, not talking. Crick sat on his horse looking blank. They finally had to unpack and shoot her. Blue Duck watched while they tried to parcel out and repack the load. He had an overpowering urge to be back in Tulsa. Back in Tulsa doing anything. In his office in the Masonic Building packing fillings, pulling teeth, making a set of Vulcanites for some old grubber with no likelihood of pay — anything, so long as the day had hope of ending and he could go home and make his dinner and read a book in the drowsy flicker of his parlor lantern. . . .

They distributed most of the valuables, left the pack saddle and panniers with the dead horse and headed on toward the tracks. When they finally got there, nobody dismounted. Belle seemed lost in thought. The tracks, flanked by a telegraph line, were straight and endless in both directions.

"We going to blow it up or what?" J. B. finally asked.

Ralph laughed. He burst out in a funny loud way and the others laughed with him. They sat around on their horses laughing like fools. All except Belle. She didn't appear to hear them. She frowned and seemed absorbed in thought. Blue Duck remembered the state she got into back at the hotel in Fort Smith. Her lips moved a little. She finally looked up. "Okay. Any of you know how to handle dynamite?"

Ralph burst out more uncontrollably, and the others laughed perhaps as much at his hilarity as anything funny. Even Crick laughed. After a minute Ralph actually seemed to be hurting with laughter, hunched down and drawn double with it. He seemed to be trying to stop. Normally close, mean, pale, sarcastic, he tottered on his saddle holding onto the horn with an agonized red faceful of laughter. Blue Duck smiled along with them but with an ominous feeling. There was something queer about coming onto a railroad line across this infinity of prairie and wondering how to blow it up. Belle had gotten down and was standing in the middle of the tracks looking north. She walked a ways, tripping once on a tie. She looked small and hot and worried.

Ralph wiped his face with a handkerchief. "Let's divide up the money and get the hell out of this place."

Belle glanced up at him and walked back down the track. "You can go any time, Ralph."

"Thank you Belle, I appreciate that." He dabbed his whole face with the handkerchief.

"If you do, the score ain't any part of yours. You understand that, I guess." She pulled her gun and without any hesitation shot above their heads at the telegraph wire. She aimed more carefully and shot again. J. B.'s horse rared. She walked off the track past them and from closer range blasted an insulator; the wire parted with a twang and fell limp.

Ralph looked at her, glazy-eyed from laughter, and shook his head slightly. He said nothing more for now.

The only one among them who had any experience with dynamite was Crick, and he wasn't feeling very optimistic. He didn't think that an effective charge could be set on a flat roadbed. They needed a bridge or a hillside to knock rocks down from. They rode north. It wasn't very far to Enid, so they needed to find something before too many miles.

The first "bridge" they came to was a squat, solid trestle over an arroyo. Crick shook his head. Belle and J. B. made suggestions and he just kept saying no. "You'll risk your dynamite," he said. "That little job ain't too breakable."

Belle was irritated. "We won't be finding anything along this track made out of stick matches, Crick. What the hell are you looking for?"

Crick was pale and he spoke quietly. "Like I said, either a sure-enough bridge or an overhang."

"I don't think there is a bridge. The North Cimarron runs east of here."

"Don't tell me we're going to camp dry again tonight," Hotsie said.

"We've got enough problems, John. Be quiet."

"We already lost one horse today."

Belle looked at him angrily. "That horse was a nag to start with. We shouldn't have brought her. All of you guys — I feel like I'm riding with a gang of schoolboys. All you do is drag your asses around in circles and look for something to complain about. Quit *looking* at me."

"Tell you what," Ralph said. He was back to his usual tone. "I don't think it's so much us as something else crossing you, Belle.

Maybe it's the moon." He raised his eyebrows slightly and one of the others chuckled.

She stood between the tracks with her hands on her hips. "You mean because it's my time of the month?"

"Oh now I didn't say that."

Another chuckle, nervous.

"Because if that's what you mean, Ralph, all I can say is it's too bad you ain't man enough to take a woman for what she is."

"What's that?"

"I can't give you a definition. Something different from what you and your boyfriends giggle about between poker games, anyway."

"Whew!" He shook his head. "She's raggin me official, ain't she boys?"

"Ain't raggin you Ralph. Just try to keep your mouth closed like Hotsie and you'll feel better. Come on. We're wasting time."

She took out at a canter alongside the roadbed. The sun was violent. Blue Duck wished that he was still a dentist. That seemed to be the theme today. Belle remained in control of herself, at least he was thankful for that. She'd gotten strange there for a while but had apparently come back to her senses. He glanced at the fat saddlebags across Zero's back and wondered why he felt protective about her. He sure didn't *like* her.

He heard a yell. Crick had fallen off his horse. Belle and Hotsie were the first ones with him on the ground. He looked embarrassed and confused. "No, it don't hurt." He grinned. "I just went to sleep, got dizzy or something. Lucky I didn't get hung up."

Belle poured a shot of bourbon down his throat and Blue Duck took off the sweat-soaked bandages to have a look at the wound. It was a little darkened, but he couldn't tell anything by it. He was still suspicious of internal bleeding. The wound was in the area of the spleen.

He sterilized and rewrapped it and they got back on the trail.

By early dusk they came onto a bridge over a dry creek cutting between low hills. Belle wanted to blow the bridge and head on north immediately. She asked Crick's advice about how to do it. Crick was grinning constantly now. He grinned and grinned. "Stack it in the struts and light the fuse, I guess. Ain't much complicated about it. You'll have to blow it more than once to get enough of it loose."

J. B. capped a couple of sticks and scrambled down the hillside and shinnied up a pillar of the bridge. For a big and normally slow-moving man he was agile. "I'm going to light it," he shouted.

"Just be sure you can get yourself down," Belle yelled back.

He started the fuse sputtering, climbed down from the bridge and hotfooted it down the creekbed to hide. The rest of them took shelter below the track. The explosion rolled out across the prairie, and they climbed out for a look. J. B. was already standing in the creekbed with his hands on his hips.

"How'd she do?" Belle shouted.

He studied it for a while. "Looks like it didn't do a damn thing." His voice sounded quiet after the noise of the explosion.

"Well get up there and lay some more. *Blow* the sucker."

Hotsie carried down four more sticks, cap and fuse, and J. B. laid it on the same spot. The explosion bounced like a giant ball this time, and J. B. climbed up to have a closer look. "Knocked some of it loose. But hell I'm going to have to set five or six more loads to get this bridge really rickety. I don't know if we have that much dynamite. What I need is an ax. I'd chop the damn thing apart."

"Why don't you blow the legs. To hell with them little struts," Belle said.

"Be hard to do." Crick sat up against a rock with his arms wrapped around his knees.

"Why?"

"Because they're two foot square. It'd take a lot of dynamite."

"Well hell, he can climb around blowing struts all day and there'll still be a cobweb of them. I say he ought to take the legs right out from under it. How many sticks do we have?"

"Twenty-some left," Crick said.

"Isn't that enough?"

Crick shook his head, grin faltering. He looked confused. "I don't know. Hell I ain't . . . I ain't . . ." One hand came up and seemed to feel the air in front of him. He looked puzzled. "I ain't feeling so good."

Blue Duck got Belle off alone to talk. "He's sick. He's bleeding inside. He won't make it riding any farther."

"What do you want to do?"

"I want to stop that train tomorrow morning and take him to Enid. You can blow the bridge after it passes."

"You want to hail a trainful of people that saw you rob a bank yesterday. That's smart. Instead of Crick bleeding a little bit you want to hitch a ride up to Enid so both of you can hang."

"Our faces were covered. I can say we're cowboys working for Circle Bar and there was an accident."

"You've got better sense. That bank job was the biggest thing that ever happened to Guthrie. Every one of the people on that train will have talked about it at dinner and supper and woke up to chew it some more for breakfast. They'll have read descriptions and meditated about it in the outhouse. You'd do better for yourself and Crick to lay your head over the tracks then to hail that train."

"If his spleen is busted, the last thing he ought to be doing is riding."

"I ain't in the mood for this shit," she spat. "I've got a gangful of green punks and a straw boss made out of pussywillow. What the hell is wrong with you? Are you just trying to get away? Is that it?"

"Crick Watson is sick. His guts are full of blood. If we get him to a doctor, maybe he'll pull through."

"I know what it is. You're worried about that train, aren't you? You're worried about a wreck."

He looked at her. "Okay. I'm worried about a wreck."

"There won't be nothing but boomer scum on that train. They're taking over this Nation like a plague. They want everything free and nothing earned. They're walking over the tribes like they hadn't ever existed, much less lived here sixty years.

They're Bible-thumping little hypocrites a-rubbing their legs and squirting and laying eggs like grasshoppers in ever inch of dirt."

Blue Duck said nothing.

"Don't give me that look. Far as I'm concerned, it's war. I thought you'd know something about that. I thought you had some backbone against these scum."

"Scum?"

"What?"

"Who's scum?" He tried to smile.

"Well ain't you the big philosopher-dentist of the Oklahoma Nation. Look, we ain't doing anything at all for Joel Mayes less we do it big."

He looked at her. Her face was strange as a mask. She looked ugly. He turned and started to walk away.

"You ain't no wild Indian," she hissed. "You don't even know what to do with a woman."

He stopped but did not turn. He looked at the ground before him and felt very tired. Exhausted. He looked up and saw the others slouching around on the roadbed, glancing over toward him and Belle. Crick sat up against a boulder like a doll, eyes closed.

18

Surrounded by treachery. She had cut this little wire between Guthrie and Enid, but all out across the Territory the other little wires were tapping and humming, singing *bank robbery, six persons, one female suspect* . . . which was okay. It was the chance she'd taken. But now they'd lost a packhorse, and to carry it all they looked like a band of gypsy peddlers weighted down with pots and pans, and Crick was sick on her and Blue Duck was stalling and Ralph Bunch was threatening to pull out and she didn't have any pills and the God damn things were more important than she had thought to keep an old woman from falling out because the headache was back and the woman complaint was nothing compared to the headache. And the silly dynamite didn't work. Whoever heard of that? It wouldn't blow the bridge down. She'd never played with dynamite, but common sense said that if you put seven sticks of it at the base of a bridge pillar it would blow it away like a toothpick in a tornado. That was not what happened. What happened was that they had one more bang, a little bigger this time, which shattered the base of the pillar all right, but not high enough up to eliminate support. And she couldn't decide whether to use the few sticks they had left on the other pillars or just to set one big load between ties in the middle of the bridge and see what happened. This was sure not the kind of dynamite she'd heard the boys talking about in the old days blowing a bank safe agog six feet off the floor. It was some cheap boomer doofud, probably made to pop off and celebrate land runs more than do any work.

J. B. went on and set more charges under the other pillars — so she guessed that was the program. The result was no more satisfying: the bases were cracked and knocked a little askew, but they would settle to the ground before the bridge would collapse. It would have to be burned. J. B. hated the idea of a fire and Blue Duck hated the idea of a fire and she hated the idea of a fire, but that was the only way. Crick hated the idea as much as the rest of them, but then Crick was not with them anymore. Crick was elsewhere.

"Get it started down that grass slope and it'll be hell to pay," J. B. said, sweating dirt and cordite. "Nobody will be able to stop it. Them cowboys will have five thousand head of cattle loose to the four winds and they won't have no way to fight it except to drag carcasses or some such nonsense. I wouldn't do it."

So J. B. had joined the others. It was a total mutiny. Her head was banging the same slow concussion over and over, like the same number repeated, one, one, one, one, and she had to go off down the arroyo and hide behind a boulder to stuff the shreds of her second shirt into her pants because otherwise it would stink and bleed down her legs and she'd lose what little control she did have, which wasn't much. She needed a bath. She needed a friend. Hotsie. But Hotsie didn't have any pull with the others. Ralph was the canker. She'd like to place a rattlesnake in his little smart mouth. She had to keep a hold on Blue Duck.

She had to keep a hold.

Her boy was the worst of it all. A woman ought to be able to look to her own children for comfort, but what had the Lord given her but one glue-brain and one whore, and what had she done but go and make it a hundred times worse.

What's wrong with you, old woman?

Crick was sitting up against the rock looking like shit soup. She wished he'd at least put his damned hat on his head if he was going to die. He was talking a lot, too, which he normally did only when he was drunk. He sounded like a line rider after six months on the range. He was talking so intensely that they were all drifting around him at a distance as if embarrassed. Just like them, the chicken-livered low-range Okie shithooks. A man talking like that needed an ear. She brushed past them and got on her knees and felt his forehead. He was cold. The pupils of his eyes were black depthless orbs and he was breathing poorly. "Crick. What the hell's wrong with you?"

He grinned — a slack string across his face. "I was telling them that I think something's kind of loose in there. I ought not to gone in there and blowed a man down with turkey shot. Ain't the best ticket out of this old carcass. I'm kind of talking I guess. It keeps me flat down. I need to be flat down. . . ."

"You're breathing silly. That'll make you dizzy. I know because I do it myself on these headaches sometime. Stop it. Just slow down and breathe regular. You're kind of pale, too. I want you to put your head down."

He carefully folded his hat — an old dove-brown felt — as flat as a handkerchief and put it on the ground. Then he put his head down and lay on his side. She had him lie on his back. "Try it quiet for a minute. If you set to spinning, I'll listen to you. I think you're going to do all right. I already see some sense coming back to your face. Just lie there like a rug. I'm going to stay here with you now. I've been nursing horsethieves all my life, I can sure take care of you. Hotsie, bring me the canteen. J. B., come here. . . . Listen to me. I want you to get them together and clear away the weeds around that bridge. Set it up to burn. It'll take some time. Take the best care you can to keep down a range fire. We have enough men to stomp out anything that gets loose. Do it now — a cleared space all the way around it."

"I don't like a fire," J. B. said.

"Every fire ain't the one that burned down your house fifteen

228

years ago, J. B. Now get down there and start earning your wages. And the rest of you — Ralph, Hotsie — go on and help him."

"How are we supposed to do it? We ain't even got a shovel," Ralph said, skulking behind J. B.

"Why don't you just go down there and talk at the bushes, Ralph; that'll be all you need to do. You'll disintegrate a square acre just swiveling your mouth around speaking in normal tones."

Hotsie laughed.

J. B. was still stalled.

Blue Duck sat on a rock looking at the ground.

The sun was setting. Crick made a gurgling noise and sat up very quickly. He looked around as if for something he'd forgotten. For a moment he looked terrified, then the grin straggled back onto his face. "A fire, did you say?"

"Lie down. We're trying to get rid of this bridge is all. Just lie down."

"Don't set no fires, for God sake. That bunch grass is gunpowder. Bushes will go up like Chinese fountains. Lightning will do it. Backfiring is rough, you got the wind and your cows to worry about, sometimes there just ain't no way. We was on the West Shawnee, I had me a gentle-broke pony cost me two years' wages, only one in the outfit had my own horse, balance, boy I mean, he was as good at cutting as any quarterhorse and even-tempered as a bell mare. . . ."

"Lie down, Crick, damn it, and be quiet a while. And quit breathing like a bellows. Just breathe smooth."

He looked at her as if embarrassed. "Think I might be in a little trouble. . . . Need to keep flat down. Things keeps a-getting round. *Round,* you know . . ."

Belle took Crick by the shoulder and laid him back.

"Sky kindly makes me to spin. Lately ain't nothing but dead cows one after another, they shit a green stream when you hit em sometimes. That's the truth, wield up that nine-pound hammer just above the eyes, they got them eyes you know, God damn they got eyes, I don't know how the Lord could put eyes like that in a creature we was supposed to eat, I have done everything you can do to a cow in fifty years of life, I mean just about everything, haze em, splay em, hunt em, doctor em, tail ride, flank, point man, smash their brains, sing to them, ain't the tune so much as the way you're feeling I've noticed that, hell I can't hardly sing a good choir tune much less these midnight solos but if you're feeling straight your voice shows it and they'll keep quiet even if it's a restless night, they say a man will shit like that sometimes when he goes out, I hope I don't if I do . . . Lord God I just hope I don't. . . . Had this horse I was saying, sharp as they come, gentle-broke you know, bought him off the old Indian that did it, nobody knows about breaking a horse like an Indian, hell this old fellow would spend the first two weeks just talking to an unbroke horse making friends, then he'd spend another week talking loud and waving a blanket at him, get him used to the idea of noise and hassle, show him it didn't hurt him none, then he'd spend a few days just a-touching him, touching him on the back and the loins and the crown and on his face and legs even, his stifle and all over, days I mean, then he'd start to putting both arms up over that horse's back, draping his arms up there and putting a little weight on him, lean against him, horse would get uneasy and bolt, well he'd just let him go, put a little more weight on him the next day until finally he'd put all his weight on him and hell by then the horse don't care a bit, he gets aboard and it's as common as a drink of water, he just trots on off, ain't no buckin to it, that's the truth. I was a contract breaker there for a while when I was still limber enough for it, and it ain't so good a method, five bucks a head, I mean I rode some maneaters, go from ranch to ranch there some weeks until my lungs was shook loose and rattling in my chest like marbles, spit blood, too. Ranch to ranch. Boy oh boy, I had . . ."

"Shut up here long enough to get this drink anyway." Belle handed him the canteen and held his head up for a drink.

Blue Duck was still sitting on a rock looking at the ground. J. B. and Hotsie and Ralph were off in a cluster.

Crick wouldn't keep down, so she moved over and put his head in her lap. He was embarrassed but seemed to appreciate it through all the fret. She put her hand to his temple and stroked him lightly. She noticed for the first time why he wore his hair long: the top of one of his ears was cropped off. Got caught somewhere thieving livestock, no doubt. And no doubt it was shameful to him — the reason why he had been living in town working wages at the stockyard.

Let them mutter among themselves. Let the dentist sit on his rock and contemplate the dirt with great seriousness. Let the scheme break up before it got a good start. To hell with it. She stroked Crick's head and listened to him. Let him talk. Let the night come and the morning come and that trainful of clods ride on to Enid. Didn't make any difference anyway. The tracks were laid. She brushed the flies off his face and resigned herself to listen. She reminded him to breathe more quietly, but it didn't do much good. He was talking because he was scared of cutting loose, floating off — hell, she could float off going to the outhouse. This headache was remarkable. It was a good thing she didn't have any Phoenix Pills or she'd be eating them like popcorn of a winter night. It was the kind of headache that reached down into her jaw. Crick's monologue floated in and out of awareness. The dentist continued to sit on his ass. J. B. and Hotsie went down by the bridge and started plucking at the weeds but not like they intended to really do the work. Ralph hovered around talking at them. She might just have to shoot that punk. How did she ever get hooked up with such a ridiculous crew, anyway? She should have paid more attention to that end of things. Now it was too late.

"Why don't you make some supper, Blue Duck?" He looked up. "If you don't have any objections, I mean."

Crick continued to augur at a hundred words a minute. She gave up telling him to quit breathing fast and just stroked his old harassed brow and held his head to her lap. She didn't know what else to do. If the dentist was right and he had a ruptured spleen, every minute outside that bank was borrowed time. He was talking like he wanted to get his whole life out, shoveling down through the memories like a miner loading cars. There was still a pitiful kind of grin to his mouth but he was talking more quietly at least now that she was holding his head.

Blue Duck went over and began wrestling with the gear. There was something funny in the air — besides the smell of dynamite. Something in the evening breeze that was striking up.

". . . and at these dances, course, it'd be hard to find much in the way of white women so we'd some of us put a neckerchief on our right arms and that meant we was a female, called it the heifer brand, be surprised how it wasn't too many of us joked about it, they was just the heifers tonight and that was it, sashaying around like a woman and then some. I played heifer, didn't hurt me none, nosir, and I sure got to dance, at a line camp out on the plain one winter I remember we run out of books and stuff and played this game called 'Know Your Cans,' memorize the labels on the tomatoes and peaches and tobacco and everything and have to recite it back, you know some of them labels got a good lot of words on them and you'd be standing up there a while to get it all out, tonic bottles are the best, they'll get a whole blamed book on one of them little labels with cures and wonders and witnesses and all such as that, only thing wrong with that horse — Jawbone I called him cause I partly had to buy him on jawbone — he was bridle-wise and balanced and smart as an angel, but he couldn't stand certain people, bit my straw boss on the face early on a trail drive, I'm not talking about the hand or arm but the face, reached out and took such a hunk out of him until he wanted to shoot him on the spot, said there was plenty of horses in the remuda, told him I didn't want no horses from the remuda, I owned that horse and he wasn't going to be shot, he said this horse is a treacherous pet that ought to be hamstrung and left to the wolves, I said well he wasn't going to be hamstrung long as I owned him, I'd pay him for the damage, and he said you'll pay all right, Watson, and sure enough I did, son of a bitch put me on the dust end of three thousand head of Devons for eight hundred miles, like to clogged my lungs before we got to Kansas, wonder if you got a little whiskey for me, just a drink I know it ain't much left . . ."

"Shut up, just hush, we'll get you some whiskey. I could use some myself." Belle eased his head down and went for the bottle. Blue Duck complained that he couldn't find anything but salt side for supper.

"Go kill a calf, then."

He looked at her over the fire with his cool and patient expression — the one that drove her into dithers. She held her voice quiet. "Send Hotsie to do it. Crick's running at the mouth. I think he needs some food. Cut a thin steak and give it a good scorch. Maybe we can bring him around with some red meat. You don't have any laudanum in that dentist kit, do you?"

"He doesn't have local pain, does he?"

"Ain't for him, it's for me."

"I don't have any. Do you still intend to burn the bridge?"

"Just fix supper. It's getting down to one thing at a time now."

When she carried the bottle back to Crick he was on all fours down the slope from where he'd been sitting. He had tried to move and fallen. She fed him some whiskey and got him to lie back and put his head in her lap. He talked and talked. After a while she heard a gunshot down the arroyo. The stars came out in the east, but the sky was clouding up in the west. He tossed and groaned, words became utterances, he receded until finally only his lips moved. She took a few nips on the bottle and tried not to think. Tonight was not for thinking.

The wind got snappy and even a little cool, and when she saw a tic of lightning in the western sky she realized what was in the air. The smell of a storm. It had been so long that the possibility seemed strange. A thunderhead. You could see them a hundred miles away out here and four out of five times never get a drop, but it sure gave the wind a nice feel. And something to hope for.

"There's a storm out there," she told Crick. His head was motionless in her lap. "It's going to rain. I see lightning, feel it in the wind. You rest up now, we're going to have us a free bath. Wash the dirt and itch off this old sunburned face. Yessir, we're going to hope for that. Rain." She put her hand on his heart and hunched down closer to him. "Rain — you hear that? And you ain't got a herd to worry about either. Just your old no-good self. Just you and the rain and nothing to sing at to keep calm. Nothing to lose. You ain't got to ride clockwise, ain't got to ride counterclockwise. Ain't got a cow to your name. Ain't got a thing but your old busted-up carcass and the rain. It's gonna feel good. Sweet. You're gonna say Lord thank you, it has done finally rained. You're gonna say Lord thank you for filling these rivers. Lord thank you for taking the dirt off my face, thank you for washing the dirt boogers out of my old stupid long hair. You're gonna feel good. Cause when it rains out here brother it don't fool around. Listen to me, Crick. Think of rain and how it's gonna be good to be clean. Lie still and wait quiet for your supper now. We're gonna feed you in a minute."

Her legs were asleep but she didn't feel like she'd better move just now. His heart was hitting light and fast. Stars were going out all across the sky, the wind picked up and lightning was beginning to rumble. Her head still felt like Sunday morning in a whorehouse and she was getting the shakes. Hotsie came over to say he had killed a calf and meat was on the way.

"You got that brush cleared away?" she asked.

"That's hard to do. We have no tools."

"Maybe this rain will come. We'll fire it then."

"How is he?"

"You want to take him over for a while? I think he's finally sleeping."

Hotsie made a funny nervous little sound in his throat. "I got to see about the horses."

"Go on then. Hurry up. Maybe a little something to eat will make him rest easier."

Unable to stand the cramped legs any longer, she stretched them out and lay back on her elbows with Crick's head still heavy in her lap. The wind was edged with rain now. Sure enough rain.

She could feel the possibility in her face and arms and all under her clothes. Lightning and thunder got closer together, dull flickers and thuds becoming trees of cracking light. Crick rolled his head and twitched and Belle had a feeling he was getting worse fast. A ball of light formed on the hill below and rolled down the incline like a blue pinwheel. Hotsie brought meat; she tried to feed some to Crick but he rejected it. She tried everything to get him to eat — down to old baby tricks — but he just shook his head and looked nauseated. She tore into her steak like a cougar. The lightning surrounded them now, illuminating the whole plain below with curtains of light. The rain came in fist-sized drops hitting the ground with hard separate thumps. It worried Crick. She needed to get away from him for a while. She had J. B. help her carry him down to the fire and went over to check the horses. Hotsie had them all hitched and hobbled and taken care of. Thunder smashed against the top of her head like a hammer on a rotten peach. She wished it would just go ahead and bust it open; it sure couldn't hurt any worse. In the lightning she caught sight of Blue Duck wrestling with something over by the saddles. He was chopping and whittling on a scrub oak trunk. She saw what he was doing immediately and set to work helping. She should have thought of it herself. They could get Crick to Enid before morning on a travois. One of them could haul him and the others could stay back here and take care of the bridge.

The raindrops were huge and still widely spaced smacks on the dust. She took off her shirt. Her skin yearned like a dry plant for water. They worked together without talking much. The water slapped her face and upper body, and she took off her pistols and the rest of her clothes, and sat down to work tying support stems on the travois. There was more than one way to take a bath. To hell with it if they could see her. They were big boys. To hell with it if they could see evidence of her woman trouble, the rain was coming.

But while the storm grew more extravagant in light and wind, the rain kept holding back. The big drops stopped entirely after a while and the smell seemed to go out of the wind, leaving nothing but bursts of dry light. She whittled and tied and heard herself talking out loud, begging it to come on. Come on and do it, wash the trail dust and nervous sweat and headache and woman trouble off of this old sore carcass, wash the sickness out of this season, remind her — remind the earth — that there's an end. Her skin sensed the air with declining hope — to the point that she felt a little silly with her clothes off. The lightning showed Ralph standing not far away looking at her, and she had the immediate urge to be closer to her pistols. She spoke to him first. "Go on about your business, Ralph. I'm hoping for a bath."

"We got more meat if you want it."

"Thanks. I'll mind that later."

She did not know how long it took them. Perhaps two hours. The wind grew hopeful again, big drops again fell, but still it refused to cut loose. The storm continuing to tantalize her, she grew increasingly aware of her body, of the dirt and sweat and grime covering her skin. She needed some pills. Pills, laudanum, something. In her itching skin, she needed it. She tried to get her mind off of it. She tied sticks together with rawhide. She cut the fenders off of two saddles and made a sling on the travois, using the gar tooth that she had tried to give Blue Duck for an awl. She tied down two saddle blankets over that. Blue Duck collared the trees on his horse and she lay in it and bounced a little. It was a piss-poor job but would probably carry to Enid.

She went over to the fire. The butchered calf lay over in the dirt. "Is he still alive?"

J. B. looked astonished. She had forgotten that she was naked. Or maybe she hadn't. Maybe she was doing exactly as she had done with that band of Crows south of the Arkansas, slinging her womanbody like a weapon against these intractable God damned slow galoots.

"*Is he alive?*"

"Yes."

"Well then get him tied down to that travois."

Hotsie turned his back and refused to look at her. Ralph spat two projectiles of saliva into the fire. "Where you going in your birthday suit?"

"To a wake. You want to come along?"

"Taking that saddlebag of money with you?"

"One of two things is going to happen. I'm either leaving out of here in five minutes with Crick and Blue Duck and that saddlebag or I'm going to let Blue Duck drag him alone and the rest of us will stay here and fire this bridge and go on up to meet them in Enid tomorrow. Now which of those do you like the best? You tell me."

"If I heard an offer, I'd make a bid," Ralph muttered.

"I don't like the idea of burning it," J. B. said. "We've still got some dynamite. . . ."

She moved up closer to the campfire, trembling with shamelessness. She could feel the blood on her leg. She came right up to the campfire, almost straddling it. The sight must have been repulsive. She would not have been able to look upon it herself. Not just the uncleanness but the whole sagging forty-year-old body, the hatchet face in light that pointed the chin and deepened the lines and sags. Her skin was itching, itching.

"Go on!" Hotsie said, back still to her.

"Go on what?" she said.

"Take him to Enid!" He sounded mad.

"Not with that saddlebag," Ralph said.

"Let Blue Duck take him then, *hotepa!* We will clean out the bushes. We will burn the bridge. *Kanima!*"

"Everybody agree on that?" she asked.

"*Kanima!*"

"Okay. Keep your britches on. Go on over there while we've got the lightning. Get it ready to burn."

J. B. had once beaten a man to death for setting a fire; it was against his nature to help with this. He tore away the surrounding dry vegetation angrily, pulling up big clumps of bush and weeds and ripping up small scrub oak by the roots and dragging them away from the bridge. He was mightily crossed by this. He told her to wait with the fire, there was still brush to clear, but she began to nurse flames in two places on the frame of the bridge. The wood was relatively green and hard to light, but she persisted and one place finally took. It was very slow in spreading. While she worked at it, J. B. kept methodically tearing brush off the hillsides and along the wash, cursing and complaining all the while. He would have preferred robbing the damn train to this. Ralph worked desultorily at clearing. Belle had given up herding him.

First light of dawn had come before the fire had spread. Belle concentrated on it for hours. It gave her a task — a consuming task for the nervous state she was in. J. B. and Hotsie used saddle blankets to beat out little grass fires that began to crop up. The possibility of a thunderstorm had not entirely disappeared. The sky remained cloudy and the wind continued to gust, making it hard to keep up with chips and cinders falling down from the bridge.

By dawn the bridge crackled and blew and rained fire onto the ground. J. B. worked like the devil stomping and smothering flames. A room-sized clump of brush caught — a torch exploding into a conflagration that threatened to spread down the grass slope onto the plain. J. B. yelled at them to take cover, took two capped sticks of dynamite and threw them into the brush. The explosion blew out the fire but spread sparks in a wide radius. He yelled at them for help. He dragged and swatted and danced on the fires that continued to spread. He tore up burning clumps of brush by the roots and threw them into the wash. He screamed at Ralph to get his ass down here with a blanket or he'd break his arm.

Belle marveled at him. J. B. did *not* want to be the cause of a prairie fire. Normally slow and unassertive, he became a wild man. He tore up bouquets of burning ironweed. He directed Hotsie and Ralph to stomp out flames wandering toward another big brush pile.

The heat of the burning trestle was much greater than what

had been expected — by all but J. B. He knew about fire. He had lived with it in his heart. Fire was his secret enemy, his public enemy, the enemy of his sleep. He had once told Belle that his dreams always ended in fire. Belle was near him when he looked up from his smoking blanket, surrounded by little fires, off at the brush that Ralph and Hotsie were supposed to be guarding. Part of it had burst into flame. In a few seconds the entire heap was a monument of flame. J. B. looked over at her. His eyebrows were singed. He looked sad. "It's shedding too many sparks. Can't keep up with it."

He dropped his blanket and stalked down the wash to the bridge pillars. Fire rained around him in chunks. He put his shoulder to a splintered pillar and shoved on it. He spread his legs out and shoved back and forth, getting his back into it, back and arms, head lowered, and it was on fire at the top and splintered and fell beside him with a mighty crack. He went to another damaged pillar and put his back to it. His hair caught on fire and he put it out with an almost gentle combing and put himself low against the pillar and shoved hard. He was trying to knock the bridge down. That didn't make sense because when it fell, he'd be under it. He had no luck with the second pillar and went to a third. The brush pile was spreading too fast to keep up with. It was walking out onto the prairie. It was hopeless. Belle went up over the track to check the horses.

"What is he doing?" Hotsie asked.

"Trying to kill himself." She went over and pulled off a shot to get his attention. He did not look up. She walked closer and he still refused to notice so she went under the bridge and stood in his face. "J. B. it's too late. We're going to have to leave."

Fire dropped around them like rain. He looked up, scorched face somehow innocent. "What?"

"It's too late! Get out of there before you catch fire."

He stood up and looked at her. He ticked a burning ember off his collar and looked at her as though he did not understand.

19

The travaux that he best remembered were the ones pulled by dogs. Faces kept coming back. The old woman with gashed and scarred legs who took care of him for a while. He remembered helping put her on a funeral platform and over the days watching her body being visited by the birds. . . . He remembered a game they used to play — three or four children standing side by side, each trying to sing a different song. And another — wearing blindfolds trying to identify each other's faces. He had been good at that. He remembered the time they spent near the agency: every day some of them would get drunk. They were allowed to buy beer and not whiskey, but many of them would get whites to buy the whiskey. They went crazy on it. They drank for the same reason that whites did — to shorten their memories — and many of them became very successful at it.

Dragging Crick Watson along the railroad track toward Enid he remembered a lot of things. He remembered more than he had in years. Names. Pictures — old women pounding and grinding bones, gossiping like sparrows; the first prairie dog he killed, so suddenly dead; standing outside in snow when a hunting party returned, with everything about their gait and posture and expression saying we have failed in a bad time, we have brought no meat, and himself conveying the message, wailing aloud, women and children inside joining him without even going to look because the meaning was obvious, they were hungry and they would stay hungry, and he was proud — the coyote was secretly proud — to be the first to see, the cause of all this noise. . . . In these memories it did not seem like he was such an outcast. Not so forlorn and lonely as he had generally grown to think of himself during those years. Perhaps he hadn't been much worse off than the rest of them.

The memories came in bits and flickers like lightning on the horizon. They did not overwhelm him.

He didn't trust the travois. In places the brush came belly-high on the horses. He got off now and then to look at Crick. Tied down and wrapped up in a cocoon of blanket and rope, he was nevertheless getting whipped and slashed by the brush. Blue Duck pulled a flap of blanket over his head like a hood. He rode on, wondering about Enid. He did not know exactly what Belle intended to do there. If news of the robbery had been conveyed in any detail, the boomers would be pretty suspicious. But then he knew nothing about the place. Perhaps it was busy and preoccupied like Guthrie.

The strangest thing about his memories was that they did not seem strange. They were just memories, sealed away by habit of mind. Small things, details. He could allow himself to remember them. He could remember them all night if he pleased. But there was one resistance, one troubling fact. They belied the story of himself as a persecuted outcast in the Tribe. He wondered if he had exaggerated the story for his teacher in order to dramatize himself for her. She had loved it, after all. She had loved it desperately. She wanted to know as much about his neglect and persecution as he could remember. She watched him with fierce, pure attention when he talked about it. Perhaps he had remembered selectively. Remembered a little extra here and there. Perhaps it became his story just for her, and by her death the truth was shut away. He could remember himself only as he had created himself for her.

He had been an orphan all right, but he probably got as much to eat as the rest of them. As a young man his vision did not come, but then for some it took many trials. He had been "coyote," yes — but for a child it was more nickname than category. He had left the Tribe nearly starving, but it was a time of starvation.

The cold exotic horror of his childhood was a fiction devised for her rapture. He had been a poor child in a poor and broken community. If his birth was a mistake, it was no more so than for the others.

The old woman's name was Iron Teeth. He remembered the ear pendants that she sometimes wore — precious rocks on long rawhide strips that hung almost to her waist. . . .

In Enid he found the doctor, a grizzle-jawed stout man who did not reply to his apology for awakening him, just followed out and stood in the dawn gloom with his hands flat at his sides looking at Crick in the travois without bending or touching or even getting near him. He coughed and spat. "That man's sick."

"He's been shot," Blue Duck said.

The doctor looked at him with floating eyes. "Where at?"

"In the lower left side of the ribs."

"Take him out of that rig and let's see what the score is." He trudged back into his shack while Blue Duck untied Crick. His lips were white.

The doctor came back out with a black bag and a stethoscope. He bent at the waist and listened to Crick's heart. He squatted down and after a minute glanced up at Blue Duck. He stood up and stuffed the stethoscope into the bag and went back into his cabin.

There was a ringing in Blue Duck's ears. A slight ringing. He stood there for a while looking at Crick.

"Come on in," the doctor said.

He was sitting at a secretary with a pen and spectacles on his nose. "Name?"

"My name?"

"Yes."

"Blue Duck."

"First name?"

"Blue . . ."

"First name 'Blue,' last name 'Duck'?" The doctor squinted at him.

"Yes."

"County or nation of residence?"

"Tulsa, Creek Nation."

"Name of deceased?"

"Crick Watson."

"Age?"

"I don't know — fifty."

"Birthplace, if known."

"Don't know."

"Occupation?"

"Cowboy."

"Place of work?"

"The Territory, everywhere . . ."

"Names of parents?"

"Don't know."

"Reason for death? Bullet wound, probable burst spleen. . . . Accident?"

"Yes."

"Did you witness the accident?"

"Yes."

"Will you sign an accidental-death form?"

"Yes."

The doctor dug in the secretary for the form and eventually found it. Blue Duck signed it.

"That'll be a dollar-fifty."

He dug out two pieces of silver and the doctor gave him his change. "There's two undertakers in town. Staley is good; I don't know about the other one." He got a pint bottle out of a cubbyhole in the secretary, took a drink and offered the bottle to Blue

Duck. He took a good swig and handed it back. The doctor took another gulp and glanced up at him. "Sorry about your buddy. Say you're a cowboy?"

Blue Duck nodded.

"Working for one of these outfits?"

He didn't respond.

"If I was you, I'd visit Staley and get my butt out of town."

"Will you sell me this bottle?"

"Sure. Give me a dollar."

Blue Duck did so and the doctor got up, went over to his bed, lay down and disappeared.

He found Staley in a shack with new pine boxes of different sizes leaning against it. He left Crick's body and a cash deposit.

Enid consisted of a few other shacks, a lot of buildings in progress and a lot of tents and wagons. Blue Duck walked up what appeared to be the main street. Then he walked back down. He squatted for a while and drank the whiskey. He felt unmoored. His body was chunky from all the riding, but his head kept floating away. When a cafe opened he went in and sat down with a cup of coffee. He poured whiskey into it, drank and stared into the cup. After a while someone was speaking to him. "Sir, do you want breakfast? We have other people waiting." The ringing in his ears came back — slight, persistent. He felt a little giddy. He ordered breakfast so he could sit here longer. Three long-bearded men in high-collar black suits sat across from him and nodded at him stiffly, one, two, three. They sat very straight-backed and kept their eyes carefully ranged, talking in German or Dutch. Blue Duck noticed that their coats had no buttons. In an odd, urgent way he felt friendly toward them.

"Hello."

"*Guten Tag,*" the elder of the three replied.

"How are you today?" he heard himself ask.

"*Sehr gut, danke. Aber wir sprechen nur Deutsch.*"

"I was just waiting for breakfast here."

"*Ja. Wir sprechen nur Deutsch. Unsere Frauen sind in* Kansas.

Alle in Kansas. *Wir nehmen Frühstück hier.*" The elder smiled with big yellow teeth.

"Oh. Well. I don't understand you but glad to have your company." He held up his coffee cup at them and took a drink. When breakfast came he knifed it into his mouth and wondered what they were talking about. They seemed happy enough for such austere dress. Europe . . . He had heard Crick talk about wanting to visit India. Many of the romances he read were set in England or Italy or Germany — castles, high costume, formal balls. . . . He poured what remained of his whiskey into the empty coffee cup and sipped on it. The black suits immediately went silent. He toasted them. "Funny breakfast, I know. Are you German?"

The elder assumed a public demeanor. Gone were the yellow teeth. "*Ja.*"

"Did you ride a fancy ocean liner?"

"*Ich bin Deutsch. Sie sind in* Illinois *geboren.*" He gestured at the others.

Blue Duck smiled. He felt like he must look silly and dirty and crooked faced from the booze, but he didn't care. "*Deutsch?* Is that how you say Germany?"

"*Ja. Deutschland,*" the elder said in a tone to end the conversation.

Blue Duck sipped on his whiskey. "I've never been anywhere like that. Used to think about it a lot. Just an idea in my head, I guess. I learn languages pretty well. . . . *Deutschland?*"

"*Ja. Deutschland,*" the elder frowned.

"Where in *Deutschland* do you come from?"

"*Bitte, mein Herr. Machts nichts.*"

"Is that north or south?"

"*Nein.*" The elder tried to retain his frown. "*Nein.*" He shook his head and was relieved when their breakfasts came. Blue Duck drank the rest of his whiskey while they ate in wordless concentration. He was looking right at them. He was quite drunk and did not feel at all shy. He felt warm toward these strange men. The two younger ones glanced at him with nervous countenance, shoveling the rest of their breakfasts down. "I'll bet it's a remarkable feeling to come all the way from Germany and end up in Enid."

When they had finished they got up, nodded again and the two younger ones went quickly out the door. The elder paused. He put down three quarters and glanced over to see that his friends were gone. He looked down hesitantly and started to speak. Blue Duck had the distinct feeling that he was going to say something in English, but he didn't. Frowning, he turned and left.

He watched the man leave. The black coat. He felt a sudden hollowness inside himself. He wanted more whiskey. More food. He needed to fill up this hole. It was like choking. He looked around. Their plates were all perfectly cleaned. Nothing was left on the table but a little coffee in one of their cups. He reached for it with both hands and gulped it down. He left some money and walked out blinking into the sun.

He rode just outside the southern end of town, tied his horses in some blackjack oak, laid out a saddle blanket and went crashing to sleep. As the day got hotter he dreamed that flies were eating his face but his arms were too heavy to shoo them off. Someone was trying to rouse him. It took a long time. Finally he was sitting with his knees drawn up and back hunched over, looking at Hotsie. Sleeping off the doctor's whiskey in the heat of the day had drained him. Hotsie asked him about Crick. No energy to reply, he handed him the death certificate out of his shirt pocket.

Hotsie glanced at it. "*Alleh.*" He looked away. "We start a hundred-mile range fire and we put Crick in the box. It is a great day." He was disgusted. "Hey, listen to me —"

Blue Duck looked at him for a while. He floated here and there. "What?"

Hotsie shook his head. "Just watch yourself. I don't know."

The others showed up. Ralph and J. B. were passing a bottle back and forth, Belle reading and cussing at a newspaper. They all looked at the death certificate — Ralph distastefully, J. B. for a long time, sitting on a rock rolling whiskey around in his mouth, smudge-faced, with singed eyebrows and a burned-out patch in his hair and a blank expression — staring at the certificate as if it was something to be deciphered. Belle was taking nips from a little medicine bottle. They had ridden into Enid separately and looked for him, then snooped around outside town to find him.

It was taking Blue Duck a while to orient himself. He felt very weak. He didn't know exactly what they were talking about. It was as if a great time had elapsed since he last saw them. They seemed strange and busy and a little crazy. Belle was fuming at the newspaper and at "Prettyman and Jim son-of-a-bitch July." He tried to remember who they were. She flopped the newspaper down in front of him and he looked at it for a while. It was not a good time for reading. It was a good time to concentrate his attention on one subject and try to forget his own stomach and head. Belle was the most lively subject for his attention, but she had a way of reminding one of his internal functions. Right now she was pacing. He had seen her in a number of extreme postures over the last few days, but this — as far as his battered head could remember — was the first time he had seen her truly pacing. She was talking with herself in an angry and frustrated way. She was saying that Prettyman was a flea-circus turd and Jim July a scurvy treacherous breed. In this state she was not a good subject for his teetering consciousness.

He tried to think about a large milkweed not far from his feet, but there was something awfully large and green and excessive about it. For lack of other comfort, he looked back at the newspaper and read it. Belle was wanted for assault, bribery and a livestock rap from some time back. Prettyman, it seemed, instead of dropping the assault charges, had gone to the law with a charge of attempted bribery. He reported to Marshal Heck Thomas that Belle Starr and her consort Blue Duck had tried to get him to drop assault charges against himself in exchange for valuable photographs. The photographer — "cunningly," said the article — went ahead and made the photographs for evidence, copies of which were now in the marshal's hands. There was no mention of the five hundred dollars Belle had given him.

Blue Duck managed to ask her where the livestock indictment came from.

"From Jim July, where do you think? He traded in his rap to witness against me on something a year old." She stopped pacing. "A month ago he was calling himself 'Starr'; now he's witnessing against me."

"What about Guthrie?" Hotsie asked.

She shrugged. "Read it yourself. They don't have much on us."

Hotsie looked at the paper. "My God, one of these articles is on top of the other. Somebody could just take a pencil and draw a circle around them."

"I am much misused," Belle said very seriously. "Much misused." An expression of what looked to Blue Duck like theatrical innocence flashed across her face. She took another swig of medicine and resumed pacing.

Blue Duck arose and walked over to a brushpile to vomit. He retched hard enough to forget that he was embarrassed. He retched on all fours until he heard himself moaning and an arm locked at the elbow around his belly and held him firmly. He was happy to accept whatever support was available.

"What's wrong with you, dentist? You ain't been on the bottle have you? You keep off of it. I got a posse of drunks already."

He allowed his head to hang down limply. It almost felt good. Specks of light floated around in his eyes. His mouth was vile. She lowered her voice, breathing on his neck. "We can't trust them. Ralph's got them poisoned. We'll have to keep an eye on the saddlebag. You stay straight. The newspaper ain't saying anything about my boy yet, but Jim July knows about this scheme. If he goes worse than he already has, all of us are hanged — my boy, you, me and these other bums, too. Who knows what would happen to Joel Mayes? Ike Parker would take and line us up all at once just like he did with Dan Evans and the Buck gang. He'd sit up in the courthouse watching through his window and I guarantee you when that trap sprung it'd warm his old fat belly better than Mrs. Parker's apple pie. He's got a white head of hair now and he ain't in the best health. He'd like nothing better than to cap off his career with a prestige hanging. As many necks as he's stretched, he ain't done much in the way of names. Look down the newspaper list of men he's pronounced and it looks like a rendering plant for drunks."

Blue Duck managed to get himself up and walk over to a log. She handed him the canteen. She was talking awfully fast, and she seemed to be speaking of a number of things at once. He found it difficult and unpleasant trying to understand her. He washed his mouth out as well as possible and sat for a while until he felt a little better composed. "Is that what I am now?" He smiled limply.

"What?"

"A name?"

"You're a name of some kind. William S. Prettyman has seen to it."

"I'm not a dentist anymore; I'm a name. I knew it was going to happen."

He sat for a while longer monitoring his internal functions, trying not to pay any further attention to her. When he felt good enough to walk, he stood up slowly and went to his horse, climbed up bareback and headed into town.

He gave the boy at the bathhouse a dollar and told him that he wanted four baths. Because of the drought four baths, he learned, consisted of four gallons of water poured slowly over his head. That was all right. He sat in the tub a while between buckets and thought of Iron Teeth. She had been a good comforter because she offered no comfort, just her very clear attention.

He went to a bar and drank a half a beer. He was trying to get used to the vertical. The sun and booze had fried his senses. He felt intensely weak, flaccid, careless. He tried the subject of food in his thoughts and was not able to negotiate. He walked out of the bar directly across the street into the largest building in town — a general store — and bought some new clothes. The manager was perplexed when he left his old clothes in a heap, but he became less so when Blue Duck bought a thirty-dollar hat.

On inspiration he bought a second shirt and pair of Levi's for Belle. He went to the communal well at the end of town and stood in line to drink a gourdful of saltiron water. Life was returning somewhat. A group of armed men lay around playing cards and sleeping under the trees behind the well. He had no energy to worry about them. He tried to imagine what time of day it was.

It completely muddled him when Belle cried. She cried when he handed her the new pants and shirt. They seemed to be tears of gratitude, but she didn't say anything, tears just came and she sobbed a little and mounted Zero and left for town. She returned in a different mood. She was clean and Zero had been fed and seen about and she was carrying a box of something in her lap. She put it on the ground and made a cow chip fire and sent Hotsie for some water and got some coffee going and put out some salt side to chew on. The boys, who'd been taking naps, gathered around for a cup. J. B. still looked like he'd just walked out of hell. Ralph had been sleeping under a bush and awakened to a drowsy sulking. Hotsie returned with a canteen of water and a mouthful of chewing wax, and they sat around slurping on extra-strong coffee and passing the wax. Belle was chipper and talkative. She kidded Ralph for being so grumpy, she combed J. B.'s hair with her own comb and made fun of Blue Duck's new hat. "Ruins your professional image," she said. "Makes you look like a bank robber." She carried over the box that she'd brought from town and handed around cans of tomato and smoked fish and some bananas.

Hotsie snapped the top off a banana and peeled it carefully. "We can't stay around here much longer. That guy Couch and his boys were at the well. They were suspicious of me. What do you intend to do here?"

"You saw him?"

"I handed the dipper to him. They were having a big powwow. Maybe a dozen men. Very serious. I think they were talking about a night burning."

"They ought to hire us," Ralph said.

"Shut up Ralph. What else?"

"Nothing. But if they catch onto us, we'll be in trouble. Those guys are not farmers."

"They're Pinkertons is what they are," Belle said. "Pinkertons or Pinkerton types. The railroad can hire fifty Pinkertons for every old raggedy bum Joel Mayes can put into the Territory. Those are the boys that are cutting the barb wire and setting the fires. We better spread out. Stay in these blackjack but not too close. Find some cover and keep your horses ready."

Blue Duck spread out his roll in a grove of locust some distance from the fire and made up for a bad day with a bad night. He was awake at dawn when Hotsie went into town for water and didn't return. They waited an hour for him. Belle finally asked Blue Duck to go look for him.

In town he saw a bunch of people at the well and headed for it. When he got there he tried to appear to observe what they were doing as matter-of-factly as possible. They had Hotsie tied by the ankles dangling upside down from a tree limb. One of them was asking him questions and knocking him around. His arms were tied up behind his back and his eyes were wide open —strange upside down. His lips were swollen. A line of blood ran out the corner of his mouth up his cheek into his hair. He didn't seem to be talking.

A man with a Winchester approached Blue Duck. "What you know, stranger?"

"What's going on here?" he asked.

"Bank robber. A little Indian. Description on the wire has him flat. They're trying to get his jaw working."

"What are you going to do with him?"

"He don't talk, we're going to hang him rightside up. That'll be afternoon. Don't do no hanging till afternoon, even with a grease-head. How about you? You from town here?"

"I'm setting up dental practice here. Considering it, at any rate."

"Where you from?"

"Eastern part of the Territory." He did not say exactly where because he didn't want to appear too ready to comply. His heart was beating hard. He did not want to join Hotsie in decorating the tree. He sidled off as inconspicuously as possible and rode back to camp.

Belle didn't ask a question or say a word. She lay back on one elbow looking at the coffeepot. "Okay," she finally said. "I've got a couple of ideas. You can add on to what I say."

Ralph spat into the little fire. "Or subtract."

Blue Duck — a proven customer — diverted the storekeeper's attention while Belle swiped the medicine out of the stockroom. He had to spill a case of nails, unroll a bolt of material and make a general fool of himself, but it worked. She stole a gallon bucket and a case of "ESSENCE OF NUX VOMICA."

They poured it bottle by bottle into the gallon bucket. "What is this stuff?"

"The doctor in Eufala calls it strychnine. Gives it when you've bad stopped up."

"Strychnine is poison."

"So is salt if you eat too much of it. If I can get these Pinkertons to grunting and hiding out in the bushes, maybe we'll have a chance." She poured out the last bottle. "Nothing will make a squatter squat faster."

He hung the bucket off his saddlehorn and headed out for the well. The plan seemed less and less tenable as he approached it. The bucket was very full with the thick red liquid. One glance and somebody would notice. Numbers of people were coming and going from the trough. He pretended to be adjusting something on his saddle until there was a pause in visitors.

They had at least cut Hotsie down. He was propped up against the tree trunk as if asleep. They were leaving him alone for now. The one he had talked to earlier and another man were at the trough. He led his horse over. "Hello. How's your little Indian doing?"

"Okay right now. Won't be doing so good in a while."

The second man looked at him with flat cold eyes.

"Ever get his jaw working?" Blue Duck took up the gourd and dipped water out of the trough.

"Claims he don't speak English."

He took a long drink and put the gourd down. "Say. You had that incisor seen about?"

"What's that?"

"That side tooth up front. Looks pretty serious."

"What side tooth?"

Blue Duck walked around the trough. "Open up."

"What?"

"Open your mouth."

The man looked perturbed but did so. Blue Duck examined him. "Very interesting."

"What do you mean?"

"I haven't seen one of those in five years." He went back to his horse and fiddled with the cinch.

"One of what?"

"They have them in the books, but you don't see them very often."

"What's he got, a still under his tongue?" the second man said.

"No. But it's no less remarkable. Look in there and see for yourself." He put one hand up on the horn.

The second man laughed. "I wouldn't look in there for all the tea in China."

"What the hell are you talking about?" the man flustered.

"An Egyptian impactment," Blue Duck said.

"Egyptian?" He looked worried.

"They're quite rare. Toxic effusions sometimes result from pyramidical impactments like that."

"I got to see this. Open up."

He opened his mouth, frowning, and the second man peered inside. "Where?"

Blue Duck took the bucket off the saddlehorn and approached the trough. Two others were coming over from the tree. He had about three seconds. "Look on the far right, lower."

He submerged the bucket and sloshed the syrup out into the water.

"Say!" One of them strode over quickly.

Blue Duck froze.

"You can't do that. Get that bucket out of there. Water horses over to the mud pond. Get out of that trough."

"I don't see no Egyptian impactment," said the second man.

Blue Duck took the bucket out of the well and stood there for a moment, hoping they wouldn't smell it or notice the color.

"It's an early stage," he said. "You should see a practitioner soon."

The man who'd come over took a drink of water and scowled. "God damned rusty nails, I wouldn't feed it to a rat."

Blue Duck was turning to leave as gracefully as possible when he noticed that Hotsie's eyes had opened. He looked like a potato sack against the tree, but his eyes were very awake, unblinking.

20

There was nothing worse than a Pinkerton. They were bounty hunters for the big boys. They were hateful because they were successful. One Pinkerton was more dangerous than any half-dozen of the marshals in Judge Parker's stable. Cole used to write letters to the newspapers right and left when he heard the Pinks were after him. Just the thought of them would stimulate masterpieces of innocence. They were private investigators on big money, after big money — no two bucks a head and six cents a mile for them, nosir. And mean. When the James boys were still loose some Pinks threw a bomb into their stepmother's house, blowing her arm off and killing her little boy.

About the only thing you could count on with that kind of man was that their mommas, at some time or another, taught them not to shit in public. She hoped.

The day was hot and steamy. Clouds. She and Ralph and J. B. waited out in the jack pines while Blue Duck kept a scout in town and at the well. J. B. was glum. Ralph rattled his mouth. They checked their guns. The horses picked up the fidgets and started snorting and raring their heads. Ralph bitched until she'd like to have shot him in the teeth. She'd drunk a little more medicine, probably, than she should have, but there was no other way to slow down her nerves. She wasn't made for this kind of work. Nobody ought to have to ride into a camp of Pinkertons, much less an old woman in a delicate state. This was not smart — that kept going through her head. Not smart. She tried to think of an approach. They wouldn't be baited easily, that was certain. You couldn't start a fire and get all of them running down the street. She might have to let them hang Hotsie. That was one possibility. But something about that made her mad. Something about it was intolerable. She tried to think back on some old Quantrill stories that were like this but couldn't remember any. Wasn't this fine? Here was an old hag suffering the monthly vertigoes, soused on medicine, with one broke-down clodhopper, a dentist and a mealy-mouthed snit to face an army of Pinkertons with. That was real good. The miracle was that Ralph wasn't just riding on out. J. B. had gotten into such a dreary mood that it wasn't occurring to him to ride out. Nothing was occurring to J. B. right now.

It was a good three hours and it seemed like fifteen before Blue Duck showed up. He got off his horse and stood there.

"Well?"

"Hotsie is being hanged."

"Let's go."

"They're making a show out of it. Trying to get him to talk. Couch is going to give a speech and so forth. But there is something strange."

"What?"

"That medicine — the people are very strange. One of them went stiff."

"Stiff? You mean died?"

"No. Just stiff. He fell over and went stiff. They're all acting kind of crazy."

"How long before they hang him?"

"Maybe a half-hour."

"All right, we ain't going to figure it out here. Let's go. Play it by ear. Just keep an eye on each other. Stay near your horses.

Blue Duck, you've got Crick's shotgun in the sheath there. It's loaded."

"What are we doing?" Ralph said.

"He was fetching our water when they caught him, Ralph. Now shut up your jaw and come on."

"You're drunk on laudanum."

"Good. It won't hurt so much when they shoot me."

Blue Duck held up his hand as if he heard something.

"What?" she whispered.

"I have an idea. I think."

"Great," Ralph said. "He thinks."

He puzzled for a moment longer. "I'll try to scatter them. Go along with me. Just hang back at first."

Holsters tied on Zero, one pistol stuck down inside her shirt, she stopped at the general store, bought a sunbonnet and headed on out to the well with her face shaded.

Hotsie's arms were being tied behind him and they were getting a horse ready. The rope was strung.

The man who had gone stiff was still that way, his back arched up so hard that it wasn't touching the ground. A bunch of men stood around arguing about what to do. Some of them were trying to hold him down. Blue Duck dismounted, went over and started giving advice about what to do with him. Belle got close enough to hear him. J. B. and Ralph stayed back trying to look like part of the crowd. They were all weird, the whole stump-jumping mob of them — stiff-necked and nervous and talking skittishly among themselves, pale-looking and hitching up their pants, staring away with preoccupied frowns on their faces, walking bandy-legged off to the brush over the hill. The medicine was cooking. Mr. Couch was talking heatedly with some of his boys. Three of them grabbed up the man who was stiff and hauled him away.

"Does that man have epilepsy?" Blue Duck asked.

"He sure don't have a cold."

"Does he have a history of epilepsy?"

"Who are you, anyway?"

"He's a dentist," someone yelled.

"I'm a doctor of dental surgery," Blue Duck stated, "and I have some acquaintance with disorders of this sort."

"He ain't had no epilepsy before, far as I know," another said.

Blue Duck looked as heavy and smart as a professor. He got their attention, he looked so smart. "Gentlemen, I must say something that may disturb you."

Couch came forward. He looked pale and mad. "I don't believe I've met you. Are you part of the community here?"

"I'm thinking about settling here, yes."

"It's unfortunate that we haven't met before. We have some important business to attend to, if you'll please stand back." He stepped onto an overturned crate and held both hands high over his head. "Ladies and gentlemen! Please give me your attention. It is a trying day. We are faced with a trying . . . task. . . ." He seemed uncertain for a moment. "This man is part of a gang of half-breed renegades who robbed the Arkansas Bank of Commerce in Guthrie, killing a valiant young guard, Mr. Fred Nelson, and — what was equally odious — slandering our enterprise, our very enterprise here in Enid. You all know that story, so I won't go over it. What some of you don't know is that the telegraph line between here and Guthrie was cut yesterday. This morning we received word by courier that a bridge on the Kansas and Western line was sabotaged and burned. Rail traffic between here and Guthrie has been temporarily stalled by this mischief. Before you stands one of the men responsible. He has refused to cooperate with us in revealing the names of his cohorts. We are fairly certain that one of them is a woman. Other than that we have little description.

"We do have good reason to suspect that this gang was hired by foreign or Texas cattle interests to terrorize the white people of the Oklahoma Territory. At the orders of rich businessmen in London or Germany, perhaps Texas, this dirty little Indian shot Fred Nelson dead. On the pay of cattle barons living in places far distant, he was sent here to disrupt our community and run us off this land. In order that rich men could . . . be . . . continue to be

. . ." Mr. Couch frowned. He stood there for a moment blank. The crowd waited.

Hotsie was mounted, the knotted rope around his neck.

Another man fell, toppling over backward like a wall of bricks, letting out one huge bellowing exhalation as if pounded in the gut by a sledgehammer, then he arched up stiff as a board.

"Gentlemen!" Blue Duck said loudly. "That settles it. We are in an emergency. Something that these men ate is poison. What food or drink have they shared? It is imperative that we find out."

For a moment the crowd was quiet, no one speaking or moving.

"They didn't share nothing. Shorty was playing cards. He hadn't even had no whiskey yet. Water's all."

Blue Duck appeared to consider that. Then he strode over to the trough and tasted the water. "This water has been poisoned."

They broke into a big argument, a hundred boomers and Pinks yelling and disagreeing. Blue Duck held up a hand. "I would advise you — all of you who have drunk from this well — to use an emetic or some technique for vomiting immediately. I would also advise you to lie down. Do this as soon as possible. The doctor should be called. Are any of you having digestive difficulties? If so, you should pay special attention to these instructions. Go back to your cabins or wagons and find a comfortable place to lie down. Loosen your clothing and do not exert yourselves in any way. You must fully rest or the poison will overtax you. I advise that you do this immediately. Do not panic. I repeat, do not panic."

At this point there was a minor panic. They ran in all directions. Some of them leaned over and stuck their fingers down their throats. Some lay down right where they were and got stepped on by others who were in a hurry to leave. A man grabbed Blue Duck by the collar and virtually tore his coat off. "I got the summer complaint. Is that what you mean? If I got that, does that mean I been poisoned?"

"Go to your wagon and lie down."

"Oh my God." The man wandered off in a daze.

Hotsie and J. B. and Belle were becoming more visible as the crowd thinned out. They would have to act soon. Couch's boys milled and argued among themselves about their bowels and headaches. Three or four of them had disappeared in the melee. Couch was madder than hell. He didn't like his little sideshow being interrupted.

Belle led Zero over and pretended to be looking after one of the men on the ground. She kept close to the shotgun side of her horse. Hotsie sat very attentively in his rope collar.

Blue Duck was talking to Couch's boys. "I would advise you — all of you who have drunk this water — to avail yourselves of a dosage of opium or powdered morphine. You should do so as soon as you have emptied your stomachs."

Couch's face blistered red. "Who in the hell are you? How did you know that water was poisoned?"

"I told you who I am, sir. I deal with medicinal and chemical preparations every day of the week. That water has a decided taste to it."

"What kind of taste?"

"Boss," one of his boys interrupted. "There's a bunch of us got the complaint. We better get us a dose like this guy says."

"You stay here, Mettery. All of you stay here."

"I stay here and I'm gonna shit on my leg, boss. I'll see you."

"All right God damn it, we're going to hang this Indian and you're going to see it done. Go in the bushes or something but come back. You'll have plenty of time to get medicine for your God damn complaint. Hurry up."

Several of them left — some into the bushes, some toward town. Couch looked around nervously. His eyes fixed on Belle. She tried to look like she was doing something for one of the men on the ground. He frowned and winced as if he had a pain in his face. He seemed to go quiet for a moment. Then he walked over to the man holding the reins on Hotsie's horse. He sidled over to the trunk of the tree and started to bend over.

Belle saw what was coming just a moment before it happened

—not quite in enough time to make her move. The man at the reins went to the horse's rear, smacked him on the buttock and yelled. Hotsie was dragged off and dangling before she could get to her shotgun. In one motion she slid it from the sheath and cocked the left barrel and pulled off a round—hitting the rope but not separating it. She pulled off the right barrel and hit again but still didn't break the rope. Hotsie dangled, legs drawing up. Belle had no time to reload the shotgun. Going for her pistol, she saw Couch and another Pink both leveling on her, but Ralph's pistol was out and blazing, tearing up the hill, knocking the legs out from under the Pink and making Couch take cover. J. B. mounted and rode toward Hotsie and in one huge reaching came up from his saddle, took the frayed rope in both hands and busted it like a string. Hotsie fell to the ground in a hail of bullets; a Pink some distance back cranked his Winchester from the waist. She took aim with the pistol and laid him down. A bullet thwapped into Zero's saddle, and before she could turn, the horse was down, shot in two or three places. She fumbled more bullets into her pistol and potshot at three coming from town. A spread from Blue Duck's shotgun scattered them. J. B.'s horse had been shot out from under him, and he and Hotsie were taking what cover they could in a depression near the tree. Belle couldn't tell what condition Hotsie was in, but she doubted that his neck was broken. He was stout-boned. He'd ridden too many mankillers in his life to have a delicate neck.

She saw now why she had put up with Ralph all this time. He had a reputation with a gun, but what she was seeing was beyond what she'd heard. When Couch showed the least of himself out from behind the tree—leveling on Hotsie and J. B.—Ralph started blowing the tree apart. It was not so much accuracy as total firepower. His guns didn't seem to need reloading. When three more Pinks came busting out of the woods, one with his britches hanging loose at the belt, Ralph set the air on fire, knocking one of them off his feet, forcing the others down. He was loading the Winchester on the ground and keeping Couch honest with the .45 when shots flared up again from the rear. Somebody behind the trough. Belle was trying to take cover behind Zero but she couldn't hide on both sides of him at once. She was pinned — they were all pinned, Hotsie and J. B. worse than her and Ralph. Where was Blue Duck? She didn't see his horse. Ralph flinched and cussed — hit — rose up with his Winchester and systematically destroyed the water trough. A man tumbled out from behind it, arms and legs jerking out like a gigged frog. Ralph took another hit and sat down hard on the ground.

Couch showed from behind the tree taking aim at J. B. and Hotsie. She discouraged him with the .44.

They had to get out of here. More Pinks were appearing out of the woods. It wouldn't be long before the whole town was on them. She hurled one of her pistols over to J. B. He'd have to take care of himself.

Zero was dead. She unstrapped her holster and the saddlebag and looked around. She loaded the shotgun and put a barrelful into the woods. Ralph was sitting on his tail cussing. He had no cover but seemed oblivious to that. He cussed and reloaded.

"Ralph, hey! Find yourself a horse. Come on." Retreating past the well she saw a gaggle of men hurrying up the road. She cut down on them with both barrels and changed their minds. The air whined around her. She got down and crawled like a pollywog to a horse that was standing on its reins. At a pause in the shooting she got aboard. Blue Duck came riding full steam out from town with two horses in tow. He let them loose to her and rode straight past Couch and the hanging tree for the brush behind, staying low to the horse's neck and whacking away with his rifle. He was trying to scatter them deeper into the woods so they would have some room to move.

That left her to take care of Couch. Ralph was sitting in a heap not looking all too well. She let the horses' reins drop and circled out a ways to try to get another angle on Couch. There was another Pink with him behind the tree. If he and most of his boys hadn't been caught without their rifles, this would have been over before now.

"Squat, you squatters!" she yelled, trying to get up her courage. She got a little angle on Couch and his buddy now and started messing with them. But nothing was coming out of Ralph, and J. B. made a break for it toward the well, which allowed Couch to circle the tree. And more of the bastards were showing up from town. She'd have to move. She spurred the horse and took out straight for the tree, down low and saving her bullets, but the Pink was shooting and her horse broke in two and started belly-hopping. He rared up backwards and she just got her boots out of the stirrups in time. Knocked breathless, flat on her back, the horse a quivering thousand pounds. Couch had her. He was out from the tree, taking his time. She saw him but couldn't move. It was a quiet moment. Then the air around him started to break apart like glass, he made a little grunt, twitched down around himself and took off limping. She looked back and saw Ralph stumble down to one knee and sit there kind of weaving, prop-ping himself with the gun.

The Pink behind the tree took out for the woods, and he and Blue Duck passed within ten feet of each other without a shot.

J. B. rounded up horses and was mounting up. A few stray bullets were coming from the rear, but for the moment they weren't under close fire. Hotsie yelled, "Get me loose!" His arms were still tied behind him. J. B. dismounted and tried to untie him but in the frenzy couldn't handle it. He put the horse's reins up on the saddlehorn, picked Hotsie up like a little boy and put him in the saddle. He'd make do; he could hold a horse with his knees better than most riders with a spade bit.

She went over to see about Ralph. She told him to get up, but he wasn't moving. The meanness melted from his expression and he looked like he was about to topple over. She tried to make the noise that came out of her throat into a gobble, but it didn't sound right. That got the shadow of a sneer back on his face. He looked at her through heavy eyelids as though he was about to go to sleep. He seemed satisfied to remain here. A bullet walked up out of the dirt.

J. B. yelled at him. "Get up!"

His face wandered off on a sweet drunk. More shots, again from the woods. A rifle.

"Get up, God damn you," J. B. Stampp said. He dismounted and took Ralph by the shoulders. "Get up, you two-bit son of a bitch, or I'll strop you on that horse like a sack."

Ralph raised his eyebrows at this.

Scowling, J. B. hoisted him under the arms and threw him against a horse like he was fighting him. He fell down and J. B. picked him up and pitched him over the saddle. He arranged him with his legs in the stirrups. "Now ride, son of a bitch."

J. B. was just back aboard when he took a hit in the head. An immense sickening crack with the roll of a rifle shot down the hill, and blood was suddenly all over his face. Belle went around on her horse, she went around again — moving — watching him. He was still aboard, his hands held up as if to feel his face but not doing it. Not touching it. There was nothing to be done. He could either ride or not. She took off.

He stayed up with them for a half-mile and more out of town, but he was bleeding all down his face and it was soaking his shirt and dripping down the saddle, and he was getting visibly groggy. The top of his forehead was shattered, the blood boiling out into his eyes, stringing down his cheeks into the wind. His legs flapped loose against the horse, the strength gone from his knees. The horse was complaining. He veered off and they herded him back among them.

Ralph was staying in the saddle okay.

J. B. was stubborn. He trailed a mile of blood before he gave up. He peeled out of the saddle at a full run and was hung by one leg, smashing and bouncing through the weeds. They didn't stop for him. They rode for their lives.

It was one thing she could do. She could do it drunk or sober or glad or mad or out of her mind or any other stinking way. She could do it better than marshals/scouts/horse Indians/Pinks. Give her anything above a jackass and she could ride. The trouble was keeping these boys up with her. No backtracking or camouflaging or any of that crap; it was a race. A few miles out, they stopped to get Hotsie untied and saw them coming over the bare hill. There were six of them riding hard. "Them guys are wasting their time. Just stay with me. You doing okay, Ralph?"

Ralph seemed to find humor in that question.

They took out flying. The idea was to get a lead and then start laying discouraging tracks. You didn't hide your trail, you just laid a bum one. The kind that riders who were careful with their horses wouldn't like to follow. You couldn't fret about broken legs or any of that. She burned horses out sometimes, but that was the difference: she didn't worry about going through them. Going through them was her life. When this one laid down, you got another one. You knew — assumed — that anyplace this side of hell there was some kind of mount to be found, and the way you made him yours was to throw a saddle over his back.

They were heading east and a little south. She didn't worry about precise direction. The main thing was distance. Blue Duck was on a nag pony and was having the most trouble keeping up. They stopped again and Belle traded with him. There was blood on his coat but he wasn't complaining. Hotsie seemed a little confused, but he was another one who could ride asleep or with his neck broke or any other way. Ralph was unchanged; he looked awful but stable.

They hit a tributary to the Arkansas and let the horses drink lightly and aimed off southward. They were in Creek Territory before dark, perhaps twenty miles from Tulsa. Blue Duck wanted to take Ralph to an Indian doctor he knew living south of Tulsa. Belle agreed. A strange thing was happening. The rain that didn't fall a couple of nights before was threatening again. The darkened sky meant little chance of night tracking, and if it came a storm their trail would be obliterated.

The doctor was an old Creek living alone in a one-room cabin. Blue Duck talked with him quietly at the door before he asked them to come in. Ralph did not get down, and it was a moment before she thought to help him. He had been hanging on the horse so long that it was hard to get him unglued. Inside, there was one bunk and a single table with two chairs, a stove and a kind of homemade cupboard with bundles of herbs and medicines stuck in cubbyholes. They got Ralph's clothes out of the way and the old doctor examined him. He was very gentle — almost delicate — an ancient bag of sticks with ancient eyes and hands that barely touched as they roamed over Ralph's body. She went outside for a drink of water.

Hotsie had taken the horses to the trough and squatted down nearby. "Come on in, Hotsie. Maybe this Indian has some greens we can cook up."

"No thanks."

"You okay?"

"*Alleh.*"

"What's wrong?"

"I got a crick in my neck," he said sarcastically.

"You ought to let this old coot look you over."

"I'm heading south, Belle. Into the Winding Stair. I want my money."

She could not see his face in the dark.

"Now."

"Then get it."

"What?"

"I said get it. It's in the saddlebag. Divide it by four and add whatever wages you're owed."

"All right."

She turned to go back inside.

"Belle . . ."

"What?"

"The *Chalakki okla* don't have shit for a chance against that. . . ." It sounded like he wanted to say more but he didn't.

"Okay John. *Anya.* Take care of yourself."

"*Anya,* Belle Starr."

21

he sneer on Ralph's face was ghostly and without venom — vain mask over his exhaustion. The old man said that he should ride no farther. He had been hit in the chest and groin and was in bad shape. Blue Duck was tired. He would have been happy to lie down now on the floor. His body was as heavy as a tree. He did not care about food. He asked the old man if they could leave Ralph here and sleep in the shed.

Belle was sitting at the table looking at Ralph. "No. We'll go out somewhere and hit the dirt. I don't want to sleep inside tonight."

They rode out a quarter-mile from the shack and got down the roll. The sky was rumbling and flickering in the west. Blue Duck didn't care if it rained or what, he just wanted to sleep. He would have preferred to be alone, but there was only one blanket. She put down the saddlebag for a pillow. He lay down and there was a rock under his back and he was thankful for it. He let it push up between his shoulders for a while, then rolled off slowly and dug it out. Belle was fooling with her clothes. The lightning was getting sharper.

"What's that blood on your coat?"

"I don't know."

"You ain't got any holes in you?"

"No holes."

"We must be lucky, Mr. Duck."

"Mmm."

"It's gonna rain on us."

"Mmm."

"It'll blow."

"Good."

"You feeling okay?"

"Okay."

She rolled over on his chest. "What do you think about it?"

"What?"

"What we done."

"I think it was a mess."

"It was, all right. . . . There ain't a name I know of, alive or dead, who would have tried it."

"Wonderful."

"Are you getting smart?"

"No. I'm getting stupider by the minute. I am satisfied to be stupid. Good night."

"Hotsie's leaving."

"So am I." He felt almost breezy saying it.

"Ride with me to Tahlequah. You got some salary coming."

"What are you going to do in Tahlequah?"

"Get our payment and get Ed out of jail."

"That's unlikely, isn't it?"

"You read the newspaper. Jim July or somebody's spilling the beans about this deal. Fatman sends the marshals over to get Ed and that'll be it, buster, nothing you can do when they get them to Fort Smith. We've got some leverage on Mayes now; I think we can spring him."

"The sacrifices are made, eh?"

Her face was close to his, appearing and appearing in the lightning. "What do you mean?"

"I am too beat to talk. I mean nothing."

She spoke as if to herself, "Mayes tried to set it up so I wouldn't see him again. We'll have to get through that. . . ."

"You never cease, do you?"

"Cease what?" She got up and went off a ways to pee.

In the lightning he saw her hunkered down. He lay back and watched the sky. He was too exhausted to sleep. A funny light energy tickled along his ribs and spine, and all of his thoughts seemed unimportant, trivial, mildly entertaining. He felt good actually. Nothing mattered. The most abominable thought was a joke. He tried some abominable thoughts. The day — the last few days — was a series of disasters. *"One should never get involved with his patients"* — a doctor in one of his romances had said that. *"One shouldn't. Really."* The wind was picking up now, gusting hard. It was going to rain. They were on top of a knoll and would probably be struck by lightning. Fried. A perfect end to his career as outlaw: fried on a knoll with Belle Starr fried beside him. Nice for the buzzards. A name. *Why, don't you know? He was a name. He became a name and disappeared that very week. Some speculate that he was fried. Remarkable.*

She was there again, lying on her side propped up. He noticed that she stank. Or perhaps it was him. He. He who stank. She had the look on her face. The smile. The mother-of-the-dead smile. Necrofilial. That was one thing that was not funny. Not funny because he did not like to fuck with her anymore. *Fucking with her had become a frightful bore* — no one ever said that in his romances. He was not a good fucker. Leave that to Jim July and Cole Younger. Leave it to the true names. The *nouveau* name was satisfied not to achieve that distinction.

Lightning burst apart in the sky. The wind rose and tore hungrily across the plain, cool wind, really cool for the first time in recent memory. For the first time ever, this wind. She was there and smiling but what could he do about it? What did it matter here? Dead men walked out the door. Her face was strange lying so very still while the light pounded the earth. . . . To be tired like this was a memory in his body — it, too, vaguely pleasant. The body assured of its continuity. He watched her face and day-dreamed, the wind finding under his clothes, sand blowing against his skin, rainsmell as thick as vegetables in the air. . . . Always a pot of meat boiling to offer visitors. She sat at the fire and he sometimes noticed her old dugs through the loosely cut arms in her dress. A favorite dress from the time when she was a mother giving milk. Three love charms on it, beads, porcupine quills — old woman in the clothes of youth. *I have made friends with this hide,* she said. . . . And the time he did not see was not when they threw him down and screwed the spikes into his chest but when he went off alone into the hills and fasted for four days and saw nothing but thirst and hunger. He came back and told them the truth. The body weak.

He was awake now and fucking her. It surprised him. She was under him with the same face. Big drops began to smatter the dirt; lightning tore at his ears. It was to get that look off her face. Rain told him he was naked. Pleading scorn, immutable in jags and unfoldings of light. The storm was moving fast, as peremptory as a common visitor. He was awake and asleep at once. (The teacher worshipped his suffering body. Not a boyman but a principle. Fearful zealous seizures of fucking. Perdition. The Garden. Oh the knowledge!)

She would not break when he did but it was all right. He snapped like a dry limb. The closest space had become rain. He roamed and smelled her body like a scavenging dog — interesting here and there, the smell of menstrual womanflesh as pungent as death, saddle and dirt and nerves curious to taste. Was she cursing? Now rivulets off her belly. Mud ponds? Tiny creatures finding shelter? The dry hide opening like the dry earth, running like the dry earth. Buckshot rain — the horses were probably having heart attacks. He looked up and could not see them in the havoc of light. Shelter was irrelevant, to move anywhere worse than staying low and riding it out. On his hands and knees he tasted what was neither pleasant nor unpleasant but so much of each that it produced in him a kind of frenzy to decide. It was a place of the world, part of the landscape. Rot, blood, nectar, the response in her, a certain strange tension that was part of the taste. He rooted like an animal to find it out, not a taste of tongue and mouth to brain but to fear, the place of twenty skulls. It satisfied and enraged him equally. Acrid. Slipping. He kept slipping away. . . . (He went to the funeral. He looked upon her. The others suspected him. The husband might have killed him. He did not care. He looked upon her. He walked out — somewhere else. He went somewhere else. . . . He ate garbage as he had done four years before. He sat on his haunches fishing dreamily in putrescence. Except now he spoke this language, now he had certain desires. The coyote dead.)

The rain slowed as suddenly as it had started. He was so very tired. He felt pulverized. Her arms were held out. She called him and he lay down with her and she was in a wild state like he had never seen her, and that was fine, he was in her and she was so very needful and yet composed, oddly, voice husky out of her throat, saying "keep on, please keep on." And he kept on until she started to break, in Cherokee now, bitter,

"What's the matter with you? Please don't. God damn you don't. God damn please kill me please. Kill me please. Kill me. Please."

She chanted the hard Cherokee words. It scared him and made him weirdly happy. Ravening, finally breathless, she bucked like a horse and threw him into the dirt. Ejected him from her body. He was not needed any longer. It made him laugh. He marveled and laughed inside. Strange and joyous — how could he feel this way? He crawled back onto the edge of the blanket tentatively, like a little boy seeking warmth. His thoughts were silly and wild like dreaming. The chair from St. Louis got up and walked with stiff dignity out the door. Books in his parlor flapped their covers, gossiping. The Masonic Building was dragged off into the sky by a giant balloon. She was brought up from the earth so that he could work on her teeth. He hammered horseshoes into the jaw. Flowers bloomed from the eye sockets. Sweet peas. How beautiful they were. . . .

Rain light and clean against his skin, quieting, he saw her

disappearing now. Leaving his presence and becoming . . . what? She must become an animal. The lessons were not clear until the beast was named.

But it didn't happen. Again it didn't happen; that was all right. His bones were clay. He died.

In barest light he awakened in his nose — air steamy, warm, portentous. Propping himself up, he saw her ten feet away from him, eyes awake under half-sleeping lids, squatting with her arms crossed on her knees looking off across the hills. Her posture was symmetrical, like she had been there a while.

For some reason he woke up quickly. "Mornin."

She looked at him and said nothing.

After while she spoke. "My boy . . ."

He lay still and waited for her to continue. "What?"

"I ruined him."

". . . 'ruined him'?"

"Yes."

"What do you mean?"

"Made him do things."

"What kind of things?"

No answer. But she seemed to want to say more.

"Why?"

"Couldn't help myself."

He waited.

"More'n once," she said.

"I'm sorry."

She stood up. Her face was so very sad. Not scattered like she had been at the hotel in Fort Smith but just sad, staring at him and at the ground. She stood there limply as if there was nothing else to do.

He got up and rolled the blanket, picked up the saddlebag and went over to her. He tried to hand it to her but she made no gesture to take it, so he laid it in the dirt at her feet and went off looking for the horses.

She rode behind him down to the shack. The old man was out front on a stump eating a bowl of kafir. He nodded good morning. On a tabletop without legs a leather pouch lay in a wad of money. Blue Duck had seen Ralph open it on the front porch at Younger's Bend. Inside it were a silver dollar, a Barlow, a needle and spool of waxed thread.

He asked the old man if he would bury him. Yes. He could keep the things. A nod — he would keep the money but he did not want the medicine. Blue Duck accepted the pouch.

She took off at a walk across the yard, through chickens.

In Tahlequah they found a hotel and Blue Duck slept like the dead. He assumed Belle did too. At ten o'clock the next morning he went with her to the government building. She walked in the place like she owned it and said she wanted to talk to Joel Mayes. The secretary frowned. She told him that her name was Belle Starr and there was something Mr. Mayes would definitely want to hear from her mouth. An emergency. His frown deepened. She went on at some length and he listened darkly. "Mrs. Starr, I regret to inform you that Mr. Mayes is quite busy right now with the assembly. The Democratic Congress is in session. . . ."

"Fuck the congress, I want to see him."

"I beg . . ."

"I said fuck the congress in their democratic butt holes, I want to see Joel Mayes. Tell him my name. If he says no, okay. You just tell him my name."

The secretary flustered and fumbled around on his desk. After a moment he left. When he returned, three Lighthorsemen ambled in behind him. "Take your sidearms off, please," one of them said.

Belle and Blue Duck unbuckled their belts and handed them to him. The two others searched them. Belle had the saddlebag and one of them opened it. He looked up from the contents. "What is this?"

"That's paper money. They print it up in Philadelphia."

The secretary's frown grew worried. "Please remain here. I will inform the Chief of your visit."

They stood around for a while and he returned, pale but still civil. "Mr. Mayes will see you on the second floor. Please escort them."

Two Lighthorsemen walked behind, one in front. The one in front went in with them. Mayes sat with his elbows on the desk, fingers touching. He rose to meet them, expression neutral.

"I'm here to report, Mr. Mayes."

"I am glad to hear it, Mrs. Starr. You may do so quite easily through the channels we agreed upon."

"There are some things I need to talk to you about. You want this Lighthorseman to hear it?"

Mayes considered that and said nothing. The Lighthorseman stayed.

"Please bring those chairs over and sit down. There is no reason to be uncomfortable."

Blue Duck brought up the chairs but she remained standing. "There's not that much to it. We robbed the bank in Guthrie. You must have heard about that. We blew up a railroad bridge on the Kansas and Western between Guthrie and Enid. You didn't tell me Couch had an army of Pinkertons in Enid. They caught one of my boys up there; we had a shootout with them. Messed up Enid some. Got some ugly rumors going. Shot Couch. Three out of five of my boys are dead. We couldn't go to Kansas to hit the *Oklahoma War Chief* or them lawyers because we were in such a mess. They were hot after us. I want to settle with you."

Mayes was silent for a moment. "Please take a seat, Mrs. Starr."

She descended slowly.

"You appear to be in a blunt mood. That is fine. I appreciate the time that it saves. Allow me to be equally blunt. The congress is meeting right now to consider the question of what we are going to do with the Outlet. There are essentially two possibilities. One is to give the entire region to the United States without argument or resistance. The other is to defend our right to lease or dispose of the land as we choose. You know I stand for the latter." He glanced up at the Lighthorseman. "If the former is agreed upon, I will no longer be of service to the Tribe."

"You'll quit or you'll be fired?"

"It doesn't matter. In my opinion nothing will matter too terribly much if that happens."

"I've got some troubles, too, Mr. Mayes. I've got a couple of weeks of dirt and some dead men walking on my skin. I know you want us out of here. . . ."

"I want to remain fully in touch with you. It is a matter, at this moment, of tactics. You are exhausted and not in the mood for my hesitations. I cannot blame you for that. You have done valiant work. But at this moment it would be very imprudent to stimulate rumors around this office. I am exerting every politic influence I can on the assembly. A rumor that recent actions in the Outlet were countenanced by this office . . ."

"I understand. Pay me and give me my boy."

He frowned.

"We did half the work; you can pay us half the money."

Mayes considered that for a moment. Blue Duck could see by his eyes that he was thinking much faster than he was talking. He was being quiet and distant and measured, as if by this to conceal Belle's appearance. "I cannot release Ed Reed. I have no power to do that. That was not our contract. We are in agreement upon the money."

"That's mighty white of you, Chief, but I want my boy. Somebody over in Fort Smith is talking. If he talks anymore, two things are going to happen. Ed Reed will get extradited and my whole arrangement with you will be on the front pages of every newspaper in the country. Those two things will happen together. Not one but both."

Mayes's expression became somewhat less disembodied. "How do you intend to avoid that, Mrs. Starr?"

"Call me Belle, please. 'Mrs. Starr' gives me a headache in this building."

They were able to smile finally, even the Lighthorseman, who was supposed to not be listening.

"I intend to avoid it by getting Ed Reed out of here. Out and gone. If anybody starts snooping around trying to connect him and that dead marshal, there just won't be anything to go on."

Mayes shook his head. "The whole town of Catoosa knows about that incident. I have seen two telegrams asking for information on a missing marshal in the Creek or Cherokee Nation. It is only a matter of time until this leaks to Fort Smith."

Belle leaned forward in her chair. "Catoosa is a swamp pit. They murder people instead of playing baseball on Saturday afternoon. If one-fifth of what happens in Catoosa got out, Judge Parker's piles would catch afire. What I'm telling you is that Ed in jail here plus my actions in the Territory are not a good combination for you. It will be better for you and for all of us if Ed ain't never been heard of nor seen in your records. . . ."

Mayes shook his head fretfully. "That's impossible. Twenty people know about his incarceration. It has been very difficult to avoid a major story in the newspapers."

"There you are. When it gets in the newspapers, you're in trouble."

Mayes spoke with careful articulation. "No malfeasance has been performed by this office."

"I don't know whether you call about ten dead men spread all over the Territory malfeasance or what, but it sure makes good newspaper copy."

"Is that a threat, Mrs. Starr?"

"This thing started on a threat, Mayes. You got me into it on a threat. I didn't come to you. You took my boy and said you'd swap legal protection for my work. It is no longer protection for him to be in jail here."

Mayes picked up a pen and tapped it lightly on his desk. "I have a question. The reason I commissioned you in the first place was to answer it."

"What's that?"

"Can we resist them in the Outlet?"

"Resist them? . . . ," she sighed. "I don't know. You'd have to get behind it bigger. That boomer shit ain't exactly what you'd call spontaneous. If you got enough men out there to make it unprofitable, it might slow things down. The only way you'll do it is with small bands. Anything big and they'll send the cavalry. Guerrillas — no armies."

"An army is out of the question."

"I guess it boils down to how unprofitable you can make it for them. The big boys are pretty common sense about that."

A sad flicker of smile crossed his face. "I am acquainted with that capacity. Who could handle it, though?"

"You mean in the field?"

"Yes."

"I can name a few dead men and men in jail who could do it. And one woman maybe."

Mayes watched her closely. "You would go again?"

"Release my boy and we can do some more midnight talking."

22

He was sullen and unquestioning about how they had got him out of jail, unmoved when she told him that Blue Duck and she were gambling ten thousand dollars in bond money on him. The trial was set for the end of November and the charge was set at manslaughter, which meant that unless Parker got wind of it and extradited him he might at worst have to bust rocks for a couple of years.

Mayes's plan was to put on the trial in Tahlequah as though the correct identity of the dead man was unknown and the killing, as far as the court could determine, the result of a barroom altercation. This sounded to Belle worse than no trial at all, for Mayes and everybody else. But there were ways, presumably, that court records could be tactfully written so that in checking territorial trials Parker's clerk would not connect his case to the missing marshal. So Mayes put it, and he was in no mood for negotiation.

Ed did not act the least surprised to be out of jail, nor happy, nor anything. She bought him an old jack to ride back to the Bend on, and he sat on it loose and hinge-backed with a sneery, loopy expression on his face. There was something perfectly aggravating about him.

A pretty baby will make an ugly adult.

How could a woman raise her children without a second thought for eighteen, nineteen years and then all of a sudden get so she couldn't take her mind off of them? He made her stomach churn. She wanted to tell him to sit up straight. Smash the silly look off of his face. She wanted to ask him if he was completely unconcerned that she had just risked her ass to get him out of jail.

When they got to the Bend the door was open and the chickens had got into the house and the old cow was bawling, about to die of milk. She chased the hens around the cabin and they ran flapping and clucking and shitting in every direction but the door.

There was a note on the kitchen table, dated three days previous. "Dear Momma, I am here for a visit. My baby is not with me so don't worry. The animals have been taken care of poorly. I milked the cow. Will stay at Eufala at the Byrds' until you get back home. It's so lonely out here. Your daughter, Pearl."

Milked the cow and left the door open for the chickens to roost in the house — just about like her. That was going to be a mess. The dentist would help keep things down. He had gone real quiet again: the hardworking solid dreamy quiet bachelor man. But he had a new look to his eye. What he'd done back on that hilltop wasn't like him. Just about the time she figured out one weirdness in him, another one would come up. He didn't like her as much as she did him, that was for certain. She hadn't worried about such a thing in a man since Cole. Not that the dentist was anything like him, thank the Lord.

She told the boy to milk the cow, got Blue Duck to haul some water and set herself to work on the cabin, which was a pitiful spidery mess. She oiled the chopping block and cleaned the dishes and mopped the floor with ashes. She cleaned the safe and threw out some bug-infested cornmeal and wiped down the zinc doors. She washed the glass windows and opened out the oilcloth windows for some air and beat the ticks and swept the floors and cleaned the chickenshit off the blankets and rugs and put them out to air. She dusted the furniture (old Tom's rocker, made to last a thousand years).

She took off her tight riding clothes and put on a beltless print dress. Same dress that he used to come up and just pull down for a drink, the smart little thing. Stayed on the tit just about till he could read and write. Not Pearl. She lay in a heap and cried. *A crying baby will make a good adult* — boy, now that was a lie. And she had been so mindful when she was carrying Cole's baby, not eating anything that might mark her, staying so clean and careful, until the old man put her in a closet anyway. . . . Her body free inside the cotton. An old hill woman like her didn't get flabby, she just dried up and tightened, got round-shouldered and flat-breasted.

The cow was still bawling like the end of the cow world. Was the boy milking her? She wouldn't let it get her cross. She would make things nice. Leave him alone.

She found a green neckerchief in the bedroom trunk and put it into her dress pocket. She started a fire in the stove and got some potatoes and onions out of the root cellar, bacon from the shack, and found some fresh eggs. She cut up the roots and fried the bacon. They'd smell that quicker than they'd hear her yelling to come for supper. When the bacon was done she dropped potatoes and onions into the hot fat. No milk yet. She didn't have the patience for biscuits anyway, sour milk or baking powder either.

It was going on night. They eventually showed up, Blue Duck and then the boy. He didn't have the milk bucket but she held back from saying anything. They sat in silence, like two bumps on a log. The dentist sat up straight as a poker and ate without expression, the boy lurked over his plate like a government Indian on payday. She tried to talk about the weather, how the grasshoppers were down, but they didn't much respond.

Always something wrong. Her head was not clear. No pills today, not a single one. Maybe she'd give up the silly things for good. Wasn't anything but dope.

She took the green neckerchief out of her pocket and gave it to Ed. "Thought you might be missing that in the slam."

He looked at it for a moment, then wiped his mouth on it. "Missed a lot worse."

"I'll bet you did."

"I'm going to Fort Smith tomorrow, Belle."

Belle? Since when did he call her that? "I wouldn't if I was you."

"Why not?"

"Because that girl's living on the row, you know that."

He picked something from his teeth and said mildly, "I'll go anywhere I want to."

She finished her plate and poured three cups of coffee. She would not get into a fight with him. Not now. The three of them sipped coffee. Outside the sounds of evening deepened — nightbirds, crickets, frogs from clear down on the river. She turned up the table lamp and poured more coffee.

His eyes met hers. Someone was coming, a ways off still. She normally had an instinct for anyone approaching but now she was uncertain. His eyes were on her.

"Get the shotgun."

He went to the other room and returned with the double-barrel broken over his arm, feeding it shells. She took it and blew out the lamp. "Spread out somewhere, both of you."

She sat at the table sipping coffee waiting. *Clack, clack* — a bad leg or hoof. Small horse, maybe a cow pony . . . stopped near the barn . . . light steps toward the house. She pulled one hammer back, then the other. She had a good idea who it was but still kept the butt of the gun on her thigh and waited until the door came open and a sulfur match was struck and Pearl stared out blindly in her own light feeling for a lamp, her face rounder and thicker and whiter and more hidden in fat than it had been before and wearing a fancy sidesaddle habit, kind of haggard and dusty, and a hat with plumes all frazzled and knocked cockeyed by the trail.

"Momma?" She felt for the lamp. "That you Momma?"

"Light the thing, child."

"Oop! That you Momma?"

"Why didn't you halloo? Save us some trouble."

"Hello Pearl," Ed said.

"Brother? Who else is here?" She finally got a lamp lit and from it lit two others. She came over to the chair where Belle remained sitting with the shotgun. "Hello Momma. You okay?"

"I'm okay. How about you?"

"Oh, I've been over to Eufala. Mr. Byrd and them put me up. I came to visit you, special. I haven't got Flossie. Left her in Fort Smith."

"I read your note. I thought you were staying in Kansas. Why Fort Smith?"

"Oh I have friends there, some of the sweetest people. . . ."

"That right?"

"Just some of the sweetest people in the world live in Fort Smith. I could stay there twicet as long as any old place in Kansas."

"Have some supper. We've got plenty left over. This here is Mr. Blue Duck."

"Glad to meet you," she smiled. "Blue *Duck?*"

"Yes."

"Well ain't that something? Blue Duck. No, I couldn't eat a thing. I took meat over at Mr. Byrd's and you know how they are. . . . I could just about have busted jiggling over here on that old pony. How are you, Momma?"

"I said I'm fine, child. Eat something. It'll put your feet on the ground."

"Oh!" Pearl sat down and rubbed at her face, careful of the face-paint that was already in disarray. "That's the most worrisome pony I've ever been on."

"Pony ain't much good for a sidesaddle usually. Sounds like he has a bad foot. You ought not to have been riding thataway at night."

"I didn't have any other clothes. Could have borrowed something from the Byrds, but I'm afraid I've gotten too stout."

Belle leaned the shotgun in a corner and went to get up a plate for Pearl. She would do things one at a time. Not let it come over her all at once. Keep a hold. Do like the dentist. . . . She put some things on a plate and handed it to her, avoiding her face. Eyes all black and gummed together, seashell nonsense clattering around her neck, lips red and enough different colored lumps of glass on her fingers until you wondered how she could open a door. She was dressed to kill — and just to ride over from Eufala by herself at night.

"Why don't you get shut of that costume and put on something comfortable. What'd you dress up for, the wolves?"

"We was having dinner at the Byrds' and somebody rode in and mentioned they'd seen you at Briartown."

"Go ahead and eat something. Ed, why don't you put the horse up."

He made no gesture to obey her. She laid a hard look on him but it did no good. The cow had started bawling again.

"Did you milk her?"

He didn't answer. He sat in Tom's old rocker smiling upon his sister, who looked somewhat flustered. "You seen Laura lately?"

"Why *yes*. Why yes indeed I *did*. I saw Laura two days ago." She glanced at Belle. "I saw her downtown. We didn't have time to talk because I was catching a streetcar but she looks just fine. She was wearing a morning bonnet with the cutest arrangement on it. Before that I guess I hadn't seen her for a while." Pearl took a bite from her plate and seemed to chew it tentatively, blinking up at her mother.

Belle's eyes went closed. Her heart was rattling away inside her like a cotton gin. Where did Blue Duck go? Outside? She'd have to change the subject. "Jim July — you seen him over in Fort Smith?"

"Why . . ." She put a hand to her mouth and tried to look thoughtful. "No. I don't believe I've seen him for a good while."

"It's a wonder."

Blinked her eyes. "How come?"

"Because you've been moving in the same society."

She blinked her charcoaled eyes now in a kind of convulsion of blinking. She glanced around the room. "No, I don't believe I've seen hide nor hair of Jim July. Has he been over there long?"

"Long enough to trade a rap on me for one on himself."

"Oh . . ." Pearl looked concerned. Then an enthusiastic smile shot across her face. "How do you like my habit? I know this hat's kind of a mess, but ain't too many can claim to ride at night in velvet. I liked this dress better than anything in the St. Louis catalogues and it was right there at the Boston Store! Would you believe it?" She stood up and held her arms out.

Belle's eyes went shut again. "How'd you pay for it, the flat of your back?"

When she opened her eyes the girl was shaking her head slightly.

"Har-har!" Ed laughed out in a loud, strange way.

"Because if you did, I'd just as soon you wear a towsack."

Pearl smiled wanly and put down her spoon. "I came over here to visit you, Momma. I left my Flossie so you wouldn't get upset. I want us to have a nice visit."

Belle turned to Ed. "Milk the cow."

He smirked. "Why don't you get that Indian to do it?"

She held still. She had to *hold herself* careful.

He laughed out in the same awkward manner. He was begging to be called. Leaning back in the rocker. Where did he get that little turn to his mouth? It was his permanent expression now, frozen in place; he must have learned it in the Tahlequah jail — the pissant smile.

Pearl was dressed up exactly to suit her occupation, not even trying to conceal it. Had she lost what poor little sense she had, swishing her tail around, wearing that old frazzled hat like it was the last word, acting the strumpet in front of her mother? Belle put both hands on the table. "Get those buzzard feathers off your head before you trip over them. And take off that harness and rest a while, why don't you. My God, girl."

Pearl looked away. "I didn't bring nothing else."

"Didn't *bring* nothing else? You've been riding around no-man's-land dressed up in all them ruffles and balloons; some of these Indians are liable to mistake you for something to eat."

"Har!"

"There was a fire in Fort Smith. Most of my clothes got burnt up. I didn't have the money to buy anything else right off."

"So now you're home. Well let's start at the starting place." Belle came around the table and took the hat off of her head. Then she started unlacing and unhooking the dress. Pearl resisted her. "No, Momma, I haven't got nothing else. I'm too stout for my old . . ." The more she resisted, the more fiercely Belle took apart the dress, until Pearl was holding up her arms to protect herself and crying and her mother was ripping the thing off of her shoulders, jerking her out of the chair, and she fell to her knees with the dress partially torn away, weeping in a fast unhurting sort of way, almost like laughing, and Belle held a piece of black velvet in her fist above the girl's head. "Don't you know what happens to a floozie? A floozie dies. From the inside out. Get up off the floor. Get up, I don't want to see you in this costume again. Get the gum off your eyes."

"Har!" Ed rocked back and forth smiling the pissant smile, real jolly.

Pearl crawled across the floor weeping.

It was all breaking up. She had intended to remain calm. Keep the peace. But it was all breaking up. Falling apart. "Get off the floor!" she roared.

Pearl staggered up and held her face, blubbering.

"It's no wonder Cole disowned us. I ought to pistol-whip you."

"You're nuts," the boy said.

"What?"

He smiled — real jolly. Blood surged inside her. Swam in her eyes. She saw spots. No pills today. Heart slamming in her chest like a hammer. The boy swam amid the spots in Tom's chair. Everything was falling apart and it was only she and her two blood children, alone.

"What?" she said again.

Over a great distance he replied, "You're a britches woman."

She was puzzled — in her mind somehow seeing him as if through one big eye over a distance. "What?"

"You're a britches woman," he repeated. Jolly nasty smile.

One big eye in her face. Seeing flat. Blue Duck, where was he? She needed . . . to look at her own face. There was a sliver of mirror in the kitchen. She went and picked it up and held it away from herself. The cruelly bitten mouth, yes, the absurd chin, leathery skin — the face a given, you look upon it and you are forty years old and you don't know how it got to be that way. The strange flickering eyes. A britches woman, yes you are a britches woman and what else could you have been? Oh but there's more, isn't there? You know more. That if you could not help it, then maybe she could not help being what she is, simpering floozie, and you know that you are punishing her for the same reasons that your father punished you. That is a fact. It is a plain fact. Yet you are not what she is. You never were what she is. All your life you have never been what she is; it is the choice you were given but didn't take.

Put down the mirror and walk outside. To the well. The stars are deafeningly silent. Pump a little water over your wrists. . . . At least you are alive and not in jail. You named your home and made your family and kept them in a place and lived this life cunningly and fiercely with your womanself in your own woman-hands, but what have you got left? They're drinking the poison, exactly the poison. She will service the marshals on the night before they ride across the Jay Gould Arkansas River Bridge into the Territory.

She pumped water on her wrists and wished she had some pills.

She waited by the well until her heart calmed down some. It took a while.

In the barn, Blue Duck was milking the cow. He had about

finished. She stood in the doorway. A coal-oil lamp sat on the floor. She noticed that he had shaved. She went over and sat down on an old split log. The cow chewed and drooled, bright eyed. Belle looked at the foamy surface of milk. "I'm in a funny mood," she said.

He glanced at her.

She tried to smile. "I can't stand those kids."

He kept pumping the tit. "How come?"

"Oh you know. The boy the way he is. I get dizzy—sure-enough dizzy in the head. Feel funny. You think I'm insane?"

He smiled. "What makes you say that?"

"I get so riled up. Tell myself I'm going to be calm and decent but then these kids just drive me *wild*. It seems like I can't be calm about them."

"You can't be calm because you won't let them go."

"Where to? Hell in a handbasket?"

"Yes." Blue Duck leaned down and smelled the milk, sat back up and milked some more.

"You're one to talk about letting people go."

He stopped and looked at her. "You're not crazy, Belle, you're just a little mean."

"Well, aren't you smart. Everybody's pronouncing on me to-night. He called me a britches woman, Ed did, just a minute ago."

"You told me that you made Ed do things."

Her heart started banging again. The dizziness threatened to wrap her head in strange distances again, she was suddenly con-fused and shy and did not want to talk about this subject. It was done, suffered, confessed. It was over. She did not want him bringing it up. "I told *you* that. Don't pull it on me."

"I'm not pulling anything on you." He let go of the tit. "I'm leaving tomorrow. I've got to go back to Tulsa."

"That's what I mean when I say crazy, don't you see? A mother who'd do that." Her hands came up to her face. Now that it was brought up, she couldn't drop it. Heart banging, banging. "So you're going to pronounce on me and leave? . . ."

"I haven't pronounced anything more than what you've asked me to say."

He looked at her with a very clear expression. It was true, she supposed; she had the odd desire to agree with him.

"This cow's better off, anyway," he said, putting his finger in the milk and tasting it. "I read once in a book, 'Accept the fathers and let go of the sons.'"

"Oh boy, the philosopher-dentist. Accept the fathers? My old daddy didn't have the sense God give an armadillo but at least he wasn't trying to commit suicide all the time. I don't have too much trouble accepting him. It's the sons give me trouble. And daughters."

"You think Hotsie will make it?"

"Nobody's going to find Hotsie in the Winding Stair. You and me might not have seen the last of those Pinks, though. You might have to take that dentist's chair and go to Wyoming with it. And I'll have to take my stupid children — somewhere."

"Better not take that boy anywhere else. He'll kill you." He raised an eyebrow, eyes twinkling.

"Ha! I thought you were the voice of reason! Shit."

He laughed. She laughed with him.

"That milk any good?"

"I think so."

"I could use some — my stomach could."

She got a dipper from the wall and hooked up some of the warm milk. It smelled a little rich. She wasn't hungry but her stomach was dissatisfied with the little that she'd managed at dinner. She got most of it down and dipped up another for Blue Duck and he drank it without a pause.

"You've got a pretty good stomach, don't you?"

"I guess so," he said.

"That's cause you work an honest living. Helps your stomach. I ain't never known a crook to have a decent stomach."

He wiped his mouth and moustache. "When I was a boy I could eat nails."

She sat back down on the board.

"Now I'm more conventional."

"I wouldn't say that."

He blushed and moved to get another dipperful of milk.

She burst out laughing. He looked up over the dipper, his newly shaved face red as a beet. She hadn't laughed so hard in a month. She laughed and wheezed. ". . . You put me in the mind of good things, dentist."

He tipped his hat and drank the second dipper down. "You want another?"

"God no. You can put the rest of it in the cellar. Would you go in with me? I mean just for a minute."

"The house?"

"Yes."

"I believe I'll sleep out here tonight. The house is kind of crowded."

"Just for a minute. Maybe I can put these birdbrains to bed. And maybe I'll sleep out here with you."

He picked up the pail and followed her inside.

23

When they walked in and Jim July was in the house, Blue Duck was as astonished as Belle. They hadn't heard him arrive. He sat drinking from a hip flask but was not drunk.

"I came up from Whitefield, left my horse down on the river. I didn't know who was up here, figured I better walk up."

Belle stood in the doorway with her hands fiddling in her dress pockets, the line of her mouth thin, tensed. "Who'd you think it might be?"

"Don't know. After what I read in the paper, I didn't know what might be going on up here."

There was a straightback chair right opposite July, and Blue Duck took his bucket of milk over and sat down. July looked down at the milk uneasily, as though it smelled bad, but not up at Blue Duck's face. "This is the first time I've been outside that damn town in three weeks. Glad of it, I'll tell you."

"Pretty rough living between the courthouse and the whorehouse, I guess."

"I wouldn't say that. I got this trial set anyway." He kept his eyes somewhere between the pail and Blue Duck's feet and took another two quick nips from the flask. "That mare of mine got loose in the stable last week, ate a barrel of oats and foundered. I'm borrowing a nag, simpleminded thing tried to rake me off under every God damned limb between here and Fort Smith."

Belle smiled a little, still leaning in the door with her hands in her pockets. "Where'd you get the bond money?"

"No bond. I turned myself in."

"Awful nice of them."

"Ain't too damn nice," he muttered.

"What's this thing on me?"

"Thought maybe you'd tell me. I don't know nothing more than I read in the newspaper."

"That puts us in the same boat."

"Prettyman, that photographer, turned you in is what it said. . . ."

"Prettyman doesn't know anything about any old livestock raps. All he knows about is a hole in his foot."

July shook his head, took another scowling drink from his flask. He was sweating. To Blue Duck he seemed much older and more serious than the person he had met on Coke Hill a week or two ago. He still didn't look at Blue Duck, although their knees were four feet apart. It was very uncomfortable. His manner was serious, nervous, purposeful, and in some odd way intimate.

For a while no one spoke, and it grew increasingly uncomfortable.

Ed reached out for July's flask and said in a strange voice, "Been getting any good pussy over in Fort Smith?"

Blue Duck glanced at Belle, who continued to lean in the doorway, no response on her face except a kind of ruffled freezing like a rooster about to fight. She went as quiet and still as a photograph. July didn't answer the question; it was dropped like an embarrassment from a child.

Belle nodded at the pail of milk. "Why don't you put that out in the cellar. There's a jar down there you'll have to wash out."

Blue Duck was glad to do so — to leave the room. He took up

a lamp and went outside. The cellar was cool and dry, with potatoes and onions on racks and a big old stone jar that smelled of rancid milk. He took it outside to rinse. The pump squeaked and complained. Jim July showing up here was completely unexpected. Belle had thought she'd have to go looking for him.

Back inside, he was asking about the work for Mayes and Belle wasn't saying much.

"You wouldn't be the ones that robbed that bank in Guthrie, would you?"

"Hell no, and I wouldn't tell you if we were."

"Why's that?" He was getting a little color to his face now. It was apparent that he needed whiskey to operate on.

"I don't think you want me to answer that question."

"Oh now don't hurt my feelings."

"What are you doing here, Jim?"

"Do I need a reason?"

"You have a reason, I'm just asking what it is."

His eyes glanced around the room, for the first time taking in Blue Duck, who remained standing back near the front door. He took another chug from his depleted flask. "Just thought I'd take a ride out and see how you were doing. Trial's next week."

"Come on Jim. Either you or Miss Laura Ziegler can tell me something about this charge, I'm pretty sure, and I don't think Laura Ziegler has enough sense to go to the sheriff."

"I didn't make no deals on you, Belle. I wouldn't be here if I had." He looked gloomy and tense.

"Tell you what's worrying me, Jim. Not that somebody might have told Mr. Thomas about any old livestock raps but that they might have told him something bigger, something about this arrangement with Mayes, and what he's calling 'livestock' is just a way to get me in. If that's happening, it's going to get pretty bad around here, I imagine."

He put the lid on his flask.

"For one thing, Mr. Rocking Chair here's going to get his neck broke," she said.

"Har!"

"You'll laugh all the way to the platform, sonny boy."

Blue Duck watched her. Her face was strangely bright. There was no malice, just a solid hatchet brightness. Sometimes in moments like this she got very quick and clearheaded and he would look at her and not be able to stop looking at her. *As a boy, he had starved himself and gone into the hills hoping to see certain beings; they would teach him and then disappear as animals, pausing so that he could see them clearly and remember them for medicine. He never saw them, he saw only discomfort and hunger, but Belle's was the face — his face — that was clear now. No message but the face itself, like a picture. . . . And where was there any wisdom in her ragged life? The schoolteacher had given him knowledge, made a literate person out of a scavenging coyote, but behind his face was more than knowledge. Not male or female, not ugly or beautiful, it told something deadcenter even though she lied and was crazy and needful and tangled in her own life. . . .*

She was looking at Ed. "How about you and me go outside and unsaddle Pearl's pony. I'm sure she didn't do nothing about it." He looked suspicious. "Won't take us but a couple of minutes." After some coaxing he finally went out with her, leaving Blue Duck alone with Jim July.

For a few moments nothing was said. Blue Duck leaned back against the wall. Finally July looked up at him with a yawing glazed intensity in his eye. "Been thinking about that dental examination you gave me."

Blue Duck watched him.

"Pretty low thing for a man to do." He smiled with his lips stiffly parted. "Been thinking about that just about every night now since it happened. Come at it about every way. And you're a name now, ain't you?"

It was apparent now what July was here for, and that he had been waiting to be alone with Blue Duck. Blue Duck tried to gauge whether he could walk out the door. It was right beside him. He'd better try now or there would be no opportunity. He took a step forward and was immediately looking down the barrel of a navy Colt. July was very fast. Still smiling. "Yeah, it seem to me like a man takes a woman away from somebody, he shouldn't add insult to injury."

"Is that why you came here?"

"Yeah."

"You going to give me a fair chance?"

"No." He shook his head once. "I don't figure a jack-leg Indian like you deserves a fair chance."

"Depends on how much of a coward you are, I guess."

An explosion showered spark and flame in Blue Duck's face: the bullet licked at his side.

"One chance you have is to ask me nice. Talk ugly like that and I'll have to stack you up, greaser." He looked at Blue Duck for a minute. "Fact of the matter, that's what I think I want you to do. Been thinking it ever since it happened. I want you to apologize to me for sticking that glass in my mouth."

Belle appeared. She took in the scene and remained for the moment just inside the doorframe.

"Momma!" Pearl called from behind the closed bedroom door.

"Right now, in front of her, I want you to say you're sorry and I want you to ask my forgiveness. If you was to put enough into it — you're such a good talker and all — I might not have to take you apart just yet."

"Put down the gun, Jim."

"Momma!" Pearl called.

"I ain't putting down this gun till I have some satisfaction. I've been thinking about this real hard. Ain't been sleeping I been thinking about it so hard."

"How can you expect to get any sleep in a whorehouse? This dentist ain't your trouble; you got a high nature is all. He ain't done that much. You was going to do him mischief, now wasn't you? Think about that. He didn't do you a part of the mischief you was laying to do him. Why don't you put down that gun and let's have a drink. I've got a jug here somewhere."

She moved and July pulled off a second shot. "*You better listen to me, Belle.*" He spoke in Creek. "*I don't owe you anything. Don't try to stand in my way.*"

"All right. If you're killing us all, you might as well admit what you told Heck Thomas. I'd like to know if this boy's going to get hanged."

July snickered. After being serious and directed and even ponderous, he now snickered and Blue Duck saw again the nervous bright mean boy he had seen in Fort Smith. "*Are you still worried about that?*"

"That's my weakness, ain't it?"

"Weakness?" He snickered again. "You going to apologize, Indian?"

"Yes."

July frowned. "Yes what?"

"Yes, I apologize."

He looked surprised. "Do?"

"Sure."

"What do you apologize for?"

"*For putting the glass in your mouth and causing you so much worry,*" Blue Duck said in Creek.

"Momma, what's happening in there?"

"Shut up child, Jim July's going to kill us is all."

July looked troubled and confused now; he had expected Blue Duck to be as muleheaded as himself. "*What will you do to make up for it?*"

"*There is nothing to do but apologize.*"

"Ain't good enough." July cocked the pistol. "Course now, you could say you was dropping her."

"What do you mean?"

"I mean you could say you was dropping her for good." He nodded at Belle. "And going back to Tulsa or wherever you live."

"It so happens I am going to Tulsa tomorrow."

Belle fixed her gaze on July. "You dilapidated low-range Okie son of a bitch, don't talk about me like I was one of your little municipally inspected floozies. You've been hanging around that bunch too long." She turned her back and went into the kitchen.

"Hold it!" July said. "I don't owe you nothing. . . ."

"Nothing but a last name, Mr. Jim July Starr," she said from the dark room.

The pistol waved between the kitchen and Blue Duck. He stood up.

"*Momma!*"

"You put any blood on the wall, so help me you're going to clean it up. No killing in this house, that's a rule." She came back out of the kitchen with a lamp, walked between them and put it on the table. She stood in front of him. "Now get on out of here. Sleep outside under the honey locust, I don't want you in the house. You're tired and drunk. We'll all have better sense in the morning. Don't roll on a sticker."

July was outclassed. The gun eventually sagged in his hand. "Hide pretty good behind a woman, don't you?"

Belle answered that. "I ain't ever known a man to do anything else, from the names to the punks. Hide behind em and run em down behind their backs."

July's face was sour and sweating. He had run out of words.

"Go on to sleep, you're riding back to Fort Smith tomorrow. I'm going to ride with you and find out about this warrant."

He eased down the hammer on his Colt. "You're riding with me?"

"To Fort Smith, yeah. If you act decent."

Belle barred the bedroom door and they lay down together. It was a while before they talked.

"You're going with him?"

"I'd rather be with him on the trail than to have him lurking somewhere behind."

Blue Duck shifted in the bed. He was saddle-sore. He didn't want to discuss Jim July. Jim July irritated him very much. "Did you talk with Ed?"

"Little bit."

"Get anything straight?"

"Oh hell . . . I don't know . . . That's between me and him, I guess." She sighed. "Looky here, we have all this money. If you're taking off for Tulsa tomorrow, how am I going to pay you? You could take your share of the bank money, then after we get this bond money back you can take your salary."

"I'm not too sure there'll be any bond money."

"Well I hope there is. . . . What do you think about riding for Mayes?"

"I think it was the dumbest thing I ever did."

"I mean again."

He looked over at her, sunk in the tick. "Again?"

"Yeah."

"You mean out there, same deal?"

"Pretty much — better put together maybe, more men . . . I might just go ahead with it on a wild hare. After the trial. Mayes will pay us that other ten to burn out the newspaper up in Kansas and a few other little things."

Blue Duck grunted. He didn't want to talk about this either. She had a way of drawing him into things.

His attention drifted. It was not so hot tonight. Perhaps the rain had broken the dog days. He was a little uncertain about the window being open. July might work himself into another fury and crawl through it. Or Ed. Ed had gotten pretty strange — emerged from Tahlequah jail like a moth from a worm — a strange, ugly, lunatic moth with a very short time to accomplish his business.

Belle stopped talking and he daydreamed — tired, tense.

"I've been wanting to ask you something," she said.

"What's that?"

"Do you feel shame for killing that woman?"

"Jesus."

"I mean you don't act it if you do."

"I'm tired, Belle."

"Yes or no?"

"You figure it out," he said, and turned away from her.

He woke up to fading, distant gunfire — memory or dream. She was gone. There was a note on the pillow: "Look in the cellar in the potato bin. There's your share. I hope to see you in Tahlequah for the trial. Yrs. B."

The house was quiet. He walked outside into the yard, through chickens to the well, pumped some water into his hands and splashed his face. No one seemed to be around. But a pony — Pearl's, he supposed — was in the corral. Back in the house he went to the other bedroom door and pushed it open.

She sat in her chemise and petticoat with a needle and thread, working on a dress.

"Pardon me."

"That's all right. I was making up something to wear. Come in."

"No . . . thank you. I just wondered if anybody was around."

"They left a while ago." Pearl looked up and smiled — pleasant fat dewlap cheeks. "Wasn't it *awful* around here last night?"

He felt his face for beard. "When did they leave?"

"I don't know. I heard them wrassling around but I didn't get up. Guess it was near sunrise."

"Did they all three go?"

She shrugged her shoulders and raised her eyebrows. "Well I guess so. Ed's acting so funny. I've never seen him so. Must have got a little touched in jail. And Jim July, I never have liked him, if you want to know the truth. I'd as soon not start the day looking at him."

A horse could be heard trotting into the yard. Blue Duck got his pistol from the other bedroom and went to the front door. The horse was riderless, wet from the trail and foam-flecked at the bit. It had Belle's sidesaddle on it. For a moment he was blank; there seemed no urgency in the appearance of the animal, although it was odd. Perhaps she had stopped for something and lost him.

But then he remembered the sound he'd heard upon awakening
— and tore back into Pearl's bedroom.

"What trail did they take?"

She looked up blinking. "Why, I don't know."

"North or south?"

"I guess they went down toward Whitefield. . . ."

Outside, he bridled and saddled a horse, no blanket, jerked the
cinch tight and headed down the steep trail to the Canadian
River. Untended, hungry, amazed at being so suddenly on the
trail, the horse slipped and stumbled and nearly pitched him
down the scrub oak hill, and he reined him hard, unconsciously,
thinking only of what he was going to do because even before he
had seen it it was spreading out before him like a bad dream. The
horse balked at the river and he put his boots into his sides and
spoke words — horse Indian words the meaning of which he did
not even remember — just words, mean, powerful — and across
the river he got onto the trail and for a moment was confused
about which direction to take — Fort Smith was east — and east,
this was east, no — and the horse went around and twice around,
walleyed and snorting, before he found the direction.

The horse was still dripping when he came to her, at the end of
a fenceline. She lay face down in a mud puddle. She was in a
dress. It was apparent before he dismounted that she had been
shot with a shotgun. The breath left his lungs, he dismounted in a
soundless world. There was only her lying there. On his knees he
turned her over. She had been shot in the back with buckshot
and in the shoulder and face with turkey shot. Her mouth
was a ragged hole, front teeth exposed. Her chest was blown
apart. Her eyes still vibrated with death. He wailed. He sat on his
knees and heard the weak sound come up out of himself.

On his feet, he tried to think of what to do. The horse had
trotted ahead and he walked it down, again speaking the strange
words. He mounted and rode east at a gallop.

Through a grove of sycamore and around two bends, someone
was ahead. He did not think of who, only that the old jack he was

riding moved at a good pace, and faster when he caught sight of someone behind him — a jogging, mule run — and Blue Duck yelled at him to stop, he didn't, and as the gap closed he tried to leave the trail and got stopped quickly in a wall of brushwood and stickers and drought-crimsoned sumac and ivy and sweetgum saplings, and the spavined old mule snorted and goat-bucked in a halfhearted way, and Blue Duck was able to rein in beside him and using the pistol as a club strike him on the back of the head and neck and peel him out of the saddle. He dismounted and with the pistol still drawn approached him while he struggled onto all fours with his head hanging down, tangled in stickers, dazed. Taking hold of the hair, he raised Ed Reed's face up to the barrel of his pistol. He said nothing yet, just held the pistol to his eyes.

"I didn't . . . ," he gasped.

Blue Duck cocked the pistol and touched it to the bridge of his nose. He looked up with his lurid sticker-slashed face and as if he had no idea of the tenuousness of his life right now — or didn't care — raised a hand and made a swipe at the pistol. Blue Duck kicked him in the ribs, reached down and took the pistol from his holster and pitched it hard over the brush into the river. Ed gasped for breath. Blue Duck noticed that the scabbard on his saddle was empty. "What did you do with the shotgun?"

"I didn't . . ." He still struggled to breathe.

"Didn't what?"

"I found her back there."

"What else?"

"Why should I tell you? For all I know . . ."

Blue Duck kicked him again; it took him somewhat longer to get up this time. "I found her like that," he gasped.

"You weren't with them?"

"She said I couldn't come with them to Fort Smith. Said she'd be back in a couple of days and we'd go together. That was crap. I followed after them. I was going down the hill when I heard the shots. Found her back there. July was gone."

"Did he do it?"

"How do I know? How do I know you didn't do it?"

"Does he have a shotgun?"

"I reckon he would. She had that old double barrel."

Still blank, buzzing somewhat in his skull, without grief or sorrow or any emotion yet reaching through to him, Blue Duck watched the boy and tried to see the murder of his mother in his face, but there was not the change that he would have expected, not the nervous triumph, nor the horror. The same gloom pervaded his expression, the same face of a prisoner, different now only in that it was gloomier and more sullen. If he had killed her to free himself, he had failed.

"Why would July do it?"

"Shit, how do I know? You know more about all this than I do. I've been in jail, remember? Let me go before the buzzards start flocking. If they catch me anywhere around here, I'm cooked."

"Why is that?"

His voice was a lamentation now — somewhat of a whine. "Everybody knows what she did. Everybody expected me to do this. But I *didn't* do it." He stood up and staggered backward two steps.

Blue Duck held his pistol level. "Why did they expect you to do it?"

He looked up, one eye hooded by an open gash. "Because they know how her and me got into it, what do you think?"

"How was that?"

The whine left his voice. "Who the hell are you, judge and jury?"

"That's right."

He sneered, "Okay. How did we get into it — that what you ask? We got into it over her always trying to make us do things she'd a' never done, that's how. Because she was a flat hypocrite and crazy to boot. That enough?"

"Real sorry for what just happened, aren't you?"

"I'm going to be sorrier if you keep me here any longer. These district people will drop us both in the slam."

"Did you kill her because she made you do things?"

Ed stopped short. "Do things? . . ." He looked down. "You've been talking to her, I guess. Well you can forget it, forget it all. She's a liar."

"You mean that it's untrue?"

Ed looked exhausted. "What fucking business is it of yours?"

"I want the truth out of you, Ed. I'll make any kind of mess I have to to get it."

"I didn't kill the bitch."

"What did she make you do?"

"Real interested, huh? I thought maybe you'd a' found out on your own. She was nuts, mister. Out of her gourd, if you can understand that. Crazy. What she did doesn't matter. The bullshit that she talked doesn't matter. She was a woman that thought she was a man — a britches woman, ever hear of that? — the worst of both." He was pale now, talking louder.

"What did she make you do?"

"What? What?" The cut above his eye was blue and puffy, his hands helpless and oddly fluttering at his sides. They turned to fists. "Shoot me. Go ahead and do it because I ain't saying a word more. Not as long as I live." He leaned forward and sneered, as if he really was reconciled to a bullet or as if he might try something, but the energy visibly leaked out of him and he looked defeated, broken, insouciant in exactly the way he had with his mother. Shoulders slumped, head down, clownish, he turned and began to trudge out of the brush toward the trail. Blue Duck held the gun on his back for a moment, trigger finger tense, and holstered it.

Ed Reed wasn't the one.

24

He *found his horse* again and rode eastward. The trail was fresh with tracks, but of more than one horse. It was a guess that July was still heading for Fort Smith. He could be going south into Choctaw country or he could have gone immediately westward. Blue Duck had a hunch, though, that if July had done what it appeared he had done, he never needed a warm bed more than tonight.

He rode all out. The sun rose, the earth heated beneath him and he scarcely noticed it. He floated above the trail, the day happening without him. His mind was not sensation but thinking, all thinking — about what he was doing and why. It was like something in one of his books. An event that people imagined. There was anger in him but not much. He did not feel it yet. He was more bemused than enraged, more curious than swallowed up. It seemed like a necessary act to follow Jim July, but he was not dying to wring the man's neck. It had to be seen about, but it was strange that he should be the one.

The horse was hungry and thirsty and at some point in the late afternoon near to balking, but he was following a set of fresh tracks from a horse that was moving fast now, and if his own horse winged and faltered and breathed like a locomotive he did not care. He was four or five miles from the place where the trail left the Canadian when he came to a barb wire gate that was partly sprung and trampled and had blood on two or three of the top row barbs. Down the trail through a row of shacks, he headed straight on without stopping to ask questions of the dirty children and baby-draped mothers who stood out front. Tracks here got lost in the confusion of local traffic, but he had a strong enough feeling now — the Missouri gate back there confirmed it — that July was ahead and running for a reason.

From a lope he cut down to a walk. The horse would be lucky to make Fort Smith at any pace. He wondered about July going to Fort Smith. Maybe there was something besides a warm bed there, some other deal. Perhaps a deal with the U.S. marshal that involved more than just information. In which case there was more than one reason to be following him.

It was still possible that Ed Reed had done it. July might just be running from the scene. The boy had every reason, after all. But something in his manner made it seem unlikely, and something else that Blue Duck wasn't clear on.

The horse remained beneath him to Red Land, where he noticed that the sky was moving into the last of sunset — serene over the Arkansas River. For a dollar the ferryman was able to remember July, and that he was no more than a half-hour ahead.

In Cottonwood he looked for a lathered-up horse but there was none. It was about three miles to Paw Paw, which consisted mostly of Choctaw saloons — shacks with tin roofs and log walls. It was on another bend of the river, and required another ferry to get across to Fort Smith. The five or six saloons at the edge of the Paw Paw bottom had a look of impermanence about them, as if constructed out of driftwood from upriver floods, and in this position on the edge of the plain likely at any time to become driftwood again when the water got high.

In front of one of them he found the horse that he'd been

following all day, lathered up and chilling in the night breeze off the river.

He tied his horse at a trough. Up the moonlighted street, ghostly shapes stumbled and muttered from one riversmelling heap of logs to another. Paw Paw was on the fringes of Fort Smith — even more ragged fringes than Coke Hill. The better-off class of townspeople preferred that Indians and Negroes and poor whites cross the river here to do their distasteful deeds. There were knife and cock fights, even an occasional duel, although that was going out of style. Paw Paw was a miniature of the Territory — outlet for what was vile and resource for income.

Needing a drink pretty badly, he aimed for the shack at the end of the street, farthest from July's horse, but knew somehow before he had got in the door that he'd made a mistake, as did the bartender, an immense man in an apron who yelled — did not pronounce but yelled — before Blue Duck had fully appeared in the door that he was to leave his gun at the bar, twice booming out that declaration before Blue Duck had clearly seen July sitting at one of the two tables in the room with a deck of cards and drink in front of him and a bedraggled woman hanging at his side hunched over and laughing soundlessly into his arm. He looked sober. He said nothing.

"I know what you got in your pocket, buddy. Don't reach for it."

July smiled. The woman lifted her head and with her back still hunched over turned her face toward Blue Duck, irritated.

"Better go powder your face, honey," he said.

"What's the trouble?" July's hands remained visible for the moment.

But when the bartender lumbered out from behind his short counter — "*Unstrop that gun, Indian. Any fighting, you'll do it outside*" — and came across in front, July threw over the table and pulled off two shots and the fat man was looking at his shoulder, hit, and the woman was screaming. Blue Duck went down at the end of the counter, but there was no way he could shoot. The bartender was making a play for something behind the counter, but two more shots and he grunted and was rolling, more or less, toward the front door. The woman's screams had become systematic, like some sort of whistle on a train. July had her by the hair and was keeping her for insurance, but the policy was backfiring: she kicked and screamed and partially knocked away the table and Blue Duck took one intentionally wide shot and July fired his remaining bullets wild, and Blue Duck lunged out from the bar into July's belly. Pummeled on the back of the head and neck and shoulders but without leverage, he was able to grapple the gun and twist it away, but now they were on the floor and July had the scrambling energy of somebody ten years younger and with twice the desperation of Blue Duck. He was all knees and elbows and flurries of fists and then he had a stick— a dowel? — in his hand and Blue Duck took it on the shoulders and face and fell backward and even as he hit the sand floor and was kicked in the jaw and knocked close to insensible he realized as clearly as if engaged in some abstract meditation that quickness was the key here and if he did not get quicker fast he was going to lose his ass. He crawled away from the kicking and stood up, stumbled and almost toppled over backward again, head buzzing like a summer night, but then he was using his feet to kick back, conscious enough to keep July away from the guns behind the bar, and it was becoming a full-fledged kicking fight, the Creek mean with his legs and Blue Duck trying to gain time for himself to clear his head, circling, on the defensive, reading July's expression which was blank and all-out, no questions or doubts. He was fighting for one purpose.

They kicked alternately, one in attack and one in retreat, then they kicked at the same time, furiously, like children bruising each other's legs; he tried to knock July down but could not. July caught his foot and twisted him over backward and was onto and all about his face again, Blue Duck could not even tell with what — fists, the dowel, kicking? — and he crawled and scrambled in retreat under the table that was still standing, but July went for the bar again — a sawed-off shotgun — and only the pause in cocking it allowed Blue Duck to get up and knock it away as the barrel roared. That set him off. Somehow it was the thing that did it — that and the recognition of what July's deal in Fort Smith was — again odd in occurring to him now out of the smoke and ringing of the shotgun, but the fact was so very simple that it could have chosen almost any moment to come clear in his mind — and July was after him with a whiskey bottle now, but it had all added up to set him off, and the quickness that he had abstractly cogitated a moment ago came out of his bones, and they were on the floor grappling for eyes and kneeing at testicles and somehow the fact of it — the simple fact — made him angrier by the second. He managed a fist-stunning blow to July's face, and the younger man hustled again for the bar on all fours, and Blue Duck came after him and kicked him in the gut hard enough to turn him over, eyes bugging out, and kicked him in the face and kicked the breath out of him and perhaps a few ribs.

"Heck Thomas is waitin for me over there —" This after he could talk, just the thing he shouldn't have said, the thing to confirm Blue Duck's suspicion.

He kicked July again, lightly, almost exploratorily, as if toeing a carcass to see if it was alive, and he grunted, "He's waitin for me right now on the other side of that river. And he ain't the only one. . . ."

Blue Duck kicked him in the face. "You son of a bitch." July found his face with his hands and spat out teeth and blood and Blue Duck kicked him in the gut again. "You trash." He got his gun from the floor and when July got his breath and tried to crawl away he jammed it into his ass, jammed it hard up partly through his pants, and July screamed like a woman.

"They know! I did it for them. If anything happens to me . . ."

"You keep saying the wrong thing." Blue Duck spoke quietly enough. "All that to get out of a horsetheft rap? Are they going to pay you, too? What are they going to pay you?"

"I didn't have any choice. . . ."

Blue Duck jammed it another couple of inches up the bush-whacker's ass.

"It wasn't me, God damnit, it was the Cherokee deal, the deal with Mayes, Thomas got orders from higher up. . . ."

"You'll have orders from higher up real soon, don't worry." He cocked the gun. There was no question in his mind as to whether he was going to blow the scum apart, no doubts, even a kind of delectation in making the moment last longer. "Any questions before I do the humane thing?"

July drooled blood and chips of teeth and whimpered, and Blue Duck felt the awfulness of it before he did it, before he squeezed the trigger, felt it somewhat as the dentist might feel it, the man who worked for a living and swept his house — and in that pause decided not to dignify the punk with execution.

He withdrew the gun and brained him. Surveying the room, he got his hat and started to leave, but it occurred to him that he should help July fulfill his appointed rounds. He threw him over his shoulder, trundled him down to the ferry and dropped him on the deck.

The ferryman came out of a shack and squawked at him, "Ain't no more tonight."

"Take this bum over and unload him. I'll give you five dollars."

"Five?" the ferryman squawked. "Ain't dead, is he?"

"I don't think so."

July moved an arm and suddenly jerked up his head, eyes glazed.

"Come to Tulsa sometime. I'll make you a pair of false teeth for eight bucks."

He turned and plodded back up the sand and found his horse shivering in sweat. Clusters of people formed in the street gossiping about the fight. He did not want to stay here. But the horse wouldn't last long tonight, so he rode back to Cottonwood, bought a bed and died in it.

He woke up to a bad-tasting mouth and took two shots of whiskey for breakfast. He worked on the horse for a while, rubbing him down and cleaning out the burrs. He was a poor excuse for an animal. Yesterday had about done him in.

He tried to think of which direction to go. Tulsa was out of the question; they'd have him within a week. He was cut free whether he liked it or not. He could slip through Fort Smith and head on eastward. It had been his ambition for so long to go east. . . . But there were things still to clear up. He thought of her dead. He thought of her alive. The boy would have to make the trial. He saddled the horse and headed west.

end

Epilogue

The historic Belle Starr was assassinated on the trail from Younger's Bend to Fort Smith on February 2, 1889. The two principal suspects in her murder were Jim July (Starr) and Ed Reed; there were no trials.

Her body was anointed with turpentine and oil of cinammon, dressed in black silk with a high waist and collar, and laid in the coffin with one hand clasping a pistol. Armed Cherokee guards served at the funeral. There was no religious ceremony besides the placing of a piece of cornbread in the coffin by each Cherokee passing by.

In 1891 the United States government made forced purchase of the Cherokee Outlet at three dollars per acre. In the summer of 1893, the land was opened for the "great" Oklahoma land rush.

The historic Jim July was shot within a year of Belle's death by Deputy U.S. Marshal Bob Hutchins. Ed Reed was killed in 1896 while shooting up a saloon in Wagoner, Oklahoma. Pearl Younger became a highly successful madam on Fort Smith's row and died of natural causes in 1925. The historic Blue Duck was commuted from a term of life imprisonment by President Grover Cleveland in March, 1895 — to go home and die of tuberculosis.

The foregoing is not an attempt to reconstruct accurately the last weeks of Belle Starr's life but to re-create her character, using both facts of history and imagination.

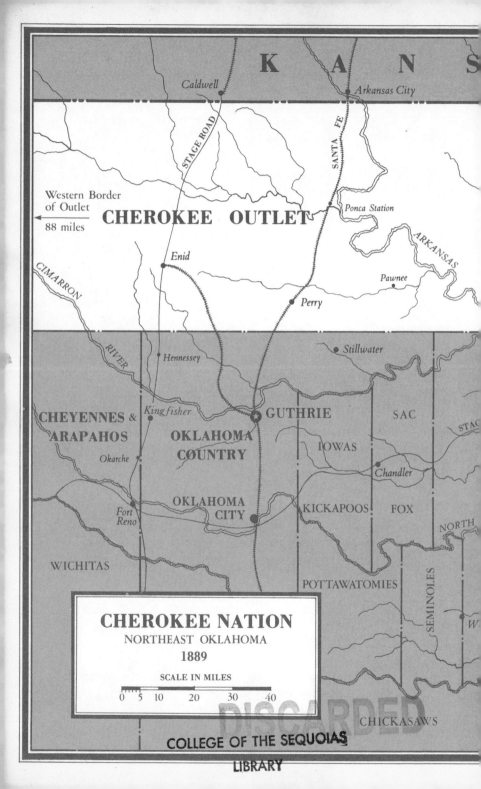

KANS

Caldwell

Arkansas City

STAGE ROAD

SANTA FE

Western Border
of Outlet
← 88 miles

CHEROKEE OUTLET

Ponca Station

ARKANSAS

Enid

CIMARRON

Pawnee

Perry

RIVER

Hennessey

Stillwater

**CHEYENNES &
ARAPAHOS**

Kingfisher

☆ **GUTHRIE**

SAC

STAC

**OKLAHOMA
COUNTRY**

IOWAS

Okarche

Chandler

**OKLAHOMA
CITY**

KICKAPOOS

FOX

*Fort
Reno*

NORTH

WICHITAS

POTTAWATOMIES

SEMINOLES

W

CHEROKEE NATION

NORTHEAST OKLAHOMA

1889

SCALE IN MILES

0 5 10   20   30   40